Waxwings

Jonathan Raban

Pantheon Books, New York

All rights reserved under International and Pan-American Copyright
Conventions. Published in the United States by Pantheon Books, a
division of Random House, Inc., New York, and simultaneously in
Canada by Random House of Canada Limited, Toronto. Distributed by
Random House, Inc., New York. Originally published in Great Britain by
Picador, an imprint of Pan Macmillan, Ltd., London.

Pantheon Books and colophon are registered trademarks of Random
House, Inc.

Grateful acknowledgment is made to Random House Children's Books
for permssion to reprint an excerpt from *The Cat in the Hat Comes
Back* by Dr. Seuss. TM & copyright © by Dr. Seuss Enterprises, L.P.
1958, renewed 1986. Reprinted by permission of Random House
Children's Books, a division of Random House, Inc.

Library of Congress Cataloging-in-Publication Data

Raban, Jonathan.
   Waxwings : / Jonathan Raban
     p.   cm.
   ISBN 0-375-41008-2
    1. British—Washington (State)—Fiction.   2. Repairing trades—
Fiction.   3. Seattle (Wash.)—Fiction.   4. Illegal aliens—Fiction.
5. Immigrants—Fiction.   6. Authors—Fiction.   I. Title.

PR6068.A22W39 2003   823'.914—dc21   2003042997

www.pantheonbooks.com

Book design by Johanna S. Roebas

Printed in the United States of America

First American Edition

9 8 7 6 5 4 3 2 1

FOR MY DAUGHTER,
JULIA RABAN

Waxwings

1.

"November," the pilot said.

Wave-crests were breaking gray on a sea as black as crêpe. Ragged nimbus clouds brushed the ship's bridge. The lone spot of color was on the radar screen, where the coastline showed as a wide brushstroke of glowing copper.

"Steady as she goes," the pilot said. "Zero-seven-five."

"Zero-seven-five." Compact, broad-bottomed, the captain was a dense blot of shadow at the wheel.

They spoke quietly, as if they were in church. Eleven stories up from the water, the noise of the engines was a distant rumor. Though a westerly gale was blowing down Juan de Fuca Strait, it was inaudible on the bridge, for the ship had been built with hurricanes and typhoons in mind, and the bronchial churring of the air-conditioner drowned out whatever sounds were being made by the weather. The *Pacific Auriga,* 51,000 tons, bound for Seattle from Osaka and Hong Kong, was too big to notice the small sea on which it now found itself, its only apparent motion a slight mechanical vibration underfoot.

"You've got the Dungeness light there, Cap," the pilot said. "Starboard. Two o'clock."

"Yes, I've got it," the captain said, a little shortly, for he was an old hand on this run, and the pilot new to him. Stepping aboard from the launch off Port Angeles, the pilot presented himself on the bridge with a cocky, affectless assurance to which the captain, a New Zealander, took an immediate dislike. Now the young American was fiddling with the radar closest to the wheel, officiously targeting echoes.

"You can go to zero-eight-zero, Cap. The spit's right on the two-mile ring. Tide's making about three knots."

"We usually see Doug—Doug Nielsen?"

"Captain Nielsen's taking the week off. Family emergency."

"I'm sorry to hear that."

Ahead of the bridge, lines of stacked containers stretched away into the darkness. The water puddled on their tops caught the light from the deck below the bridge and glistened like a wet highway, blinding the Captain to the sea beneath the ship.

"Better slow her down to eleven, twelve knots—whatever's comfortable," the pilot said, voicing what the Captain had already decided. "We're in no hurry. You'll be dropping the hook for the night in Elliott Bay: they won't berth you at Harbor Island till five at the earliest."

"Your cabin's made up—the purser saw to it. David?" the Captain said to the lounging shadow of the Third Officer. "Could you rustle up a fresh pot of coffee? Coffee for you, Mr.——?"

"Warren," the pilot said, "Warren Kress," speaking his name for the second time in fifteen minutes. "You have decaf?"

"We're out of decaf," the Third Officer said. "I can make you a cup of tea, if you want."

"My wife's got me on decaf these days," Kress said. "I'll take a glass of water, though." As he moved away from the radar, he unfolded himself, slowly, in sections, and stood as tall as a basketball player. From somewhere above the Captain's head, he said, "Yeah, the funeral was today."

"Sorry?"

"Captain Nielsen's grandkid."

"Not the little girl? He was talking about her last time he was on board. She—*died?*"

"Yeah, she got killed. Five years old. It was just a couple days after her birthday."

"Oh, Jesus. What was it—a car accident?"

"A cougar."

The brand of car that ran her down? the Captain thought. *Why does he have to say that?*

"A mountain lion," the pilot said. "She was killed by a cougar."

"How?"

"She was at her day-care. In Sequim. It's a Montessori place in a new development out there, real close to the woods. Ashley—the kid—was playing by herself in the yard, a ways off from the others, and the cougar dragged her into the bushes. Teacher was in the bathroom—and I wouldn't care to be in her shoes right now. The other kids say they never heard her yell or anything. She just disappeared. First they thought she'd wandered off, then that a child-molester must've abducted her. They were running around looking for a man, and it was half an hour before they found her. A clean kill—one bite severed the carotid artery. Her right arm was gone, torn right out of the socket. Port fifteen, Captain: zero-eight-zero."

The pilot, his voice level and dispassionate, sounded like a radio announcer reading from a bulletin.

"They got the cat. The Fish and Wildlife guys treed and shot her about a mile away. They were lucky to find her, but the day-care's toast: they were meant to have a chain-link fence around the yard, according to code, and the subcontractor fouled it up. They'd only been open since Labor Day. The family's bringing suit."

To starboard, the low black hills inched slowly past, pin-pricked with tangerine lights. Sequim.

"Everyone's in shock. More'n a thousand people showed up for the funeral, so I heard."

"Poor bloody Doug," the captain said.

"Yeah, he's taking it hard. He was on a Korean bulk carrier outbound from Tacoma when it happened, and they broke it to him when he came off in the launch. Captain Nielsen, he's an older man—"

No older than me, the captain thought.

"—he lived for that kid, after his divorce. When he wasn't at work, he spent all his time around at his son's place, babysitting. It was kind of a joke with us, Doug and his babysitting."

"I didn't know he was divorced."

"He never talked about it. Wife left him two, three years back, and went down to live in Santa Barbara. Or Santa Fe. Santa someplace. His son's a realtor—got an office out on Highway 101. But now that Ashley has passed on—"

Passed on? Hunched over the wheel, looking out into the dark, the Captain was picturing the animal, a tawny shape-shifter, padding soundlessly through damp leaf mulch, and the child, talking to herself, absorbed in her play. "Passing on" was not the phrase he would've chosen for what was going to happen next. Though he didn't know Doug Nielsen well, he could feel his grief as a distinct hollow in his own gut, and didn't at all care for the young pilot's manner, in which there was a trace of something close, almost, to amusement.

"Coffee's up." It was the Third Officer. The Captain took his mug from the tray with a distracted grunt. "We're talking about Doug Nielsen," he said.

"Doug the pilot?"

"He lost his little granddaughter. The funeral was today."

"It was an accident waiting to happen," the pilot said. "When we logged the old-growth, we degraded that whole habitat. Now we're into third-growth, and a third-growth plantation just doesn't have the sustenance these critters need. By the end of summer, they're starving, so they come into the cities to scavenge—you can't blame them for doing what they need to survive. When you get cougars killing kids in school-yards, it's a wake-up call." He peered for a moment into the hooded radar. "It's a wake-up call," he repeated, rolling the phrase as if he'd just minted it.

"That's how she died?" the Third Officer said. "A *cougar?*"

"And it's not just out on the Peninsula—it's happening right in Seat-tle. They've got cougars in Issaquah, garbage-bears in Woodinville. Around this time of year, the local news starts looking like 'Animal Planet,' with everybody shooting home videos of the wildlife in their yards. People used to get a thrill out of seeing a raccoon, but nowadays you're talking bobcats, skunks, black bears . . . critters that ought to be out hunting in the mountains. Instead, they're living out of trash-cans and Dumpsters in the 'burbs. You got the fairway buoy there, Cap.?

There's a whole new generation of animals that's being raised on left-over pizza and burgers and fries."

The buoy was a cat's-eye flash of yellow in the darkness. At half speed, lying low on its lines, heavy with cargo, the *Pacific Auriga* made a wide turn to starboard.

"One-two-zero."

"One-two-zero."

As the ship slid southeastward into the gullet of Puget Sound, the Third Officer watched the radar painting echoes on the screen. He could put names to the echoes—Wilson, Marrowstone, Bush, Double Bluff—now that the ship was coming into familiar water. Familiar water, but queer land. Though he'd never given much attention to the perils of the sea, the Third Officer was horribly alert to the perils of the countryside. When he saw green fields, he instinctively thought of pawing bulls. A spell of shore leave at his sister's house outside Brisbane had been turned into agony by a casual warning about spiders in the toilet.

This had been a rough trip, dogged by small misfortunes of timing and weather, and he'd been looking forward to his layover in Seattle. But even though he meant to go no further from the ship than a ten-dollar cab ride (split with the Radio Officer), the thought of wild bears stalking the suburbs upset him greatly. To fight his phobia, he was forever telling himself that his fears were irrational—but that would cut no ice now, not in this city.

"Take your urban coyotes—" the pilot said.

Please, let's don't, the Third Officer thought.

"They're interbreeding with the domestic canids. Take a look at the dogs around here—at their jaws and the way they carry their tails. You'd be surprised by how many of them are half-coyote. You're getting German shepherd–coyote mixes, lab–coyote mixes, collie–coyote mixes . . . and you wouldn't want to meet these guys on a dark night, I'm telling you."

On the water, the copper-colored land mass was squeezing in around the ship. Bush Point nicked the one-and-a-half-mile ring, though its light failed to show in the thick weather. Gazing into the dark, the Third Officer populated the invisible coast with wild and vicious beasts and felt a pang of homesickness for the tame streets of Stoke-on-Trent, where his parents lived, and where, touch wood, he'd be back in time for Christmas. His mum and dad always expected stories from him—an expectation he could rarely satisfy. But now he had a story to tell them over the Christmas pud and brandy butter.

In the house on Queen Anne Hill, the wind rattled the panes of the sash window in the bathroom where Finn was in the tub, decorating his upper lip and chin with gobs of fleecy foam.

"Where's Daddy?"

"He's out to dinner with a friend of his. From England."

"Ho, ho, ho!" Finn said in his deep Santa Claus voice.

"He won't be back till after you're asleep," Beth said from behind the green dinosaur towel she was sniffing, which smelled not unpleasantly of Finn, old soap, and chlorine from the public pool. It was Tom's turn to do the laundry—as she'd remind him with a Post-it note on the fridge.

"You know what?" In a movement that a yogi would have found hard to emulate, Finn lifted his right leg from the water and brought his foot close to his face for inspection.

"What, pumpkin?"

Squinting between his toes, he said, "I've been thinking."

"What have you been thinking?"

"It's a problem. Where would I be if I wasn't here?"

"You mean here in this house?"

"No." Finn studied his pink sole, frowning impatiently. "Where would I be if I wasn't here?"

"I don't know." Beth had been fighting a headache all afternoon, and a pile of work was waiting in her laptop downstairs. "Where would you be?"

"I wouldn't have a brain if I wasn't here." For a split second, Finn's face looked as it did when a hamster or a gerbil died, crumpling inwards like a dynamited building, but this time it crumpled into a fit of the giggles. He sat in the tub, engrossed in some huge private joke, idly popping bubbles with his forefinger.

Beth sat on the closed lid of the toilet and put on her largest, most reassuringly maternal smile. "Is this something you think about a lot, pumpkin?"

"What?"

"Like where you'd be if you weren't here?"

"Oh, I think about it all the time." Finn went on popping bubbles. "My toenails are too long."

As people said, Finn had his father's hair—not Tom's thinning, white-pepper Jewfro, but a thornbush of tight dark curls that made him easy to spot in the preschool swarm. It was a nagging worry to Beth that, along with the hair, Finn had inherited the mind that went with it.

Tom had a Jewfro without being Jewish, and a British accent without being British—at least not exactly. He wasn't Hungarian, though he was born there, and living in the United States certainly hadn't turned him into anything remotely resembling an American. It was his unplaceability—or, as she saw it now, his existential vagueness—that had so attracted her when they first met. He was like no-one she had ever known. The trouble was that after eight years Beth still had days when she didn't quite know who Tom was. When she saw stories about women who'd been unknowingly married to men who turned out to be mild-mannered spies or serial killers, she instinctively understood how that could be.

Clipping Finn's toenails, she saw out of the corner of her eye that he was playing with his penis. She pretended not to notice, then saw that he'd caught her out and was watching her, slyly, with the funny, lop-sided smile that was a copy of his father's. "Finn Janeway!" She stood up, spreading wide the dinosaur towel. "Come on. Out of the bath!"

"I'm not Finn Janeway," he said. "I'm Finn Szany."

She wished Tom hadn't told him that. "They're the same name, silly. 'Janeway' was just the way they said Szany in England."

"No it's not. It's different. Szany, Szany, Szany, Szany! I'm Finn Szany!"

She plucked him from the tub and bundled him into the towel.

"Can I have a cookie now?"

Later, after she'd read him a chapter of *Otis Spofford*, she lay with Finn under the covers in his bunk bed, listening to the house creak and grumble in the wind. Pitched high on the hill and facing south, it was exposed to the full blast of winter gales as they came barreling up Puget Sound. When the wind got under the eaves, it made owlish *whoo-whooing* noises, and Beth could hear it prowling through the junk in the attic. They needed to call in a roofer or one day soon the whole damn thing was going to fly right off—and the roof was only one of a hundred things that needed fixing.

Beth habitually thought of the house as more Tom's than hers. It was old and cranky, the southward tilt of the floors so pronounced that a ball of Finn's would roll from one end of the house to the other across warped boards of varnished fir. In three small earthquakes—mild premonitions of the promised Big One—she'd felt and heard the massive timber pilings grind deep in the shaly dirt of the basement, sounding like the teeth-on-wood gnawing of a tribe of super-rats. The floors rippled, books fell from their shelves and pictures off their hooks. A long S-shaped crack appeared in the plaster of the bathroom wall. After each earthquake, the balls rolled a little faster. "It's just settlement," Tom had said, but to her it felt more like progressive collapse.

She wriggled her arm out from underneath her sleeping son, pillowed his head on Squashy Bear, and slid sideways out from under the covers, then gently eased his thumb from his mouth. His lips opened and closed in a string of damp, unrequited goldfish kisses before he rolled away and again was gone. Finn went to sleep like grown-ups went to Bangkok or La Paz, taking off for a destination for which he alone had the currency and the ticket. He'd leave Beth feeling a little despondent, as if she'd just dropped a lucky friend at the airport and now had to make her way back to the office through heavy traffic. Reporting on his travels, he was no more vivid than the writers of most vacation postcards. "I had a dream about dogs," he'd say over his bowl of Cheerios, but you never heard what the dogs had been up to in his dreams.

There was a fiery crackle at the window as a rain squall hit the glass. Treading softly, Beth tidied Finn's discarded clothes into his laundry basket, checked on the hamsters, Oliver and Nancy, and the stick-insects, plugged in the night light, a grinning blue moon, and went downstairs to face the tangle of unedited copy about to ambush her on the screen of her notebook.

The house shivered around her in the wind. Even down in the kitchen, where she sat prodding distractedly at the keyboard, she could hear what sounded like burglars up in the attic. She found the Yellow Pages and looked up "Roofers"—not that anyone would come. They wouldn't even bother to return your call. You were in deep trouble if you lived in a falling house in this fast-rising city, where every contractor was otherwise engaged. You could get a venture capitalist on the line in five minutes, but trying to find a plumber or a carpenter was about as hopeless as locating a reliable daguerrotypist, shepherd, or ivory merchant.

Beth left voice-mail at five numbers and was dialing the sixth when Finn came down in his tartan pyjamas, carrying Squashy Bear.

"I woke up. I heard scary noises."

"Oh, pumpkin, it's only the wind." She opened her arms, and he sat in her lap, sucking his thumb. Through the jungle of his curls, she could see a line of print on the screen.

suits hang out with flowies at Cafe Ho on 12th and Caesar

"Come snuggle with me," Finn said, and then, after a long pause, "Please?"

They were halfway upstairs when the phone rang. For a mad moment, Beth thought, *Roofer!* and raced to field the call, but it was a recorded male voice saying, with monstrous jollity, "Got dings on your windshield? Call Magnolia Auto Glass at—"

"Fuck off," Beth whispered, and slammed the phone back into its cradle.

Finn watched her from the stairs, his eyes big as a lemur's. "Was that Daddy?"

"But of course," David Scott-Rice said loudly, with his new fanged smile, "they don't know how to live, Americans."

The solo Japanese diner, hunched in a booth across from the two Englishmen, risked a glance but met the eyes of Thomas Janeway and quickly found his plate of salmon deeply interesting.

"It's funny, but I've always thought that 'living' is something Americans generally tend to shine at, like synchronized swimming."

"I meant the writers," Scott-Rice said, with a touch of huffiness.

They were eating late—late for Seattle, anyway—at the Painted Table, where Scott-Rice could charge the meal to his hotel bill, and to the New York publisher who would be footing it.

"They're like exiles in their own country, half of them. Pynchon, Salinger, Roth . . . Who does Roth talk to up there in Connecticut? He's a recluse. Or What's-his-name, Gass. No, not Gass—the other one. Gaddis. Lives in a shack up a lane somewhere on Long Island . . ."

Seattle was the tenth and last city on Scott-Rice's book-tour, and he had the punch-drunk bravado that so often came with spending too long aloft at 39,000 feet, looking down at America. By the time English writers reached Seattle, they usually had the United States figured out from top to bottom, and Tom had spent a good deal of time having his adoptive home explained to him by these haggard, jet-lagged visitors.

"I'm afraid Gaddis has other problems on his hands. He died last year. And anyway, he had the reputation of being quite the party animal."

"Dead? I never heard that. Of course, it's different for you—you've always been an exile. It's so sexy to be an exile these days. Everybody wants to be one."

"Exile? I'm not an—"

"Oh, come on, what about Czechoslovakia?"

"Hungary. I was only two then, and that's a painfully self-absorbed stage. You know, I don't remember a blind thing about Hungary—too busy having tantrums, I imagine—and you can't really be in exile from a country that you have no memory of at all. As for here, just about everybody comes from somewhere else, so one can't even be an outsider, exactly. My mum's an exile, though. She's a real exile. You could go and visit her—she's got a flat in Romford now—but I can't imagine that you'd find her all that sexy."

Scott-Rice winkled a dime-sized Olympia oyster from its shell and twirled it on his fork close to the flame of the rushlight that burned on their table. "Funny little buggers, aren't they?" He blinked at Tom, his lashless blue eyes enlarged by thick wire-rimmed specs. "You know? I heard you on NPR—in Minneapolis. 'All Things Considered,' is it? Anyway, you were talking about 'food courts.'" His voice was comically severe. "You liked them."

"Yes. They're Finn's notion of the perfect restaurant."

"I'd never even heard of food courts. I was intrigued. I got my escort to take me to one for lunch." He pronged another tiny oyster. "It was quite ghastly."

"Yes, they do rather vary."

"Can we get this straight? On the radio, you said . . ." Scott-Rice pantomimed the act of recovering a memory from the deep: he threw his head back, pursed his lips, half-closed his eyes, then raised his forefinger and wagged it at Tom. "You said these places were . . . multicultural-blah . . . democratic-blah . . . liberty-and-the-pursuit-of-blah. You quoted—actually quoted—Thomas Jefferson."

"Ironically."

"It's a tease, isn't it? This unnatural affection for all things American. Food courts! It's a put-on. You just do it to annoy." He slapped vaguely at his clothing, then rootled in a trouser pocket. "It's your 'schtick,' right? You don't really believe it—"

"Didn't it remind you of picnics you had as a kid? Only indoors?"

"What?"

"Your lunch at the food court."

"We didn't stay to eat," Scott-Rice said loftily. "We found a perfectly nice Italian place. With proper wine." He fished a pack of cigarettes out of his pocket, shook one free, and tapped its end twice on the tablecloth. An unfiltered Camel, slightly creased around the midriff.

This was another new thing about Scott-Rice. In London, a smoking city, Tom had never once seen him smoke, whereas Tom himself couldn't work, or even talk, without the shield and solace of a Benson & Hedges close to hand. He'd quit—"for Finn's sake," as Beth put it—but four years off cigarettes hadn't freed him from their thrall. Working alone, he still chewed on tablets of nicotine gum. His secret fantasy was that when the four-minute warning sounded, he'd cadge a cigarette from someone in the street and enjoy one last heady blameless smoke before the Bomb.

A spurt of flame from a plastic lighter, and Scott-Rice took a cautious hit. He quickly exhaled, smoking like a novice. Tom thought he was probably doing it only to *épater* the Americans: when in Rome, do as the Greeks.

From behind his penumbra of enviable smoke—at once alien and intimate to Tom, like the recorded voice of a dead friend—Scott-Rice said, "An uncle of mine once ran into Guy Burgess when he was in Moscow. The poor sod—"

"Sir, I'm afraid this restaurant is not a smoke-friendly environment." Their waiter, a boy of college age, too young for his uniform of black silk shirt and black butcher's apron, had materialized beside their table, head dipped confidentially close to Scott-Rice's ear.

"Oh?"

"I sympathize. I must tell you, sir, I'm a smoker myself."

"Really?" The full wattage of his astonishingly blue gaze turned on the waiter, he lifted the Camel to his lips and sucked on it reflectively.

His voice rising, the waiter said: "What I'm telling you, sir, is that this is a no-smoking area. Smoking is not permitted in this restaurant."

"Got you." Scott-Rice smiled his crooked smile, disclosing large gray teeth. He searched the table item by item, then lightly stubbed the cigarette into the last of his Olympia oysters, which for an instant seemed restored to life. As the glowing tip of the Camel touched it, the oyster wriggled, in a tiny spasm of offended flesh.

"Shall I remove that, sir?"

The bent cigarette was darkening as it soaked up brine.

"Yes, why don't you do that? Thanks."

The Japanese man now leaned back in his seat, watching the Englishmen as if they were the after-dinner cabaret, as the frozen-faced waiter loped off toward the kitchen with the violated oyster shells, the skirts of his apron swishing officiously against his pants.

"Don't you love the way they talk?" Scott-Rice said. "Sometimes dealing with Americans seems rather like trying to have a conversation with a speak-your-weight machine."

Not for the first time, Tom was relieved that Beth had cried off dinner: David Scott-Rice was an acquired taste, like Marmite or black pudding, and he doubted if Beth would've seen his point. Tom, though, had always had a soft spot for him. He'd never actually finished one of his books, but he liked the pugnacious book reviews, the gossip column in the *Times Literary Supplement* that ended in a libel suit, the late Eighties TV show "The Book Biz," where Scott-Rice genially insulted poets, publishers, agents, novelists, English dons, newspaper critics, and stage-managed such happy confrontations as the one between George Steiner and Gore Vidal. A dangerous young turk in those days, Scott-Rice popped up everywhere, attracting abuse, mockery, and more fear than people liked to admit. When he did a hatchet-job on a book in the *Observer,* notice was taken, and a string of little hatchet-jobs usually followed in its wake.

But that was long ago, and since moving to the U.S., Tom had rarely seen his name. A strangely mild piece in the *New Yorker;* a "Diary" column in the *London Review of Books;* some so-so reviews, all in the

British press, of his two novels (Tom bought the first) that came out in quick succession in the early Nineties. He seemed unknown in America, so Tom had gone to his reading at the Elliott Bay Book Company expecting to find a scattered congregation far outnumbered by a host of empty chairs. But Scott-Rice had drawn a nearly full house. (As it turned out, he'd been on both "Charlie Rose" and "Fresh Air" the day before.) Several of Tom's students in the M.F.A. program were there—Mary Ellen Girthlin, Todd Levitt, Hildy Blom. A bit mystified, he waved to each of them across the room.

Before going downstairs to the reading, Tom had bought a copy of *Crystal Palace*. Sitting in the back row, he studied the dustjacket. Scott-Rice had changed his name. The book's author was Dave Rice, and the short bio on the back flap claimed he was born in 1956 and "grew up in south London." Nothing about Oxford, where he'd been at Balliol. Nothing about his long, louche literary career. Nothing, even, about the two novels that had come out in England. Between his south London childhood and his appearance this evening, he might have spent his entire time in jail. In America, Dave Rice was a brand-new man—and it dawned on Tom that on Sunday he'd skimmed a review of *Crystal Palace* in the *New York Times Book Review,* but had seen no reason to connect Scott-Rice's last-minute phone call with the "engagingly bold new voice in English fiction" discovered by the *Times.*

Dave Rice, when he ambled up to the podium, turned out to be twice the size of the old Scott-Rice. Cerise shirt unbuttoned halfway down his chest, he looked like a dugong bloated on too plentiful a diet of sea parsley.

Head cocked to the right to catch the performance with his best ear, Tom listened to Rice read from his book in a peculiar accent that was half West Indian, half East End. Before beginning, he lit a lawless Camel and placed it beside him in a saucer, where it burned slowly, untouched, into a sagging worm of ash. Speaking in the character of someone named Caz, Scott-Rice delivered a kind of ventriloquial tirade—a sequence of riffs on the workings of the London Stock Exchange, the Spice Girls, New Labour, the cult of Diana, scooters, mad-cow disease, Lymeswold cheese, the Lottery, Madonna, and the decline of the Gunners, the Arsenal Football Club. This Caz character was meant to be in his twenties and employed by a shady brokerage firm to make cold calls, selling high-risk shares to gullible pensioners.

The telephone (as he read, Scott-Rice cupped an imaginary one between his shoulder and his cheek) was what the M.F.A. crew would have called a structural device, meaning that the book consisted mostly of Caz's cold calls. When not on the phone—and, quite often, on it—Caz dabbled in E and crystal meth. Hence the title.

Scott-Rice being Dave Rice being Caz was a hit. Tom was laughing along with the rest of the audience, though the printed text seemed a little flat to him, and the narrative thread tenuous at best. Every so often, he glanced over at Hildy Blom, who was from Spokane, and could hardly have heard of Peter Mandelson and the brouhaha about his house in Notting Hill. Yet when Caz laid into "Mandy" and his puppy-dog, she heaved with giggles—and Tom realized that never before, in eight weeks of classes, had he seen Hildy Blom laugh. It was a nice laugh, too. He'd try fishing for it in the future.

The funniest thing about the evening was that Scott-Rice got away with what in America usually counted as murder. Had a middle-aged white writer from New York showed up to read in the comic, exaggerated voice of a black kid from the projects, the room would have been loud with the censorious scrape and rattle of emptying chairs. But Dave Rice had them eating out of his hand. They adored listening to the out-of-shape Brit with his trademark cigarette read his broad-brush travesty of a street-smart boy from Battersea Rise. Scott-Rice was old enough (and surely he was born in 1950, not 1956) to have fathered half his listeners, yet he somehow managed to stand before them as a brat after their own hearts.

When question-time came, Scott-Rice went on speaking in character. His questioners, and they were many, called him "Dave," and it was in a Daveish voice that he replied—a nasal, throwaway, south-of-the-river whiffle. His signing-line stretched in a long, patient conga around the perimeter of the room, and it wasn't until he got back to the hotel, where Tom was waiting for him in the bar, that he reverted to an Oxonian drawl, 1970s variety, with the requisite fine shading of London-suburban.

After congratulating him on his reading, Tom said, "So how's the book done in England?"

"It's not out there yet," Scott-Rice said. "Marketing strategy. They're waiting on the buzz from the States." The way he said this, and the speed with which he changed the subject, seemed shifty, but Tom didn't pry.

Scott-Rice was soon busy digging into his rack of lamb with a wooden-handled butcher-knife. Then he pronged a neat cube of rosy meat and held it in mid-air. "You're playing your cards close to your chest," he said. "What are you up to? You're sitting on a five-hundred-page manuscript, putting commas in in the mornings and taking them out in the afternoons? You've got terminal block? You're racing towards the home stretch? The natives are getting restless."

"Oh, I don't know," Tom said. "I've got a lot of . . . stuff. I think there's probably a book in there, somewhere. It just hasn't quite jelled."

"You know, after *Tunnels,* I was afraid you were going to be a one-book man. Tour-de-force. Bloody marvelous. But I couldn't see where on earth you could go after that. Didn't seem to lead anywhere. *He's written himself into a cul-de-sac,* was my thought. But then you did your war book. Knocked my socks off."

"I'm afraid your socks are quite safe from me for the moment."

"Does it have a name?"

The box into which Tom threw notes, quotes, scraps of dialogue, newspaper cuttings, and the rest of the stuff that still hadn't quite jelled had once contained wine from a vineyard in Idaho. The side of the box was stamped HELL'S CANYON 1994 CHARDONNAY.

"*Hell's Canyon,*" Tom said, and laughed.

"Well, that sounds like a strongish start."

"The book wouldn't live up to it, unfortunately. I hate titles that promise more than they can possibly deliver. When I was fourteen, I borrowed *Howards End* from the library. I thought it was going to be about someone called Howard, whose end, I imagined, would be sticky in the extreme. Instead, it turned out to be about a bloody house, in Hertfordshire of all places. It was acutely disappointing. But I did like *Wuthering Heights* . . . as house books go. The trouble is that other people have already bagged all the really good unassuming titles. What I'd really like to write is *Diary of a Nobody,* or *The Man Without Quali-ties.* I think my ideal book is one where you're pleasantly surprised when anything happens at all."

They were the restaurant's last customers. The Japanese man had vacated his booth long ago, and their waiter was going from table to table, flicking each one meaningfully with a napkin. Between flicks, he put the evil eye on Scott-Rice, who eventually got around to dealing with the bill.

"What's the usual tip here?"

"Double the sales tax."

"I just tripled it. I want that horrid boy to feel a stab of remorse."

"He won't."

"Nightcap?"

There was a poignant reek of smoke in the bar, but Scott-Rice's Camels remained in his pocket. Tom had planned to mooch one, for old time's sake, and it was all he could do to stop himself from observing who was now supposed to be the great smoker.

Wading into the Armagnac, Scott-Rice said, "I imagine you have some gigs for visiting writers at this university of yours? Lot of people passing through?"

Dulled by wine, Tom was slow on the uptake. "We're a poor school. We haven't had the money for that kind of thing. But we've just had a windfall, so now we're trying to get Don DeLillo for a month."

"A windfall?"

"An avalanche, really," Tom said thickly. "Four and a half million dollars. This . . . Internet entrepreneur. He's giving it to the program, quite out of the blue. He founded a company that makes a sort of switch for Web sites. It's based in Menlo Park in California, but he's building a house here on Lake Washington and says he wants to give back to the community the same money that his house will cost him. 'Outreach,' he calls it. Claims his first love has always been literature. He's an Indian."

"A *Red* Indian?"

"No, the other kind. He's an Old Harrovian."

Scott-Rice carefully did up a button on his shirt. "So he ought to look pretty favorably on English writers."

"Oh, English, Japanese, South American—you name it. He wants UW to establish a global footprint in the world of modern writing. That's the way he talks."

"This guy went to Harrow?"

"I think he went to Stanford after that. Or Middlebury. Some place like that."

"How much are you offering DeLillo?"

"We started at thirty-five thousand, but might have to go up."

"Christ." Scott-Rice looked hungrier than he had all evening.

It would be hard to tell him, Tom thought, that when Shiva Ray said "writers," he meant winners of, or at least famous candidates for, the Nobel Prize, not people like David Scott-Rice. It had been hard enough to sell him on Don DeLillo.

Scott-Rice smiled vaguely into his brandy. "I didn't know Web sites had switches."

"I didn't either. Beth explained it to me, but I've forgotten how it goes."

"Four and a half . . . fucking . . . million."

"Welcome to America—the land you despise."

"And what does DeLillo have to do for it?"

"A public reading. Afternoon office hours with students. Nothing much. He'll be here basically to hang out and show his face—if we can get him."

"And you'll go up—to what? Fifty? Sixty?"

"Something like that. We're also writing to Bellow." Tom tried to drive home the point. "And Toni Morrison. And Günter Grass."

"And all expenses covered, accommodation and so forth?"

Tom nodded dolefully. The agreement with the university, which by now should've been signed, was still in the hands of Shiva Ray's lawyers. "We're just putting out feelers at present."

"You want another?" Scott-Rice already had his hand up, signaling the bartender. "The air fare would be first class, of course?"

Shortly before midnight, Tom recovered his VW from the valet-parker. The rain had ceased, though the wet streets dazzled, and stoplights tossed in the wind on their overhead wires. Watching the wing-mirror for police cars—Scott-Rice's publicist would surely be impressed by the bar bill they'd run up—he soft-pedaled his way around three sides of the block, and turned cautiously north on First Avenue.

A rift in the speeding clouds revealed the young moon, hazy and tarnished above the wide blackness of the bay. At this hour, the streets of rich Seattle belonged to the poor, who trudged in ones and twos, hunched against the weather, past the lighted boutiques, oriental carpet shops, and galleries of antique artifacts from Oceania. In every doorway, a ragged sleeping form. The walking homeless, with their backpacks and bedrolls, sported wild shovel beards and greasy broad-brimmed hats, like hapless prospectors left over from the Gold Rush.

At the red light on First and Pike, two such characters shambled across the street in front of him. One wore a Seahawks cap, the other what looked like a bona-fide Stetson and full old-timer regalia—knotted bandanna, plaid lumber-jacket, jeans, and disintegrating cowboy boots. A guitar was slung across his back, and he pushed the remainder of his—or their—worldly goods in a Safeway supermarket cart. Shamed by the loose talk about money that evening, Tom dug out his wallet and found two twenties, then rolled down the window. "Hey, guys? Perhaps you could use this?"

Seahawks stepped over to the car and took the bills. "Thanks, pardner. And you drive careful now." When he held up the money so his friend could see it, this ossified survivor of the Old West made an approbatory O with forefinger and thumb for Tom, who gave him a thumbs-up sign in return. The man's grinning face caught the light from a street-lamp, and Tom saw he was a Pacific Islander—Samoan, probably—and, as the light changed to green, heard the clatter of the cart wheels on the cobbles that led down to the Pike Place Market and its food-rich Dumpsters. The Samoan, who had now seen that his bill was a twenty, called, "Good luck, man!"

Tom hardly felt in need of good luck nowadays. His new American life—and after eight years, he was surprised by how it still retained the gleam of novelty—had happened to him rather as a child's Christmas might fall suddenly, unheralded, out of season. For a man long used to solitude, irregularly punctuated by flings and affairs that blazed, then fizzled out, like fireworks on Guy Fawkes Night, marriage and fatherhood were the big gifts. The job—if being the Weyerhaeuser Distinguished Professor of Creative Writing could be called a job, exactly—had liberated him from the quiet panic and exiguous dodges of freelancing, and left him able to enjoy those gifts in all their unanticipated luxury and profusion.

Visitors from London and New York might think his affection for this city a pose, but Tom was happy in Seattle, whose ambiguities suited him perfectly. It wasn't all that big, but it wasn't all that little, either. Though gratifyingly remote—the Pacific Northwest was something like

America's own Outer Hebrides—it was also central to the big world in ways that made London, at least, seem provincial, to borrow Scott-Rice's tiresome word for Seattle. And unlike most American cities that Tom knew, there was a *here* here, where herring gulls were a traffic hazard and all streets led down to the water, where the older buildings pursued a guileless infatuation with the architecture of Ancient Rome, and ungovernable greenery—bramble, vine, salal—rose up defiantly from every crevice and scrap of waste ground, as if to strangle the city fathers' vain Roman ambitions.

Living in Islington (Holloway, really, but the neighbors called it Islington), Tom had never felt this warmth towards London. There, he was most at home in the city of Victorian novels, the London of *Tunnels,* his first book, but a quick foray to, say, the Pentonville Road of 1980 made him feel a fugitive. He'd scurry nervously from shop to shop, noticing little, coat pulled up around his ears, then escape back to the flat overlooking Arundel Square and his forest-green Olivetti with the overflowing ashtray beside it, to London *circa* 1850—the "rookeries" of Saint Giles; Savoury Dock, where Bill Sikes met his death in *Oliver Twist* and the great cholera epidemic started in 1849; the old Garrick Club in King Street, with Thackeray, Trollope, and Millais; Jack Black, the Queen's Ratcatcher; Tyburn and Marshalsea . . . Through this fog-ridden world of insanitary tenements, gin palaces, and scented West End drawing rooms, Tom moved, when things were going well, with a citizen's confident swagger, but the London that stretched away beyond the double-glazing of his study window remained a gray enigma to him.

It was in Seattle that he had at last learned to live in the present, more or less. He had his lapses, but nowadays mostly stood fair and square in 1999. He knew where Costco was. He enjoyed trekking out, with Finn and Beth, to the Northgate Mall. He had his elevenses at Starbucks. He'd taken Finn to see a Mariners game at the Kingdome, just a few weeks before the stadium was blown to smithereens. Though the Olivetti still occasionally saw active service, it spent most of its time in retirement on a bookshelf while Tom jiggered away at the new Compaq, Pentium III–fuelled, writing, or trying to write, about the here-and-now. In his radio commentaries, he talked of himself as "an analogue person in a digital world," but that was a faux-modest mask. Though he wasn't quite yet there, Tom was going digital.

Laboring in third up the Counterbalance—how he had dreaded the gear-shifts involved here, when Beth was teaching him to drive—he could now name each passing street: Aloha, Ward, Prospect, Highland, Comstock. At Galer, he turned left and allowed the car to find its own way home.

On Tenth West he parked on the street, under the big sycamore in front of the house, for Beth's new plum-colored Audi now commandeered the garage. The storm had piled the leaves in soft drifts across the sidewalk and pavement, where they shifted like uneasy sleepers in the warm salt-smelling wind that thrashed the branches overhead. The house was dark, and the bulb in the porch-light was burnt out. Fumbling for his house-key, Tom stepped back into the street and stood under one of the repro gas lamps the city had installed in a recent blitz of urban prettification.

His keys were—as Beth would say—an issue. Two jumbo-sized, interlinked steel rings' worth, they formed an irregular lump of clinking ballast in his right-hand trouser pocket. "You're so anal-retentive it's not funny," she told him. "Those stupid keys. They're so heavy they tilt you sideways when you walk. They wreck your pockets. It takes you hours to find the right one. Couldn't you just take a deep breath and toss, like, your thirty least-favorites?"

He had keys to hotel rooms, to London flats unvisited in twenty years, deposit-boxes in railway stations, long-abandoned suitcases, tennis courts, filing cabinets, his parents' old house in Ilford, his student digs in Brighton. The difficulty was that each one summoned a precise image of the lock it used to fit. In a way he couldn't bring himself to explain, they still opened doors for him. So he hung on to the key to Sue's place in Onslow Square, long after she'd married and moved to somewhere down in Hampshire. He'd tried to segregate them, moving his American keys to one ring, and planning to exile the European collection to a drawer in the study, yet they remained obstinately coupled. Without their familiar weight, Tom felt strangely insubstantial. He shuffled, unhurriedly, through the Yales and Chubbs until he found the Ace he was looking for. No key had ever been so precious to him.

When they first caught sight of the house—even before Beth turned off the ignition—Tom had known it was the right place for them. On a block of grandiose remodels involving clerestory windows, wraparound balconies, azure-tiled roofs, fake adobe, and basement carports, the house stood out like the lone honest burgher in a line-up of con artists. "Prairie-style, 1910, in need of some minor refurbishment and modernization," according to the spec sheet, but what Tom saw was amplitude and solidity—the generous overhang of the eaves, the massive square timber pillars of the porch; an air of bluff, unpretentious, American self-confidence. You'd trust a house like that. You'd buy a used car from it.

Standing with the realtor in the bare-earth basement while Beth's footsteps sounded—very faintly—overhead, Tom admired the great rough-cut fir pilings that held the house aloft. "They don't make them like this anymore," the man said. "Sturdy. Deep-rooted." Just the qualities for Tom.

The realtor told him that it had been built by a well-known Seattle shipwright, and there was a shiplike woodiness about it—the paneled walls with high box-beam ceilings, the stout window-seats, a black carved fireplace that would've looked well in a fair-sized Elizabethan manor. Pointing at the handsome triangular shelving built into a corner of the dining room, the realtor said, "Your china hutch." Yes, Tom thought, they'd need china, and in an instant he'd filled the hutch with craquelure Wedgwood.

The rooms at the back looked out at Elliott Bay and the Sound. On the third floor, there was a single bedroom with a gabled window; an eagle's perch, with its aerial view of the miniature Manhattan of downtown, the miles of sun-speckled open water, islands like floating clumps of moss, and, beyond the islands, saw-toothed mountains, snowcapped even on a mid-August afternoon. Here, in this amazing eyrie, Tom had stood hand-in-hand with Beth and said, "I'll take it," smiling because that was a line from a Larkin poem, and funny in this context. But it would take too long to explain.

Back in the car, Beth said, "You didn't talk him down!"

The asking-price was $192,500—within a whisker of what Tom had got for his two-bedroomed leasehold flat in London N7, in a grimy stucco-fronted building that looked like a birthday cake on which the mice had been at work. In just three words, Tom had transmuted base metal into gold, and to have haggled over the price would have wrecked the magic of the exchange.

"It's a bit dark," Beth said, but he could see only sun on snow, and the mercurial dazzle of the sea.

*　　　*　　　*

Stepping quietly into the dark hall, he stumbled into Beth's old bike, which slid from wall to floor with a dream-wrecking crash. Tom listened, but heard nothing from the sleepers upstairs. He switched on the light and, carrying the bike as carefully as if it were constructed of spun glass, moved it well clear of the front door. Its chain was off, and the brakes seemed to have locked solid on the front wheel. Beth hadn't ridden it in years, but it had become part of the furniture of the house, like the hutch, for which they'd never bought china, and which now housed a miscellany of stuffed toys, paperbacks, CDs, board games, and Disney videos, along with Orlando, the goldfish, who swam alone amid the bright green plastic foliage in his bowl.

Tom shucked off his loafers at the foot of the stairs and tiptoed up to look in on Beth. Her reading lamp was still on, but she was huddled under the comforter, a scrap of razored blonde fur visible against the pillow, her book splayed open on the carpet. He picked it up: *Your Hyperactive Child.*

"What was the noise?" Her voice was groggy with sleep.

"Your bike. Sorry."

"—Take it to the dump . . ."

He sat on his side of the bed, stroking the nape of her neck.

"Mmmm," she hummed, then settled back to sleep again.

Finn's eyes had welled with sudden tears when she came home with her new buzzcut, but Tom had felt a rush of tender excitement. People talked of the boredom of marriage, but Beth was always surprising him, and never more often than now, when each day seemed to call forth from her some unexpected grace or favor. Her familiar footfall on the porch steps was still rousing for him, this sound of news from the outside world, of treats, and jokes, and bombshells. Before, Tom struggled with the idea of love much as he had with trigonometry at school, getting the general drift without ever quite mastering the details, but Beth had made it seem as easy as two-plus-two.

Lately, she'd been surpassing herself, with her new hair, new car, new job, new language, even. Just this evening she burst through the front door to announce, "There's a jihad on at work!" her knotted face looking exactly like some fundamentalist holy warrior's. Last night, he bent over her while she was working on the laptop from which she'd become inseparable; nodding at the screen, she said "Bitstorm!" and he'd kissed her wonderingly. She was amazing.

Not yet ready for sleep, and anxious not to disturb Beth in hers, he padded next door into Finn's room, where the blueish astral gleam of the night-light showed him asleep on his back, arms wide, fists lightly curled, head pillowed on Squashy Bear, his mouth a candid O. He was not, surely, *hyperactive?* Tom pulled the covers up under his chin, moved—as always—by the trustful unguardedness of his sleeping child. No adult slept like that. He and Beth adopted the same defensive fetal crouch: some nights, he cuddled up behind her, some nights she did the same for him, his right hand spread wide on her bare stomach or her left hand on his. "Why do we sleep as if the Furies were after us?" he'd once asked her. But Finn had no Furies. His body lay any-old-how, wide open, in a posture of reckless surrender. A circular patch of drool the size of a silver dollar darkened his pillowcase. Tom brushed his forehead with his lips. This love, too, was easy—far easier than he ever could have guessed. In London, he'd thought of fatherhood as a burden borne by other men, not his sort of thing at all. Yet in this, as in so much else, what had seemed true there had been proved false here. American alchemy again.

He stood at the window and watched the storm blowing itself out. On the Sound, the broken water was ribbed with streaks and gashes of reflected light. The last ferry from Bremerton, lit up like a chandelier, was moving fast across Elliott Bay, and the traveling blaze defined a matte-black rectangle closer inshore, a big ship lying at anchor almost within spitting-distance of the house. The shadow became substance as, bit by bit, the winking waves pricked out its silhouette: twin radar domes atop a high bridge near the stern, containers piled almost to the level of the bridge, a stubby foremast on the blunt bow.

Studying the motionless black ship and listening to Finn breathe in his sleep, Tom was struck dizzy by the thought that he wanted nothing else than to be here, now.

2.

At 5:20 A.M., the *Pacific Auriga,* loosely attended by one
small tug, docked at Pier 28 on Harbor Island. Two hours
before dawn, the fierce sodium lights of the container terminal made it look like a giant illuminated stage with all of
Elliott Bay as its darkened auditorium. In windless calm, the
ship slid quietly backwards into the berth—the sea boiling
briefly white under the stern—and stopped within inches of
the pier's concrete wall. Heaving-lines were passed to the
half-dozen men waiting on the dock, who silently hauled
the massive warps ashore and dropped their spliced eyes
over the iron bollards.

Up on the bridge, the pilot said, "Nice."

"New bow-thrusters," the Captain said, his face flushed
and tautly smiling. "The old ones were gutless and she was
a pig to handle at close quarters. Last refit we had, they put
in new thrusters. That made all the difference."

"What's your tonnage? Forty-five?"

"Fifty-one." Coffee mug in hand, the Captain looked up at the tall pilot. "Remember me to Doug, will you? Tell him I was shocked to hear his news."

Out on the wharf, two INS agents sat in a parked Camry with government plates, waiting to board the ship. They'd stopped at a gas station with an espresso stand and were sipping Americanos from paper cups emblazoned with the Torrefazione logo.

"After dial-up, you wouldn't believe it, it's so damn fast," Refugio Martinez said. "I mean, it's click and you're *there*."

"You install the modem yourself?" Stacy Sakiyama said.

"Wasn't nothing to it. They send you a kit, and you just follow the instructions."

"When it comes to that stuff, I'm clueless."

"I could put it in for you. You'd love DSL, it's magic. You have to be inside of fifteen hundred feet from the main cable, but where you live that's no problem."

"Uh-huh. Boarding ladder's down. Looks like we're on."

The agents set up a temporary command post at a table beneath the electronic dart-board in the officers' lounge and processed the crew's passports, which the purser had produced in a rubber-banded bundle.

The Captain, still buoyed by his textbook docking operation, stopped by to play the amiable host. "Coffee? Biscuits?" he said. "I mean, cookies to you."

"We already got coffee, thanks," Sakiyama said. "Cookies would be good. You're going to be seeing more of us today than you probably want to, Captain. They're sending out S.A.'s to do a spot check on the cargo. They should be here at eight."

"I've got a lunch date at noon with our agent here," the Captain said.

"I don't think so," Martinez said, not looking up from the passport he was studying. "Rest of the crew can go, soon as we finish this, but they'll need you and the loading officer."

"You hear about Long Beach yesterday?" Sakiyama said. "Seventeen Chinese in a container. That's Long Beach, Vancouver, *and* L.A.— all in the last couple weeks."

Martinez stamped the passport and scribbled his initials over the stamp. "There's a rumor floating around the Chinese community that the President's going to declare an amnesty for illegals on the first of January. That's what the snakeheads are saying, anyway, so I guess business must've slowed down—and now everybody's trying to sneak in before the deadline."

"Everything normal on this trip, Captain"—Sakiyama glanced at the passport.—"Williams?"

The Captain snorted. "I don't know what you call normal. We ran into some funny weather on the trip out, which put us three days late in Hong Kong. Then we were five days late out of Osaka, where a Maersk ship got ahead of us in line. When we finally left, we had a big tropical storm just to the north of us, and it kept us company all the way to Juan de Fuca. We were meant to be in here last Tuesday and out of here yesterday. We're eight days off-schedule."

"I meant with the containers. You didn't see or hear anything?"

"Weather we had, they could've thrown a rock concert down there and no one would've heard a thing."

"You take on any rag-tops in Hong Kong?"

"There may be one or two down there. You'd have to talk to Bob Stenhouse, the loading officer."

In the corridor, passport in hand, the Captain met the Chief Engineer, already dressed for shoregoing in raincoat and rollneck sweater.

"We've got the Black Gang with us for the day."

"What's up?"

"Spot-checking for illegals. You're all right—you can go. But I was meant to be having lunch with Tony Andressen—"

"Captain?" Martinez called from the doorway of the officers' lounge. "We'll need the cargo manifest."

"Go fetch . . ." the Chief said.

In his cabin on 9-Deck, David Pilbury, the Third Officer, was readying himself to face the wilds of Seattle. Freshly shaven, in peek-a-boo Grinch boxer shorts, and smelling powerfully of Old Spice, he wriggled into his purple-striped Rugby shirt and faced the big decision of the morning: Levis or leathers. He settled for the leathers.

At six, Beth was up and showered. Leaving the autodrip coffeemaker to hiss and splutter on the kitchen counter, she brought in the *New York*

Times from the porch and glossed the headlines. The Cuban boy was still the big story—only two months older than Finn, and the poster child for the last battle in the Cold War. Of course Elian should go back home. The Miami Cubans were a pain in the ass—their hatred of Castro now righteously disguised as sentimental love for a little boy whose life they were only too happy to turn into some political game-show. She skimmed Maureen Dowd, then filled her insulated beaker with coffee and turned to the Business Section to check on how her stock was doing in the Nasdaq. Down ⅛, up 162½ on the year.

On a blue Post-it, she wrote:

T—
It's pool day today—pack F's swim-things. Don't forget goggles (!)
Laundry?—pretty please? Back 6-ish.

She signed it *XOB* and pinned it to the fridge with a plastic-asparagus magnet, then washed down a quartet of vitamin pills with a swig of bitter coffee.

Outside, she waded through a slurry of fallen leaves. Lights were on in half the houses on the street, and a gang of early-rising crows had set up a raucous parliament in the trees. Tom's VW was parked askew under the sycamore, its front wheel up on the curb, its windshield splashed with a glob of creamy, speckled crow shit. Triggered by the remote, the ancient machinery of the garage door groaned and clattered as it canted back to disclose the dark spectre of the Audi.

The locks clicked. The interior lights bloomed. Beth snuggled down her coffee beaker in the cup-holder, turned on the ignition, then faced the constellation of red lights and dials, more like the control console of a 747 than of any car she'd known, and breathed in the Audi's good air. When she touched the glowing button of the CD player, an explosive ripple of drums and percussion led to a few bars of melody picked out on twelve-string guitars and the low, raw, sleepy-talking voice of Lucinda Williams singing "Right on Time."

The *whomp, whomp, whomp* of the bass line throbbed with a jackhammer pulse that found an answering reverberation in her own bones. The car had eight hidden speakers and a subwoofer—and whatever *that* was, it did it for her. Beth was right in there with the band. The intimacy of it was freaky: she *was* Lucinda. Turning the volume up a notch, she eased out of the garage and was soon afloat, the Audi's tires seeming to not quite touch the uneven surface of the street.

The car was six weeks old, with 1,143 miles on the clock. Its purchase ranked high among the big events of her life. Most of the important things had just sort of happened to her: going to Smith, coming out from Brooklyn to Seattle (that had taken nine days in Chad's rustbucket Ford Galaxy, and they'd split almost the moment they arrived), then meeting Tom and getting pregnant with Finn . . . But the Audi was entirely her own adventure, and the most reckless act of self-indulgence that she'd ever dared to commit. She was still unnerved and excited by her own audacity, as if in buying the car she had opened up a whole new world of impulse and extravagance. What next? Sky-diving? Canoeing down the Amazon?

Her pleasure was tempered by a vague, generalized alarm at what the car had uncovered in her character. Certainly, it went against what she had always believed to be her natural grain. In the showroom, she'd been astonished at herself. It was surely not her but a third person who'd felt that stab of hungry desire at the sight of the bone-colored leather seats with blue piping. It was only upholstery, for godsake! Yet the ache to make it hers was as intense and blind as the promptings of sex—or sex as she remembered it, from rather long ago. This, she'd lectured herself, was like a high-school romance—and you can't have a crush on a fucking *car*.

She mentioned it offhandedly one evening, while Finn was watching "Rugrats," expecting—hoping, really—that Tom would laugh her out of it. Feeling more than faintly absurd, she passed him the fat brochure that she'd come away with from the dealership. He studied it carefully, reading each page like it was *Our Mutual Friend* or something. Every so often, he glanced up at her with the crooked, private, British smile whose meaning she could never securely fathom. "What are puddle-lights?" he asked.

Beth shrugged.

"Performance and panache," he read, "visceral in its appeal. Like sculpture, worthy of long, loving, and knowing looks from any angle. Every angle." Speaking in his "radio" voice and rolling his r's, he gazed at her over the tops of the half-moon glasses that added ten years to his age. "So which are you going to get, the manual or the automatic?"

Feeling satirized, she smiled and shook her head, but two days later went back to the dealership for one last look. This, she thought, would purge her of her longing, and she could walk away light-heartedly, but the blue piping did its seductive thing again. She got the automatic, because they didn't have the manual in her color, which was Andorra Red. When she wrote the check, she scribbled it out fast, as if it were for groceries at Thriftway. After the trade-in (an '87 Dodge Spirit with a long gash on the driver's side) and with tax and license, the Audi came to—she wrote this bit especially quickly—*thirty-six thousand, eight hundred twenty-four and* $^{oo}/_{100}$ *dollars.* It looked like the price of a house. Still, she had nearly $19,000 left over from her first batch of vested options, with the next instalment falling due in less than six months' time.

At work, the new car was of no account at all. Where the scarred Dodge had looked suspiciously like a statement, the Audi shrank modestly into the lot where Steve Litvinof parked his silver Mercedes SL500 and the tech staff rolled up in new Porsche Boxsters and Lexuses. It was at home that Beth felt prickly and protective of it. She hid it in the garage, with the door that stuck as often as it creaked open, to save it from the cynical gaze of Tom's UW friends. When the three of them were out *en famille,* she chose to ride as a passenger in the Volkswagen, even though this meant yielding the front seat to Finn.

With the Audi came the realization that she had never until now had a real place of her own. Between roommates, Chad's apartment, more roommates, and Tom, she'd always fitted in as best she could to other people's spaces, taking for granted their music, their pots and pans, their books, their posters from the Louvre. Her junk and their junk got boiled up together in a stew that was everybody's and nobody's. She and Tom had furnished the Queen Anne house together, but it was he who nearly always paid and often exercised his right of veto. This Beth accepted as one of one of life's givens, like the weather.

Now she had climate control and programmed the Audi to produce a constant temperate summer of 72 degrees, even with the power sunroof open. Here she was the sole proprietor of her own estate, and from the driver's seat began to see vistas that reminded her of that long view from Blenheim Palace, the year before Finn was born: the turf cropped close by sheep, the misty elms and oaks, the soothing distance of all those acres whose only function was to please the eye and invite the mind to roam. Gazing out, she'd said, "It's heaven!" and truly meant it, thinking of the astounding artifice and labor that had gone into the making of something so beautifully useless, and an echo of that feeling was awakened in her now. The office was a ten-minute drive down-town from Queen Anne Hill, so for nearly two hours a week, between the house and her corner cubicle in the Klondike building, Beth could revel in this strange and ducal view.

Like a gull on the wind, the Audi, in light traffic, went swooping down the Counterbalance. Only the luminous pointers on the dials betrayed the workings of the four-liter engine, the interior as insulated from the outside world as a padded recording studio. Cushioned in blue-piped leather, glancing at the trip-computer, Beth sipped at her coffee and drank in the sound of Lucinda Williams getting right in time.

After "Arthur" on the TV, after the battle of the Froot Loops and the doing-up of the difficult button on the jeans, after the abrupt U-turn to retrieve the forgotten swim-things and the encounter with the fascinat-ing banana slug on the sidewalk and the guarded exchange of fire with Amy's mom, who was taking an extension course in Advanced Fiction, and with Sally, who was in charge of the Sunshine Room, Tom got back to the house just in time to hear the phone ringing in his third-floor study. Gasping from the sprint upstairs, he picked it up and said hello.

"Thomas. It is Shiva. Shiva Ray."

Though he was said to be in his thirties, Shiva Ray's voice had little more than a trace of an Indian lilt and belonged to an older generation of Englishmen. It was the voice of the Pall Mall clubman, or the BBC newsreader—Alvar Liddell!—of the old, fruity, Oxbridge kind.

"I am in the air," he said gravely. "I am flying from DFW to JFK."

His phone calls were nearly always made from planes, giving the impression that a brief moment of leisure was possible only in the sky. Tom took these calls with some unease. He wasn't the department chair—that was Bernard Goldblatt, the ineffectual eighteenth-century scholar—but Ray had announced, during a conference call while he was stranded by bad weather in Denver, that Tom was his man. "We shall understand each other's jokes, you see?" So far, however, there had been no jokes, at least none that Tom had managed to detect.

"I have been brainstorming again," Shiva Ray said. "Gabriel García Márquez!"

Well, Márquez was still alive, unlike some of Ray's earlier candidates, including Graham Greene and William Golding—"You know, the *Lord of the Flies* chap."

"It's a thought," Tom said, distracted by a sudden glimmer of turquoise in the holly tree below the gabled window. Then the Steller's jay took wing and fled from sight.

"You think he'd bite?"

"I doubt it, somehow. But we can always try."

"Pessimism bores me, Thomas. I am always the optimist. Our doubts are traitors, and make us lose the good we oft might win, by fearing to attempt."

So many of his literary quotations came from *Measure for Measure* that Tom suspected the play must have been Ray's A-level set text at Harrow. "I can find out how to reach him," he said. "But you know, Shiva, I wonder if perhaps we shouldn't aim for just a little more in the way of balance ."

"Yes, balance is good."

"I mean, suppose we get Márquez, or Bellow, or Morrison? It would be wonderful, of course, for the students to be able to actually meet and talk with them, and I can't think of a more inspiring gift for young writers. But to meet only the great, who also tend to be the old, could be a shade inhibiting, don't you think? If we could sort of alternate the great with the good, and bring the students into contact with some lesser stars—but still stars, definitely—then we'd be introducing them to people they could *identify* with a bit more, you know? Than with Saul Bellow, or Márquez."

"Who do you have in mind?"

Tom was suddenly stumped. The jay had reappeared in the holly tree. "Well, I was at a reading last night, a lot of students were in the audience. They turned out in force to hear this English writer—David . . . Dave Rice."

"That rings a definite bell."

"He's got a book out which seems to be enjoying a kind of cult success."

"I like 'cult.' "

"He'd be the wrong person for us. Too old, for one thing, and his writing isn't really up to scratch. But it was the audience reaction that interested me. They could see themselves in Dave Rice's shoes, in a way they'd never see themselves in Saul Bellow's."

"Title?"

"Oh—*Crystal Palace,* but I wouldn't bother. I was just pulling his name out of the hat as an example. But it's not the right example. Assuming that DeLillo says yes, do you think we might look around for one or two people who are a little less exalted and maybe a little more accessible to students? The other thing of course is that they'd come cheap."

"Thomas—I do not like 'cheap.' I do not think cheap. Money is easy. Money is cheap. We are talking about Modern Literature here, and one can't build a global platform with the shillings and the pence. Ah, Tennessee!"

Oh, God, now Williams, Tom thought. Still chasing the dead.

"We're over Tennessee, I think. Yes—those are the old Smokies, I am certain of it. Quite beautiful, though I wish I were there in Seattle. I dream of it, you know, my little house on the lake? I have been *harassing* my architect. He is so slow, and I hate slow. I love fast. But when at last my chappie pulls his silly finger out and the miracle happens, I am going to be happy there. I know it. I see it every day—the shore, the water, the shaded patio . . . Yes, there I shall Write. And—"

But as so often happened with Shiva Ray's calls, the connection broke off and Tom was left listening to the long-distance crackle of the skies. The question he always wanted to ask, and never did, was whether these curious conversations were conducted from a seat on a scheduled passenger flight or from Ray's personal jet. He thought it funny that this prince of the virtual world spent most of his time haring around the actual one, when the Internet was always said to have dissolved geography. You'd think Ray could've done it all with his famous switches. Or something.

A few minutes after eight, an ultramarine Jeep Cherokee with a barred cage built into the back arrived at Pier 28, carrying Special Agents Quillian, Kiminski, and Lai, along with a trained beagle. An hour later, the dog found something deep in the *Auriga*'s hold—a canvas-topped container, one of six, visible only through the foot-wide crack between containers down on 3-Deck. The beagle lodged its head in the crack and jubilantly yodeled, its tail beating as fast as a hummingbird's wings. There was no getting at the container until the cargo above it had been craned out of the ship and the hatch-plates lifted. Three dock-cranes and two Mack forklift trucks were on the job, burrowing into the ship and stacking the unloaded containers on the dock. The port police had cordoned off the *Auriga* with yellow crime-scene tape. A knot of paramedics hung out beside their two ambulances, and a Seattle Police Department squad car was parked, headlights glaring and doors open, at an oddly self-important angle to the rest.

Captain Williams, chalk-faced and in shock, clung to a clipboard with the cargo manifest. To make himself heard over the racket of trucks and cranes, he shouted, "It says 'Seasonal Ornaments.'" He'd already said as much to the INS agents, a port policeman, and two of the paramedics. The pages of the manifest flapped wildly in the breeze that had sprung up since dawn and was raising dust-devils up and down the docks.

The Chief Engineer—who'd changed his mind about going ashore—turned to Bob Stenhouse. "Worse things happen at sea."

"I wouldn't tell the Captain that if I were you, Chief."

During the long morning, two more squad cars showed up, followed by an INS bus. The quarantined ship drew an audience of off-duty longshoremen and delivery-drivers, each of whom stayed long enough to smoke a cigarette and trade a joke or two, then drifted off because nothing much was happening. It wasn't until after noon that a space had been cleared around the container found by the happy beagle.

A padlocked chain wound through the metal door on the container, but the Chief Engineer cut it loose with a pair of enormous shears. When Agent Kiminski lifted the securing bar, the door swung open, releasing an enormous bubble of foul gas.

"Jesus Fucking Christ," Kaminski said.

Their first sight was of faces—bloodless faces, blank as stones—crowding at the doorway.

"No one goes in there without protective gear!" Kaminski shouted. "Stacy! Get on the phone! We need haz-mat gear! Masks! Stacy?"

One of the faces became attached to a body. It tottered into the dark rectangle of the doorway: a sexless, ageless thing in sneakers, jeans, and a raspberry-pink anorak. Quillian reached out his hand, and it came stumbling forward.

"Today!" it said in a thin dry voice.

A second creature stepped out—a man, this one, wispily bearded, with eyes so far receded in their sockets that they seemed on the verge of disappearing altogether behind pouches of bruise-colored flesh.

"Count them!" Kaminski yelled. "I need them counted out!"

Quillian helped a third man from the doorway. His head was bowed, his shoulders shaking, and someone handed him a Kleenex.

"Half an hour," Sakiyama called. "They say they can get the gear out here in half an hour."

From behind the waiting faces, there was a sudden animal explosion, a squall of stink, and where there had been three, there were a whole lot more than anyone could count.

"Holy shit!"

"Get him!"

Like a kitten climbing a curtain, one was halfway up a ladder on the side of the hold before getting picked off. Hobbling, scuttling, others tried to bolt behind the remaining containers. A port policeman stood guard over the sobbing heap he'd chased into a grimy bulkhead corner. Martinez got two so entwined with each other that at first he thought they were one.

All men, it now appeared, they were cuffed and led to the bus with barred windows. Paramedics were looking after those who couldn't walk. The SPD was sending out two German shepherds with their handlers.

"Today!" It was the first to leave the container, the blankness on his face gone, replaced by a look of shriveled woe.

Special Agent Lai spoke to him in Cantonese, and he talked back in Fujianese.

"He says there are two dead guys in there. 'Two die' is what he's saying."

"The fuck there are," Kaminski said, gazing into the repulsive cave beyond the doorway.

"They died of seasickness, he says."

"No one dies of seasickness. It makes you want to die, but you don't—and *that's* the problem."

The man was jabbering in a high-pitched, metallic whisper.

"He doesn't know how long ago they died. He lost count of the days. Maybe a week, maybe more. One die a day before the other . . . One he know—Chen Xianshen. The other, he forgot his name. First they threw up . . . Everybody was throwing up . . . Then they tried to drink, but they couldn't hold it down. They got weak, and then they died, is what he says."

"It was rough," Captain Williams said, his voice a croak. "We ran into some funny weather, this tropical depression . . ." He began to cry.

Sakiyama touched him on the shoulder. "It wasn't your fault. You couldn't have known."

"No one goes in there," Kaminski said. "Tracy? Get an update on the haz-mat stuff, will you?"

"I'll call Pathology," a cop said, "on the car radio." He made his escape up the ladder from which the stowaway had been plucked minutes before.

Everyone gave the container a wide berth. Overhead, the cranes and trucks had stopped working, and aboard the ship a spooked silence was broken only by the mechanical heartbeat of the generators.

"Mostly they ate crackers," Lei said. "Crackers and apples."

The last of the Chinese were carried off on stretchers, then a minibus came with protective clothing. White-masked, space-suited, carrying black rubber flashlights, two policemen, then Kaminski and Quillian, entered the container in single file.

Inside, the flashlight beams wandered, crossed, and came to a brief, shuddering halt whenever they found something recognizable in the putrid darkness of the container: a scarlet JAL airline bag; a car battery, evidently dead, with wires running to a six-inch fan and a lamp clipped to a metal flange above the doorway; a heap of empty plastic water cans; four stacks of thin mattresses, ranged along the wall like a low couch, with neatly folded blankets on top; a disheveled magazine; a backpack; a toothbrush; a plastic bucket.

The soles of the men's shoes made a crackling noise as they came unstuck from the floor with each new step. The flashlights showed a surface glazed with something that had once been liquid but was now so thickly embedded with crumbs, hair, and dirt that it had taken on the texture of an old and filthy carpet. There were still enough pale flecks of color to identify it as a layer of dried vomit.

Nearly half the container was occupied by a mountain of swollen garbage bags with knotted tops. What had begun as a pile in the far right-hand corner had climbed and spread, crowding the stowaways into a space that must have grown smaller by the hour. Rivulets of goo trickled from the myriad folds and creases in the bags' distended skin. Some attempt had been made to sop up the mess at the bottom with rolled-up blankets, now black and sodden with the stuff that was leaking from the bags.

"Shit!" one of the men said, his voice muffled by the mask.

Below the bags in the far-left corner, a thin blanket was contoured to the shape of two bodies, lying as close together as lovers. One of the police bent down, reached out a long fastidious arm, and pulled at the blanket.

"Leave that! Leave it to Path!"

The blanket was dropped.

When the story was reported in next morning's *Post-Intelligencer,* the cause of the two men's deaths was still unknown. Fifteen survivors were now in a secure ward at Harborview.

Eight of the 15 fled, but were caught yesterday afternoon, said INS spokeswoman Irene Mortensen. "Seven of them turned themselves in willingly," Mortensen said. "The rest were running around on the ship. But we are pretty sure we got everybody."

Ping. Ping. Ping. E-mails were erupting on the screen at Beth's workstation, where she was talking urgently on her telephone headset. Within the last minute and a half, two messages had popped up from Robert, her assistant, whose industriously bobbing head she could see over the top of the Sheetrock partition that divided their cubicles.

"No," she said. "They have to live there. We've tried using outsiders, but they turn in 'travel writing' and that always sucks. Can't you find some bright kids who work for the *Observer* or the *Voice?*"

"Hi, Liz. *Liz?*"

She glanced over her shoulder and saw Steve Litvinof. At least two weeks had passed since he had last been seen on the ninth floor, which Editorial shared with the gym and massage room, and his unannounced visits were always alarming.

He smiled at her—an economical twist of the lips that was over almost before it had begun.

"Sorry, I have to go. I'll call you right back," she said into the phone, then swiveled around on her chair.

"I've been looking at Phoenix," Litvinof said. "I like what you're doing there, Liz. Good job."

Rake-thin and narrow-faced, Steve Litvinof was bald on top, with the back and sides razored to a blue shadow. He was not the usual start-up boss. His background was Money, not Tech, and it showed: winter and summer he wore identical black two-piece suits, tailored in light-weight silk, and white shirts buttoned to the top. The absence of a tie was possibly a gesture of informality—his concession to the khakis and T-shirts worn by every other male in the company—but in combination with his suits it made him look, as Robert had once said, like an Iranian cleric with a taste for Italian fashion.

"But," he said ominously. "Here, scoot over for a moment, will you?" He wheeled her spare chair over to her terminal, and sat down at the keypad. Scorning the mouse, he typed and Entered, typed and Entered, until he reached Phoenix. Thick black hair sprouted from beneath the French cuffs of his shirt and framed the blue dial, rimmed with gold, of the watch on his left wrist. Beth was close enough to read the lettering: PATEK PHILLIPE, GENÈVE.

"See?" He nodded at the screen. "The tours are kind of samey. And the neighborhoods have to be more hip. We need more upscale property, but that's not your problem—I've got them working on it. I want to see Phoenix looking more like San Francisco, which is working great."

Checking his beautiful watch, he slid the chair back. "You have kids, right, Liz?"

"Yes—a boy, Finn. He's four and three-quarters."

He held up three fingers. "But only one's still living at home with us. She's a senior at Bush."

"Finn's at preschool on Queen Anne," Beth said, wondering why, after thirteen months, they were suddenly having this domestic exchange, especially since Litvinof still didn't seem to know her name.

"We should see more of each other," he said. "*Socially.*" And then he was gone.

What could that mean? Surely not. It was always said of Steve Litvinof that he led a blameless suburban life out in Issaquah and was a creepily devout Episcopalian. Whatever this was about, Beth felt half-flattered, half-disturbed, and throughout the morning she found herself returning to the image of Steve's wrist-hairs surrounding his midnight-blue watch like otter fur.

She checked Robert's second message, which said: *"steves coming!!!!!!!!!!"*

Beth and Robert were among the nearly two hundred peons who occupied five of the ten floors in the Klondike Office Plaza, formerly the Klondike Hotel, which had been closed down in 1994 after the bodies of murdered prostitutes began turning up in the bedrooms on a regular basis. The new landlord had gutted the building, tearing down walls and replacing them with orange-painted steel joists. A few plaster moldings, the Cutler mail chutes, and the regal brassbound elevator cages were all that was left of the old hotel, which had been Seattle's grandest when it began life in 1901. Now it was Start-up Central. Most of the companies it housed moved in and out almost as fast as hotel guests, but Steve Litvinof's had stayed and grown. He'd begun with half a floor but currently was rumored to be negotiating the outright purchase of the whole building.

"We're evolving a new paradigm here," he said when Beth was given her ten minutes of face-time with her new employer in October of 1998. Everybody was evolving a new paradigm then, but Litvinof made it sound believable.

"Every retail site on the Web is transaction-based. We're content-based. I like to fly in the face of conventional wisdom, and I don't like the margin on retail. So we're a content-based retail site, which sounds kind of screwy. Think of what Jeff does over at Amazon, then think the opposite. *We're* the opposite.

"Jeff liked books—low unit-cost, easy to package, small in size, and big multiplicity of choice, right?—but now he's got people wrapping up lawnmowers in Atlanta. What I like about houses? You'll never have to mail a house by UPS. So there goes your shipping and your warehousing. Plus, I don't want to sell anyone a house. That's a realtor's job, and they can do the sweet-talking better than I can. And the paperwork."

He glanced down at her résumé. "You are not here to sell houses, Liz. Our revenue-stream derives from content, and what we sell is talk, attitude, customer interaction, and community. And we keep it very cool indeed, because cool sells."

At the end of the interview, at which Beth had barely spoken a word, Steve Litvinof said, "Okay, now you get to drink the Kool-Aid," and gave her a brief, terminal smile across the desk.

Her job title was Executive Editor (Neighborhoods). The company's name was GetaShack.com, which sounded ridiculously clunky, but it had been market-researched and people remembered it. The techies liked to call it the Big G, a phrase that really set Beth's teeth on edge. The site was up and running in Seattle, Portland, the Bay Area, Santa Barbara, San Diego, Dallas, and Denver, with Phoenix and Kansas City running close behind, as Litvinof pursued his policy of eastward expansion. He intended to cross the Mississippi in the first quarter of 2000, into what he called Indian Country.

From her big corner cubicle, Beth commanded a tatterdemalion army of freelancers across the West, most of them writers for alternative weeklies. These foot-soldiers were paid a dollar a word to genially disparage their own neighborhoods in the offhand, knowing style that was the company's hallmark. Her job was to keep the tone laid-back, to iron out displays of unseemly enthusiasm, likely grounds for libel suits, and all uses of the first-person singular.

Visitors to the site clicked on a city for a general briefing, then on the neighborhood of their choice, where they were whisked off on a tour conducted by one of Beth's cool young mercenaries. They could watch a video of their journey, in letter-box format, at the top of the screen. Below it, on the left-hand side, the accompanying text unscrolled, while to the right a tiny black convertible—a 1957 T-Bird, if you looked closely—motored along a large-scale street map. The visitor stopped the car to check out supermarkets, movie houses, clubs, delis, newsstands, flower shops, restaurants, and other businesses, each of which contributed to the site's revenue stream. The tech staff on the tenth floor were still working on the problem of how to persuade the T-bird and video to make turns in sync: sometimes they did, and sometimes they didn't. The standard response to customer complaints was "We are working hard to extend the technology platform."

Whenever the car passed a house that was on the market, a red FOR SALE logo would flash on the map. Click on it, and you'd get a video shot of the house in question, whether a "Roach-infested Victorian fixer-upper" or a "Gruesome 1950s Stepford Wives Rancher." One more click led you to a realtor's site, where the description of the property would be more conventionally fulsome. Each time a visitor clicked on the See More button, Getashack would automatically collect a flat fee of $12.50 from the realtor.

Traffic on the site was heavy, and also exceptionally sticky. In the third quarter of 1999, the average visitor remained on the site for seventeen minutes—up by nearly two minutes from the previous quarter. What mostly kept them lingering, and why realtors clamored to get their listings on GetaShack, was the Virtual Starbucks in every neighborhood. Howard Schultz had invested heavily in the site from the beginning, seeing it as a useful test-bed for actual cafés. The virtual coffeehouses were crammed with prospective house-buyers, idle passersby, and bona-fide neighborhood residents, who hung around, often for hours at a stretch, swapping local knowledge. They gave out names and numbers of contractors, posted warnings of impending construction projects, rated the nearby schools and teachers. If a newly released sex-offender was moving into the neighborhood, you'd hear about it in the Virtual Starbucks, as you'd learn of deaths, divorces, break-ins, babysitters, hair stylists, potlucks, yard sales, problem kids, reading groups, and AA meetings. Actual dates were made in the virtual cafés, and sometimes actual fights erupted from them, as neighbors left their PC screens to confront each other angrily in "the physical venue," as the real world was known inside the Klondike building.

Beth, a journalist, was still a stranger to the online world. The inner workings of the site were as obscure to her as to a casual Netsurfer, and the techies were no help at all. Riding up in the elevator with a gang of slouching boys destined for the tenth floor, she was aware of how they looked straight through her, as if she didn't exist. She felt too young to be made to feel so old and out of it. And when the techies did talk, it was literally in code, their speech sprinkled with impenetrable acronyms.

Sandwiched between Tech on the floor above and Finance on the floors below, Editorial was regularly attacked from both the air and the ground. Beth and her colleagues had no arcane science of their own with which to defend themselves, and so the programmers and the number-crunchers, incapable of making sense to each other, usually settled their differences by laying into the dopes on the ninth floor. For a while, they'd fire volleys that went clean over Beth's head, about leveraging operational efficiencies or optimizing bandwidth utilization. Then, because everyone could read, they'd turn on Beth. Make it sexier, they said. Cooler. Or looser. Tighter, funnier, more serious. More ironic—or less. More like the kind of stuff they read in *Architectural Digest, Rolling Stone, Wired, Islands, Salon, Gourmet,* the *National Enquirer,* or whatever rag on which their eyes had last briefly paused. Or. Or. Or. Or. She emerged from these meetings feeling stoned, bruised from head to foot by these salvos of stupid *ors.*

She opened her next e-mail, from Harriet Zimmerman, who sat on the other side of Robert's cubicle.

> *hi beth! this from rachel wu who pete said was great—i dont think its right for us but will you read please? Thanx. ;) harriet*

She clicked on the attached *Mill Valley.doc,* and scanned the file:

> *Once the California capital of hot-tub parties and wife-swapping, Mill Valley is now the woodsy Bay Area enclave for white, college-educated liberals. Towering redwoods shade wood-and-glass homes that cling to winding canyons. Picture sneaking a post-dinner-party Davidoff on a redwood deck, walking the Dipsea Trail with the Bichon Frise, and Sunday cycling expeditions to Peet's to compare gear, sip decaf, run a hand over the silvered Clooney cut, or bemoan deer-damage to the baby vegetable garden . . .*

Of course it wouldn't do. Woodsy enclaves and homes that cling were not what anyone wanted to find on GetaShack, let alone that Bichon Frise. It sounded as if this Rachel person hadn't even bothered to visit the site. Beth hit Reply.

> *You're right. It doesn't make the cut. But she's obviously tried. Get her a kill-fee and find someone else.—B.*

The INS did not, in fact, get everybody. When the others, starved of natural light for so long, scuttled across the open deck and tried to climb their way free, one went down, instinctively reaching for the dark. Practised at this, he could flatten himself into a shadow, knowing that in stillness and silence a man can disappear.

Squeezing himself into the friendly gloaming behind a container, pressed close against the ribbed plates of the ship's hull, he found a semicircle of pure darkness at his feet, and the handrails of a companionway dropping to the deck below. He didn't immediately trust himself to the ladder, but waited for the next bout of yelling and stamping from the men on the far side of the container. When it came, he found the top rung with his foot and let himself down into the darkness, gingerly feeling for each toehold. Heights scared him, and the ladder was greasy, the soles of his sneakers slipping on the iron rungs.

The ladder went deeper down into the ship, but he stepped off at deck level, and took his chance among the containers, wriggling his bony shanks between them whenever he found space, losing himself in the labyrinth, thinking of the dogs. At the far side of the ship, he rested for a moment against the cold wall of the hull, panting thinly, shivering, in his T-shirt and New York Jets windbreaker. Then he set off again along the side of the ship, looking for the next ladder.

The opening in the deck-plates was lighter than the last one, and light frightened him. Moving like a slug on a grass blade, he crawled on his stomach toward the hole until he could peer out. He'd guessed right: below him, Land Cruisers were lined up, dangerously distinct, on the car deck. He cursed the whining of the generators as he scrutinized the dark perimeter of the shadows for a movement or human silhouette.

There was little of him left to disappear—sneakers, jeans, windbreaker, baseball cap worn back to front. There had been more to him once. When—so long ago that it was in another life—he had stepped into the container, clasping his airline holdall of belongings to his chest, he was definitely somebody. He was Jin Peng, from Lianjiang. He was twenty-four. Under interrogation, he could still have found these facts, but now they were dead husks, like discarded peanut shells that one might crunch underfoot in the street.

Now he was only the wheedling, angry pain in his gut; his thumping heart; the fizz of excited blood in his veins. Lying by the opening in the near-dark, craning his neck to search for enemies on the deck below, his breath came back to him in a sudden rank gust—a sickly zephyr from a cesspool. This is me! He thought, I am this stink!

He stood on the ladder above the opening, willing himself to go down. Like an abseiling spider on its thread of gum, he made his descent, feet pattering against the rungs, hands dry-burning on the rails. Ducking low, he scooted toward the closest vehicle, and crawled between its big wheels to take stock. No one came running. The puddles on the deck were deep enough to drown the rivets; he could smell the sea salt in the water. When certain of his solitude, he crept out and, treading carefully from puddle to puddle, so as to leave no scent, made his way between the cars, putting as much distance as he could between himself and the ladder on which he'd skinned his palms. He chose his vehicle for its appearance of looking lost in the crowd, and because it stood in a puddle as big as a pond. He looked quickly up and down the line—the same covert, split-second survey that he used to make in the streets of Fuzhou—then squatted behind the tailgate, unbuckling his sagging belt and pulling it free of his jeans. The pin on the buckle was filed blade-thin, for business. After wetting it with his fingers, he worked the pin inside the lock on the tailgate. It was a babyish lock: the wards sprang easily apart, and it clicked open. He made another quick reconnaissance, and was into the car and out of it in a short moment, having released the lock on the left-hand rear door. He closed the tailgate quietly, watched and waited, then scrambled back into the Land Cruiser, locking the door behind him.

Inside, the car reeked of beeswax, machine oil, and perfumed leather—a rich-man smell. He shrank himself under the welcoming overhang of the backs of the front seats, and clung there, fearful, spectral, a long smear of dirt in the gloom of the lavish interior. He breathed meagerly through his nose, concerned by the foul odor that came out of him whenever he opened his mouth. He mustn't smell-up the car.

Before he entered the container, self-extinction had been his useful craft: now it was something that had happened to him, like catching a disease or being in a bus accident. He had the dim but terrifying sense that sometime during these last days he'd ceased to be a person.

In the beginning, the men had talked, confided their stories, shown their family photos, argued, quarreled. There'd been two fights. Then the noise began: the shunting and booming, the groan of flexing metal, the crashes, like tall buildings toppling into rubble, the constant rippling thunder of the sea. The men were flung against one another like carcasses of meat. No one could stand. No one could talk. When someone shouted, it was always a curse. Sleep was a raging phantasmagoria, from which waking to exhaustion was a merciful release.

Time had no meaning there. Some of the men had watches that told the date, and to begin with they watched the days stack up with building hope. The snakehead had promised a six-day voyage. On the fifth day, the men believed this must soon end, that they were close now to the USA. But it did not end. First one man died, then another. He thought he might die. He didn't mind: all he wanted, if he could still want anything, was an ending.

After the men died, the battery died. They hadn't rationed their use of the fan, whose blade revolved slowly to a stop. The clip-on lamp they'd fixed above the door went dim and they were in darkness, although the filament inside the bulb continued to glow. First it burned like a firefly in the night, then it turned coppery, revealing itself as a wire, hair-fine, bent into an octagon with a missing side. Through the incessant crash and rumble, he watched the wire. Once, in delirium, he found himself praying to it—the last and only light in the world. Waking from a mad sleep, he saw it was gone, and was certain he was going, too.

It was long after the wire went dark that the ship suddenly steadied and was quiet, and he heard the human noises. Every man was moaning, each after his own fashion. Nobody talked, nobody cried. One man's moan was a twiggy crackling in his throat, like the wind in a dead thornbush. Another mewed like a starving cat. Another made a reedy nasal singing sound, like an old monk.

He listened to his own noise—a painful, rasping *awww!* Each time he exhaled, his protesting breath burred and croaked in his dry larynx. *Awwww!* When he tried to speak to his neighbor, he felt his swollen tongue filling his mouth. "Caw!" he said, like a rook on a telephone pole.

The men shared the last of the water. He drank, and stole enough to rinse his face and swab his reeking armpits. In the new quiet, he dozed, oscillating between moments of sleep and appalled wakefulness. When at last the Americans opened the container door, he was in better shape to make the break than the others, and waited for the first two escaping men to be caught before he sneaked out, under the cover of the running and shouting.

He clung miserably to the underside of the car seats, the adrenaline leaking from his body, replaced by waves of nausea and exhaustion. He couldn't even remember why he'd run. He wanted to be found. They'd give him food, surely? And let him sleep? They'll be here soon, he thought: an ending. So he waited, taking a wan comfort in his own indifference.

It was the dog he heard first, an echoing *halloo* that rang down the street-long deck from far up front, then the men moving slowly through the cars. He didn't tighten his hold, but lay quietly—almost relaxed now—on the soft carpet. He was tempted to struggle to his knees and show himself, and only the habit of evasion stopped him. He wasn't a man who helped soldiers, police, or officials to do their work. These were people to be dodged and hidden from, to be shown a face as blank and void of feeling as a shovel.

This realization cheered him. He had habits—he was a person—and hadn't lost himself entirely in the black container. With suddenly renewed assurance, he gripped the back of the driver's seat. He knew what to do, and became a shadow. He heard a voice answered by a laugh—a loud, snorting, *gweilo* laugh, full of phlegm and spittle. Laughter was good, he thought. It meant the men weren't searching for anyone in particular. They sauntered casually along the deck, and their dogs were quiet, though he could hear them moving, claws on steel. Quick as a minnow, moving in darts and jerks, the narrow beam of a flashlight made a cursory pass over the car's interior, then the men passed on. He heard more laughter.

Later, when the great hatch-door at the back of the ship was cranked open, a wash of sudden daylight flooded the deck, and more men came, to drive the cars off one by one. He readied himself for a journey, but the car stopped only a minute or two after it had started, and the driver—a heavy man, whose weight pressed against his face through the upholstery of the seat—left, slamming the door behind him.

He listened to the hungry bubbles bursting from his belly. Not very long ago, when no one else could eat, he'd crammed his face with crackers, then chomped down the rotting core of an apple he'd thrown away some days before. Now all that was left in him was gas. Not yet daring to move, he lay low, farting painfully, and waited for nightfall.

*   *   *

Fingers pattering quickly on the keyboard, Tom wrote:

> *Every morning without fail, my wife—like so many people here in this virtual city—performs a tribal ritual. As soon as she's put her coffee on to brew, she rescues the skinny national edition of the* New York Times *from our front deck, skims the headlines, then turns to Section C to read her fortune.*
>
> *Being the sort of paper that it is, the* Times *doesn't have an astrologer on its staff. But it does carry the Nasdaq listings, which are the next best thing to Madam Sosostris or Gypsy Petulengro, and there in the fine print of numbers and fractions, my wife discovers her future.*
>
> *For Beth has options . . .*

The form of the NPR commentary was tight as a sonnet: Tom had four minutes, or 480 words, a tiny room into which he was always found trying to stuff far too much furniture.

For this piece, he had Pope's *Collected Poems* (in a battered green Nonesuch edition) and Swift's *Gulliver's Travels* open face-down on the floor beside him. For he meant to get, somehow, from Seattle in 1999 to London in the 1720s, and back again, in his four minutes; taking a whirlwind tour of Swift's fantastic schemes (extracting sunbeams from cucumbers) and Pope on share-mania ("Instead of Scandal, How goes Stock's the Tone / Ev'n Wit and Beauty are quite useless grown") in order to say something about start-ups and stock options. At 108 words (Word Count was his new best friend), the Beth-stuff was already out of control and would have to be fiercely cut down.

Although both *Tunnels* and *The Few* had been published as novels, Tom didn't instinctively think of himself as a "novelist," exactly. "Bookworm" would be closer to the mark. For him, writing had always been a continuation of reading by other means. *Tunnels* had begun life as a winning entry in one of the *New Statesman*'s weekly literary competitions. Competitors were invited to submit accounts of imaginary meetings between well-known characters in works of nineteenth-century English fiction. Tom sent in a prickly exchange between Dorothea Brooke of *Middlemarch* and Becky Sharp of *Vanity Fair*. After that, he found himself compulsively inventing more encounters, which came to him unbidden when he was riding on the Tube or trying to get to sleep.

He scribbled some of the funnier ones into a notebook, and soon he was writing a book, of sorts, about Victorian London, or it was writing him.

The tunnels of the title were the London sewers, described with voluptuous relish by Henry Mayhew in *London Labour and the London Poor;* they were also the tunnels that the bookworm-author excavated from book to book, so that General William Booth of *In Darkest England and the Way Out* could make his way into Dickens's *Little Dorrit* and attempt to enlist Amy in his Salvation Army, or Sergeant Cuff, retired from his job in Wilkie Collins's *The Moonstone,* could delve into the unsavory past of Trollope's magnate-from-nowhere, Augustus Melmotte of *The Way We Live Now.* Tom had no conscious style of his own, but found that he could slip into the style of Charles Kingsley one day, George Gissing the next, with a feeling of release and discovery, like a character actor losing himself in a part. Reviewers were wrong to call him a parodist. He knew what he was: a fan, a mimic, a *pasticheur.*

The success of *Tunnels* took him by surprise. Space was made for it on the syllabus of "postmodernism," though Tom's self-diagnosis was that he was incurably premodern. The American advance on the book more than paid off the mortgage on his flat, and between answering letters from graduate students, he busied himself, in a lazy sort of way, with another antique enthusiasm—stories of the Second World War.

As a student in Brighton, he was a secret devotee of television reruns of 1950s films about the war, especially those that starred the young, or youngish, Kenneth More. Other people liked Antonioni. He liked *Reach for the Sky.* From the 10p boxes outside secondhand booksellers' shops, he fished up books to match the films, most of them in dog-eared yellow Pan paperback editions: *One of Our Submarines, Two Eggs on My Plate, The Last Enemy, Ill Met by Moonlight, Doctor at War, Safety Last, Anything But a Soldier,* and tales of escape from POW camps (plenty more tunnels there) like *The Colditz Story, The Wooden Horse, The Great Escape, Escape or Die.*

In 1988, Tom reread all of these over a long and happy summer. He collected more books, printed on browning war-issue paper and cheaply illustrated with woodcuts, designed to foster a sense of patriotism among men serving overseas. They were about English churches, the English countryside, English canals, and English counties, written in a prose that was indigestibly rich—as near as words could come to a farmhouse tea of scones, clotted cream, and lumpy strawberry jam. He also bought every book he could find about Bletchley Park and the Cambridge dons who cracked the Enigma code.

The code that Tom tried to crack in *The Few* was the enigma of England, as it was refracted through these films and books. At the center of The Show, as the war was known in Tom's book, he placed a debonair young officer-type named (too obviously, he worried) Kenneth. One of the last chaps left on the beach at Dunkirk, Kenneth flew Lancasters and Spitfires, broke out of Colditz, donned frogman's gear to plant limpet-mines on enemy warships, sailed in a corvette on convoy duty, served with Montgomery at El Alamein, landed at Anzio, was in France for the liberation of Paris and in Germany for the fall of Berlin. Clean-cut Ken, a paragon of decency, modesty, and niceness, was not very bright. The question was: What did he think he was fighting *for*? And why was he the star of The Show?

The Few was a best-seller in Britain, though the letters from graduate students gave way to an even larger mailbag from colonels and brigadiers (Retd.), who sniped at Tom from assorted foxholes in Wiltshire, Kent, and Hampshire. In the U.S., the reviews were generally strong but sales flat: America had its own war stories, and none of them starred Kenneth More. Going coast to coast on his eight-city tour, Tom met no one who remembered seeing *Reach for the Sky*.

But he did meet Beth.

An arts reporter for the *Post-Intelligencer,* she came to interview him, somewhat at a loss, in his room at the Alexis Hotel. She'd never heard of Douglas Bader or "Bomber" Harris, but she had read *Daniel Deronda* at Smith, and *Tunnels* had been a set book in her Victorians course. So mostly they talked about Dickens and George Eliot. After his reading at Elliott Bay, he—or his publisher, rather—bought Beth dinner at the Painted Table, and one thing led to another. Auden said that poetry makes nothing happen. But *The Few* made something happen. Eventually, it made Finn happen.

It was Beth who learned of the job at UW, and Beth who talked Tom out of his sense of fraudulence in applying for it. Making the short list was as much as he could hope for—ten sweet days with Beth in Seattle, when he was summoned across the Atlantic for the interview. Because the Writing Program was a colonial dominion of the English Department, Tom was grilled by a bevy of English profs about his knowledge of, and willingness to teach, Victorian Lit. He was, in effect, two for the price of one. Besides, as Beth heard later, the committee was split rancorously down the middle between supporters of the novelist Jed Wing, whose eloquent black comedies had been tarred with the phrase "coarse misogyny," and those of the poet Camilla Taruk Sanchez, whose work was denounced by the contrarians as artless agitprop. So Tom rose to the top as the only candidate about whom no-one was in violent disagreement. From the start, he knew, via Beth's Filofax of contacts, that he'd got the job because he was thought to be relatively harmless—a reputation he'd tried to live up to ever since. He never stuck his neck out, never got embroiled, was always on time for his classes and punctilious about office-hours. Enjoying the sociable back-and-forth of teaching, he encouraged, criticized without causing hurt, and had the knack of finding unexplored possibilities, if not merit, in every piece of writing that he read; so the few courses that he taught were always oversubscribed.

The Hell's Canyon Chardonnay box was brimming, now, with writing all about the present—or at least it had been about the present when Tom put it there. The box was his America, as the Victorian stuff had been his London, and the Kenneth More stuff had been his War. Sometime soon, he thought, he'd read carefully through everything that was in the box, and see if the next book was ready to hatch from that eight-year accumulation of paper. But not quite yet. What he really needed was a second box.

A late yellowjacket buzzed against the windowpane, and Tom raised the sash to set it free. Beyond the window, city, water, and sky were the same frog-spawn gray. Until a couple of weeks ago, Tom had enjoyed an unhindered view of the Klondike building, but it had disappeared behind a rising office tower, still sheathed in what looked like bubble-wrap. He'd always been able to see where Beth worked, first under the big green globe of the *P-I,* then at the Klondike. When lost for words, he'd look across the bay to her for help—a trick that nearly always worked. Now the new construction returned his gaze with a loutish wink of polythene and steel.

He touched the Backspace key, wiped what he'd written from the screen, and began again:

Every morning, first thing, my wife reads her fortune in the paper . . .

*   *   *

"*Arf!*" Finn said. "*Arf! Arf! Arf!*"

He and Spencer were in the boys bathroom being dogs, Finn a large woolly black poodle, Spencer an Alaskan malamute like his family dog, Balto.

"*Roof! Roof!*" Spencer said. "I seen Balto drink water from the toilet once."

Finn, on all fours, reared up and planted his paws on the rim of the bowl. "*Wurra, wurra, wurra!*" The water inside was still swirling, since Spencer had just flushed it.

"I seed him do it," Spencer said, as if expecting contradiction.

Finn took a deep breath and dunked his head in the toilet. Then he tilted his face ceilingward and yodeled.

"You didn't have done!" Spencer said admiringly.

"*Arf!*" Finn shook himself, spraying Spencer's sky-blue corduroys and Pooh Bear T-shirt with toilet water.

Spencer was laughing so hard he was sliding down the wall. "You wet me! Bad doggie! No, doggie!"

"*Arf!*" Panting, tongue hanging out, he sprayed Spencer some more.

"Don't!"

"Spencer? Finn?" Teacher Sally put her head around the open door, "Bathrooms aren't for—"

"Finn drank water out the toilet! Finn drank out the toilet!"

"I didn't *drink*. I—" Then Finn remembered that he was a dog. "*Arf!*" he barked at Teacher Sally. "*Arf! Arf!*"

"Your hair, Finn! And, look, it's all over your face—"

"It's just water," Spencer said.

"*Grrrr!*" Bottom up, forearms on the floor, Finn snapped at Teacher Sally's feet.

"There's fecal coliform in there! The germs! You'll get *E. coli!* Oh, shit—"

"You said a bad word. That's a bad word." Spencer stage-whispered to Finn, "She said 'shit.'"

"I'm sorry, Spencer—I didn't mean to, and I'm really sorry. Now, Finn, will you please stand *up?* Surely you're old enough now to—"

"*Arf!*"

"Stop that! Come over here!" She wrenched at the loop of towel hanging from the machine, but it locked solid on her.

"You're making me feel sad," Finn warned her. "You're making me feel really sad."

"We're going to have to call your parents. Right now. You'll have to see a doctor—both of you. I'm serious, Finn."

"I'm serious, Finn," Finn said, holding his ground. He wasn't afraid of Teacher Sally. She was stupid, the stupidest teacher in the whole school, and she was being super-mean.

"Finn!"

"*Woof,*" he said, but it was more sob than bark, and he began to blubber, silently, his cheeks running with toilet-water and tears.

Later, after the boys were carted away by their respective parents, after the forced smiles and *just-to-be-on-the-safe-sides,* Midge, the principal, said wearily: "This can't go on. That child needs treatment."

It was like a city, but with no windows or doors. Containers, stacked three-high, formed the blocks, with a grid of bare-earth streets between them, all of it harshly lit by floodlights on towers. Choosing his route carefully, finding shadows just wide enough to hide him from the glare, he stole cautiously from corner to corner, getting as far away as possible from the illuminated checkpoint, where uniformed guards were positioned in tall glass booths. Anticipating the crackle of gunfire, he watched for each next sheltering wall. Once, he flattened in terror at a sudden movement on the ground, but it was the shadow of his own hand, caught for a second by the floodlights.

After letting himself out of the Land Cruiser, he'd found a clump of weeds and munched his way through two big mouthfuls of leaves, washed down with water that had collected in an abandoned hubcap. He was doing okay. No problem.

He reached a street-end and saw the real city, only a few kilometers off: skyscrapers, like New York—a dozen glittering sticks of light packed close as sheaves of wheat. The sight roused a sudden swell of excitement that left him fearless and elated. It was like the videos. It was like he was in a video. The rush of it made him grin. *Heh, not bad, huh? No shit!*

Twenty yards of open ground separated him from the perimeter fence, which was tall, with a barbed-wire overhang, but was meant to keep people from getting in, not getting out. Baulks of concrete, chained together, had been placed between the posts, so no one could drive a car out through a hole in the fence. He'd get his start from one of these. The fencing was attached to the posts with wire ties, forty or fifty centimeters apart: skimpy things, but they'd work as toe-holds. The big problem was the lights. Clinging to the shadows, he moved toward the next corner, searching for the right patch of fence to make his break.

Several corners later, he found it: a shady juncture between the pools of white light, well screened from the guards by the container-city, with a useful pile of builders' sand on the far side of the fencepost. Crouched on his haunches, he went through his moves, then, quick and bony as a squirrel, sprinted for the fence, his muscles thinking for him. His fingers clawed at the chain-linking, and his right foot got a purchase on the first of the wire ties. *Yes!* There was no weight to him as he squirmed his way up. *Yes!* He grabbed the iron flange of the overhang, got his left foot out on to the second strand of barbed wire, and pitched himself forward.

Ouf! The wet sand knocked all the breath out of him, and he was in America.

The terminal lights showed what looked like a Special Economic Zone—same wilderness of construction, same mud, same dirt-mountains, same yellow diggers, same flappy red plastic temporary fencing pegged out with metal stakes. Good cover. Keeping low, he crossed an unfinished road to the shelter of a digger. His ankle hurt, and he'd torn the sleeve of his windbreaker on the barbed wire. Squatting underneath the cab, shivering with cold, he peered out at the tall and incandescent city, where cars sped like shooting stars on an aerial highway and every light meant money.

The air smelled empty—not like a city, more like soap, with its faint tang of woods and sea. That's how money is, he thought: it smells of nothingness. It smells like America.

He waited patiently in the darkness below the digger. It wouldn't be long now, he thought, before the workers came and he could melt into the crowd. When he sensed the approach of dawn, he left his shelter and sidled along a line of plastic fencing to where the construction site ended, at a paved road under the massive concrete pillars of an over-head highway.

He'd been watching the spot intently for some time. This was the approach to the terminal, and the traffic on it had been thickening steadily. He'd hoped to see people walking on the roadside, but nobody came. He was alone with the trucks, frighteningly conspicuous in his solitude. Hands thrust deep into his jeans pockets, staring fixedly at the ground, he tried to look as if he knew his own business and destination. He didn't dare to look over his shoulder, and with each step he expected to be seized from behind, slapped, cuffed, and tumbled into a van.

He was rocked on his feet by the windy gusts thrown off by the passing trucks. Their brakes hissed, their motors snarled and throbbed, but he was spooked by the absence of something. Then it hit him: *No horns!* In America, he had not heard a single horn.

No horns, no people. *Where were the workers?* Already the sky had paled to gray, and he was still the only person out on foot. How was it possible to be in a city and yet feel so baldly exposed? He had to keep walking—there was nowhere to hide—but now he knew how the walk would end, with policemen, a beating, and jail. This knowledge steadied him. He was not afraid of jails.

Limping a little from his fall, he hurried across a too-wide street, turned left towards the tall buildings in the distance, and felt suddenly at ease. He was no longer responsible for what would happen. He'd made the attempt and done his best. Now things were out of his hands.

There were fewer trucks on the street, where cars swam past him silently like giant fish. A single bicyclist went by—he heard the *tick-tick-tick* of the chain on the machine's sprockets—but it was an athlete, not a worker, in a helmet and a skin-tight, many-coloured costume.

In the eerie quiet, he found himself listening to the noise of his own body—the creaking of his jeans and windbreaker, the spongy smack of his sneakers on wet concrete. He was used to being a trick of the light, a whisper, a presence so attenuated that it was hardly there at all, but America had made him suddenly loud, obtrusively visible, like a fat man with a drum. *Bang! Bang! Bang!* Here I am! He would never have guessed this from the videos.

He had walked two kilometers at least before he saw them—people, on the street, going nowhere in particular. The first thing he noticed was how far apart they stood from one another. Each had his own space, like so many statues on a square. Then he saw they were as poorly dressed as he was. *Poor?* In America? He slowed his step. They were *gweilos,* certainly . . . but Americans? Perhaps they were villagers—if they had villages in America, which was something he'd never thought of before.

He hung back, watching. The street had led him to a sudden frontier, where concrete and wire gave way to dusky brick, to flights of steps, fire-escapes, dark corners, and parked cars, to all the sheltering nooks and crannies of a real city, just as he had imagined New York, long ago, in another life. The villagers stood right on the edge of a world—now so nearly within his grasp—that he might yet make his own.

A short distance ahead, the street converged with the waterfront on one side and the line of the great aerial highway on the other. The ragged villagers were scattered under the arches of the highway, where they leaned against the pillars, talking, smoking cigarettes, and scratching at their sores.

He was going to have to speak to them. He knew English. He'd studied it one year in school and learned the characters, or most of them. He'd chanted, in chorus, "This is Mister Brown. He is reading a newspaper and smoking his pipe," and, "The power of the river creates electricity for the people of the town." More to the point, he'd picked up a lot of English from the videos. He knew the word he needed now, and mumbled it several times, to make sure of its pronounciation.

If something went wrong, he had an escape route marked out in his head: over the metal barrier, through the first rank of parked cars, across the narrow street, up the steps, into the street above, where he could lose any pursuers in the traffic. He was quick, like Chen Yang, ball at his feet, tearing through the line of Shanghai defenders. He could lose anyone in traffic, and nearly all the villagers looked old and sick.

Staying close to the barrier, ready to leap it at the first sign of trouble, he approached, watching them closely, but no one looked up to catch his eye. They had bad skin—so bad, some of them, that he wondered if they were lepers.

He chose a man with a pigtail of gray hair who was propped against the far end of the barrier, an old man, too slow and heavy to be a danger to him. "Please!" he said, his first American word. "Chinatown?"

"What?"

"China—town!" Surely he had it right? The snakeheads always said "Chinatown."

After a long vague moment, the man began to gabble and point. He smelled of alcohol and curdled milk. Though it was impossible to follow what he was saying, his hand gestured uphill and through the streets.

"Hey! Man, thank you." He was back in the video now, on the move, dodging and weaving through the many-chambered honeycomb of the city.

It didn't take him long to find the chilly grid of almost-empty streets, smelling of aniseed and cinnamon, where the Chinese restaurants were. First terror, then excitement, had numbed the tormenting hunger in his gut; now he was dizzied by the sudden ferocity of the pain. His stomach was hemorrhaging for want of food. Not caring who saw him, he tore through the garbage in an overflowing trash-can, and at last came up with a paper carton nearly full of orange-stained rice. He shoveled it down, both hands packing the cold gluey stuff into his mouth. Burrowing deeper, he found a half-eaten chicken leg, part of a hamburger bun, a 7-Up can with a mouthful of soda still left in it, a crescent-moon of a burger that had once gone with the bun, some flakes of fish adhering to a brown paper bag, a mess of bean shoots, and a barbecued spare rib.

Grunting for breath between swallows, he wept as he ate. He carried the spare rib across the street to a small park with a painted toy pagoda and a drinking fountain. Hunched over the fountain, he gobbled furiously at the slender trickle of icy water that welled from the spout, so cold that it felt like a tendril of fire in his throat. Then he washed himself, rubbing hard at the dirt around his mouth and eyes. He picked up the spare rib from the edge of the fountain and sat on a stone bench, where he slowly gnawed the meat off the bone. Pigeons scuffled around his feet, and when he was finished, he threw the dry bone to the birds.

The quiet alarmed him. It was like something bad had just happened here. Though it was deep into the morning now, the streets held only a few hurrying, solitary figures. The signs in the restaurant windows were strange, the cooking-smells were wrong. Half the store-fronts were empty—cleaned bare of everything except a bleached poster for an old Jet Li movie, fallen thumbtacks, dust, dead flies. He passed a grocery as poor-looking as any in Fuzhou. On a corner, he spotted two men talking; from a distance, it sounded as if they were speaking Cantonese, but drawing closer, he couldn't make out a single intelligible word.

Up an alleyway, he found a pet shop—a long, low, narrow cavern lit only by an overhead bulb and the green glow of its bubbling aquariums. No one was inside except the owner, a wizened, slippered man who was shuffling from tank to tank, feeding his fish.

He felt safe in this dark place. Pretending to study a school of guppies, he spoke to the owner without turning his head.

I have a message for my uncle. He works in a restaurant here. He is from Nanping, in Fujian.

You had better ask them at Restaurant Hoi Sun. Everyone there is from Fujian.

He had to listen hard to understand what the old man was saying. His voice was quavery, and the words were twisted out of shape, like echoes in a tunnel.

Now I remember. Hoi Sun. He works there. Thank you. He tapped on the aquarium, causing a small explosion of fright among the guppies. *You have some pretty fish.*

He had passed the Hoi Sun just a few minutes before. He returned there now, and tried the door. Locked. But the restaurant backed on to an alley, where a cook in a sauce-and-blood-splashed apron was tipping food into a garbage can. It looked like good food, too. He marked the can for later, made his apologies, and asked the cook if his imaginary uncle, Kai Chao from Lianjiang, was a waiter in the restaurant. The cook replied in Fujianese: no one by that name worked at Hoi Sun, but there was a restaurant in Tacoma where the family came from Lianjiang. Digging behind his apron into a trouser pocket, he came up with a packet of American cigarettes.

You smoke?

He hated to smoke—it spoiled the wind—but accepted a cigarette. Cupping his hands around the flame of the cook's lighter, he dipped his head and sucked gingerly at the filter-tip. The toxic smell of lighter-fluid masked the faint herbal odor of the tobacco.

Health regulations! The cook laughed. Usually, he said, he smoked inside, but when Madame Han was in the kitchen . . . He nodded over his shoulder. *Wah! You'd better watch out, then!*

He tried to contain the smoke in the front of his mouth, puffing it out between pursed lips as fast as seemed consistent with good manners. In the cold, dead air of the alley, the smoke from the two cigarettes lingered around the men's heads in an acrid mist that reminded him of the early days in the container before the smokers ran out of their supplies.

The cook was friendly, but he was a rude, incautious man. He asked personal questions—Where from in Fujian? How long in U.S.? Where living now? He deflected each question with a polite obliquity and, head bowed, patiently worked the conversation round to a question of his own: suppose someone were interested in a position—a lowly position, like washing dishes—at Hoi Sun, to whom would this person need to speak?

The cook dragged deeply on his cigarette and consulted the mottled gray sky. *That*, he said, *would be a matter for Mr. Han.*

Where was Mr. Han?

Not here. Later, perhaps. One could never tell with Mr. Han.

The cook, and the alley, swirled abruptly into soft-focus, and he had to lean against the wall to stay upright. First he thought it was the smoke, then realized that his bowels were giving way.

Toilet! Please? You show me the toilet?

He sat, whimpering softly, in the windowless dark closet. It felt as though his whole being had turned to liquid and was discharging into the bowl in an unbroken stream, cascading out of him like scalding tea. He wouldn't have believed that one starved body could contain such a burning flood of excrement. The diarrhea dribbled to a brief halt, then started to pour again, hissing as it hit the rising lake of shit in the bowl. He was afraid it would overflow onto the floor, imagined it seeping out under the door and pooling in the hallway. They'd see the puddle of filth, open the door, and find only a tangle of sodden clothes.

Though it rose to the rim, it didn't quite spill over. He had to flush the toilet four times to get rid of it, then, swaying on his feet, colliding with the walls, he cleaned himself up as best he could. When at last he got outside, the cook had gone. He leaned back against the brick, a papery shadow of himself, fearful that a gust of wind down the alley might blow him clean away. Gasping for air, he closed his eyes and prepared to wait for Mr. Han.

3.

Tom's morning was getting wrecked by the *whomp-whomp-whomp* of helicopter rotor blades. He faced a hefty pile of student work, including an unexpectedly fine story, "Meredith," by Hildy Blom, set in a trailer-park in eastern Washington. But the choppers dismembered her sentences almost as fast as he could read them, and he kept on going back to the first page to begin again. The upstairs study shuddered as the beastly machines—a whole fleet of them, by the sound of it—flew low over the house, the branches of the holly tree gesticulating crazily in the downdrafts from the rotors. This had been happening, on and off, for the last hour.

He carried Hildy's manuscript down to the scrubbed gloom of the kitchen, where he chewed long and hard on a fresh tablet of nicotine gum, then tried to switch off the mayhem in the sky and allow himself to be transported across the Cascades to the scorched desert plain of her story.

Meredith was a suburban college girl from Mercer Island, but Hildy's sympathies were with Meredith's country cousins, who lived in a double-wide out in the dusty boondocks west of Spokane. The story was written from their point-of-view and took place one baking summer Sunday after service, at the Ritzville Church of God, as the stiff-suited cousins waited uncomfortably for Meredith to show up for lunch.

It was a lovely subject. Hildy had created two distinct landscapes: one wet, green, and affluent; the other dry, brown, and poor. The cousins, staunch Christian Rightists, feared Meredith as the avatar of godless liberalism. They envied her, too, of course: for the SAT scores that were broadcast through the family via the jokey Christmas bulletin from Mercer Island deftly parodied in the story; for the white Jeep Wrangler that was her high-school graduation present; for her friction-less ease of passage between their world and hers. Yet come-uppance awaited her there in the trailer, where an overhead fan slowly stirred the suffocating air to no great purpose, and on top of the TV a plastic puzzle spelled out the name JESUS in silver blocks six inches high.

It had its rough patches, and the opening wasn't quite right, but "Meredith" was the first student story Tom had read in ages that would have excited him had he run across it in a magazine. Lank-haired, painfully shy, thickly bespectacled, Hildy Blom was a real writer—better by a long shot than David Scott-Rice, on whom she'd squandered her strangely merry laughter. If she could improve on the first two or three pages, Tom thought he'd try sending it, without telling her, to the *New Yorker*. With his known weakness for trailer parks, Bill Buford ought to be susceptible to this second-generation dirty realism. And if Buford actually bought it, Tom could use the credit due to himself as rain-maker: to get a student published in the *New Yorker* would be one in the eye for Lorraine Cole.

The lazy revolution of the fan-blades in the trailer-home grew suddenly louder and more urgent, and metamorphosed into the unearthly racket of another bloody helicopter, which was immediately joined by the querulous pealing of the phone. Though he recognized his wife's voice over the noise of thudding rotors, he couldn't understand a word of what she was saying.

"Sorry—we've got a helicopter gunship in the bedroom—I can't hear you."

She yelled something about "murder."

"Beth! What did you say? Darling?" He crawled under the kitchen table and blocked his free ear as the helicopter passed directly overhead.

Beth was saying that two men had been shot dead at a shipyard on Lake Union. "It's all over the TV."

"Ah—that explains the plague of helicopters."

"I think you'd better pick Finn up."

"I'm a bit busy at present—marking. There's a girl in my class from Spok—"

"Tom: there's a killer on the loose."

"Well, not here there isn't. You said Wallingford—"

"Tom—"

"Well, of course if you're really worried, I'll go and get him now."

"Thank you," she said, in a tone, Tom thought, of needless exasperation. "And call me when you get back home, will you?"

He flicked the TV on with the remote. Sandwiched between the words BREAKING NEWS at the top of the screen and LIVE IN WALLINGFORD at the bottom, a woman was talking from behind her espresso stand.

". . . I used to not be afraid of anything. I feel like there's nothing I can do about it—a little bit of powerlessness."

"Baristas" was another name for these coffee vendors, and in this city they'd displaced cab-drivers as the main source of instant public opinion. Whatever happened in Seattle, you always heard what the baristas had to say about it.

"You can't be inside and hide, you just have to be very careful of your surroundings."

The camera swung around to frame the reporter on the scene. "Dan, that's what some of the folks in this quiet residential neighborhood are saying about the tragedy that's happened here today. Reporting live from Wallingford, this is Michelle Terry."

Back in the studio, the news-anchor said: "Thank you, Michelle. We'll be back with you in Wallingford momentarily." He then did a recap. A man had walked into the shipyard office, shot two men dead, wounded two others—one critically—and had disappeared into what Dan the anchor called "the tree-lined streets of Wallingford."

Tom usually passed that shipyard on his way to the university—it was less than two miles from the house. Yet Wallingford was elsewhere; on the far side of the Ship Canal, over the Fremont Bridge, safely beyond the ken of Queen Anne Hill.

Dan said: "Police describe the suspect as a light-skinned man, five-feet-ten to five-feet-eleven, in his late twenties or early thirties, with a moustache and a scruffy beard. Police say he was wearing sun-glasses, a dark cap, and a dark trench coat over camouflage clothing."

Up came an artist's sketch of a generic Wanted Man that to Tom's eye was identical to the ones issued for the Unabomber and Timothy McVeigh's accomplice in Oklahoma City. By the time the police artists finished with them, their own mothers wouldn't know them.

Driving to pick up Finn, he switched on the car radio, and got another update from Wallingford.

"And this just in: The police tell us that a man has been arrested near the Tacoma Dome. They stress that he is only a person of interest, and not a suspect, at this time, and that the gunman may still be at large."

If she glanced to her left, Beth could look down over the streets of actual Belltown even as she navigated virtual Belltown on the site.

Belltown had always been a problem. Its text had been written and rewritten as often as the script of a Hollywood movie. Writers—moon-lighting from the *Stranger*, the *Weekly*, the *News Tribune*, the *Times*, the *P-I*, the defunct *Rocket*—had come and gone, and still it wasn't right. This was partly because actual Belltown was changing so fast that it had no settled character. Looking up the line of Second Avenue, what you mostly saw was scaffolding and beetling construction cranes. Even its name was a recent invention. In the nineteenth century, it had been Denny Hill, but during the civil megalomania brought on by the Alaskan gold rush, the hill was sluiced into Elliott Bay, and when Beth first came to the city, it was called the Denny Regrade. "Belltown" might well prove another temporary alias. NoVi—for North of Vir-ginia—would suit it just as well.

Restaurants down there opened and closed so quickly that by the time you got a reservation, the place had changed from French to Afghan. Sometimes, driving down Second, Beth had the impression that new condo blocks were built by the wrecking-balls of the demolition crews, so instantaneously did they spring into place. It was no wonder, really, that the neighborhood on the site never seemed to jibe with the physical venue visible from her cubicle window.

She launched the console for the video-stream: the pictures were hopelessly out of date, but that, mercifully, was not her province. She left-clicked on the T-Bird to make a turn on Bell, checking the text as she went. There was a spelling issue that needed to be settled site-wide. *Dot-commers* or—as here—*dot-comers?* She liked the latter, with its echo of "newcomers," but it looked a little odd on the screen.

For the second time that afternoon, she called home and got Finn.

"What are you and Daddy doing now, pumpkin?"

He paused to consider, then said, "I'm eating a cookie. And watching TV. Daddy's reading a book."

She prayed that Tom would have the sense not to let him watch the coverage of the Wallingford shootings. If Tom had even registered them.

"What are you watching?"

"'Scooby-Doo.'"

"Can I have a word with your daddy?"

Talking with Tom, she continued her tour of virtual Belltown, turning right on First. On the west side of the street, two FOR SALE signs flashed on the map. She clicked on the first one, and a caption came up: "Just another condo block. So what did you expect?" Lame.

Into the phone, she said, "I should get home before six . . . You, too. Bye." When she clicked again, the transition from the GetaShack site into the Belgrave Realty site was seamless. She'd show Steve this one: it was a model for how things ought to work, but so rarely did. Usually one got a crumby Web page, probably designed by the realtor himself, with a jumble of typefaces and some amateur flourishes courtesy of the Windows Paint program. But Belgrave's home page was so glitzy that it was like opening a door on wino-strewn First Avenue and finding yourself inside a palace.

You stood in a tall pillared lobby, with a marble waterfall as its centerpiece and a chamber orchestra playing in the background. Mozart or Haydn? Tom would know, but she didn't. Superimposed on the sound of the music was the sound of splashing water. The words "Welcome to Belgrave Realty" were posted in admirably small type over a reception desk in the upper-right-hand corner, where an animated virtual realtor pointed to the Enter button.

It was the coolest fucking home page she'd ever seen. "Hey, Robert," she called over the Sheetrock partition. "Come over for a sec. I want you to see this."

In khaki cargo pants and a Polo polo-shirt, he came sloping round the corner. He still walked with his entire body, as Finn did; and sometimes, like Finn, he fell off chairs.

"Look." Beth clicked back into the GetaShack site. "We're in Belltown. On First Avenue."

Robert instinctively looked out the window, at a white rectangle between the buildings that was possibly the top story of the Belgrave Realty condo block, but that was not the point.

"No, look at the screen . . ." She clicked the FOR SALE sign, and this time the what-did-you-expect line worked a lot better, given the sumptuous surprise of what was to come. The music played. The water trickled. The little animated realtor even had a striped bow-tie.

"Cool," Robert said.

"That's what I thought."

She clicked *Enter*.

Three days in America, and he had a name.

At Hoi Sun, Mr. Han paid him $2.50 an hour to mop floors, scrub the long tables in the kitchen, wash pans and dishes, and clean the car of Madame Han.

I am being kind. I treat you like family. This is very good pay for a man with no ID.

He slept overnight on the fire-escape, wrapped in an old coat lent to him by the friendly cook.

Then, early the next morning, Mr. Han came to the restaurant. *You go. Now. You must go away.*

Government officials had raided three restaurants on Jackson Street the previous evening, checking papers, looking for illegals. "Eye-enness!" Mr. Han kept repeating. "Eye-enness!"

You must not come back. Ever.

He opened the till and handed him two bills. Forty dollars, U.S.! Big money.

I am too kind. Madame Han must not hear about this. Now go. Out the back.

That afternoon, he got American clothes: jeans, shirts, socks, underwear, even two bedsheets and a torn towel. He found them in a dryer
at a Laundromat. The man who'd left them there—and he'd measured
him carefully by eye, from behind a newspaper he couldn't read—was
just his size, and the linen bag he'd left atop the machine was good quality, too.

Keeping his distance, he trailed the poor people—not villagers or
lepers, he'd learned, but a wandering tribe instantly recognizable by
their wild hair and ruinous teeth and skin. They were thickest in the
parks and around the street-market, where they drank from bottles,
shouted, scuffled, and openly clamored for money from passers-by.
Instinct told him to stay nearby these rowdy beggars: if the police left
them alone, why would they bother him?

From across the street, he watched the shabby building, a kind of
clinic, which people entered through one door and came out through
another, carrying food in their hands. He would have liked to join the
line, but feared that officials inside would demand of him a name,
papers, maybe a government license.

He let his bag of laundry rest on a sidewalk. Rich Americans were
striding past, their faces pink as shrimp, stinking of cologne, looking
straight through him with no suggestion in their eyes that they saw a
man in the space where he was standing. He felt mysteriously gifted.
The thought crossed his mind that if he were to look into a mirror, there
might be no answering reflection in the glass.

His invisibility excited him. He knew there must be power in this
ability to remain unseen in broad daylight on a crowded street. Putting
his new discovery to the test, he selected an old woman who was walking alone with a stick. He stared her in the eye, grinning fiercely at her,
ready to run if need be; but her gaze traveled clean through the middle
of his face. To her, he wasn't even a ghost. So that was why he had been
able to walk unchallenged down the long road from the terminal. He
hugged his secret to himself, moving boldly now, a sighted person in a
city of the blind.

From the poor tribe, he learned how to climb into Dumpsters and
find things to eat. In the early evening, when the street-market closed,
there was plenty for everyone. He was amazed that people threw away
stuff so green, so fresh, so new, and loaded his bag with bananas,

apples, cooked meats, pastries, bread. No one paid him any attention. He was, it seemed, invisible even to the poor.

He spent his first night on the streets walking and dozing, walking and dozing, always careful to stay in the footsteps of other burdened shadows. He did not dare to do what many of them did and curl up in a doorway; by dawn he was shivering in a park overlooking the sea, where a drunken man was being sick into a bush.

Later that day, he found a place to live. For much of the morning, he'd kept his eyes on two men and a woman. Younger and cleaner than the rest of the foragers, they had about them an air of easy competence that he admired. He watched rich Americans give the woman money, which she later shared with the men. They had no bedrolls strapped to their backs, and didn't push a wire cart. They were high-class beggars, clever and quick on their feet. When they wandered away from the street-market, he hung far behind, but kept them just in view as they wandered past the waterfront beneath the aerial highway along a winding ribbon of wooded parkland. The moist, gauzy air, not quite rain and not quite mist, softened their outlines and made their bodies wreathe and taper like spirals of smoke.

Past a ship dock, they came to an industrial zone of railroad marshalling yards flanked by warehouses, sheds, and factory workshops, but the place was muffled in that eerie American silence—no hammers, no whining saws, no voices. There were rows of new cars parked outside the buildings, but the only man in sight was the driver of a single empty forklift, and the loudest noise the rustling of great polythene tarpaulins in which these people sheathed their dirt-piles.

It was like the Dumpsters. What things Americans abandoned! Rusting machinery, old boats, and cars that would need only a little fixing to make them run, or good wood, all left out in the open for anyone to carry away in the night. Wherever he looked, he saw neglected valuables, half-buried in grass: tires with plenty of life left in them; a car battery; a long metal step-ladder; a whole family of refrigerators; wooden pallets; a child's car-seat; a pair of gas cylinders; a baby tractor, its seat gone to pieces but its engine still intact. He reflected that the only thing a man would truly need in this country was a pick-up truck.

Ahead, the walkers were crossing a patch of waste ground under the overhead tangle of a highway interchange. Beyond them lay a dense thicket of masts and radar-scanners, and a bridge, clogged with traffic, reaching out over what he took to be a wide stretch of water. From five hundred meters he watched the three cross a one-track railroad, scramble up an earth embankment, and disappear into the shadows under the bridge.

He waited, then followed them slowly through the brambles and gorse, his head filling with the drumming thunder of the traffic up above. He could see the harbor below him now—maybe one thousand big fishing boats packed hull-to-hull like seeds in a box. At the top of the embankment, he peered cautiously through the bushes and saw tents pitched on the soft, dry, crumbly soil underneath the bridge, perfectly hidden from the outside. He counted seven altogether, thinly scattered over a low-ceilinged space almost as large as a soccer field. A fire smoked in the far corner, against a concrete pillar. The people he'd been following were there, and two other men.

He put his laundry bag down and walked toward them open-handed, eyes lowered, smiling, and very scared. They stared at him, but seemed, he thought, more curious than hostile. "Okay?" he said. "To make sleep?" He pointed back at his bag, more than twenty meters away from the nearest tent.

One of the men shrugged. "I guess."

"You got a reservation?" said another.

"Please?"

"Forget it."

"Thank you." He went back to his bag. Opening it, he saw them watching his every movement. The reverberation of the bridge was quieter here—a continuous deep rumble that muffled the people's voices, but not their sudden, barking laughter. He spread a sheet on the ground and laid out on it his food and new clothes. With the other bedsheet, he, too, would make a tent. Trusting his possessions to the people beside the fire, he went outside to hunt for a stick to prop up his tent with, and when he came back, everything was as he'd left it. The watchers watched.

When they saw what he was trying to do—and he had no experience of tents—the woman and one of the men came over to help. They found him a better stick, rooted it deep into the dirt, and the woman produced string with which to tie the sheet to it. Then they pegged out the edges of the tent with rocks.

"L.L. Bean," the woman said.

He grinned at her. He could tell from the man's face that what she'd said was funny, not unkind.

"Po-lice?" he asked. "Po-lice come?"

"Don't trouble us none here," the man said.

He pointed at the clump of bananas on the sheet, their skins barely flecked with brown. "You want?"

They shook their heads. The man said, "Know where the wash-room is?"

He smiled uncertainly.

The man pointed down at the harbor. "Right there. In the terminal. They got showers."

Later, after dark, when flames from the fire played against the concrete and he saw the people as cut-out silhouettes, he heard them calling him: "Hey, you! Chink!"

Chink!

They were cooking sausages, holding them to the fire with forks. They offered him one, and he squatted on his haunches on the outskirts of the group. When he bit into his sausage, it tasted unexpectedly of fish.

A growling voice said: "How'd you get over here, Chink? In a container?"

"Please?" Wanting to spit out the rancid mouthful, he forced himself to swallow it. Then he said, "San Francisco." He gestured to the yards behind him. "Railroad."

"San Flancisco," the growling man said, and honked. "Wailwoad."

A bottle came to him. By the light of the flames, he spelled out the name on the label . . . Thunderbird . . . and passed it on without drinking.

Back in his tent, he slept in fits and starts, woken by the violence of his dreams. The laughter stopped and the fire died out. In his waking moments, he lay on the oil-smelling earth, and listened to the furious caterwauling of the police sirens over the roof of the encampment. Each one had an urgent appointment, but not—tonight—with him.

"Tell me a Mister Wicked story."

Finn's dad was great at telling stories, and most of them were about Mister Wicked, who wore a black hat, with a broken top like a lid, a black jacket, black silk underwear, black pants, and pointed black shoes with tassels on them. His rainbow-striped bow-tie spun like a propeller when he turned the hidden switch in his pocket. He lived in a penthouse on Pioneer Square. Finn wasn't sure what a penthouse was, but from its high windows Mister Wicked could see everyone in Seattle. With his extra-powerful binoculars, he could see right into Finn's bedroom on Queen Anne Hill. Mister Wicked's one great friend was a witch named Moira, who lived with her cat in a houseboat on Lake Union and could fly unseen across the city on her magic vacuum cleaner.

"As was his wont," Finn began.

"As was his wont, Mister Wicked was still in bed at noon on Saturday, wearing his black pyjamas—"

"—drinking champagne—"

"—and smoking a fat cheroot with a gold band."

Finn's mom's stories were about a little Indian boy called Laughing Water, but he much preferred Mister Wicked.

"And, as was his wont, he was reading the classified ads in the *Seattle Post-Intelligencer*. With his red ballpoint pen, he drew a neat circle around a particularly interesting advertisement, which said—"

"Old Boeing jets for sale?"

"No. This time it said, 'Super Glue Powder. Wholesale, by the truck-load. Fifteen dollars a ton.' And Mister Wicked began to ponder on the many, many wicked things that might be done with a truckload of Super Glue Powder."

Finn excavated a knotty booger deep inside his left nostril. His dad never seemed to notice when he picked his nose at bedtime.

"An idea—a rather wonderful idea—took shape inside Mister Wicked's wickedly inventive head."

"What was his idea, Daddy?" Rolling the booger between forefinger and thumb under the covers, he snuggled up against Squashy Bear.

"Patience! Hang in there, Finbow. He picked up the black cordless phone at his bedside—"

"He's going to call Moira—"

"Correct. And on the second trill, Moira answered. 'Ambrose?' she said—"

"She knows it's him by magic."

"No, she has caller ID."

"She never had it before."

"Well, she has it now. It came in the mail on Thursday, in a cardboard box. It's her new toy. She surprises everybody with it by telling them who they are. 'You're drinking champagne in the morning again,' she said. 'I can tell. I've got caller ID.' And Mister Wicked, chinking his champagne glass against the phone, said, 'Toodle-oo, bottoms up!' At the other end of the line, in her houseboat on Lake Union, Moira pulled a face. Like *this*. 'It's Bollinger '79,' she said, 'but I hate champagne. It tastes like cat pee.'"

Finn giggled. "How can she tell?"

"I told you, she's got caller ID. Anyway, back to Mister Wicked's wonderful idea. 'Moira,' he said, 'isn't there a big sailboat race on Lake Union this afternoon?' 'Yes,' Moira said, 'it starts at three, and we're having a dock-party here to watch it. I'm baking toad-entrail cookies for it right now.' And Mister Wicked said, 'No time to lose, then. I'm off to buy some glue.' And he leaped straight from his bed into his black silk underwear."

"I know what's going to happen. He's going to put the glue into the lake. He'll turn the whole lake into glue."

"Right on the money, Finbow. But with stories, it's not the *what*, it's the *how*. So Mister Wicked . . ."

Finn closed his eyes. Lulled by wickedness, he was asleep within the minute.

Socially. What Steve Litvinof meant by that was made plain when, at 6:45 A.M., Beth found waiting for her on her keyboard a stiff cream-colored envelope addressed to her in the extravagantly seriffed handwriting of Steve's assistant, Lisa Mayo. Inside was a card headed "Northwest Festival of Early Music," and, inside the card, an invitation, printed on opaque rice-paper, to a dinner at the Juergensen Home and "featuring" the Madrona Dowland Consort. The hosts were Soraya and Bill Juergensen, and Joyce and Stephen Litvinof. At the top, Lisa had written *"Elizabeth Rourke and Partner,"* beside which was scrawled *"Hope you can make it!"*—Steve.

At nine, she broke off work to call the RSVP number. "This is Soraya?" Mrs. Juergensen said, and then, when Beth told her that she and her husband—whose full name she had to spell twice—would love to come, she issued driving directions from I-5, adding that "you can give whatever you like, of course, but most people are sending a thousand dollars each. It's going to be wonderful, and we're so glad you can come. You can send the check here, made out to the Northwest Festival of Early Music. See you both on the twentieth!"

For several minutes, Beth sat nauseated at her work-station, then she fished out her checkbook from her bag. She hated herself, it was so fucking obvious: Lisa must keep Steve regularly supplied with the dates on which every senior employee's options vested, and then, whenever someone cashed out, he'd hit them up for a fund-raiser. And she thought he'd meant sex.

At seven-thirty, Chink was prowling along a potholed street beside the wide canal, looking for Dumpsters he might revisit after dark, walking past cranes, timber-yards, ships and boats in and out of the water, and—for the first time in America—workers. This place was alive with men in dirty dungarees, and he felt comfortable here, where the sound of hammers rang from sheds, and the air was tinctured with sawn wood, paint, and creosote. Every waterside business had its own sign, and he read each one carefully, practising his English.

"Chink!"

He thought it must be someone from the encampment, but it was a stranger, a big grizzled man in corduroys and a fleece coat.

"You're looking for the job?"

At the word "job," he nodded slyly.

"The Mexicans are late. You ever worked with asbestos?"

"Little bit, maybe."

"'Little bit,' huh? Well, it ain't rocket-science."

"Please?"

"Eight-fifty an hour."

Chink stared at him.

"Eight dollars." The man held up eight fingers. "Fifty cents." He pulled two coins from his pocket.

"For one hour?"

"You got it."

The Mexicans—five of them—came in a pick-up truck, and the big man spoke to them in Mexican, talking very fast. To everything he said, they replied *Si* and *Okay* and *Entiendo*.

"Chink," the big man then said, pointing to him.

"Hi, Chick," one of the Mexicans said, holding out his hand.

"Chick" was an American name; he'd heard it before, on the videos. He thought, *Okay, I am Chick now.*

Walking in single file, they followed the big man along a narrow wooden dock to a gray military-looking vessel, more ship than boat, and clambered aboard. The man led them down a companionway ladder to the dark of the engine room, turned on a light that did little to dissipate the gloom, then slapped at the labyrinthine tangle of lagged ducts and pipes, saying, "Asbestos, asbestos, all asbestos."

Their job was to cut away the insulation and load it into black garbage bags. The man provided them with knives, and showed them how to work the hose, wetting down each duct before they made the first cut. The Mexicans, their faces covered with knotted red handkerchiefs, looked like bandits. For Chick, the man brought a white mask.

One of the Mexicans pointed and said, *"El puerco!"* and the others laughed while he took his place among them, watching closely for cues.

The engine room stank of diesel and the rotten-vegetable odor of bilge-water. The bad smell, dank cold, and meager light made him think of jail. The Mexicans hosed down the burlap that was wrapped around the asbestos lagging, spraying each other and yelling like small boys. He slashed at the burlap with his knife, raising a puff of white smoke. The tiny fibers stayed aloft, drifting and swirling on the vagrant currents of air, and against the bare electric bulb he could see them teeming in millions, like flying chaff at harvest-time. Though they kept wetting-down the asbestos, the dust thickened until the entire engine room was filled with a dense white fog. He ripped out armfuls of disintegrating fluff, stuffing them in the bags.

Sometimes the big man was there, wearing a mask like his, sitting at the top of the companionway or, occasionally, wielding his own knife to gather twice as much asbestos with one slash as any of the Mexicans. Chick copied him—cutting and shoveling, cutting and shoveling, knotting each bag when it was full, and tossing it, like a great soft pillow, into the corner.

Late in the morning, the big man called a stop to work, and led the gang to flat boxes of hot pizza and cans of Coca-Cola up in the wheelhouse. Sitting by himself, Chick wolfed down the free food.

"You do a good job of work, Chink," the man said.

"No 'Chink.' *Chick.*"

"Okay, Chick. I like your style."

Then they were down in the white fog again, sneezing and coughing. The men took turns, two at a time, driving the truck away once it was filled with bags. On one of these excursions, the big man ordered a Mexican named Lázaro to take Chick along.

They drove across the bridge, over the top of his encampment into a new quarter of the city, where there were even more docks, warehouses, and industrial buildings. They stopped near a Dumpster. After looking around, Lázaro put one of the bags into the Dumpster, and drove quickly on. Several Dumpsters later, there were still three bags left in the truck.

Chick gestured at the bags and the Dumpster. "Why no—?"

"Is the law," Lázaro said, and laughed. "Asbestos. No good. No legal. Is *illegal.* Like me!"

When they got back to the ship, it was dark and the job was finished. The last bags were loaded onto the truck, and the big man paid off each man in turn, peeling the money from a fat billfold. He paid Chick last, when the Mexicans were climbing into their truck. Seventy-six dollars and fifty cents—for one day's work only!

"You do painting?"

"Please?"

"Know how to paint?" The man mimed, conjuring a can, a brush, a wall.

"Oh, yeah! I paint! I paint . . . real good."

"I thought you might. Come back tomorrow. Eight o'clock. You just got yourself a job."

"Eight dollars and fifty cents—one hour?"

The big man, hands deep in the pockets of his huge fleece jacket, gave him a squinting smile. "Right. Same as today."

In the deep back pocket of his new jeans, he had $116.50. That was his secret. When he returned to the encampment, the woman asked where he had been. "I go walk . . ." he said, pointing vaguely in the direction of the street-market, fearful that someone might have seen him in the truck with Lázaro. But the people sprawled by the fire asked him no more questions.

In the dark of the morning, while the others still slept in their tents, he packed everything back into the laundry bag and tiptoed out from under the bridge. He knew of a safer place now, where he could be alone with his American money—there was even a toilet and real beds. No problem. He'd live on the asbestos ship.

"Actually," Tom said, "it was Hildy's story, 'Meredith,' that sent me back to the first chapter of *The Portrait of a Lady* . . ."

He usually began his classes with a ten-minute sermonette. Things got very airless when students discussed only each others' work, and Tom wanted to remind them that they were apprentices in a long tradition of marvelous achievements. Comparing Hildy Blom with Henry James was rather a stretch—and Hildy herself, sitting at the far end of the long table, frowning grimly into her notebook, looked as if she were in the early stages of prolonged root-canal surgery.

Each of the eight students had photocopies of both "Meredith" and the James chapter, but Tim was pleased to see that four of them—not Hildy, though—had bought *The Portrait of a Lady* in the black-spined Penguin Classics edition. At the back of the room, tall stone-framed windows with leaded panes, vaguely ecclesiastical in style, and designed to import a whiff of Ivy League and Oxbridge to the Far West, let in three shafts of pallid November sunlight. The blackboard, which ran the full length of the narrow room, was covered in Cyrillic characters, along with the single English word "Chivaree."

"James's English country house and Hildy's eastern Washington trailer park may seem to be pretty remote from each other, but James had a genius for opening scenes, and I love the way he begins *The Portrait of a Lady*. As in 'Meredith,' we're waiting for the main character to arrive. Isabel will show up in Chapter 2. But Chapter 1 is wonderfully rich in inklings as to what the novel is going to be about—clues, if you like, laid cunningly through these pages by an artist working at the very top of his form.

"You'll have noticed that at first we don't see the characters themeselves, only their lengthening shadows on the lawn. They're all still the shades of the people they'll eventually become, and you may have seen in James's preface to the book—this is the one where he speaks, famously, of the 'house of fiction'—that he describes his first conception of Isabel Archer as 'the mere slim *shade* of an intelligent but presumptuous girl.' This is a novel of shades and shadows, and those of you who've read it will know that Isabel moves from being a creature of light to one trapped in the darkness of a terribly mistaken marriage.

"Nothing is quite what it seems. It's a classic afternoon tea—a female ceremony, as James describes it—but the shadows of the tea-drinkers turn out to be cast by men, and although it's a classic English house in the country with an English lord in the picture, the house is owned by an American. And while it's an outdoor scene, the garden is 'furnished,' James says, 'like a room,' with rugs on the lawn, books and papers, cushioned seats. It's as if the inside of the house has been moved outside, into the sun.

"Well, why do you think James spends so much time on this physical description of the house called Gardencourt? The lawn slopes down to the River Thames, and here James plants another clue. Later in the book, when the real shadows close in, Isabel is going to find herself locked inside another house, with another lawn, sloping down to another river."

"The Arno," said Todd Leavitt, who'd spent the summer backpacking through England, France, and Italy. His copy of the book looked as if it had been in his possession for a very long time indeed.

"Right. In Chapter 22, page 278, you'll see James's description of the Italian house of Gilbert Osmond, the dreadful husband who is Isabel's eventual destiny. And the front of the Osmond villa is 'the mask, not the face of the house.' The view of the Arno is behind the house, and James suggests a sort of sinister back-to-frontness about this other house, which is almost a perverse mirror-image of Gardencourt as he describes it in Chapter 1. At Gardencourt, everything's out in the open, even the furniture, while at the Osmond villa everything's enclosed. Long before Isabel gets there, we've been taught to see it as a jail. Look at those 'massively cross-barred' windows, James's 'jealous apertures.' You can read *The Portrait of a Lady* as a tale of two houses, if you like: the light and the dark. And in another unexpected twist, gloomy England, with its Seattle weather, turns out to be a lot brighter and saner than Tuscany, with all its celebrated Italian light.

"You see where I'm going here? The trailer-home at Ritzville . . . the waterfront mansion on Mercer Island? And Meredith herself, another 'intelligent but presumptuous' young woman? Eastern and western Washington counterposed like Italy and England?"

He saw Hildy gaping at him—not pleased by this comparison, but as if he'd booked her on a charge of plagiarism.

"Listen, I'd better say now that I think 'Meredith' is possibly the best story I've ever read by a student in the M.F.A. program . . ."

The doubt in Hildy's eyes was fierce. Tom felt himself scrutinized through those preternaturally thick specs—for what? Sarcasm? A low ulterior motive? There was even perhaps a hint of contempt, as if what he'd said was so foolish as to disqualify him from the ordinary respect due to a professor.

Trying for appeasement, he said, "But I do think there's a problem with the opening."

Chick soon found out that the big man—Mr. Don—was cunning, and to be feared.

At the end of his second day of painting, he went to collect his pay. The office—up a flight of steps in the big machine-littered shed at the head of the dock—was cramped but cozy. Warmed by a kerosene stove, Mr. Don sat at an ancient rolltop desk, his dog Scottie at his feet.

"Yeah, sit down," Mr. Don said without looking up from the sheaf of papers he was studying by the light of a green-shaded glass lamp.

Chick sat in a chair that had lost most of its stuffing. The office smelled of the dog and of Mr. Don's cheroots. Scottie—a tousled black rug with a graying muzzle—watched him with one sleepy eye.

He waited in the silence as Mr. Don grunted over something in the papers. Chick looked at the pictures of old tugboats on the wall, and at the spider-web of wrinkles on the side of the big man's sun-browned face, until he finally finished what he was reading and reach for his billfold.

"There you are. Sixty-eight."

Chick counted the money. "Mr. Don—you say eight dollar, fifty cents. For one hour."

Mr. Don studied his papers. "Rent, Chick. You thought about your rent?"

"Rent?"

"You're sleeping on my ship, pardner."

He'd hidden everything away, and had crept off the ship in the dark, long before Mr. Don arrived at the yard in his Mercedes. No one had seen him—he was sure of it.

"I cold," he said.

"Yeah, it's getting to be that time of year." For the first time, Mr. Don looked at him squarely. In the green lamplight, his face had the hooded eyes and leathery wattles of an old sea turtle. "See, it's like this. You ask permission to sleep on my ship, could be I say yes. Maybe I let you live there for free. Maybe. But you didn't ask, you just set up house-keeping aboard my torpedo retriever without my permission. Next time you ask—got it?"

"Okay, I ask. No problem, Mr. Don."

"Good. You know how to work the marine toilet on that thing?"

"Please?"

"Toilet." Mr. Don mimed wiping himself, then pumping a handle up and down.

Grinning, he said: "I figure."

"I thought you would." Reaching for the calculating machine at the far end of the desk, Mr. Don turned back to his papers.

That night, lying in the bunk of the cabin marked ENGINEER (2), Chick thought of the letter he wished he could write to his family in the village: *I am in America. Doing okay* . . . But he had talkative uncles. If his family knew he was all right, it wouldn't be long before the snake-heads knew, too.

Had things gone as planned, he would now be in New York, in the noodle factory, working to pay off his debt. He owed $37,000, payable over thirty months. The snakeheads forgave nobody. They killed people who did not pay, starting with their families back home.

He would pay, somehow. He'd spent $7.60 at the 7-Eleven store near the yard and now had $253.40. It was a beginning, but he saw the distance between that and $37,000 as an endless, lonely trail, strewn with rocks and fallen trees, bogs and caves, up a great snowcapped mountain of money. And until he had the money, everybody must believe that he was dead.

"Yes, we have coverage . . ."

Beth was on the phone in her cubicle, looking out over the riot of construction along First and Second Avenues. That white building *was* the Belgrave Realty condos. She'd checked.

"Dr. Eusebio was recommended by his preschool. I mean, he's very bright—he reads already, but he's acting-up at school. They say he's disruptive, especially in the afternoons. I got this book on AD/HD . . . I don't know. I think he has some of the symptoms, though I'm not really sure. So it'd be great if Dr. Eusebio could see him . . ."

Despite the three-week waiting list, Beth felt better for having made the call—and armored, at least, against her next encounter with Midge at Treetops. She'd tell Tom that she was taking Finn in for a regular check-up. He'd had one last month, but Tom never kept track of such things. She'd face the "psychiatrist" issue if and when Dr. Eusebio came up with a diagnosis of AD/HD.

Listening to Tom on this subject reminded her of the time she'd been stuck in a cab on the Long Island Expressway one sweltering Friday afternoon, with a driver determined to convince her that the *Apollo 11* moon landing was a charade staged by NASA in the Arizona desert. *Proof!* he kept on saying. *Proof!* Her head had grown tired with wordless nodding, just as it did when Tom talked about what he liked to call the therapy industry.

On the tar-paper roof across the street, a man was taking in potted plants from his eighth-floor garden. He had a patio table up there, and a single chair. Beth watched as he folded the chair and took it inside for the winter. Then she swiveled around to face the screen, where she was having major problems with Phoenix.

The babysitter—a checkout girl from Ken's Market—was late.

Beth was wearing her new strapless, floor-length, black silk-rayon dress by Calvin Klein, Tom the suit he'd bought in London four years ago for his father's funeral. He blinked at Beth, took off his glasses, and kissed her bare shoulder. "God, you look good. There's just one problem. It makes me want to unzip you like a banana." Finn, wrinkling his nose in scorn, said, "Bananas don't have zippers," and went off to watch "The Planet's Funniest Animals" on TV.

Courtney finally showed up, lilac-lipped, mascaraed, and clumping on heavy platform heels, looking as if she, too, meant to go out to dinner. Beth had written the Juergensens' number on a Post-it by the phone, and she opened the door to show Courtney the pesto sauce and fresh spinach-and-gorgonzola ravioli.

"Great," Courtney said dubiously. "You got any ice-cream in the freezer?"

"Chocolate chip cookie dough, but wait till Finn's asleep, okay? This isn't an ice-cream night for him."

"Sure, no problem."

They took the Audi. When Beth switched on the ignition, Terry Allen was in the middle of "Gone to Texas." She killed the music and said to Tom: "It's on Lakeside Avenue, just north of Dearborn."

Tom read her the directions out of the street atlas. The Juergensen place was on the Seattle side of Lake Washington, its graveled drive lit by carriage lamps planted among rhododendrons and old firs. The long-established greenery led Tom to expect some Tudorish mansion, circa 1925, and it was a surprise to see, at the end of the drive, a low-slung, cantilevered building of stone and glass, its weird geometric angles making it look like a partially-solved woodblock puzzle. When they found a place to park among the assembled Range Rovers and Jaguars, he saw that the long sloping lawn, with a chink of lake just in view around the side of the house, had been laid so recently that it was still a checkerboard of sods, its grid-pattern unkindly exposed by the blaze of house-lights.

While they were waiting for someone to come to the door, Tom said: "Gardencourt! Remember, in *The Portrait of a Lady?* I was—"

"Oh, do come in! You're just in time—the musicians are tuning up."

Various plinks and whines could be heard in the far distance as Tom and Beth shucked off their coats and handed them to the pinafored domestic. Then Mrs. Juergensen led them through a glass-roofed atrium, with two full-grown coconut palms in vast wooden tubs, to a door that opened into what appeared to be a corporate convention hall.

With twenty or so guests, plus the musical consort, the room still looked empty. People were scattered in armchairs and on sofas, each a long way off from their nearest neighbor, like passengers in a sparsely occupied departure lounge.

"Can I bring you drinks before they get started? White wine or Evian water?"

"Wine," Beth said, with a peculiar intensity of emphasis, and Tom concurred.

The Juergensens had obviously tried to tame the wide-open spaces of their gigantic room. An enormous blueish, pinkish, mauveish blown-glass Chihuly piece was suspended from the ceiling, representing either a tropical marine life-form or the biggest vulva in the world. Beneath it, a free-standing table, around which at least eight people might have been seated for dinner, held a collection of framed portrait photographs, all enlarged to folio-size and beyond. Two great earth-colored abstracts hung on either side of an open hearth in which a whole ox might easily have been roasted. Yet these gestures, rather than shrinking the room to manageable proportions, served only to underline its gross enormity.

Passing the back of a massive white armchair, Beth was intercepted by a bony outstretched hand and a blue wristwatch. When the occupant rose to his feet, she seemed shocked to see him.

"Steve?" she said. "Oh—this is my husband, Tom. Tom, this is Steve Litvinof."

"So glad you could come."

This man didn't fit Beth's description of her boss at all. Thin, tan, and bald, he wore a pigskin jacket over an apple-green shirt unbuttoned halfway to his midriff. Seeing Steve made Tom realize that he was the only man in the room who was wearing a tie.

Litvinof leaned towards him and whispered, mysteriously, "Liz is a treasure!"

They found two chairs, and Tom pushed his closer to Beth's. The wine arrived, he touched her hand. "Liz?"

"It's what he calls me," she said, her voice suddenly wan.

The recital began with a counter-tenor, accompanied by a lutenist, singing Morley's "O Mistress Mine." The pure, thin, choirboy voice seemed doubly amazing, given that it issued from a florid red-bearded man who looked as if his vocal cords were lubricated with six-packs.

> . . . *O stay and hear, your true love's coming*
> *That can sing both high and low.*
> *Trip no further, pretty sweeting.*
> *Journeys end in lovers' meeting,*
> *Every wise man's son doth know.*

Between pieces, a musician stepped forward to give a potted lecture on his or her instrument. "The lute is a descendant of an ancient Arab instrument called the *oud*. *Ouds* were first brought to Europe by the Moors, when they conquered Spain early in the eighth century A.D.. . . ." The lutenist spoke in an upsy-downsy voice, as if he were addressing a class of rather dim kindergarteners, then the consort played Byrd's "My Lord of Oxenford's Masque." It was, Tom thought, more Western than American, this irritating habit of talking-down. In a fluid, ever-shifting society of people who were mostly strangers to one another, nothing was tacit, nothing could be assumed in the way of prior knowledge or experience. Everything had to be stated plainly and underlined. Irony was out. So one was landed with—

"The viola da gamba means literally 'leg viol' in Italian. It received its name because it is played between the legs." This speaker's own bare legs were—not to put too fine a point on it—sturdy, and could have supported a concert grand. Tom reached for Beth's hand and held it through a brisk performance of "Nutmeg and Ginger."

The music was beautiful. The talks—on the dulcimer, the theorbo, and the sackbut—though none lasted for more than a minute, were a pain, but Tom clapped along with the others because he didn't want to let Beth down.

At the end of the recital, Steve Litvinof came over to introduce his wife, Joyce, who filled every available inch of her sky-blue jersey pantsuit and might have passed, at a distance, for Steve's mother. Clasping Tom's hand, she said, "Wasn't it interesting—learning about all the different instruments in the orchestra?"

Holding Squashy Bear, Finn snuck downstairs in his pyjamas.

On the living-room couch, Courtney was wrestling with her friend Josh, who'd arrived immediately after Finn's mom and dad had left.

"You're winning, Josh!" Finn said.

Courtney's T-shirt was pulled right down, so one of her boobs was hanging out. Her nipple was brown and stuck straight out.

"Finn!" she said, pulling her shirt back up. "How long have you been standing there?"

Finn smiled at her, wishing she'd take her boob out again. "I can't sleep. I need a snuggle."

*　　　*　　　*

Going in to dinner, a thirtyish woman laid her hand on Tom's sleeve. "I've heard you on the radio—so droll and provoking!"

He would've been happy to have seen more of her, but when he found his place-card, written in an extravagant calligraphic script, he saw that she—and Beth, too—had drawn a chair far down the long table. He was on his own, feeling self-conscious about his tie.

After the giant reception room, the dining room appeared to belong to another house altogether. Narrow and candle-lit, it had the proportions of a corridor, with an epic glass wall on its lake-facing side. Catering people were moving up and down behind the guests, serving what promised to be a lackluster sort of dinner. From his seat, Tom looked across a half-acre of lawn to a lighted dock, at which a sea-plane and two white motor cruisers were moored.

Eyeing the plane, Tom turned to the woman on his right, "So who was it who flew here tonight—or is that the Juergensens'?"

"Jack and Marcie," she said, nodding across the table at a man who looked like one of Tom's grad students.

Jack looked up and said, "It saves you the hassle of 520, which at rush-hour is a total bitch."

Everyone seemed to know everybody else, and Tom was content to listen. The main drift of the conversation was about distances. When someone complimented Soraya on the pink stone ("So warm!") used in the construction of the house, she said, "We trucked it over here from this quarry we discovered up in Maine." Then the young man sitting next to her said: "Our stone came from India, but we had to ship it to Italy first. The Italians are still the best stonemasons in the world . . ." A woman announced that she'd run into this "very special" landscape gardener in Romania, and flown him out from Bucharest to supervise the shaping and planting of her lakeside backyard.

Tom picked at his plate of dry Pacific salmon and limp asparagus. He had a trick for summoning whole passages from books. It was quite simple: you had only to picture the position of the quote on the page, recto or verso, top, middle, or bottom. He was now mentally thumbing through the pages of the Penguin edition of *Our Mutual Friend*. Recto, definitely. A chapter-beginning, set about a third of the way down the page . . . He had it.

Mr. and Mrs. Veneering were bran-new people in a bran-new house in a bran-new quarter of London.

In pre-bubblewrap days, of course, everything came packed in bran.

Everything about the Veneerings was spick and span new. All their furniture was new, all their friends were new, all their servants were new, their plate was new, their carriage was new, their harness was new, their horses were new, their pictures were new, they themselves were new, they were as newly married as was lawfully compatible with their having a bran-new baby, and if they had set up a great-grandfather, he would have come home in matting from the Pantechnicon, without a scratch upon him, French polished to the crown of his head . . .

Wonderful! He gazed benignly down this unending table of neo-Veneerings and tried to catch Beth's eye, but she was talking with Joyce Litvinof.

After the strawberries, which tasted blandly of November and hydroponics, most of the men wandered out on to the bran-new lawn to smoke cigars. The man named Jack offered Tom one. "Cuban," he said. "I fly 'em in from Vancouver."

"I daren't," Tom said. "I'm a reformed addict. I'd inhale." But he enjoyed the cigar-flavored air.

Jack turned to the man standing next to him. "Larry—isn't Shiva Ray building just up from here?"

"I don't think so. I believe he's over in Medina." He pointed at a spot on the far side of the lake, where the water was rimmed silver with lights. "Pretty much dead in the middle, between Bill's house and the Simonyi place."

"I thought it was Leschi."

"No, it's definitely Medina."

"I know Shiva Ray," Tom said.

Both men turned on him in candid astonishment.

"How?" said Jack rudely.

"He's donating money to the creative writing program at UW. I teach there."

"Ah," Larry said.

"He calls me up once or twice a week to talk about how we're going to spend the money. But it's funny—he only ever calls from airplanes."

"That sounds like Shiva Ray," Jack said.

Twenty minutes later, inside the Audi, Tom said, "So that was a fund-raiser."

"Yes."

"How much did we raise, then?"

"Oh, four hundred bucks."

"Each?"

"No. Two hundred a head."

"Well, that's not so bad. The music was rather wonderful, I thought." Then he briefly attempted a falsetto: "O mistress mine, where are you roaming . . ."

"They must've had a lot more wine up at your end of the table."

"I suppose they need the money for more shawms and psalteries and things."

"No, they want to bring over lots of bands from Europe for their festival."

"I don't think they call them bands."

"Whatever."

"What does that Juergensen guy do, exactly?"

"He used to be a v.p. at Microsoft, then left to start his own company. He makes digital smells."

"He *what?*"

"Don't ask. Please don't ask. It's what he does."

"Perfect." Tom peered through the window at the traveling darkness of the Arboretum.

Beth was in a fume. Litvinof had suckered her twice: first with the invite, then with the fraught hour at Barney's, where she'd bought the embarrassingly over-formal Calvin Klein thing. Someone really might have mentioned to her that Steve and his cronies were in the habit of undressing for dinner.

When they reached home, Courtney appeared both subdued and somewhat disheveled. She declined Tom's offer to walk her back to her parents' house, and clumped noisily down the porch steps. Tidying up in the kitchen, Beth found a used condom in the garbage can under the sink. Couldn't she have wrapped the damn thing up, at least? Then Tom came into the room, carrying a copy of *Our Mutual Friend*. *That* felt like the last straw.

Wearing earphones, Tom was sitting alone in one of KUOW's new studios on University Way. From behind the glass of the control cubicle, Ned the engineer gave him a thumbs-up, and the voice of Miriam Glazebrook, his producer, came down the line from the National Public Radio studios in Washington, D.C.

"Hi, Tom. How are things in rainy Seattle?"

Miriam always said this. She did it to annoy.

"Very Seattleish. Beth and I went to a fund-raiser last night. Our host was a man who left Microsoft to start his own dot-com. He sells digital smells. There's a box-thingy you plug into your computer. You probably have one . . ."

"The things people do out there."

"That's a bit rich, coming from D.C."

"Trish says we've got good level here. We're rolling."

"Every morning, first thing—"

"Sorry, there's a glitch at our end. Okay, now we're rolling again."

"Every morning, first thing, my wife reads her fortune in the paper. We take the skinny national edition of the *New York Times*, which doesn't have a resident astrologer, unfortunately, but . . ."

4.

"... unfortunately, but Beth makes do with Section C ..."

The rush-hour traffic was gridlocked on First. Tom's voice, relayed by eight hidden speakers, was grotesquely larger than life. Talking for the radio, he rolled his r's in what Beth supposed must be the Hungarian fashion. At the best of times, this struck her as an annoying affectation; now she heard it as a mocking affront. Her hands tightened on the wheel, and the anger inside her felt like pond-water curdling into ice. How dare he say these things? He'd never said a word about the piece. She'd happened on it by accident, looking for the news.

"Thomas Janeway teaches creative writing at the University of Washington. His regular commentaries come to us by way of member-station KUOW in—"

She hit the Power button to kill the jabbering announcer.

He knew nothing—nothing!—about the company, couldn't even find his way around the site. He hadn't a clue about how the revenue stream was generated, and for him to talk—ignorantly, complacently, with his fucking rolled r's—about "burrrn rrrates" was insufferable. Swift? Pope? That South Sea fucking bubble? As for bringing her and her options into it—it was condescending, humiliating, unbelievably pompous. He no more understood the online world than he did particle physics. All he knew or cared about were his stupid Victorian novels and his even stupider World War Two stories, yet he had the fucking shameless audacity to broadcast his worthless opinions about the "New Economy" and the company in which she was daily struggling to keep her own head above water. People listened to "All Things Considered," for godsake! How was she supposed to face the ninth floor next morning? "My wife, Beth"! She might just as well be his fucking lab rat. Would Robert have heard it? Would Lisa? Would *Steve*? She felt sick at the thought.

Instead of turning left on Galer, she continued north on Queen Anne Avenue, driving for driving's sake, trying to recover some shred, at least, of ordinary composure. By the time she crossed the Fremont Bridge and was climbing the slope of Phinney Ridge, she'd returned, more or less, to herself.

There was no real malice aforethought in the man. Tom was just utterly thoughtless in his bookish self-absorption, believing himself to be observant because he could observe things that happened in novels. In reality, he was so blind that someone ought to make him carry a white stick. It wasn't even his *fault* that he could do something like this to her; that would be like blaming a kitten for unraveling a ball of yarn. He was, in his way, incorrigibly innocent. Once, she had thought him brilliant.

Well, she thought, *live and fucking learn.*

When, half an hour later, she got back to the house, Tom and Finn were on their hands and knees in the living room, making animal noises at each other.

Tom clambered to his feet to kiss her. "How was the day, sweetheart?"

"Fine," she said.

*   *   *

Chick studied American men, wanting to look right, to blend in with the crowd. The smartest-looking guys his age nearly all had the same style: their hair was trimmed to a dark shadow around the skull, they wore neatly groomed moustaches, and most of them had a gold ring in the lobe of one ear.

He began to grow a moustache, and paid a barber $10 to shave his head. He begrudged the money but was pleased with the haircut. Catching sight of himself unexpectedly in a store window, he saw an American—although the moustache would take many patient weeks before it achieved the glossy luxuriance he had in mind.

He was still sleeping on the ship and doing jobs for Mr. Don—either on his own or with Lázaro and the other Mexicans. He was learning things from Lázaro. Most days now, he bought the *Seattle Post-Intelligencer* from the 7-Eleven on Nickerson. He hoped to improve his English by trying to read bits of it, but always turned first to the "Deaths" column, looking for young men with Chinese names.

"Have you noticed?" Tom wrote. "People are getting nostalgic about money. Like so many middle-class Americans, I'm a fan of 'Antiques Roadshow' on PBS—the last refuge of real old-fashioned money.

"We live in a world now where money is nearly always expressed in decimal points, with little *m*'s and *bn*'s at the end of it. To drum up interest in a TV game show, the winning contestant now has to come away with a cool million. Only on 'Antiques Roadshow' does money that you or I might earn in a day, or a week, or a month, or a year, have any real meaning."

The night before, he'd watched an elderly man bring in a painted glass beer stein, circa 1890, put out as an advertising gimmick by a Milwaukee brewery. His granny had kept string in it. When the appraiser estimated its value, the old man cracked up. Tears dribbled down his cheeks, and in a shuddering, weepy voice, he said, "Oh . . . Oh, my . . . Two thousand dollars?" Across the country, Tom sensed, millions of viewers were tearing-up in sympathy.

That was the real secret of "Antiques Roadshow": it restored value to sums that were important to people—as they certainly were to Tom— but which had become contemptuously devalued in the public discourse. GetaShack's "burn rate" alone was running at $2.7m a month, according to Beth, while its assets were said to be $4.1bn. No wonder, then, that the audience ratings for "Roadshow" were themselves expressed in the kind of figures that—

The phone went off at his feet.

"Thomas? It is I—Shiva. We've just taken off from LAX. I'm on my way to D.C."

"Funny, some people were just—"

"Thomas. I have been reading Reisz. I think I am turning into a fan. He has extraordinary irony and pathos."

"Sorry—who?"

"Reisz," Ray said, sounding offended. "Dave Reisz. *Crystal Palace*."

"Oh, that. Really? I thought it was quite funny, but—"

"Thomas, you sound blasé. I don't like blasé. We are living in a world nowadays where there is far too much blasé, and far too little passionate enthusiasm."

" '. . . the best lack all conviction, while the worst are full of passionate intensity,' " Tom said, playing Shiva's usual game.

"What is that?"

"W. B. Yeats. 'The Second Coming.' "

"I do not agree. In my business, I have time only for people with the passion. I chose to talk with you because I thought you had the passion. For literature."

"I don't think you could accuse Yeats—"

"No time for Yeats. Here I am busy, busy, busy. To come to the point: will Reisz play?"

"Well, I'm sure he would, but—"

"Get him. You know who his agent is, his man of affairs, or will you write to his publisher?"

"I've got his e-mail address."

"You have?" Ray sounded surprised and admiring. "For a man like Reisz, I think we could definitely push out the boat. You think he might say yes if we offered him a lakh? One hundred large?"

Resisting temptation, Tom said, "Yes, I really think he might."

"For a writer of this calibre, Thomas, one must be willing to go the whole hog."

"I'll write to him today. Shiva—we were at dinner the other night, and there was a great debate about where your house actually *is* on the lake. The entire party divided between the East Siders and the West Siders, Medina or Leschi. Where is it, in fact?"

"Ah," Shiva Ray said. "I oscillate. Furiously." Then the connection was lost.

When Tom had finished writing his commentary on money, he wrote to David Scott-Rice, offering him some. The exact amount was hard to arrive at, and he kept on changing it, but finally settled on $21,500, which he thought looked nicely precise and should set something of a barrier against flighty upward negotiation. When—as must inevitably happen—he had to raise it to $25,000, he wanted it to seem like a hard-won concession. Still, he wished he hadn't mentioned Don DeLillo's offer over dinner, and wanted to imply that he'd wrested this lesser sum out of the authorities in the face of substantial opposition.

> *Dear David,*
>
> *Emerging—only slightly scarred—from the briar patch, I'm thrilled to say that, following our conversation in the bar, I can now report back that . . .*

His message ended:

> *We can arrange accommodation for you on campus (a quite prettily furnished one-bedroom apartment), or, if you preferred, we could put you up at the University Inn. I have the feeling that you'll be happier in the apartment, and we can arrive at a reasonable per diem. As for airfare, I very much doubt if we can run to Business Class, but I will of course do what I can.*
>
> *I greatly enjoyed our vinous evening in Seattle, and very much look forward to seeing more of you here in the spring. You can count on our house as a home-from-home, and I badly want you to meet Beth and Finn.*
>
> *My best,*
> *Tom.*

Scott-Rice had a demon return-of-serve. Barely ten minutes later, Tom's computer pinged, and the stamped-envelope icon appeared on the bottom of the screen. There were a couple of opening pleasantries, then a sentence that began "Given my American reputation . . ." He was busy, just starting a new book, and holding out for $40,000, with Business Class assured. He wrote: "I don't suppose you happened to see the review of *CP* in the *Times-Picayune* did you? They put me in the best possible company . . ." *And which company was that,* Tom wondered sourly, *Homer and Tolstoy, or IBM?*

He checked the time. At 3:25 P.M. in Seattle, it was thirty-five minutes short of midnight in London, so Scott-Rice was likely to be in a vainglorious mood after taking in a skinful, and with any luck the sober morning would find him in sackcloth and ashes. Tom decided to do nothing for the next couple of days, then respond late in the evening so that Scott-Rice could reappraise his American reputation over his breakfast coffee.

"See, it's like this, pardner. Properly speaking, you don't exist."

Mr. Don was chewing on his cigar, and the dog Scottie gazed at Chick with rheumy, blameful eyes.

"Twelve bucks an hour is a big chunk of change to give somebody who's no better than a spook."

"Please?"

"Spook. Ghost-man. Like you say in Chinese, *gweilo.* Funny, that. You see, Chick, you're the *gweilo* around here now, and the way I look at it, you got a pretty good deal for a ghost. You got a nice place to live, you got eight-fifty an hour, cash. You thought about the IRS?"

"INS?"

"That's a whole different outfit. The INS, they just lock you up and send you back where you came from. But the IRS, they take your money and *then* throw you in jail. So between the INS and the IRS, people like you get kind of squeezed, especially when the ghosts get uppity and start talking twelve bucks an hour. See what I'm saying, pardner?"

"I think, Mr. Don."

He leaned back in his chair, blowing smoke. "It strikes me that you're a pretty sharp guy, on the whole. But you've got a lot to learn about some of the institutions we have in this country. The INS and the

IRS, the EPA and the FBI, the SSA—and that's just the federal ones. Then you got to think about the state and the county and the city—and all of them got their own institutions. You run a little business like mine, you got every one of these fine institutions on your back. I take a piss in the dock, I get the EPA after me. I even talk to a *gweilo* like you, pardner, I'm in big trouble. That could get me put on McNeil Island for a good part of the rest of my life. McNeil Island's a jail. You know about jails?"

"Yes, Mr. Don."

"I figured you did."

Chick was saddened by this interview, having hoped to reach a compromise, to make a deal. For the last two days, Mr. Don had put him in charge of the Mexicans, so he was a manager now. When the Mexicans slacked off, he goaded them. Under his supervision, they worked twice as hard as they'd done before. A manager ought to be making $10 an hour, *minimum*.

He had now saved $1,914.50. He kept it in a long inside pocket he'd sewn into his jeans. At night, he rolled them up tightly, and used them as a pillow in his cabin on the ship.

His haircut and moustache were working wonders for him: on the streets, people now treated him as an American, and not a homeless American, either. The men, especially. Often now, he saw them smiling in his direction. Sometimes they brushed his hand with theirs. He would smile back, but walk on. His English, though improving fast, with many new words learned every day, would betray him; yet he felt the day would soon come when he'd be able to stop and talk with one of these friendly men.

But Mr. Don was right. He had no identity, and in this country a man without identity would never go far. Lázaro had one, and still was paid only $8.50 an hour, but Lázaro was slow-witted. Chick knew he could do a whole lot better than Lázaro, if he, too, could get ID.

On November 27, he found what he was looking for in the *Post-Intelligencer*. Charles Ong Lee—born 02/13/74 in Tacoma—had died in an automobile accident on Highway 99. From talking with Lázaro, he knew what to do now.

The helicopters were back.

From the gabled window of his study, Tom saw seven or eight of them hovering above downtown, like a flock of chicken vultures circling a carcass. One appeared to be buzzing the Klondike building. Tom dug out the binoculars he'd bought for spotting American birds when he first arrived in Seattle. The 'copter shimmied in the glass, the word POLICE stenciled in large blue letters on its pod. Anxious, he called Beth.

"Oh," she said, "it's just the WTO demonstration."

"The what?"

"Tom: people have been talking about nothing else for weeks. The World *Trade* Organisation!"

"Ah. Yes, I suppose I did know about that."

"There's a parade of old hippies going by right now. It looks kind of fun. Apparently, Madeleine Albright can't get out of her hotel." She laughed.

"Are you sure it's safe?"

"I put it in the underground garage this morning."

"I didn't mean the car. I meant—"

"Of course it's safe. We've got a grandstand view from up here. Now there's a lot of people in turtle-costumes marching by."

Tom went downstairs and switched on the TV, where it didn't look safe at all; it looked like Kosovo, or worse. A ragged line of masked police with riot shields was holding off the crowd with tear-gas. As grenade after grenade exploded at the heels of the running demonstrators, the gas stained the air a brownish ochre. It was bewildering that Beth should make such a fuss about the shipyard shootings yet be so flippant about this. He gazed at the picture on the screen: familiar streets rendered scarily foreign by the stampede of people holding caps and scarves up to their faces as they bolted from the gas. A panicked reporter was yelling into the camera, which in a sudden lurch turned the street completely upside down.

Back in the newsroom, the anchor was badly rattled. "Brian? Brian!" he shouted, and the reporter's head bobbed briefly back into view before being lost again in the scrimmage. Over the image of the swirling street, the anchor announced: "We're just hearing now that Mayor Schell has declared a state of emergency . . ."

The news burst through in distraught fragments. "Anarchists and looters" were sacking McDonalds, Starbucks, Nordstrom, Niketown, Planet Hollywood. Christ! Tom thought: if Starbucks is a symbol of global capitalism, what does that make GetaShack.com?

He dialed Beth again.

"Hello, this is Beth?"

"Beth!" He bawled over the noise of the riot on the screen.

"Yes? What's up now?"

The words came tumbling out of him—*tear-gas, looting, state of emergency!*—and then he heard Beth's impatient sigh at the other end.

"You know how the media is—"

"—*are*," he said, immediately wishing he hadn't.

"Well, thanks for the grammar lesson. But honestly, Tom, I'm hideously busy right now."

After hanging up, Tom decided that she must be in shock. This was how situations of extreme stress often took people: they went numb to it, and behaved with exaggerated ordinariness. Like that scene in *Sink the Bismarck* where Kenneth More . . . He gazed at the TV, at a group of policemen mustered behind their lines; with their gas masks off, they looked scrawny, young, and terrified. Then there was a shaky hand-held sequence involving a blazing Dumpster and some black-hooded characters smashing the windows of a department store with sledge-hammers.

It came to him that he really ought to rescue Beth, if only from herself. That defensive cool was liable to crack at any moment, and who knew where that would leave her. The trouble was, the police were closing all the downtown streets—and he had to pick up Finn from Treetops at five sharp. Feeling quite maddeningly powerless, he dialled Beth's number again and got a busy signal. The second he replaced the phone in its cradle, it warbled shrilly.

"Beth!"

"Tom? It's David here. You got my e-mail?"

"I can't talk now. There's fighting in the streets, and Beth's right in the thick of it!"

"Really? In laid-back Seattle? Is Beth some sort of urban guerrilla, or is she—"

Tom slammed the phone down. On the screen, protesters were pitching rocks and bottles at the police, who were firing back, said the reporter, with rubber bullets. In the background, Tom thought he recognized the ornate molded frieze of the Klondike building. He pressed the Redial button—still busy. Yet Beth had voice-mail—she was always "on the other line"—so maybe the whole system was down.

He raced upstairs and typed a frantic e-mail:

Beth—please acknowledge. Are you okay? Call when you get this. I'm so worried for you. Take care. All love—Tom.

The message did not immediately bounce back to him as undeliverable, which he took as a good sign, but the phone stayed silent as he raked the downtown waterfront through his binoculars. Apart from the helicopters, everything looked normal.

He returned to the living room. A police car had been rolled over, and people were trying to set it alight. Farther down the street, there were more fires. Tom gazed at the TV for thirty seconds, then ran back upstairs to his computer, clicked on Send/Receive, and got a message from rourkee@getashack.com:

T—do stop fussing, PLEASE. Everything's fine here. When you get Finn, can you stop at Ken's and pick up . . .

A brief shopping list followed. He scanned it with wonder. At a time like this, how could anyone possibly be thinking about arugula?

The following day, Beth worked from home, to Tom's huge relief. And when he went up to his study after dropping Finn off, he found a decently craven message from David Scott-Rice, who'd "had no idea" of the seriousness of the situation when he called, and realized that he must have sounded "callow and heartless." Since then, the events in Seattle had been at the top of the news on BBC TV and on the front page of the *Guardian*. He was very sorry to hear that Beth had been caught up in the mêlée, and hoped that she was now safe and well. *Etcetera.*

It was a pretty good letter, considering; and it showed a sensitivity to Tom's reasonable concerns that was bafflingly absent in Beth when she had arrived home the evening before on the dot of six. Her chief line was one of self-congratulation for having the good sense to put the Audi in the underground garage. One of the techies had left his car in the open parking lot. "They totaled it," she said. Otherwise, it was all turtles and marijuana smoke—and not a word of acknowledgement that Tom had been half out of his mind with worry.

All this made him feel a sudden kinship with Scott-Rice, who from a distance of more than four thousand miles nonetheless seemed to understand. Tom had no difficulty upping his offer to $32,000, and even paused over the ridiculous demand for premium air travel, then wrote: "It'll have to be Economy, I'm afraid. But we'll pay the full fare, so it may not cost you the earth if you want to upgrade."

An hour later, Scott-Rice accepted, without a haggle. When Tom e-mailed Shiva Ray with the good news, he didn't say anything about the money. In the mid-afternoon, a three-word message came back from shivaray@home.com:

VIRTUE IS BOLD!

Tom needed to consult the *Oxford Dictionary of Quotations* to confirm that it did, indeed, come from *Measure for Measure.*

"As was his wont . . ."

That night, Mister Wicked, poring through the small ads in the *Post-Intelligencer,* bought a wholesale consignment of white mice, an African parrot that could say bad words in five languages, and the world's biggest, loudest, most embarrassing whoopee cushion.

When Finn was asleep, Tom came down to the kitchen to find Beth tipping the last of the bottle of Syrah that they'd shared over supper into their two glasses—more into his than hers—and sliding it across the butcher-block table.

"You may need this," she said.

"Oh?"

"I'm buying a condo. In Belltown."

"What for?"

"Tom—don't make things harder than they have to be. What do you think?"

"Not as an investment, then."

"No."

"Oh."

"And, no, before you ask, it's not 'another man.'"

"A woman?"

"Hardly."

"What about Finn?"

"Well, obviously we'll have to draw up a parenting agreement."

"But we're Finn's family. You can't just—"

"It'll be better for Finn. Better for all of—"

"—unilaterally . . ."

"Half his friends at Treetops already live in two houses."

"That's not true."

"Scott? Amelia? Taylor?"

"Christ."

"He's still at that adaptive age. It would be tougher on him next year, or the year after. That's one of the reasons—"

"I had no idea."

"That's what's so wrong with us."

"What is?"

"Your having no idea."

"But—"

"You'll see it's for the best when you get used to it."

"I thought . . . it seems bloody ridiculous to say it now, but I thought, I actually thought, we were happy."

"I'm sorry, Tom. I'm sorry."

Crouched on his haunches at the top of the stairs, Finn listened to his dad making these funny gasping noises, like he was crying, and his mom saying "Tom" over and over. He knew what they were doing.

He and Spencer had talked about it loads of times. Spencer knew all about it because Spencer's mom was going to have a baby sister for him. When people made babies, the dad grunted a lot and then the mom yelled. It was bad to interrupt people when they were making babies: Spencer did it once, and there hadn't been a baby.

So Finn just listened.

Spencer was wrong about one thing. He said the mom and the dad always did it in their bedroom. He'd tell Spencer tomorrow: his mom and dad did it in the kitchen.

*   *   *

"... because of something I said on the bloody radio?"

"Please don't shout, you'll wake Finn. No, of course I'm not. I was just using that as an example."

"I didn't show it to you because you've been so busy lately that talking to you about anything at all has seemed like an intrusion."

"Okay, forget the radio thing. It was trivial anyway."

"It didn't seem trivial three minutes ago."

"Well, it is now."

Tom was fossicking in the cupboard where the liquor was stored, but there wasn't much: a boxed bottle of champagne with a pink ribbon tied round it that Miriam Glazebrook had sent him last Christmas; two more bottles of Syrah, and one of Chardonnay; a tablespoonful, perhaps, of The Famous Grouse; and the bottle of Dutch gin, still unbroached, that he'd bought at Schiphol Airport last year after a conference at the University of Utrecht.

He slopped geneva into his empty wineglass. "Gin?"

"No, thank you. I'll stick with water."

The only thing to be said for geneva was its alcohol content. He swallowed the oily, herbal stuff like medicine, thinking, *I shall always remember this as the taste of devastation.*

"Tom—we've been going in different directions for years."

"For one year. Maybe."

"I've been growing up."

"Is that what you call it?"

"Don't be cheap. Look, I know you want someone around, someone to come home to, someone to read your pieces to. But that's not love, it's babysitting."

"That's so unjust."

"Is it?"

"It's not 'someone' I want. It's you."

"But you don't know who I am."

"Eight years!"

"Hey, I played along. I tried. I did the wife thing. 'My wife, Beth.' I learned all my fucking lines."

"But—Finn!"

"I won't let you use him like a weapon."

"I'm not trying—"

"This is about me. And it's about you."

"It certainly seems to be about you, but I don't see how I come into it at all."

"You live in a world of your own construction, Tom. Half the time, you don't even live in America, much less with *us*. Finn and me, we're like characters to you, like in a book you never quite get around to writing. You make us up—'my son,' 'my wife.' Well, I've had it up to here with being a figment of your fucking imagination."

"Beth!"

"Well, I have, I'm sorry."

They wrangled until after midnight. Tom cried twice. Then Beth cried. Then, in the temporary lull at the center of the hurricane, they discussed custody. It was agreed—though *agreement* was hardly the word for it—that once Beth's purchase of the condo was finalized (requiring his signature on several documents), Finn would spend Monday and Thursday nights in the house on Queen Anne and weekends would alternate; Tom would pick him up from Treetops on Tuesday and Wednesdays and have an hour or two of playtime before Beth whisked him off to Belltown for the night. This arrangement was, she claimed, "non-prejudicial."

Tom stared at her, slack-jawed. "You've been talking to a lawyer."

"Yes," Beth said.

Once he had the birth certificate, the rest was easy.

He paid Lázaro $100—$20 for each of the Mexicans—to use their address in Greenwood. They were careless, and never stayed long in one place, anyway, so this was no real inconvenience. A hundred dollars was a lot of money, but it would have been dangerous to use the address of the yard. He was having enough problems as it was with Mr. Don, who'd found a buyer for his asbestos ship.

"You got seven days to get your shit out of there, pardner. Come Tuesday, say around dark o'clock, I want you *gone*, okay?"

"Where I sleep then?" Chick asked.

Mr. Don looked up from his papers. "You seen my sign outside there?"

"Yes."

"What's it say?"

"It say 'Dahlberg Marine Inc.'"

"See, I'm in the marine business, not the hotel business or the homeless-shelter business. If I ever try that out, I'll be in touch—but right now I'm selling ships, not renting rooms. Got it?"

"Yes, Mr. Don."

Some days Mr. Don seemed like his friend; other days, he bullied him. First smiley-smiley, then loud shout. That was the trick of his power—you could never be sure where you stood with him—and Chick was fascinated by the way he could suddenly veer from gentle to fierce. When Mr. Don turned rude, he watched his face to see how it was done. Then he practiced on the Mexicans.

They were stripping paint off a tugboat. Chick was in charge.

"Lázaro," he said. "In Mexico—you got kid?"

Lázaro reached into the back pocket of his jeans and from his bill-fold took out a buckled snapshot of his little girl, Ria.

"Nice," Chick said. "Now move your ass."

There was much to learn from studying Mr. Don, but Chick was looking ahead to the time when he could have a business of his own. After his Social Security card came, he'd go for a driver's license, and then he'd be legal, almost, as Charles Lee. Free of Mr. Don, he could start making real money.

He had saved $2,312. Compared to the Mexicans, he was already rich.

Finn had to be told.

It was an ice-cream night, so they waited until he'd finished his bowl and "The Crocodile Hunter" was over. He was sitting at his own table in front of the TV in his little red chair.

"Pumpkin, we've got something to tell you," Beth said, squatting beside him with an arm around his shoulder.

"Yes?" he said expectantly.

"Your daddy and I have been talking, and we've decided—"

"I'm going to have a baby brother—"

"No, Finbow—"

"A baby sister?"

"No, honey."

His face began to crumple. He'd already told Spencer that he was going to have a baby brother.

"But we're going to get another apartment. So we'll have two houses!"

"We already have a house," he said angrily. "I don't want another house."

"Pumpkin, the new apartment's near the Aquarium—and the Science Center."

"I don't care."

"You'll have your very own room—"

"I want to watch 'Amazing Animal Videos.'"

"You see—"

"I heard you making a baby." Finn's lower lip stuck out, and he blinked back tears. "I thought you were making a baby."

As Beth said later, it hadn't gone well, but at least they'd sown the ground, and Finn would soon get around to asking about the condo in his own good time.

"It's nowhere near the Science Center," Tom said.

Sleepless and jumpy, he was trying to teach his weekly morning class. The Cyrillic writing on the chalkboard had been replaced with Italian, the beams of weak sunlight had disappeared, but otherwise all was the same, though everything was different. He was talking, as kindly as he could, about Alan Wurtz's story.

". . . I did find myself pausing, rather, over that long stretch of dialogue on pages 4 to 6. It's all weighted one way. I felt throughout, really, that Lance was being starved of the kind of authorial attention he deserved, and I was reminded of something I once heard said by V. S. Pritchett, the English short-story writer. If you don't know his stories, you really ought to. He was a sort of Russian realist with a powerful libertarian streak and a magnificently impish sense of humor. Very observant, very funny, very humane. Try reading 'The Saint,' or 'The Wheelbarrow,' or 'The Camberwell Beauty'—wonderful pieces of writing, rather neglected now, but they'll come back.

"What Pritchett said . . ."

It must have been—what, 1983? He'd gone to the party with Sue, in a dark, packed, and smoky flat in Paddington. Sir Victor was in his

chipper eighties, wineglass in hand, pipe clamped between that mouthful of incongruous teeth. Scott-Rice was somewhere in the picture, too.
But Pritchett, older by a quarter century than anyone in the room,
seemed younger, merrier, than the thirtyish crowd around him.

His pipe puffing like a traction engine, he'd said: "I'm not really
much of a one for 'tips,' but there's a tip I sometimes give myself, and
find quite useful. Whenever I think up a good line—a 'clever' sort of
line, you know?—I always try and give it to my least-favorite character."

Tom quoted this to the class. Hildy Blom scribbled on her pad, but
the rest looked back at him with faint, indulgent smiles, as if such
advice was a bit on the elementary side.

"You'd never catch V. S. Pritchett using a term like 'characterologi-
cal,' I'm afraid," Tom said. "But it's a luminous remark, and if you think
about it in relation to Alan's story . . ."

He taught on autopilot, his mind elsewhere. Talking of Pritchett
made him think of Waugh, who wrote, when his first wife left him, "I
did not know it was possible to be so miserable and live." Misery was not
what Tom felt. Rather, he was wonderstruck. Beth, with her reliable talent
for surprise, had pulled the floor out from under his feet, but the force
of gravity hadn't yet kicked in, and he was left standing on empty air,
like one of Tiepolo's massively fleshed, absurdly buoyant rococo angels.
Tom supposed it would not be very long before the laws of physics were
restored and he'd come hurtling down to earth. For now, though, he
was in a giddy, weightless state akin, strangely enough, to happiness. It
was like that first fortnight with Beth in Seattle, when he'd flown over
for his interview at the U. Same lack of sleep. Same jittery high. Same
sense of looking at the world through intensifying hangover spectacles.

He heard himself saying, "Alan, if you were able to grant Lance sufficient wit to speak that early line spoken now by your narrator—you
know, the one about their father flying low over their lives like a crop-
duster spraying herbicide on fields of young wheat? See how that
would open up the dialogue?"

It wouldn't really, of course. Alan's story was unrescuable, but the
principle of the thing was worth exploring.

"We always want to claim the best lines for ourselves, or for our
stand-ins. That's only human. What I love about Pritchett's remark is
that it argues for generosity on the part of the writer. In American
terms, I suppose you'd have to call V. S. Pritchett a 'socialist,' although I

doubt if he ever defined himself quite like that. But he did believe in a general redistribution of verbal wealth, in taking good lines from the haves, and giving them to the have-nots—an impulse at the heart of his kind of liberal realism . . ."

When class was over, walking in the rain back to his office, Tom was deep in the past. The party had been in Westbourne Terrace—it must've been at Greg Harbison's flat, when he was still with Tessa. He and Sue had gone in Sue's old Mini—and Sir Victor was there because Scott-Rice had brought him. They'd come in a taxi together from Shepherd's Bush, where David had been interviewing him for "The Book Biz." Tom remembered seeing that interview, though Pritchett had said nothing as memorable as his "tip" on dialogue. It would be something to remind David of when he came to Seattle.

On Sunday morning, the three of them drove to Belltown to see the condo. They took the Audi.

Finn was given a quarter and two dimes to throw into the lobby fountain, and allowed to press the button for the eleventh floor in the elevator. It was hard to know how much—if anything—he understood about what was going on. *Mostly* had been the key word, so these new arrangements might sound comfortingly slippery and provisional. Mommy was going to live *mostly* in the condo, to be nearer to her office; Daddy was going to live *mostly* in the house on Queen Anne, because he needed the space and it was closer to the university. And Finn was going to get two of everything, where before there had been only one. Beth and Tom alike made it sound as if Finn had won the lottery and was on the brink of a sudden, spectacular enlargement of life that would make him the envy of everyone at Treetops.

Beth was encouraged to see that he certainly liked the fountain.

In the elevator, she said, "Won't it be cool, riding to our house in an elevator?"

The condo was a maze of interconnecting white compartments. The developer, Tom thought, must have wanted to economize on doors, and there was an insistent generic resemblance between these rooms and the cubicles in the Klondike building. On the woodblock floor of the main living space were piled half a dozen huge, unopened cardboard boxes from Ikea.

"Ah, the furniture's come," Beth said.

Someone would be spending many hours with incomprehensible assembly diagrams, L-shaped keys, and a Phillips screwdriver. Tom feared it would be him.

"Look, pumpkin—our breakfast bar."

Beyond the Ikea boxes, a sliding glass door in an aluminum frame opened onto a small concrete balcony with a view of more condo blocks and a compact rectangular slice of Elliott Bay. Tom craned to see if the house was visible from here, but it was just hidden by the curtained picture-windows of somebody else's corner apartment.

He heard Beth saying, from one of the bedrooms, "Well, it's not really big enough for Daddy to live here, too. He needs his upstairs office at the house."

He stepped back inside. Even on a day of pearly overcast, the condo was bright. In sunshine, it would be blinding—like living, he thought, in a hospital operating theatre, or on the set of a shadowless TV sitcom. He walked through the tiled kitchen area and joined Beth and Finn in the smaller of the two bedrooms, which smelled pungently of its snow-white fitted carpet.

"If your bed goes here," Beth was saying, "you'll be able to sit up and look out the window in the mornings. And we can go buy some really cool posters to put up on the walls."

"Can Daddy come, too?"

"Well, of course he can—if he wants to." Over Finn's head, she said to Tom: "You see why I had to have it?"

Her smile was cloudless, unforced, and Tom realized with a pang that it had been months since she'd last smiled at him like that.

"Yes, it's nice."

"The light," she said, prompting him, "and that *view*."

View? What view?

He found himself instinctively hunching his shoulders beneath the too-low ceiling. Cramped, sterile, and anonymous, the condo looked more like a fate than a choice.

"I thought I'd look for a big mirror to go on the long wall in the living room," Beth said, still smiling absentmindedly.

A mirror would only multiply the horrors. Tom thought of the generous amplitude of the house on Queen Anne: what must it say about her feelings towards him that Beth could scorn that for *this?*

Down in the lobby, Finn begged for more coins and tossed them in the fountain.

As they were leaving, the uniformed doorman said, "See you, Beth. Have a great afternoon—"

Tom bristled slightly, for the man's easy, accustomed use of her name gave this other life of hers an unwelcome solidity. In the bathroom, Tom had spotted a toothmug, a hair-dryer, and some lipstick and stuff, already in residence on the faux-marble countertop; in the kitchen, two bottles of some herbal power drink, one of them empty. He'd noted these objects without any definable emotion, but the memory of them now provoked a sudden apprehensive stab of discomfort, like the first, exploratory burring of the dentist's drill.

When they were back in the Audi, with Finn up front in the passenger seat, Tom said from the back, "Why all those things from Ikea? There's plenty of furniture in the house that you could take."

"I wanted a fresh start," Beth said.

Finn stayed oddly silent until they were halfway up the Counterbalance, then he said, "You know what?"

"What, sweetie?"

"I have an idea."

"What idea, Finbow?" Tom said, playing along with Finn's irksome habit of demanding to be put through an F.B.I.-style interrogation in order to disclose the simplest piece of information.

"Well . . ."

"Spit it out, pumpkin."

"I really like the condo—and the fountain. But."

"But what?"

"It's a two-person condo, and what we need is a three-person condo. Can't we get a three-person condo? Please?"

Tom, trying to glimpse his expression in the rearview mirror, could see only his frizzy black bird's-nest of hair.

They were on Galer and Seventh when Finn said, "Are you having a divorce?"

Dr. Eusebio's office was on the fourteenth floor of the Medical and Dental Building on First Hill.

The waiting room, furnished like a nursery with bean bags, puzzles, unpainted wooden toys, old typewriters and adding machines, was drenched in astral New Age Muzak. The bookshelves held the usual kids' books, many of them beaten half to pulp, along with such adult titles as *The Indigo Child, When Children Grieve, Families Are Forever, Positive Discipline, Beyond Ritalin, The Life of the Bipolar Child,* and *Straight Parents, Gay Children.*

Beth had been waiting here for fifteen minutes while Finn was in with Dr. Eusebio. Her exclusion from the interview had come as an unpleasant surprise, as had the doctor. Beth had expected someone older, to whom she could naturally defer, not the elfin blonde in a bold forsythia pantsuit who met her new patient with the words "Hi! I'm Karen," then barely acknowledged Beth's existence before whisking Finn off into the consulting room. The Muzak clearly had a purpose: over the sobbing noises of the synthesizers, you'd never hear your own child cry. The whole set-up had a sinister aura about it, as if Dr. Eusebio's suite of rooms was infected by the anger and unhappiness of all the disturbed children who'd passed through.

Beth leafed through an antique copy of *Vogue,* too on-edge to look at the pictures with any comprehension, listening through the Muzak for any noises from the far side of the wall. When she checked her watch, two minutes had gone by

Finn was comfortably sprawled on a scarlet bean bag, while the psychiatrist sat cross-legged on the floor beside him, scribbling notes on a pad of lined yellow paper.

"*Penthouse?*" she said, her pen moving rapidly across the page.

He was fascinated by Karen's suit. She had big pouchlike pockets on her jacket, and more pockets down the legs of her pants. It must be great, Finn thought, to have so many pockets to keep things in.

"And he does 'wicked' things."

"Yes," Finn said. "*Really* wicked."

Karen had a nice face and a cloud of fluffy pale hair. There seemed to be very little of her inside her bulky suit. Her wrists were as slender as his own, and she was more like somebody's big sister than a teacher or a parent.

"Where does he do these wicked things, Finn?"

"Oh . . . everywhere. Sometimes he does them in parks, like Discovery Park. He's done lots of wicked stuff up there."

"And who does he do them with?"

"Kids, mostly. Sometimes with grown-ups. And a lot with Moira. She lives on a houseboat on Lake Union. She's a witch and flies around Seattle on her vacuum cleaner."

Dr. Eusebio made more notes. "You know, Finn? Don't tell anyone, but I still love to play with my dolls. Do you like dolls?"

"Maybe."

"If we keep it a secret between us, would you like to play with my dolls?"

"Okay."

"Great!" She put her forefinger up against her lips. "I keep them in this cupboard here. Very few children know about my dolls."

From the shelf where the dolls sat in a long line, Karen selected a mommy doll, a daddy doll, and a little-boy doll. Then, from a cupboard full of doll furniture, including, Finn saw, some doll toilets, she brought out two beds, a table, and three chairs. "Here, Finn—you help."

All the dolls were fully clothed. But when they were undressed, they were anatomically correct in every essential detail.

5.

At ten on Sunday morning, Tom's mother telephoned from Romford.

"They're both fine," he said. "Fine. They're . . . out at present."

His mother had sent off Finn's Christmas presents—a book, a stuffed dog, winter clothes—more than a week ago.

"Don't worry, Ma. The mail's always a bit slow at this time of year. It'll come. I'll call you as soon as it arrives."

Katalin Szany (she'd never taken to Janeway) had refused Tom and Beth's offers to fly her to Seattle, and her image of the United States was firmly rooted in the films of her girlhood. He imagined her imagining the parcel of goodies from Marks & Sparks being conveyed by stage-coach through Apache country.

Tamás, she kept on saying. *Tamás.*

It was worrying. After his father died in 1995, Tom had

helped her sell the Ilford house and move into a ground-floor flat in Romford, where she could walk to the shops and was only a five-minute bus ride away from the Nagys, Judit and Andras, who'd come to England on the same Hamburg ferry as the Szanys. This move had taken Katalin just seven miles to the east of the old house, but her eastward migration had continued ever since. Each time Tom talked with her over the phone, it seemed that her accent had grown a little thicker, her grasp of English more unsteady, and she nowadays appeared to have entirely forsaken Romford, Essex, for—where? Budapest, where she'd met his dad? Or Eger, perhaps, where she'd grown up? He no longer knew where she was, only that she had ceased to live at her official mailing address.

Her accent was disconcertingly contagious. Tom would have been hard-pressed to come up with twenty words in Hungarian, and had never made the ritual trip to the country of his birth, yet now found himself falling into the rhythms and intonations of his mother's broken, weirdly accented English. "Good luck with the eye-doctor, then, Ma," he said. "Take care. Lots of love." But when he hung up, his words lingered in the air: *got lok . . . lotz off loff.* It was all right, though. His mother wouldn't have noticed, any more than she would've detected that things were amiss between him and Beth—a piece of news that he meant to keep permanently hidden from her.

He went back to *Dr. Wortle's School.* Tom loved Trollope, not least because you could go beachcombing through out-of-print titles and discover novels as good as this one, written in just three weeks with a furious intensity of focus and concentration. He read more, perhaps, than Trollope had intended, into the scenes between Peacocke, the English clergyman and "man of letters," and the American woman who was not quite legally his wife. In these short, dark days, time hung heavily on his hands. The university quarter was coming to an end. He felt no urge to write. Trollope was his best distraction, and he lined up *The Macdermots of Ballycloran, Ayala's Angel, Lady Anna,* and *Linda Tressel* to read when he was done with Dr. Wortle and the bigamists.

The small van that Beth summoned to the house had STARVING STUDENTS painted on its sides, though the two movers appeared to be neither starving nor students, and they'd left almost all the furniture behind. The most conspicuous absence was that of the hamsters, who now lived in Belltown, while the stick-insects and Orlando the goldfish stayed at Queen Anne. Wherever Tom looked, he saw things that belonged more to Beth than to him, which reinforced his instinctive conviction that she wasn't gone but away on a visit, taking a breather in her hotel-room–like quarters at First and Lenora.

Even so, picking up Finn from Treetops, or trawling through the shelves at Ken's Market, Tom felt a marked man now. It was clear from their looks that the moms all knew—though what they knew, or thought they knew, was something he preferred not to think about. Spotting Amy's mom as she crossed the far end of the aisle, he tucked his head between his shoulders and made a show of reading the fine print on the packets of chicken-flavored Ramen noodles.

He hid himself away in the house with his books. On his first evening alone, it occurred to him that he could call someone up and go out for supper or a drink, but when he paged through his address book, he realized there was no one to call. He and Beth were on two rosters— his colleagues and hers—of flat little dinner parties. The people they met regularly on these occasions were known, for convenience' sake, as their "friends"; but they were really no more than fellow toilers in the same vineyard, fellow parents, neighbors with little more in common than their zip codes.

The closest that Tom had come to friendship here was with another Englishman, Ian Tatchell. A lean, sixtyish, denim-shirted alcoholic, Ian was a Marxist in the E. P. Thompson–Eric Hobsbaum line, and had been in the History Department at UW since the early Seventies; but his serene lack of ambition and his failure to complete his great book on Chartism had stalled him at the rank of Associate Professor. Tom enjoyed the skirmishing between Ian and his wife, Sarah, that usually went on well past midnight in their farmhouse-style kitchen, fuelled by three-liter bottles of booze. Beth did not, and once had labeled the Tatchells "co-dependent old farts."

Flipping to the *T*'s in his address book, he nearly dialed Ian's num-ber, then thought better of it. When he got together with Ian, they wrangled happily about Shelley, Thomas Hood, Hardy, Gissing, *The Ragged-Trousered Philanthropists,* Dick Francis, Tony Blair, but did not talk about their marriages. Their nearest approach to personal inti-macy was when Ian confessed that he'd gone through a prostate-cancer scare.

As a snatch of birdsong in a theatre defines silence, so Ian's presence in the landscape defined Tom's friendlessness. If he couldn't talk to Ian, he could talk to nobody. He thought, *This must change.*

He tried to take lessons in equanimity from Finn, who seemed to be taking the new regime comfortably in stride, regaling Tom with atrocious puns and double-entendres.

"A panda bear walked into a bar . . . *Ouch!*"

"Groan!" Tom said.

"Why did the chicken cross the playground?"

"I don't want to know—"

"To get to the other slide!"

But Finn now spoke of Beth as "my mom," as if Tom might not have made her acquaintance. At first he'd construed this as a diplomatic gesture, then decided that Finn was only laying claim to what was rightfully his own—*my* mom, *my* dad—in an attempt to glue his disintegrating family back together again. Otherwise, he seemed ebulliently cheerful, commuting between Belltown and Queen Anne, with Squashy Bear in his backpack, like a seasoned straphanger.

Without Finn, Tom was in uncharted waters. Evening by evening, he steered a faltering course from one hour to the next. In the past, he and Beth had watched TV programs like "Jeopardy!" and he'd happily called out "What is Chile?" or "What is a manicurist?" in the arsy-versy, question-for-answer style of the show—a charade that now seemed tinny and moronic. He glared unsmiling at the screen through an episode of "Seinfeld," and switched off "NYPD Blue" when the first batch of commercials appeared. PBS was no better, with "Elton John's Greatest Hits" and quarter-century-old reruns of "Are You Being Served?" He supposed it was preferable for the federal government to subsidize Elton John's wigs and the faded camp of John Inman instead of nuclear missiles, but only marginally so.

Although Tom sometimes bought books via Amazon or Bibliofind and had dickered around on the GetaShack site, he'd never spent much time on the Internet, yet every night now he crossed the Atlantic by mouse. He printed out the crosswords from the *Guardian* and the *Times,* then holed up in the kitchen, trying to figure out "In the past, you once strayed disastrously (9)." At 10 P.M. he'd go up to the study with a glass of wine to click through to the BBC and listen to tomorrow's news, live on the "Today" programme with Sue MacGregor and John Humphrys. At eleven, he'd return to the United States downstairs, with the local news on Channel 7. Never had he been so well informed about the trivia of the moment—from the parrot in County Durham who saved a family of six from burning to death by shouting "Help!" (though the bird itself, a red Amazon, died in the blaze) to Ken Griffey Jr., the Mariners' star center-fielder, who was standing firm on his refusal to be traded to the New York Mets, prepared to be sold only to the Cincinnati Reds.

Around midnight, he'd go upstairs again, to sleep as best he could, sprawled diagonally across the king-size bed, waking at frequent intervals to Beth's coldly palpable absence. For these spells of unwanted consciousness, he kept a pile of funny books on the bedside table: *Jorrocks' Jaunts and Jollities,* the collected short stories of Saki, *Work Suspended and Other Stories, The Inimitable Jeeves.* Surfacing with a jolt, he'd grab whichever one of these was closest to hand; at three and four in the morning, the important thing was not to surrender a minute to dangerous introspection.

It was when he came home after teaching his last class of the quarter, and his guard was down, that he made his most upsetting discovery.

The day was unusually bright for December. A dry and frigid wind was blowing out of continental Alaska, and through his classroom window Tom enjoyed the fifty-mile-long view of Mount Rainier with its raspberry-shadowed slopes of blinding snow. On Tenth Avenue, the sunshine was cruel to the porch, dwelling on its scabbed green paint and the holes in the planking where the wood had rotted away, and he reminded himself that sometime over the Christmas break he must go on another, most likely fruitless, hunt for a contractor.

Inside the house, he was taken suddenly aback by its darkness, dirt, and clutter—the junky yard-sale furniture, its upholstery badly clawed by Hodge, the cat which got run over on Finn's fourth birthday, Beth's busted bike, the litter of newspapers and magazines. There were dead sycamore leaves and Jiffy Bag fluff on the carpet, and Finn's tartan pyjamas on the ravaged couch. The window, through which the low southerly sun was striving to effect an entrance, looked as if it had been smeared with lard. The house was—and here came the discovery— exactly like 127 Ladysmith Road.

127 Ladysmith Road, Ilford, Essex, England, Great Britain, Europe, The World, The Universe, Space.

Appalled, he watched his parents' house take shape inside the walls of his own. He'd always thought they were binary opposites—systole and diastole, east and west, yin and yang—but now he saw they were one.

Coming to England with nothing, the Szanys hoarded everything. Long before they moved to Ladysmith Road, they'd filled their council maisonette with silver paper, string, old newspapers, cardboard. Every emptied jam-jar was rinsed out, dried, and shelved against the day when jam-jars would be as valuable as gold. In 1959, when Tom's dad, formerly a teacher of mathematics in Budapest, landed his job in the accountancy department at Rowntrees, the candy factory, and Harold Macmillan won the general election on the slogan "You've Never Had It So Good," the Janeways (as they had now become) bought their own house on a twenty-five-year mortgage.

It was pronounced, dolefully, *Ze moeur gauge.* Tom was seven when he first heard the name of the angry and jealous god who came to preside over the Janeways with unforgiving vigilance. The Moeur Gauge was the answer to every important question: Why can't we get a car? Why can't we stay at the seaside? Why must I wear these old trousers to school? Fealty to the Moeur Gauge brought the Janeways not possession but conditional occupancy of the narrow, bay-windowed, pebbledash-fronted, semi-detached castle of dust and dinge that was the house on Ladysmith Road. All these houses were inclined to pokeyness; veiled behind identical net curtains, their dim front rooms were inadequately warmed in winter by coal fires. Ladysmith Road was at its best in the great fogs that still sometimes blanketed the London suburbs, when the lighted houses came into their own as cosy refuges from the noxious gloom of the outside world.

But No. 127 was a special case, its pokeyness different from the rest. It was—as Tom came to understand when he entered his teens—a small corner of eastern Europe marooned in the Essex commuter belt. Walking through its front door was like passing through Checkpoint Charlie, the boiled-cabbage smell in the hall announcing that you were on the threshold of a new economic system, a new philosophy and politics. The Szanys had fled "Communism," yet had established on Ladysmith Road something uncannily like a threadbare Soviet satellite. Their stockpiles of precious rubbish, their much-repaired clothes, their terror of spending money for fear of some nameless cataclysm to come, set them a world away from their English neighbors, who referred variously to the Janeways as "the Hungarians," "the Russians," "the Czechs," "the Poles," "the Romanians," The one fact obvious to everyone was that they came from—and belonged to—the wrong side of the Iron Curtain.

Yet in their own fashion, they were good capitalists. When Tom's dad died in 1997, he left just over a million pounds, including a £100,000 trust for Finn's education and £50,000 for Tom, who was named as the eventual inheritor of the Janeway estate—unless he should predecease his mother, in which case everything would go ultimately to Finn. For Katalin, her stewardship of this great pile of money was a source of terror, as if she had it in her to casually fritter away a million pounds. The thought of Katalin plundering Harrods on a credit card was, for Tom, enjoyably bizarre. When he suggested she might find it fun to go on a Mediterranean cruise, she was shocked.

"I be such a crazybones? Tamás!"

The house on Ladysmith Road had sold for £278,000, and the flat in Romford had cost £162,500. Tom went over the arithmetic with his mother, pointing out that a two-week cruise could hardly come to more than, say, £4,000.

"No, I cannot. I would feel such a bad waster."

So she spent her fortune on boil-in-the-bag cod in white sauce, her Senior Bus Pass, and the weekly bottle of Harveys Bristol Cream sherry that had always been her only genuflection to the high life.

Holding Finn's pyjamas, Tom stood in the living room face-to-face with his mother, in a floral housecoat, in the front room of the house on Ladysmith Road, circa 1962. Her hair was pinned up in a disheveled black haystack, her lips thinly rouged to the outline of a cupid's bow. She'd have been thirty-four then, a dozen years younger than he was now, though her knotted brows and fast-emerging spiderweb of anxiety lines made her look already old. The brown rubberized cord of the Hoover lay heaped in serpentine coils at her feet, though there was little trace of its passage through the house.

Shamed, Tom fished out the Miele from the closet under the stairs and marched it from empty room to empty room, trying to suck the gloom and neglect out of the place. Shoving its blunt nose as far as it would go under the cat-ravaged couch, he hardly knew if he was in Ilford or Seattle.

He was the family interpreter. Left to themselves, his parents spoke Hungarian. At Rowntrees, Ferenc Janeway spent his days in the borderless language of numbers. In English, Tom was grown-up, his parents the children. When they had to deal with tradesmen, solicitors, doctors, teachers, he was their short-trousered ambassador, negotiating glibly with the girl from Radio Rentals or the man from the gas board, then translating everything back into bare kitchen-English. His airy command of idiom—much of it found in books, and twenty or thirty years out of date—won him admiring plaudits from his parents.

"The whole shebang!" his father said, rolling the phrase hesitantly around on his own tongue. "The cat's pyjamas!"

Tom, though, caught the flicker of amusement in people's eyes when he was talking. Though as fluent as any Essex-born child of his age, he was slightly, indefinably off-key. English wasn't exactly his second language, nor was it quite his first. He was encouraged by his parents to think of it as an exotic possession—a chest of treasures he could store up in his bedroom at the back of the house, along with his fishing tackle and his model-aeroplane kits from Keil Kraft. His parents had their language; he had his, and he loved its cadences and quirks of phrase, spending rapt hours alone, enlarging and polishing his word-hoard. In Mrs. Atherton's class at Rose Lane Primary, his fellow-pupils yawned through her by-rote vocabulary drills, but not Tom. He added each new precious item to his collection—those merry grigs and quiet church mice, the charm of finches, the clamour of rooks, the pride of lions, the murmuration of starlings, the covey of partridges, the exaltation of larks.

In the Bloemfontein Avenue branch library just around the corner, Tom entered a truly foreign world, tagging along behind a tribe of marvelous children quite unlike any to be seen in Ilford. They all lived in extended families, in big houses in the country, attended by cooks, gardeners, gamekeepers, and dogs. The boys went to boarding schools— wild, colorful republics run from top to bottom by the boys themselves, from whom Tom picked up the glamorous argot of "fagging," "keeping cave," "fains I," "beaks," and daydreamed his way into the Lower Remove. On their epic summer holidays, these super-children sailed boats, solved mysteries, tickled trout, rode on horseback (the girls had their own ponies), and mounted fantastically elaborate practical jokes.

Halfway through *Swallows and Amazons,* and vainly trying to imagine what would happen if a girl named Titty were to show up in Mrs. Atherton's class, Tom realized for the first time that England was another country, and Ladysmith Road not so much a part of it as a colonial dependency inhabited by an inferior people. The England of the books, the real England, began somewhere in London and stretched out westward from the city into a rich, dappled landscape of green hills, brambly footpaths, oak trees, and half-timbered Tudor villages, where gnarled rustics leaned on five-barred gates and every crackle in the night was a poacher up to no good.

In Ilford there were no hills, no hedgerows, no nature, unless you counted the reservoir where Tom went fishing with his dad—just council estates, shopping parades, and long identical streets of bow-fronted semi-detacheds. On rare family day trips to London, he felt he was standing in the foyer of a legendary country, privileged to be allowed a peek inside.

In Hamley's, the toyshop, a fair-haired boy about his age interrogated the shop assistant in a loud, bright, cut-glass accent, as if she were not an authority but a menial. The boy's mother, a perfumed, willowy woman in a hacking jacket and tweed skirt, watched over him with a distracted smile. "Oh, really!" he said, pronouncing it *rully*. "Hadn't you better look it up in the Hornby catalogue? We haven't got all day."

That was England. So was the changing of the guard at Buckingham Palace, where Tom and his parents stood in the crowd craning for a glimpse of trumpets, drums, and busbies, the sound of the marching band blurred by the whirr of home-movie-cameras and the pigeon-chatter of people talking in a dozen different languages. Tom knew instinctively that this was where Janeways belonged—with the dazed and passive tourists for whom England was a pageant and a mystery, viewable only from a respectful distance.

Going home at Christmas after his first term at Sussex, he took the train from Liverpool Street and watched the sooty grandeur of London fray out through Stratford, Forest Gate, Wanstead Flats, and Manor Park. Smoke from chimneys was pasted low over the housetops by a fierce easterly wind blowing in off the North Sea. At Seven Kings, a fox watched the train go by from a hillock of blackened shale, its greasy pelt mottled with bald patches. Though the diesel locomotive, jolting to a stop at every station on the line, made the most of the journey, it was, at most, only ten or eleven miles. As a child Tom had believed the distance to be immense, and London a glamorous elsewhere half a world away, but now he surprised himself with the thought that he'd actually grown up as a Londoner without ever knowing it, and that his sense of provincial exclusion was a peculiar gift bestowed by the capital on its citizens in order to keep them in their proper stations.

Lugging his twin suitcases down Ladysmith Road that December afternoon—the Antler cases, found by his mother in a summer sale, were a lurid clan-tartan, and a cause of serious embarrassment—he felt himself to be a stranger of a different kind. Before he could ring the bell of 127, his mother flung the door wide, and they kissed on the step. Her hair, cut in a ragged bob, was graying now, and her web of wrinkles put Tom unchivalrously in mind of the cracked moonscape of Auden's famous phiz.

Her happiness left him tongue-tied. She was in the middle of making the dinner she always cooked for momentous occasions, goulash with dumplings and paprika potatoes; and he spotted the bottle of wine, Bull's Blood of Eger, on the sideboard in the dining room. Dicing an onion in the kitchen, wiping her eyes with the back of her hand, she was a torrent of excited talk. Ten weeks away among the English-born had spoiled Tom's ear, and he could barely follow what she was saying.

"Oh, *drágám,* Papi come home early tonight, he is so . . . But you sit in your coat, like you not stay, is so cold? *Vékoni!* Too thin! Papi, he want so much to talk with you. He saves up. I know all night will be *politikai* talk. Oh, Tamás—*egyetmista* already, is hard to believe! *Profeszor* next! You're hungry, yes? What you want to eat? *Pirítós? Toasty?*"

He'd sat there with a guilty, shit-eating grin on his face, taking in the shabbiness and clutter of the house with the detachment of a visiting stranger. Toppling stacks of *Manchester Guardian Weekly*s were piled against the kitchen wall, hundreds and hundreds of copies, going back into the 1950s. You could dig through that yellowing mulch, and find the Suez Crisis, the space dog, the Cuban missile stand-off, Kennedy's assassination . . . Each weekend, Tom's father would work his way slowly through the latest edition, cover to cover, like a textbook, before filling it in the dank archives along the kitchen wall.

Tom's mother passed him a mug of tea, and he had to excavate a space for it between the piled bills and circulars on the table. The bare forty-watt bulb overhead didn't so much light the kitchen as expose its wilderness of fast-darkening shadows, with his mother moving among them like a badger in its sett.

"Three weeks!" she said. "Tomorrow we go to Judit and Andras house—always, they ask about you, and how are your studies."

Twenty minutes at home, and three weeks sounded like an age. Tom tried to shorten it by naming to himself the books he had to read before the beginning of the new term—*Gawain and the Green Knight, Troilus and Criseyde, Shakespeare Our Contemporary, Comus, Clarissa, Tom Jones*. He thought, already longingly, of his square, sunlit study-bedroom in Park Village on the campus: the Hockney swimming-pool poster on the wall, the color-coded spines of the Penguin Poets on the shelf, the mandala-patterned Indian bedspread, the scent of freesias (Nuala's contribution, but she would be far away in Larne for the entire Christmas vac).

"Papi buy two tickets for the football game on Saturday. For him and for you."

"That's great. Who are they playing?"

"Oh, Tamás—I don't know. I thought you would know."

It was his closest tie with his father now—the shared fiction that both of them were passionate fans of West Ham United. Several times a season, they'd make the trek to Upton Park and roar with one voice for Geoff Hurst and Bobby Moore. At first, Tom believed that he was humoring his soccer-crazed dad, then that his dad was humoring him; lately, he'd come to realize that each of them was aware of the other's lack of real interest, and that this secret knowledge bound them more intimately than mere fandom ever could have done.

So they kitted up in striped blue-and-claret football scarves—Tom hiding most of his inside the RAF greatcoat that he'd bought at the army-surplus shop—and cheered themselves hoarse from the stands when Moore, in midfield, sent the ball soaring across to Hurst, who headed it smack into the visitors' net. When the Hammers pulled off a truly brilliant goal, father and son hugged each other tight—something they never ever did at home.

At Upton Park, it didn't matter that Tom was going to Sussex to read English, rather than to Cambridge to read mathematics. For all his dad's efforts to demonstrate the logical beauty of simultaneous equations, Tom had failed 'O' Level maths first time around. When the results came in the post (eleven passes, one fail), he saw the tragic disappointment in his father's face, that the passes counted for nothing, and the fail for everything. Only when West Ham beat Arsenal 3 to 2 the following Saturday were Tom and his father reconciled.

Funny, that, Tom thought, switching off the Miele in the house on Queen Anne Hill: when they were dropped from First Division football in England, both Geoff Hurst and Bobby Moore landed up here, as the geriatric stars of the Seattle Sounders. Ian Tatchell had seen them in the late Seventies, playing to thin crowds of English expatriates and American curiosity-seekers.

"They had bandaged knees, and sometimes the bandages came unraveled: it looked like the escape of the mummies from the British Museum."

He also claimed to have spotted Bobby Moore, captain of England and hero of the 1966 World Cup, standing forlorn and unrecognized in the checkout line at Ken's Market.

"What was he buying?" Tom asked.

"A six-pack of Coors, a carton of Luckies, and a frozen pizza."

His cleaning efforts made no more impression than his mother's used to do. The ingrained shabbiness of the house defeated him. You could rearrange the stuff in the rooms till kingdom come, but they'd always look like a pig's dinner. There wasn't a stick of furniture that didn't conjure the image of the yard sale where Tom and Beth had found it, but it was like adopting feral kittens or abused Russian toddlers: feral stayed feral, and the flinty scowl of the state orphanage remained on the children's faces long after they'd been dressed in new clothes from Gap Kids and fed on peanut-butter-and-jelly sandwiches. So it was with these cast-offs. Abandonment was in their nature, and it showed. Eyeing the cane-back rocker in the living room (U District estate sale, 1993), Tom saw just why Beth had taken virtually nothing from the house and turned to Ikea for furnishings.

He pushed the Miele back into the closet. Even on this brightest of winter days, the ground-floor rooms needed electric lights to alleviate their sullen timbered gloom. Give them horse brasses and hunting horns, and they'd pass as bars in some dusky Tudor pub—the Old Bull & Bush or the Goat & Compasses. "It's a bit dark," Beth had said after they'd viewed the house. Dark? It was bloody sepulchral. How peculiar that it had taken him eight years to notice what Beth had seen in a glance.

He saw it now, though, and he was excited by the novelty of standing in her shoes, looking out through her eyes. Moving stealthily, like an intruder, not wanting to break the spell, he set out on a tour of the house, seeing what she must have seen when he was down in the basement talking with the realtor.

To him, its age—ninety was historic in this young city—had always meant solidity, permanence, but now he saw it as infection and decrepitude. Who'd want to take on a house where so many slights and sorrows must have festered unspoken in the L-shaped kitchen, and so many doctors and undertakers' men must have gone up and down those stairs?

He remembered the sound of her footsteps on the bare boards overhead while the realtor banged on about how the house was built like a ship. Trying to retrace her footsteps, Tom became aware of details that he'd never paid much attention to before: the hairline crack in the exposed brickwork of the chimney, the tipsy slope of the floor, the failure of any of the doors to hang quite true. She'd stopped—just here—and thought, *This place is a fucking liability.* He was certain of it.

He climbed the stairs to the half-landing, where a dead yellowjacket lay on the dusty sill of the tall stained-glass window. With its leaded panes of scarlet and dark green, it might have been looted from a church. It turned sunshine into a somber, multicolored twilight—useless as a window, though handy, perhaps, if you had the sudden urge to fall to your knees and say your prayers. He felt Beth's pang of dislike for its shabby ecclesiastical pretensions, and remembered how for him the window had been a selling point, lending a splash of grandeur to the house. Why hadn't they got rid of the stupid thing years ago? The house was starved of light, and a single sheet of plain glass would brighten up the whole ground floor. He'd find a glazier. It was a simple job—an afternoon's work, at most.

In Finn's room, he saw at once that the glum beige of the walls had to go. Painting them white was within even Tom's limited capacity in the home-improvements department. He'd let Finn help. Across the hall, he opened the door of his and Beth's bedroom, and took in the heavy old-gold drapes that had come with the house; the sash window with its broken cord, now propped partway open with a book; the repro "Chippendale" vanity with a blemished oval mirror (Ballard, '94), that Beth had never used.

Turning back, chastened, into the hall, Tom had an out-of-the-body experience, or something uncannily like it. From a distance of ten feet or so, in the gloaming he caught a distinct glimpse of himself, shoeless, unshaven, in wrinkled denim shirt and baggy corduroys. His woolly-headed avatar was heading upstairs to his sanctum on the third floor, the hog. That room was the only one in the house with a normal supply of natural light.

So up he goes—off to spend another day in Cloud Cuckoo Land.

Well, of course she'd moved out. Having seen what he'd seen, Tom would've moved out on himself. The condo was Beth's message to him, and he understood it perfectly; every syllable made sense. She'd given him a sideways glimpse of his own bloated self-absorption, and he was shocked but grateful. His first thought was to phone and tell her about his discoveries—how he saw it now from her point of view, and how . . . But show was better than tell. He'd show her. Going down the stairs, he was light on his feet, brimming with energy and purpose, riding the surge of his enthusiasm like a surfer on a steep Hawaiian wave.

On the half-landing, he stopped in front of the offensive window. The dimpled lozenges of colored glass were impossible to see through, and the fussy trelliswork of lead mullions took up half the entire window space. The seventeenth-century Puritans had railed against stained glass, seeing it as man's vain attempt to divert God's all-seeing gaze with tawdry art, and suddenly Tom found himself of one mind with Cromwell and Cotton Mather. If a brick had been handy, he'd happily have pitched it through the bloody thing.

More light!

After dark, the condos of Belltown became a dense aerial honeycomb of illuminated rooms, each boldly exposed to the gaze of the others. Though the windows were routinely fitted with featherweight ivory venetian blinds, they were rarely closed, except in bedrooms late at night. At any one moment you might see people with bodies already in perfect shape working out on home treadmills and exercise bikes; Web sites blooming on computer monitors; familiar movies playing out on jumbo-sized DVD screens; pizzas arriving in white cardboard boxes; intense, gesturing figures, like maestros conducting imaginary orchestras; physical intimacies between men and men, women and women, and sometimes between men and women. After the public preliminaries of sex in Belltown, and there was plenty of sex in Belltown, the scene was more likely to fade to black at the turning of a dimmer switch than it was to go white with the rude closure of the blinds.

Since everybody took turns being observers and the observed, the condo-dwellers took pride in the increasing refinement of these nightly performances. Whatever compelled them—love, grief, health-maintenance, pulling an all-nighter at the terminal, or hanging out with a friend—was done with a keen awareness of the watching audience, so that in Belltown even raw unhappiness took on a shiny professional finish.

Seeing the lighted rooms, a newcomer might think that he—or, statistically more likely, *she*—was watching Belltown "life," but these radiant *tableaux vivants* were more like commercials for the product than the product itself. You could measure their effectiveness in bottom-line terms: the price of a Belltown condo was rising by a steady 35 percent per annum, thereby comfortably outperforming the market and running slightly ahead of the blue-chip standard set by waterfront property on Lake Washington. So the flirtations, treadmills, pizza deliveries, and rare scenes of abject despair all helped to add to the wealth of the Belltowners, most of whom were now paper millionaires.

In the southwest-corner apartment on the eleventh floor of Belgrave Pointe, Finn's venetian blind was squinched tight shut, but the rest of the condo was on display in the multi-screen extravaganza. The casual viewer would probably miss the toys strewn across the living-room floor and the nest of cardboard boxes in the far corner, seeing instead the twin powder-blue couches facing each other across a low glass-topped cane table, where a dozen white roses stood in a water jug beside an open laptop and the New Millennium issue of *Vanity Fair*. Seated on the couches were two women, one dark and curly-haired, the other a razored blonde. Between them, a bottle of Blanc de Blancs had been broached, but the level of the wine had sunk only an inch or so past the top of the label, and they'd moved on to mugs of blackcurrant tea.

"He's losing it," Beth said. "It's totally unlike him. Totally."

"Is he on medication?" said Debra Shumaker.

"Alka-Seltzer? Ibuprofren? He's got a phobia about doctors. He hasn't seen one in years."

It had been a delightful surprise to find Debra waiting for the South elevator. They'd both been on staff at the *P-I,* when Beth and Tom and Debra and Joel had sometimes gone out to dinner as an awkward foursome. Debra, newly divorced, now worked at Oroonoko.com, a women's adventure-travel site, and had a studio apartment on the fifteenth floor, though Beth had yet to see it. The flowers and wine had come with a card: *"To the best days of our (single!) lives, Love D."*

Tom and Joel should have found something in common—they were both teachers, after all—but were like oil and water, with Tom always trying to talk to Debra, and Joel to Beth, so that conversation between the women was hopelessly fractured by the men's needy, attention-seeking interruptions. "They have to strut their stuff," Debra had said after a bad evening at the Dahlia Lounge, and Beth had instantly seen the two husbands as a pair of gobbling turkey-cocks with spurred legs and scarlet wattles. That was the last of the dinners.

"I remember that window," Debra said. " I liked it."

"Me too. It used to sort of sprinkle the light through the house . . . I was shocked."

"What was he thinking of?"

"Goethe."

"What?"

"When I went to pick up Finn, he had this creepy smile on his face, and all he said was 'More light!' Goethe's last words. Except they weren't. I got to learn all about it. According to Tom, what he actually said was something like 'Can you open the shutters, please?' but they shortened it down to 'More light' after he was gone. Can you imagine? It's dark outside, this frigid wind's howling through a gaping hole in the side of the house, Finn's shivering in a Pokémon T-shirt, the guy from Glass Doctor's on his cellular, trying to locate a bigger sheet of glass, and I'm getting a tutorial in German poetry."

"Oh my god, that's so Joel—"

"He's into Goethe?"

"No, the Great Man thing. They all do it when they go into hypomania—obsessing with celebrities, like Hitler, or Jesus. With Joel it's FDR. He did his master's on the New Deal, so he's the ultimate know-it-all on

Roosevelt. He knows the first inaugural speech by heart. It used to scare the shit out of me, hearing that the only thing I had to fear was fear itself."

Perched on the couch, bare feet tucked under her haunches, she sipped at her tea like a shy chickadee at a feeder. "Joel has this favorite armchair. He'd pretend it was a wheelchair and trundle around the room in it, smoking an imaginary cigarette. In a *holder.* Joel hates to smoke—I had to quit when we first started dating—but when he was manic, he'd puff and puff on this make-believe cigarette until he was actually wheezing."

"That's funny."

"Maybe now, but it wasn't funny then. You know, most of the time he's the decent, self-effacing high-school teacher—and Joel's good. The kids love him, and they stay in touch long after they've left Garfield. He's always getting e-mail from history majors in college—he's still critiquing their term papers, and sending them reading lists. Oh, as a teacher, he's just *adorable.* But every year, around the beginning of summer break, like he can frickin' schedule it, he turns into Godzilla."

Her voice was sandy, dry, midwestern, with the ring of the family farm in it. Outside her *P-I* cubicle, she'd hung a South Dakota vanity license plate (DEBRA!) to announce just where she was coming from. One of her assignments had been to crank out "The Dish," Friday's showbiz column, a scattershot recital of Hollywood splits and pairings, lawsuits and breast-cancer scares, billion-dollar contracts and spells in Arizona rehab clinics, quarried from press releases and the supermarket tabloids. Beth, who sometimes had to fill in for her, never quite managed to catch the column's trademark tone, the artful mix of dizzy fandom and jaded *weltschmerz* that came effortlessly to Debra. Listening to her now, Beth thought, *It's "The Dish"—she's doing "The Dish."*

"He swells right up. He literally gets bigger. You can practically see him grow. Then he stinks the place up because he's too preoccupied with running the world to bother taking a shower. Does Tom get to the point where he needs no sleep at all?"

"Sleep's never been Tom's problem."

"Because that's another big sign. When Joel's high, he goes two, three days without a wink of sleep. I'd get up to use the bathroom in the middle of the night and he'd be sitting in his stupid wheelchair, puffing away, and lecturing me about the Brain Trust—all these great minds, like his, right? It didn't sound insane, and it wouldn't sound insane to you, not if you didn't know. The history lesson from hell."

"I've had a few of those."

"You know that spooky look they get behind their eyes? When they seem to be telling you 'This isn't me'? There are two people there. One of them's plumb crazy, and the other's just heart-breakingly sad, like 'Please: let me outta here!'"

No, Beth thought; *that's not Tom—that's never been Tom. What he suffers from is lifelong blind self-involvement, and that's* culpable. Tom didn't deserve the exoneration of mental illness. To feel good about the condo—and Beth loved its bare, clean, uninfected space—she had to be certain of his maddening brand of sanity.

"I've been there, Beth. You've got compassion fatigue—"

Debra hiccupped, quite loudly, and Beth looked up to see that her face—always so sharply defined—had gone soft and wobbly. Shoulders quaking, she said, "Oh, fuck it. Sorry." She bared her teeth in a ruinous grin that fell apart as soon as it was framed, then wiped her clenched fist across her eyes. "I don't give a shit. Honestly. Now I've lost a fucking contact—no, I got it . . ." Slotting the lens back under her lid, she was shaken by another temblor. First she seemed to be having a fit of the giggles; then she began to make a low *whooing* noise like a distant train whistle in the night.

Still unused to the basic layout of her new life, Beth got up too quickly, painfully barking her shin on the corner of the table, knocking her glass over. Wine pooled on the tabletop as, hobbling slightly, she reached the far couch and gathered her friend clumsily, self-consciously, into her arms. "Debra? Deb?"

She seemed lighter than Finn, all air and bone, like a beaky fledgling fallen from its nest.

"I never cry," Debra said. "Ever. It must be something I ate."

"Poor baby," Beth said, just as she'd say it to Finn.

"Hey, coach, you get to cry next time. Deal?"

"Deal."

It was a very Belltown tableau—the blue couch, the fair woman cradling a dark one in her lap—and would ordinary have drawn no one's attention. The interesting feature was to the right, where a boy in pyjamas had flattened himself against the short dividing wall that ran between the kitchen and the living area, his hair showing as a ragged splotch on the white paint. Standing stock-still with his back to the wall, his throat stretched taut, the small figure looked less like a boy than a spider, a black widow, ready at any second to scuttle out from his hiding place and bite.

Carved gargoyle pumpkins left over from Halloween collapsed and rotted in the December rains, their crumpled faces turning to soft mush. Strung along porches, on bare cherry trees and ink-black cypress hedges, Christmas lights twinkled fiercely in the sullen dusk of noon. Santa, the obese clown-god of the winter solstice, now reigned. Santas walked the streets, clanking bells. They stood, moulded in plaster, in front yards; padded and perspiring, they worked the malls; they were stencil-painted in store windows, and rode illuminated sleighs on suburban rooftops. With his drunkard's cheeks and Abrahamic beard, Santa was patriarch and prodigal, half Jehovah, half Falstaff. Tom thought of him as the dad from hell.

Though not a believer, Tom did miss the baby Jesus in the all-purpose bacchanal known as "the holidays," meaning Chanukah, Kwanza, the Wiccan Yule, the end of Ramadan, the arrival of the 1999 Beaujolais Nouveau, and, more afterthought than centerpiece, the virgin birth in Bethlehem. In the ubiquitous din of seasonal music, herald angels, mangers, shepherds, and magi lost out to the honky-tonk-tonk of sleighbells and red-nosed reindeer. Tom's NPR piece about the grotesquery of Saint Nick in America provoked his largest stack of hate-mail yet.

With the Nasdaq promising to pass 4,000 by the end of the holidays, even the worst restaurants were booked-solid with office parties. The GetaShack party was held aboard *The Spirit of Puget Sound*, rented by Steve Litvinof for a moonlight cruise to Poulsbo. In the event, there was no moonlight; a full gale was blowing in the sound; the boat never left the dock, where it lay, lurching, sometimes wildly, through the festivities. Yet the evening was held to be a wild success when Steve, in his usual black silk suit, clinging to a pillar like a toper to a leaning lamp standard, made the surprise announcement of a three-for-one stock split. After delivering a stern homily on "sustaining shareholder value," he waved a champagne flute at his whooping employees, and said, "To

Y2K. And to our new frontier. Next year, we cross the Mississippi. March, we open in Chicago. June, Philadelphia. September, Boston. We got a busy millennium on our hands, guys, so Happy Holidays, because they're going to be the last holidays you'll see before we hit my old home town, New York." The small ship gave a sudden jounce, and four young women from Editorial lost their footing, made a grab for each other, but landed among a herd of shambling techies. "And you can cut *that* out," Steve said. "Leave the office sex to Amazon. I got a basic piece of math for you. Y2K equals 24/7."

Meanwhile Beth, who'd been doing some hurried math of her own over the last sixty seconds or so, realized that she was gazing at Steve with such a wide and silly smile that she had to raise her hand to wipe it from her face.

Tom braved the leering Santas, hideous music, and combat-hardened shopping grannies to buy presents for Finn: a box of magic tricks, an electronic walking dog said to possess artificial intelligence, and a host of five-dollar bibelots and tchotchkes for stocking-stuffers. Sheltering from the rain under the wind-torn awning of an antique shop on First, he noticed in the window a Victorian glass paperweight—a limpid globe housing a surreal butterfly of many colors. *Beth,* he thought, and went inside.

"Baccarat," the clerk said.

"What?"

"It's Baccarat, the butterfly. Quite gorgeous. Are you a collector?"

Given a credit-card slip, Tom registered the price for the first time, and it was just short of astounding, but it was too late to pull out now and he signed with a flourish. When the woman was packaging it, in a silver cardboard box and a fuss of tissue paper, it occurred to him that perhaps he was no longer obliged to buy a Christmas present to be delivered to a condo in Belltown . . . "It's for my wife," he said.

"Lucky lady," the clerk said, handing him a stiff, rope-handled brown paper bag that might have held a ball of lead.

The wrapped parcels on the back seat of the VW looked to Tom like virtue itself, and he drove back to the house feeling that he'd escaped the holiday battlefield with honor and was owed the just reward of the

good soldier—guiltless hours under the lamp with a book, and a bachelor lunch of toasted cheese and a bottle of warm Bass. His rosy mood
was barely tarnished by the discovery that his usual parking spot under
the sycamore was occupied by a scrofulous pick-up, once white, now
rust, and that a man unknown to him sat on the bottom step of the
porch, evidently awaiting him. He found a space thirty yards ahead of
the truck, and walked back, laden with his parcels.

"Belong to you, mister?" The Asian-looking man gestured at the
house with what seemed to be deep sorrow, and for a moment Tom
thought he must be the bearer of tragic news.

"Yes?"

"Nice place. But need work." Glancing up and down the street, the
man said, confidentially, "Green on roof."

"Moss," Tom said crossly.

"Moss!" the man said, echoing Tom's accent and pronunciation like
a mynah bird. "Moss!"

Was this some kind of derisive parody? Tom looked at the guy, trying to stare him down. His Mariners cap was worn back to front. Hair
sprouted thinly from his upper lip, less a moustache than a tentative
pubescence. He was encased in a voluminous sky-blue Gore-Tex jacket,
apparently brand-new but far too big for him and incongruously
sportif—a riddle of zips, toggles, and Velcro flaps, the sort of garment
designed for anally-retentive weekend mountaineers. It hung on the
man like a rustling tent. He was all skin and bone, except for the twin
swags of fatty flesh above his eyes, which gave him an expression of
sleepy woe.

"Moss bad."

To get into the house, Tom needed to find his keys. To find his keys,
he had to put his parcels down. He stood irresolute, halfway up the
steps, willing the man to go away, but his visitor only stared patiently
back at him. "Thank you," Tom said, in as terminal a tone as he could
manage.

"Need new roof."

A messenger from Beth? Surely not.

"You want, I fix."

Daring himself to do it, Tom placed his two biggest parcels on the
deck and reached for his keys.

The man instantly gathered them into his arms. "Rain make wet. I hold for you."

At least he was still standing there, not running for his pickup, and Tom had the paperweight, but the man had the dog and the magic set as hostages. He grinned, exposing snaggle teeth, their enamel tinged with green. The street was empty. There was no one to call to for help. Tom had to go through the usual performance with his keys, shuffling through the English ones before he reached the American.

"That one, he good," the man said, and—most disquietingly—he was right. Carrying the parcels, he followed Tom through the door, where he immediately spotted Beth's busted bike leaning against the wall. "Wah!" The explosive sound was a call of recognition, like someone shouting to a friend seen in a crowd.

"Okay, take it away with you. I was meaning to drive it to the dump. *Thanks*." Tom held the door open, but the intruder was on his knees now, feeling the twisted front fork of the bike with both hands. Even in his fury, Tom was reminded of how gently the vet had handled Hodge, their cat, after the accident, and of Finn snuffling beside her, his eyes aghast, saying "Poor Hodge" over and over again. He'd never before seen anyone show tenderness for a bicycle. When the man raised his head, there was a look of moral accusation in his pouchy eyes. "Can make good. I fix for you."

"I don't want it. You can take—"

"No problem," the man said. He sounded insulted.

It was preposterous: the fellow had wormed his way into the house like a sneak-thief, yet Tom felt called on to somehow make amends to him for his—for Beth's—neglect of the bicycle. Against all reason, he found himself giving way.

"Where are you from?"

"Everett."

"No, I meant before that."

"Everett," the man said in his hurt voice, wrong-footing Tom again.

There were, of course, immigrant communities so self-contained that whole generations could grow up inside them learning little more English than this guy appeared to have at his disposal. But perhaps he was brain-damaged. If so, then his alarming prescience with the keys might bespeak an idiot savant. As a child in Ilford, Tom had known a certified lunatic who, given a date, any date, could tell you what day of the week it was. You'd say "January twenty-fourth, 1895," and he'd say "Thursday." He was never wrong, but he couldn't go to the bathroom on his own.

This bicycle-fixated idiot got to his feet and wiped his hands on his jacket, leaving smears of black oil on the virgin Gore-Tex. "Name is Chick," he said. "I give you pager number." He looked around the room with the entitled air of an invited guest. "Wah, books! You teacher?"

"Well, yes, sort of."

"Hey! Maybe you teach me a thing or two, huh?" He cackled, and in his laughter Tom now heard an insufferable mockery. From one of his jacket's many zippered compartments, he got out a pencil and notepad, on which he scribbled laboriously.

When finished, he tore off the page and presented it to Tom, but Tom found far less than he'd expected, just "Chick" and a seven-digit phone number. Still, it looked like hate-mail. "Thanks," he said, meaning "No thanks," and stuffed it away in his trouser pocket along with the balled-up credit-card slips from his morning's shopping.

"You want quote, you call. Right?"

"Quote?" Dazed, Tom thought, *I told him he could have the fucking bike.*

"For roof, mister. New roof."

"You're a—roofer?"

"I got men," Chick said in a new, lordly voice. "Mexican boys. Work like shit. I ride them herd. They do nice job, and fast, fast."

During the last ten minutes, Tom had seen Chick as a messenger of doom, a pest, a likely mugger, a figure of pathos, and now he tried to view him in an altogether more flattering light, as a contractor. The effort of doing this was very nearly beyond him, considering the ruinous pick-up, whose flat-bed held two gas canisters and a suicidal-looking stepladder. Yet better that, perhaps, than the new Range Rover with pigskin seats and double-decker ski-racks driven by the last contractor he'd tried to hire—or, rather, had been interviewed by, and rejected out of hand. In these times of raging plenty, beggars couldn't be choosers when it came to contractors, and Tom was way down in the beggar class so far as contractors were concerned.

"I give good bottom-line," Chick said as if reading Tom's mind.

Tom wanted to believe, but Chick defied belief. He didn't like Chick. He didn't get Chick. Chick frightened him. But—and as buts go, it was a

big one—Chick was volunteering to do the roof, and had Tom sub-
scribed to the doctrine of preordination, he might have thought that
Chick had somehow been *sent*.

"I'd like to think it over."

Frowning gravely at the books on the shelves, Chick said, "Think
too much, maybe I go some other guy's house . . ." He picked up the
injured bicycle and carried it out to the porch, where he went poking
into the spongy patches of wood on the deck, letting out grunts and
puffs of distress to signal his findings, as if each small outbreak of rot
were a malignant tumor. Then he stood up, holding between his thumb
and forefinger a fibrous splinter of black fir a few inches long and half
an inch thick; rubbing the wood quite gently, he squished it to pulp.

"You got insurinx, mister? Guy come up"—he pointed to the steps—
"stand on wood and *whoosh!* he go down hole. Big-ticket item, right?
Hey, maybe he die!"

Tom thought of Olin the mailman, built like a manatee, a three-
hundred-pound hulk in his crumpled Postal Service blues. From his
office at the top of the house, he could hear Olin pounding the deck
each morning, a great amiable reverberation, now to be anticipated
with dread. He'd have to buy a mailbox and mount it on a post by the
sidewalk . . .

"I fix for you, no big deal." He broke off a piece of sun-bleached
green siding from the corner of the porch and held it out. "Time to
make new!"

You couldn't go ripping the siding off people's houses like that.
"What do you think you're—"

"I show." The contractor snapped the tile in two like a cracker,
releasing a few grains of pale floating dust. "Asbestos," he said in a
whisper. "Illegal."

"Really? I've never heard—"

"Real bad stuff. They hear you got asbestos, you get the city on your
butt—"

"Back. You get the city on your back, not your butt."

"See? What I say to you? You *teacher!*"

Still cackling, he hoisted the bicycle aloft and bore it off to his truck.
Before he climbed into the cab, he turned. "You have a good one, now!"

But all good had drained from Tom's day. Sadly, he hid the Christmas presents in the closet under the stairs. Sadly, he lunched off a can of lukewarm clam chowder and smoothed out the crumpled page with Chick's name and number on it, fixing it with a magnet to the fridge door. Sadly, he found the receipt for the glass paperweight and stared at it with disbelief: the horrible sum at the bottom now looked like the price of a new porch.

He made a pretence of picking up his book under the reading lamp, but the print made barely more sense than if it had been written in Chinese characters. He tried to conjure the willowy figure of Trollope's Lily Dale, but saw instead the massive, inert body of Olin the mailman, fallen from the deck into the shadows of the basement and lying in an untidy nest of spilled mail. Drafty zephyrs stirred the strewn letters, lifting the pages of catalogues and magazines, rearranging the slithering piles of introductory 0.0% credit card offers, supermarket coupons, *Have You Seen Us?* missing-children flyers, bills from AT&T and Puget Sound Energy, along with the rare handwritten envelope with a real stamp on it. The mail was alive; but from Olin—whose son was a second-string linebacker for the UW Huskies—came neither breath nor peep.

At five, he picked up Finn from Treetops. As soon as he was buckled into his seat, Finn said: "Knock, knock!"

"Who's there?"

"Lucy."

"Lucy who?"

"Lucy Lastic makes your pants fall down!" In Finn's manic screech of laughter, Tom heard Chick.

"*Groan!* Oh, hellacious, ginormous groans galore!"

"Knock, knock."

"Who's there?"

"Sam and Janet."

"Sam and Janet who?"

"Sam and Janet evening you will meet a stranger!" Finn guffawed, then said, "I don't really get that one."

"It's a famous song." Tom sang it, in a fruity baritone. "Across a crowwwwwd-ed room . . ."

"I still don't get it. You don't sing as good as my mom."

"So what are you, a music critic now?"

"What's a music critic?"

Tom cooked pasta while Finn watched "The World's Funniest Animals" on TV, then they played Pokémon, a game whose rules neither of them adequately understood, and Tom was glad to see his last hairless pastel-colored warrior creature destroyed by the venom powder of Finn's Venomoth. At bedtime, Tom coasted through an episode of the current Mister Wicked story, but he could feel the narrative flagging as he spoke. Wind fluted in the eaves and crackled in the timbers of the roof. Even with his arm around Finn, and Mister Wicked up to no good on Lake Washington's palatial eastern shore, Tom was dogged by the mocking figure of the contractor in his incongruous blue coat.

He watched the eleven o'clock news on Channel 7. A man "of Middle Eastern appearance," thought to be Algerian, had been arrested in Port Angeles when he tried to drive his rental car off the Victoria ferry. Inside the trunk, the spare-tire well was crammed with bags of urea, jars of nitroglycerine, and four black boxes, each containing a circuit board, a Casio digital watch, and a nine-volt battery connector. According to the female customs officer who'd stopped him, "His car looked too big for him, and he was kind of sweaty and agitated." The man had a reservation for one night at the Best Western motor inn on Eighth Avenue in Seattle, and a ticket for a flight to London. "Reporting live from News Control," a solemn reporter said that the FBI believed the man was involved in a plot to blow up the Space Needle. Taking down the Space Needle struck Tom as an eccentric and circuitous way of challenging the imperial might of the United States, but this was an easy country to misread: perhaps the conspirators had seen too many television reruns of *Sleepless in Seattle*.

The KIRO people were high on their story of the swarthy foreigner, too small for his big American car. Tom saw in it a radio commentary about how aliens were figures as necessary as cowboys to the national mythology. In the great polyglot sprawl of America, people constantly needed to be reminded of their Americanness. The Treetops day began with small voices reciting the pledge of allegiance to the flag. One nation *indivisible?* Come again? The children had to say this each morning because it was such an entirely unlikely proposition—a profession of faith in a mystery that confounded the observable facts of the case. So America required strangers as proof of its own always-slippery existence.

Canada—"our big dumb neighbor to the north," as Beth liked to call it—helped. So did Hollywood extra-terrestrials, Mexican wetbacks, and industrious green-card seekers. But nothing made America feel more American than the arrival on the doorstep of a bona-fide Arab terrorist carting a bomb in the trunk of his rental brown Chrysler sedan. This guy—now safely under guard in the Clallam County jail—was a trophy alien, someone so satisfyingly other that everyone could feel a patriotic glow in the American-as-apple-pie Port Angeles officer who'd noticed his shaking hands, thick French accent, un-American size, and nailed him as the enemy.

Writing idly in his head, Tom fell asleep in front of David Letterman.

The next morning, driving home from Treetops, he was still at it, and eager to try the piece out on the keyboard. There was a rift of blue in the sky, shadows—faint, it was true, but definitely shadows—striped the pavement, and Tom had very nearly persuaded himself that Chick was a transient nightmare, mercifully banished by the sunlight. But the contractor was waiting on the porch steps, where he sat cradling Beth's bike.

He acknowledged Tom with a verdant but quickly curtailed grin. "Hey, how ya doin'?"

The bicycle gave Tom a jolt. Yesterday it had been invisible to him, just part of the house's fixed structure, to be stepped around without a second thought. Today—wiped clean, oiled, its chrome bits glittering in the pallid sunshine—it seemed to insist on its own presence, its self-important bicycleness. Tom saw Beth astride it; laughing, in high summer. The splintered basket was full of books. Beth's fair hair was up but escaping in all directions from her tortoiseshell barrette. Skinny-legged, in tank top and jeans, she looked like a student. He hadn't seen her laughing like that in years.

"See? I fix. Is good like new." Chick lifted the front of the bike and, with a grubby forefinger, set the once-frozen wheel in motion: it spun, and went on spinning, true as a gyroscope. "Now, you drive." He thrust the bicycle at Tom, who took it cautiously by the handlebars as if it were a cat with a reputation.

"Wait!" He produced an adjustable wrench from his jacket, which appeared to have aged badly over the last twenty-four hours; it looked slept-in, the blue Gore-Tex mottled with grease-stains. "Too little." He wrestled with the saddle. "You big boy." He wrestled some more, staring at Tom's crotch from beneath the violet bags that overhung his eyes. "Wah!"

There was no arguing with him. Shoulders hunched, scowling, gnomelike, he gestured impatiently at the street.

Conscious of the pathetic figure he was cutting, Tom mounted the bike. He hadn't ridden one since his first few days in Islington, when he'd been scared half out of his wits by speeding lorries on Liverpool Road, a quarter of a bloody century ago. Fearing a painful crash-landing, he put his weight on the pedal. He wobbled atrociously but stayed upright, more or less. There came back to him the unexpectedly familiar clocklike purr of bearings and sprockets. He pedalled up against the shallow gradient, his knees doing novel things as he strained to keep aloft and on the move. It was like people said: you didn't forget. Head down now, grunting, he passed Galer, remembering in a rush the Sussex lanes where he and—what was her name?—*Anne Wilshawe!*—used to cycle out from Brighton to look at churches, then to smoke pot and snog each other silly in hayricks. He laughed aloud at the memory. Strange how those dark and frowsty churches, their air ripe with the scent of hassocks, Rentokil, mouldy hymn books, and bone dust, had turned them on . . . At eighteen, nineteen, the close proximity of the dead was an essential preliminary to going—nearly—all the way.

He stopped, walked the bike across the street, and freewheeled back. Between the houses, fragmentary views of gray wind-frosted water and whitecapped mountains sailed past his right shoulder. Inhaling the salty breeze, Tom thought, *I could get used to this*. He braked, and clattered to a halt beside the contractor.

"He go good now, right?"

"Excellent!" Tom was thinking of Anne—no, no, Annette—Wilshawe, the dampness of hay, the twined braid of smoke rising from their shared joint.

"Excellent!" The mynah-bird copy of his voice came back to him. "Excellent!" Chick fished out the notepad and pencil from his jacket. "You write down."

The page was full of English words and phrases, each written in a different hand, and, beside them, neat sprays of hieroglyphs in Korean, Chinese, or whatever language it was that they spoke in Everett. Tom read *win-win, prioritize, dickhead, sweat equity, divvy up.* He wrote *excellent* and handed the pad back.

The contractor stared at the word, frowning. "Eggs-kellent."

"No. Excellent. The c is silent."

Still looking dubious, Chick stowed his dictionary in his jacket.

Tom got out his wallet. "What do I owe you?"

Chick flapped his hand dismissively. "Nothing." *No ting!*

"Oh, no, that's not fair—" He fingered a twenty. Two twenties, perhaps?

"No ting!" His voice had taken on the insulted tone that Tom was coming to dread. "Fix for friendship only."

"Well, that's awfully . . . kind of you, Chick."

The contractor, unappeased, wore a wounded scowl. "Now I make you quote for roof," he said, and stomped off to the truck, where he made a sullen show of liberating his stepladder from the flat-bed, using the gas canisters as percussion instruments.

In the upstairs study, Tom pretended he was working. He typed on to the screen *Like cowboys, or Pilgrim Fathers, aliens,* and voided it with the Backspace key, listening to the scrape of *his* alien's sneakers on the composition tiles overhead. He could hear him talking to himself in a soft and mournful-sounding warble, punctuated by sudden astonished exclamations. There was a tearing noise, and something—not a bird—went tumbling past the window into the yard. Alarmed, Tom went down to find out what was going on.

Looking up, he saw Chick astride the roof-peak, notepad balanced on his knee, intently scribbling.

"Everything okay up there?" Tom called.

The contractor had the abstracted air of a poet in thrall to an imperious muse. For several seconds, he went on writing, then treated Tom to a long silent stare. Some fifty feet separated the two men, but Tom could've sworn there was a look of contemptuous pity in the pools of shadow that were Chick's eyes.

Half an hour later, Chick, ignoring the bell, was hammering on the front door. When he stepped inside, he placed his hand—too familiarly, Tom felt—on the seat of Beth's bike and fondled it in a *droit du seigneur*ish sort of way. He came quickly to the point. "Under roof, wood go all to shit. Must have new."

It was as Tom had feared—and as Beth had kept on saying. His whole house was rotten. In this wet and wooden city, houses were as ephemeral as sand-castles. They were washed away in mudslides, or collapsed back into the soil in a soggy mulch of decomposing Douglas fir. They needed to be looked after with the care of a mother for a chronically sick child—which explained why so many of Tom's colleagues in the English department appeared to spend half their time in carpenters' aprons, repairing, remodelling, trading elaborate tales of stuff they'd found in the Home Depot on Aurora. For years, he'd been in denial; now he was in for it.

"Big trouble." There was an infuriating note of satisfaction in the contractor's voice. He handed Tom a folded sheet of paper, torn from his notepad. "I make quote."

Tom hardly dared to unfold it. His house was a tear-down. But the lot, at least, must be worth something. Frozen-faced with apprehension, he read what Chick had written:

> ROOF
>
> *$4150 WORK AND MATERIEL INCLUDE*
>
> *CASH*

The number was a fraction of what a real contractor would charge; even he knew that much. "And the porch?" Tom heard himself say in a supplicant whisper.

"I'll make you a deal, mister," Chick said in fluent American, as if his fractured language had all along been a pose. "For porch and roof? Five grand, even."

At her work-station in the Klondike building, Beth opened her Drafts folder and, for the sixth time in two days, read through the letter she'd been writing to Tom. It wouldn't do. In its present version, it all sounded far more complicated than it should; he was bound to take it the wrong way, jumping to stupid conclusions. What she needed to say must be plain, simple, factual, leaving no room for argument, doubt, or—worse—laughter. If she'd promised herself anything over the last few weeks, it was that never again would she expose herself to Tom's shallow and destructive cynicism, to that curled Hungarian lip, that supercilious eyebrow with its white hairs crowding out the black. That snigger. She wasn't going to let him get to her, not anymore.

It angered her that Tom should still have the power to put her on her guard like this. Why did *she* have to be so fucking diplomatic? Indignation mounting, she scanned the draft on her screen:

Hi Tom—

Finn's counselor [and make that "doctor," for a start] has sug-gested that we put him on an oligoantigenic diet—chicken, fish, potatoes, rice, pasta, bananas, apples, and green vegetables. No-nos include chocolate, and any foods with synthetic dyes, like cupcakes, candies, colored breakfast cereals (no more Apple Jacks!), and striped toothpaste. Also to avoid: apricots, berries, tomatoes, milk, wheat and corn, and eggs (he doesn't like them much anyway).

He's got a problem with yeast overgrowth—best treated with probiotics (good bacteria), like lactobacillus, which comes in live yogurt. (But make sure it's live—commercial yogurts usually aren't. Queen Anne Thriftway carries the live stuff, on the top shelf, above the Yoplaits, etc.)

When Finn gets "hyper," it's because of an excess of free radicals in his system—unpaired molecules that tend to run amok if they're not neutralized. I'm giving him blue-green algae capsules (one in the morning, one at night). Look for the bottle in his backpack.

Sorry if this sounds a hassle, but the diet is the safe alter-native to Ritalin. (I can tell you the horror stories . . .)

—Beth

She printed it out, then clicked on New Mail. Furious now at Tom for wasting her time and exhausting her patience, she typed:

Tom: Finn's doctor has put him on a diet, and we're all counting on you to cooperate.

A single terse graph of instructions followed. Not wanting to give her-self a chance to weaken, she sent it immediately. He deserved it, didn't he? For once, she'd stood up to him, leaving no clever loopholes for him to escape through. Watching the message leave her computer, Beth felt a just pride in her own temerity.

Later, though, she fished the damned thing out of Sent Items, winced at its tone, and sent a note that began "Sorry, I was in a rush at work when . . ." And for making her write it, she hated him.

Tom woke in pitch darkness to what sounded like the quarrelsome tail-end of a drunken party in his yard: men's voices, shrilling at each other, and the noise of heavy falling objects. Bodies? The luminous LCD of the alarm said 07:00. With Finn at Beth's, he'd planned to sleep in, but now groggily clambered into shirt and pants. The loudest of the voices outside belonged to Chick. *"Más rápido!* Move your ass, man!" he shouted, then, *"Mierda!"* This was quickly followed by the sound of something like a head-on car smash, which in turn was followed by a terrible low groan from below the bedroom window. After a moment or two of silence, there came derisive laughter.

When Tom ventured on to the porch for the *New York Times,* he was met by his contractor, who gestured at the tumult of shadows behind him, and said, "Mexican boys," as if that explained everything. Then he showed Tom his open palm. "Today, you give me one thousand dollar."

The demand, while fair enough, was voiced like a threat at gun-point.

"I'll need to go to the bank to draw—"

"When bank open," Chick said. It was not a question.

As the darkness paled into a drizzly half-light, Tom saw that "boys" was entirely the wrong word to describe this gang of shambling men with tragic faces, beside whom Chick looked like a kid. In the dank chill of midwinter, the Mexicans went sockless in flappy plastic sandals, their feet black with mud. Their headquarters was a red pick-up truck, conspicuously newer and shinier than Chick's rusted hulk; here they retired at intervals to smoke cigarettes and swig from a shared Thermos flask. There seemed to be a lot of them—a dozen at least, by Tom's rough estimate, though when counting them up, he never got higher than five.

During the course of the morning, and apparently of its own

accord, there grew up one side of the house a perilous folly of driftwood logs, broomsticks, lengths of drainpipe, a boathook, some bamboo, the side of what had once been a ladder, two-by-fours, and a pole to which a 2 HOUR PARKING sign was still attached, its countless joints lashed with raffia. Seeing the man named Lázaro trust himself to this flimsy scaffolding, flitting from perch to perch like a budgerigar in a cage, Tom—who suffered from vertigo at the best of times—felt an ominous convulsion in his stomach and thought of Chick saying "insurinx." Was he *liable?*

The men took casual possession of the house, leaving their routes through it clearly posted in mud. When Tom went to the bathroom, he found the door open and a Mexican inside, shaking his prick dry over the toilet. Perfectly unabashed, the man greeted him with a wan, misshapen smile. At noon, in the kitchen, the whole crew assembled round the butcher-block table to gnaw at wings from Kentucky Fried Chicken—the first fruits, Tom assumed, of the thousand dollars he'd given Chick in a wad of new fifties.

Then the devastation started. They were up on the roof, armed with crowbars, slinging tiles and timber into the yard. The house shook to the din of pounding, rending, splintering, and the steady rain of falling wreckage. Above it all, Tom heard Chick goading his hapless "boys" more loudly than the howler monkeys in Woodland Park Zoo. How the Mexicans put up with this treatment was a mystery to Tom—he felt vicariously outraged on their behalf—but they appeared to accept Chick's tyranny as a fact of American life, like its unkind weather.

To escape the noise, he wheeled Beth's bike outside and pedalled the hazardous three-quarter-mile to Ken's Market—an adventure heightened by his near-death experience with a silver Nissan Pathfinder. On the return journey, he heard the house long before he saw it. Coasting downhill toward the racket of demolition, he spotted a rotund figure standing in the middle of the road, and recognised it as Suzanne Somebody, a not-so-close neighbor, in tight cherry-pink running gear, her hand cupped above her forehead as she gazed at Tom's roof.

He dismounted and began to apologize for the noise, but she broke in before the word "Sorry" had left his mouth.

"How clever of you! Where *did* you find them? Did you have to spend an age on their waiting-list?"

He searched her face for indications of malicious irony.

"We've been looking for two years, but nowadays you can't find anybody to do a thing."

Together, she and Tom stared upward at the marvel of men doing things. A baulk of rotten timber bounced off the porch guttering and exploded at the bottom of the steps. From his command post, wedged between the brick chimney and the slope of what was now left of the roof, Chick fired off a rapid volley of multilingual abuse. "Muttafukka!" was the only word Tom understood.

"Lucky you," the woman said. "If—when he has a spare moment—you could possibly put in a good word for me?"

Tom felt a sudden rush of protectiveness toward his contractor. "Well, of course I'll *try*. But I gather that he's pretty much fully booked." Then he added: "Through next year and well into 2001. So he was telling me."

"They always are."

"But I will ask," Tom said. This was now the way of the world. No sooner did you find a contractor than some unscrupulous neighbor bribed him away in the dark of the night, leaving you with a wide-open hole for a roof. Beth had told enough sob-stories about flighty contractors that he knew they were prone to decamp at the first hint of a more profitable berth. To keep them faithful, you had to be always at the ready with sweet-talk and lies. This Suzanne was a grim reminder that he had to stay on Chick's good side.

All day, piles of rubbish had been rising around the house. They were now a good deal taller than Tom, and he had to scramble between them to gain access to the porch, from where he had a view of dark junk-mountains, dust rising like volcanic smoke in the thin drizzle. Chick was fast turning the place into Boffin's Bower. Leaning on the porch rail, looking out over mounds already big enough, surely, to contain the ruins of an entire house, Tom saw himself for a happy moment as Nicodemus Boffin, magnate of dirt, the Golden Dustman, in black pea-coat and gaiters; "rather a cracked old cock," as Silas Wegg observed of him.

He was still smiling when he collected Finn from Treetops.

"Did you eat your fruit at lunchtime, Finbow?"

"Yep."

"What was it?"

"Kiwi."

"You ate a whole kiwi?"

"Cross my heart, hope to die, stick a needle in my eye."

Back at the house, the contractor's men were draping tarps and pieces of plastic sheeting over the exposed rafters, with Chick holding a builders' clip-on halogen light on an orange extension cord that disappeared into Tom's open bedroom window.

"Oh my God!" Finn's whole face seemed to swell up and go out of focus.

"Finbow, love, I'm so sorry. I should have told you. We're getting a new roof."

As he hugged Finn's shivering body tight, Tom heard a long gurgling sob, as if he was about to lose his lunch; and it took a little while to realize that Finn was quaking and heaving with laughter as he took in a view of chaos and destruction beyond even a four-year-old's ambitious dreams of mayhem.

"Holy shit!" he said admiringly.

"Finn!"

He spluttered out: "My mom says that all the time."

"Really?"

"It's so cool!"

By lamplight, it was a scene from the Blitz; the rubbish piles forming the jagged rim of a bomb crater and the crazy scaffolding up the right side of the house resembling rooms torn open in the explosion. Down through the staging, monkeying from branch to branch, came Chick.

"Hey, how ya doin'?" he said to Finn, dusting off his hands.

"Good," Finn said, gazing up at the great anarch with something close to worship, and setting an exploratory foot on the mounds.

"Don't!" Tom said. "Don't climb up there, it's dangerous."

"Soon all be go," the contractor said. "Mexicans take away. Night is good." Then, as Finn climbed up on the porch, he nodded in his direction. "Grand kid—"

"Yes, I think he's a keeper," Tom said, arriving a few seconds late at Chick's meaning. "No, no, he's my son."

"Son? You—son? Wah!" Shaking his head, he laughed in Tom's face, baring his horrible teeth.

Thinking of Suzanne, and of the crowd of predatory neighbors for whom she stood, Tom kept his composure and made himself smile back. "Funny, but true," he said.

"You old man!"

"I'm forty-six." This with gritted teeth.

The contractor chuckled, as if at a transparent fib.

Later that evening, the wind got up, and the loose tarps and plastic sheeting thunderclapped overhead. Refusing to stay in his own room, Finn colonized Tom's bed, where he stayed awake till after eleven, demanding ever more episodes in the new Mister Wicked story, which involved the hijacking of an amphibious tour-bus carrying a party of pre-schoolers on a field trip. Tom eventually managed to bore him to sleep. Late-night whisky in hand, he peered out between the drapes of the bedroom window: the mounds had vanished, though he'd heard no sound from the Mexicans, only irregular drumrolls and cannonades from the roof.

Finn had somehow filled the bed with elbows, knees, and feet. Tom dozed shallowly, in fits and starts—a hectic and distressing ride through a succession of inhospitable dream-landscapes. He was a confused tourist, lost in a multi-story parking garage, then among ruins that might have been East Berlin in the 1950s. He was a pedestrian walking the breakdown-lane of an American freeway that became the tunnels of the London Tube. He was with Finn, in a fast-moving crowd at an airport much like Chicago's O'Hare, where Finn disappeared and Tom was running, crying out his name. In his last dream, he was in a house besieged by shouting men. He woke to find himself in a house besieged by shouting men.

Riding through the dark in the red truck, cruising Dumpsters, Chick, in the passenger seat, discussed his theory with Lázaro: the kid wasn't really the American's son, but the son of a relative, perhaps a cousin, who had gone abroad or died.

But Lázaro disagreed. The boy looked like him—"Same hair they got!" In America, he explained, he'd seen many such cases. The wife left the husband, and took all the money. Then she went gambling. "She in Las Vegas now. She play the slots."

"Las Vegas?" Chick said. "In Mexico?"

"No. U.S. Like California."

"Wah! California I like to see."

The truck shuddered on a deep pothole. They were on an unlit street by the edge of a lake, driving past workshops, cranes, boats sitting high and dry on blocks.

Across the water, the tall city was a dazzling blur, its myriad lights all run together in the rain. Lázaro braked for a Dumpster. "My uncle, he go to California. Anaheim. Now he in jail."

"INS?"

"No, he *legal*," Lázaro said. "He do vehicular homicide. Drink too many beer, go on highway, make accident, lady die, get three years. Not young lady—old crazy lady. She drive like—" His hand fish-tailed through the air. "But police test Uncle Luis. Point-two-five percent. Three years."

Chick liberated a toaster-oven from the Dumpster before they filled it with trash. "I fix," he said.

"You fix that TV yet?"

"Sure. He go good. He *color-TV*."

"The guy?" Lázaro said. "He got one TV alone, and *poco*, fourteen-inch. Some homes they got TV for every room, and the big wide-screen for NFL. Like I say, guy got no money."

"Don't like the TV. He teacher, he have to read his fuck books."

"The wife, she take the TVs, all that good stuff. Now he got nothing."

"He got house—"

"He got mortgage. He got kid." Lázaro laughed. "Wife got the money. She go to Vegas, man. Spend, Spend! Hundred-dollar slots!"

"He got money," Chick said.

"That VW he drive is piece of shit. Wife got Buick Park Avenue 2000, and *loaded!*"

Chick knew otherwise. The ATM slip he'd found on the bathroom floor said, "Current Balance: $41, 389.17." That the American could leave such personal secrets lying around the house could only mean he was very rich. Everything about the American intrigued him. A whole family—maybe twenty, twenty-five people—should be living in his house, but it was just him, sometimes the boy, sometimes not. Chick couldn't figure it out—no family, no friends, no noise, no nothing, except for books, and Chick had never seen so many books. A man would go blind reading them.

He said he was a teacher, but he never went to school.

He was so large and clumsy that he couldn't even ride a bicycle, tottering all over the road like a decapitated chicken. It made Chick laugh.

But he had the money.

The American possessed one skill, so far as Chick could see: he talked beautifully on the telephone. When he got going at that, he was a champion. Chick sometimes hung out on the stairs that led to the top of the house just to hear him talk. He used long words—learned from his books—and every word was different from the others. He'd lean back in his chair, look up at the ceiling, and the words would come rumbling out of him, all hooked together like boxcars in a train that seemed to have no end to it. It was impossible to understand what he was talking about, but to Chick's ear every word rang like money.

And what he'd found in the American's garbage! Seven eggs in a carton made for twelve; a whole bunch of bananas, their skins lightly freckled; purple grape-wine in a green bottle, nearly full, with a cork in it; a tube of toothpaste, barely squeezed; a loaf of sliced bread in a bag; a wedge of cheese, half a kilo, maybe; and tomatoes, sausages that tasted of chicken, chocolate wrapped in foil, red-and-white-striped candies, and a whole box, unopened, of a breakfast food named Apple Jacks.

Only a rich man would toss such things out, yet the American's toes poked through holes in his socks when he walked around the house without shoes. Seeing him in his wrinkly pants, with little clumps of unmown stubble under his chin, you'd think he lived in the encampment under the bridge. He was rich and he was poor—like a hologram you tilt under the light and see now one, now the other, but never both at once.

When Chick reflected on his fascination with the American, he remembered the *gweilos* who paid money—big money—to see the bamboo bear. He'd laughed, in his other life, about how they'd go up into the mountains and spend whole weeks looking out for bamboo bears. It rained all the time. If they got lucky, they'd see a bear eating bamboo shoots. Mostly, all they ever saw was piles of old bamboo-bear shit—thousands of dollars, U.S., just to look at shit. Shooting a bear would be something, every skin worth 2 million *yuan*. But for looking only?

The American is my bamboo bear, Chick thought. *I stare at his shit, like a stupid gweilo.*

The truck was stopped at a red light. Lázaro said: "Drop you same place?"

"Yeah, same place good."

"You get in trouble, man—"

"Is okay. Nobody see nothing."

Lázaro whistled in disbelief as he stepped on the gas-pedal. Half a mile later, he let Chick out of the cab. In the darkness and rain, all that was visible was his blue coat, sailing away down the sidewalk. Lázaro wound down the window and shouted to the coat, "Las Vegas!"

"I see you've joined the shadow economy." Beth had to raise her voice to make herself heard through the racket of construction coming from above. "I doubt they've got a single Social Security number between them, but they look like they're doing a fairly good job. Considering."

"They're surprisingly reasonable," Tom said.

"Just remember Zoë Baird." Beth laughed. "And what's with the gay Chinese guy?"

"What makes you think he's gay?"

"Everything. The Castro look."

"He doesn't look like Castro."

"The Castro. The San Francisco Castro."

"Oh."

"You know what he said? He was sitting on the porch steps with Finn and said, 'We chew the bleeze.' He was feeding him candy."

"I'll have a word with him."

"I already did. Is Squashy Bear in the backpack?"

Finn came into the kitchen, dragging a ragged bundle of roofing-felt behind him on a length of string. "I like Chick," he announced. "I really like Chick. He gave me this dog. His name's Anthony."

Beth looked across at Tom; an any-wife-to-any-husband telegram that read, WHAT DID I SAY? Its tone was threatful. To Finn, she said: "Cool, pumpkin."

"He killed a cat. He ripped its insides out. Then he ate them."

"Finn!"

"Anthony *hates* cats. He chases them up trees. Sometimes he kills them. He's a German shepherd. He's only got one eye." Finn wandered out of the kitchen toward the open front door, trailing his killer hound.

"Well," Tom said, "I've been giving him his blue-green algae," rolling the *r* in "green" to get a rise out of Beth.

"You're still telling him those Mister Wicked stories?"

"Are you still letting him watch the Cartoon Network?"

Warming to the now-familiar exercise, they began to row in earnest.

Chick liked the sound of hammers. The forestlike silence of the city set his nerves on edge—like people were watching and waiting for something real bad. When the Mexican boys got going, tacking down the plywood sheeting and the felt, he was comforted by their homely noise. The five men fell into a rhythm like some Beijing rock band like Cui Jian: *wah*-da-da-da-da, *wah*-da-da-da-da. Chick conducted with his fists and feet, grunting in time to the hammers as they fell in sequence. *Heavy metal!*

Tom relocated to the kitchen. He stuffed his ears with cotton wool, turned up the volume of the stereo and played Mahler's Fifth. That didn't work, so he tried the Britten "War Requiem," then the "Ride of the Valkyries," but the hammers smashed the music into a chaotic rubble of disconnected noises. Fleeing the house, he drove out to the university campus, where the underground parking lot beneath Red Square had been emptied by the holidays. His office was cold; the few books on the shelves—Strunk & White, a College Webster's, *Sister Carrie, The Pushcart Prize XIX*—had the random air of titles abandoned to a garage-sale. He turned on the frigid radiator below the window; as the water knocked and rattled in the pipes of the antique heating system, Tom heard a tiny gang of undocumented Mexicans banging away with hammers.

His office took an age to unfreeze. He sat at the black metal desk in his old Burberry tweed overcoat, trying to think of entertaining things to say, within the space of four minutes and forty seconds, about aliens in America.

For Beth, the idea of life after Tom had always included—in a woozy, abstract sort of way—dating. When she thought about it, which wasn't very often, she saw a waterfront restaurant, floating votive lights on the tables, the menu hard to read in the near-darkness (she'd go with the sea bass), and candid, ardent talk between grown-ups, untainted by the niggling, evasive ironies that made real conversation with Tom impossible. And afterwards? Well, that would have to take care of itself, though there would obviously be an afterwards.

But it looked as if thinking about it would be as near to dating as she'd ever get. Most of the men she knew were boys, like Robert, in baggy cargo pants and over-engineered running shoes. The rest were married, gay, or neuter. On the evenings when she didn't have Finn, she found herself hanging out with Debra, eating take-out Chinese one night, take-out Thai the next. One night, they went to the Crocodile Cafe to listen to a new band, but they both needed to be up at the crack, and had to leave before the music started.

Five days after the company Christmas party, a David Ziegler called her at the office. Though everyone on the boat had worn nametags, she couldn't place him. Was he that stooping, spindly Californian from the ad agency who'd gone on about the miseries of the Seattle winter? Or the bald, pugnacious attorney who'd gone to college with Steve, and wanted to talk boating? To David Ziegler, she said that of course she remembered him, and that she hadn't seen the new Woody Allen yet.

They agreed on the next night, which suited her parenting schedule. At six o'clock, at Von's, he was already sitting at a table and signaling to her as she walked through the door, and she immediately remembered him—or at least his glasses, which were oversized, with rainbow frames. She associated nothing off-putting with these whimsical specs, though she couldn't recall a word of what had passed between her and the trim, pink, fortyish Mr. Ziegler.

The waiter arrived at the table just as she did. Mr. Z.—white teeth, thin lips—gave a brisk, compact smile and gestured for her to order first. She asked for a Dirty Martini, on the rocks, with a twist. He told the waiter to bring him a Perrier, which made her wonder why he'd suggested Von's, where the air itself, foggy with the smoke of several packs of Marlboro Lights, had sufficient alcohol content to fail the Breathalyzer. Presumably, he'd assumed that this was the sort of place that she liked, which it wasn't. She cast her mind back uneasily to the party, where, she now remembered, her champagne glass had been kept topped-up by an over-attentive flunky from the caterers. He must've thought she was a lush. *Oh, god.* She made a point of ignoring the Martini when it came, and in the twenty minutes before they had to leave for the movie theater she tried to artfully draw out Mr. Z.—no, *David*—on the question of who he was, and why he'd asked her out on a date.

He'd retired this summer from the licensing division of "the big M" and since then had been setting up a non-profit. Steve Litvinof was on his board.

"Our aim," he said, as if this was a public meeting, "is to span the digital divide and put new technology into the hands of the underprivileged." Relaxing only slightly, he described a pilot project that was already up and running in the Central District. He was getting black kids online, giving computers to grade schools and youth organizations, and establishing a film co-op so the kids could make documentaries about their neighborhood.

So he was the compassionate type, if a bit stiff—or maybe that was just shyness in her company. Smiling, she took a swig of her olive-brine-flavored Martini. If drink was meant to be her weakness, it might be a good idea to show a little now. She seized on the film co-op as the most promising item in the package, and asked if the kids had started shooting yet, how much adult supervision they were being given, whether any local film-makers were involved.

"You'd have to talk to my project manager about that. I'm just the meat-and-potatoes man. You know, funding."

Oh. Yet if David Ziegler seemed on the surface to be colorless, his teasing rainbow glasses seemed to promise that something more fun lay beneath the surface. She asked what had drawn him to the Central District. He appeared to be momentarily puzzled by the question.

"Well, I have a house in Leschi, so I drive through it most days. On Yesler. It was an obvious market niche. If the program works out there, I'm planning on moving into other cities. Oakland . . . South Central L.A."

Like Steve, restless for territory. "East St Louis? Roxbury? Harlem?" Beth said.

"That kind of thing."

As they crossed the street to the theater, he said, "We're calling it

TechReachZ." Inside the cinema he took stock of the rows of empty seats and said, "Woody's turning into a nonprofit too."

Beth laughed, rather too loudly, feeling that at last, in the kindly half-dark, the rainbow specs were beginning to come into their own.

The movie was slight but pretty to watch, with Sean Penn as the second-best jazz guitarist in the world. Set in the sepia-colored age of the Great Depression, it had gangsters, vintage automobiles, and swing music that sounded good on the Dolby sound system. Beth tapped her foot to "Sweet Sue" and "I'm Forever Blowing Bubbles." Though the script was a bit short of really funny lines, she noticed that she and David laughed at the same moments. Penn, in the role of artist-as-engaging-jerk, was upstaged by an actress who played an adoring mute; Beth had never seen her before, but thought, *Take note, Soon Yi.* Halfway through, she felt the distinct pressure of David's shoulder against her own, and without turning her head from the screen she swiveled her eyes sharply to the right, but saw that he was only digging into his trouser pocket for a handkerchief.

When it was over, he remarked, "It's a mystery to me how he always gets these big-name stars. How much do you think a movie like that would gross? Ten million? Fifteen?"

"I liked it," Beth said. "Do you know the name of the woman who played Hattie? I didn't recognize her."

"Samantha Morton. She's a Brit. Maybe that's why she got to play a mute."

Thinking of Tom, Beth giggled, but wasn't about to explain the joke.

David had booked a table at Wild Ginger, on Western. The night was dry and mild, and they walked the half-dozen blocks down towards the waterfront. Between the old brick and stucco buildings that flanked Union Street, a departing ferry showed like a suspended jack-o'-lantern. On the corner of Second, four black boys, in black-and-silver parkas and matching Raiders caps, barely into their teens, stood leaning against the wall, smoking.

"My clients," David said when they were safely past.

"Do you have children of your own?"

"No," he said—in the same tone, she thought, he might've used if asked if he had herpes.

She felt that she ought to make her status plain. "I have one."

"Yeah, Steve said."

So he'd been doing some research—which meant that Steve must also know that she and Tom had separated, which meant in turn that—

"A boy, right? Philip?"

"Finn."

"As in Huckleberry."

Again David Ziegler seemed to know more than he ought to. Finn's name had been Tom's idea; she'd thought the literary allusion pretentious, but eventually went along with his enthusiasm. "Actually, no," she said, "I'm half-Irish. It's a family name." Which was half-true.

Her unease deepened when they stepped inside the restaurant and the maitre d' smiled at David and said, "Your usual," then showed them to a corner window-table. So she sat down in the cane chair assigned to all his dates—weeks and months and maybe years of women taken to the movies before a dinner interview. She wondered what percentage of her predecessors in this seat had ended up in his bed.

But a date was a date, and—rusty at the exercise, long out of practice—she played along. Looking over the long menu, she said, "Do you want to share things?"

He glanced up and smiled. He had a good smile. "Okay," he said. Then, "I eat vegetarian."

Giving the sea bass a regretful miss, she settled for squash-and-sweet-potato soup, the satay of sweet onions and Chinese eggplant, asparagus and black-bean sauce, tomato and tofu, and Sichuan green beans. When she asked for a glass of Sauvignon Blanc, David said, "I'll have the same," which pleased her to a degree she found faintly embarrassing.

"Even when he isn't acting in them," David said, "all his movies are really about Woody."

"Yes!" Beth said, surprised by the crispness of his judgement, and feeling encouraged to talk about this Samantha woman's performance, which to her seemed to project all of Allen's misogynistic fantasies.

David nodded as she spoke. "It's essentially about a self-absorbed artist whose shabby treatment of women can be excused because he's got more important things on his mind."

And she'd thought him colorless. She gazed at him across the table, censuring herself for her recklessly premature judgement, and David caught her gaze, his pink face further pinkening. For a couple of seconds, their eyes locked, and Beth felt a heady rush of affection.

"Well," he said, "at least that's what it said in the *New York Sunday Times*. Kind of."

She masked her disappointment as best she could.

Over the soup, he talked about how he was living in a rented loft above Pioneer Square while his house was being remodeled—gutted and rebuilt, it sounded like. His architect was named Julian, his contractor Emerson, which put Beth in mind of Tom's ragged crew of illegals, whom she spun into a story. Laughing, she told of the crazy scaffolding, the hysterical Chinese guy on the roof, the sad-sack Mexicans, and conjured a picture of extravagant destruction, in which a bunch of inept roofers transformed an entire house into a pile of smoking dust. Referring to Tom, she said "my ex"—a phrase she'd never used before but which suddenly seemed to define him.

David smiled, though his face was serious. "He could get in trouble."

Beth was in no mood to worry about Tom's potential misfortunes. "Oh, he always muddles through. The absent-minded-professor act seems to get him out of everything."

David's chopsticks hovered indecisively over the tomato and tofu, then pounced, like a raptor plummeting out of the sky to snatch a mouse. "He does commentaries. On 'All Things Considered.'"

"He used to write novels. Now he just does his radio things."

"I've heard him. He's . . . quite funny."

The conversation had taken a seriously wrong turn, so Beth steered it firmly back in the direction of Julian and Emerson; the trials and adversities of remodeling were of no inherent interest to her, but David proved easy to steer. The builders were nine weeks behind, the cost-overruns vast, his Pioneer Square tenancy a kind of "exile," and he missed his view of the lake—all very commonplace perhaps, but Beth preferred this to fan-talk about Tom.

Munching on green beans, he talked of converting his bathroom into a personal spa, complete with hydrotherapy jets, sauna, Jacuzzi, and bidet. "This suite I had in the Tokyo Hilton last year was a revelation. Have you been to Japan?"

"No, not yet."

Looking strangely relieved, he discussed tiles, at length. His personal spa apparently was to be tiled—ceiling, floor, and walls—in malachite.

"Do you know about malachite?"

"Well, you know, *vaguely*."

"Here . . ." He rummaged in the side-pocket of his brown silk jacket and produced a flat piece of stone about two-inches square, which he handed to her like some very fragile, precious object. "It's a kind of copper ore."

Her first thought was that it was beautiful—a veined swirl of dark but lucent green that put her immediately in mind of Douglas firs seen in a low summer-sunset light. It was the precise color of the Pacific Northwest. It was brilliant of him to have—

"It comes from Zambia," he said. "They've been quarrying it there for centuries."

Out of left field came her second thought, which was that the tile was perfectly ridiculous. Zambia? This sly boasting about stuff being shipped halfway around the world only to adorn some Microsoftie's palace! It was just like . . . and then she remembered this was one of Tom's gibes after the fund-raiser. *Everything has to travel—even the bloody grass.*

She was still collecting her feelings when David rose abruptly from his seat— "Excuse me," he said, "I just have to go to the men's room"— and she was grateful for this interval of solitude. Once he was gone, she ordered a second glass of wine—the level in his glass having sunk by, at most, a half-inch.

She was furious at Tom for having barged, uninvited, into her date, annoyed at David for having laid himself open to his mockery, and angry at herself for thinking like this, with a cynicism that wasn't hers at all, but *his* ghost intruding on her feast. She considered David's work in the Central District. His impulses were generous and good, and if he felt like tiling his bathroom in Zambian copper ore, who was she to mock him for it? She looked at the square of stone in her palm, at the wavy, pale striations in the forest-green. It was beautiful. It was exactly right for this part of the world. It spoke for his taste, like his intelligent take on *Sweet and Low-down*—even if he had cribbed some of it from the *New York Times*.

But. Her wine came. She gulped at it, glad that David wasn't there to observe her, and tried to name to herself the things she liked about him: the even, unaccented tone of his voice; his thatch of straw-colored hair, tamed by expensive layering (and did his barber use tints, or was it naturally so variegated?); his air of quiet, prosperous self-containment; the humorous glasses. There was, she told herself, more to David

Ziegler than met the eye. She took another gulp of wine and glanced at her watch. He'd been gone at least five minutes.

His absence had stretched well past ten when the waitress asked, "Do you think your friend's finished?" Beth said she didn't know, but that she was done, thank you. Staring into the rippled green depths of the malachite, she suddenly remembered Chad in Brooklyn, coming back jazzed and relentlessly talkative from restaurant bathrooms, having spent an age doing lines in there. Was that David's game, too? Beth was more pleased than not that she had no idea at all; that he might be snorting-up in the men's room only added to her sense of the unexplored largeness of his character. If he did have a habit, it was obviously under tight control. She prepared herself to be surprised.

And was. He came back to the table, his face white and papery-looking, with a desperate glued-on smile. "Sorry," he said. "A case of the runs. I sometimes get them. The wine, I think . . ."

So Beth turned from date to mom. She walked alone up to Fifth to get her car from the garage, picked up the limp and ailing non-profit from Wild Ginger, drove him to where his car stood at a meter on Seventh, and not until she got back to the condo did she realize the square of malachite was still in her bag.

It was only nine forty-five, not too late to call Debra, who was just back from Dubrovnik, working on an Oroonoko.com feature about the revival of tourism in the new Croatia. Beth reported that her evening had been a wash, and moments later they were drinking Slivovitz nightcaps in the fifteenth-floor studio. Debra inspected the malachite tile. Having already taken her contacts out, she had to find her old reading glasses to see the patterning in the stone.

"The whole bathroom, in this? You know, that's so unbelievably tacky."

Beth knew that she'd known as much all along.

News of Tom's contractor spread fast and far. Entreaties began to arrive on his answering machine—the first from Pam Lendau, the asthmatic deconstructionist and gender-theorist. Since he barely knew her, that call was easy enough not to return. More worryingly, Chick showed up one morning in a new truck, which turned out to be his old truck transformed. The rust-holes in its bodywork had been filled, it had been

resprayed black, and stenciled red lettering along the sides announced
EXCELLENT CONSTRUCTION, with the pager number nakedly advertised
below in white.

Tom had now paid out $3,700—money for which no receipt was
forthcoming. "No paper, no tax," Chick said, with a crafty you-and-me
grin, as if they were arranging to hold up a liquor store together.
Although there was still work to do on the roof, the Mexicans had
already demolished the porch, leaving the house with the appearance of
having had its face bashed in and its front teeth scattered to the winds.
A cement-stained builder's plank was propped at a 45-degree angle
between the front door and the yard below, but the only safe means of
access was around the back, through the laundry room. A plastic mailbox, attached to a two-by-four stake, stood just in front of where the
porch steps used to end, though Olin preferred to walk the risky plank
and stuff the mail through the letter-slot in the door. The yard was a
muddy devastation, and the tall holly tree beyond Tom's study window—once the resort of bluejays and bushtits—was lavishly decorated
with discarded roofing tiles.

The place looked irreparable. Tom knew that he was now entirely at
Chick's mercy. One wrong word, and he'd be left helpless and alone
with his ruins. Whenever possible, he'd heap insincere praise on the
contractor's progress for fear of losing him, but Chick gazed back at
him with a morose, noncommital stare. Sometimes, Tom was certain
that he was reading his mind, and despising what he found there.

On December 22nd, he took out $300 from the bank, in fifties.
When the men were assembled in the kitchen for their lunch break, he
distributed the bills between the six of them. "For Christmas . . . like a
bonus, you know? To thank you for your work . . ."

Lázaro gave him a laconic smile. The others shrugged and stuffed
the money in the back pockets of their jeans, while Chick held up his
bill against the light, evidently doubting its authenticity. The scene
hadn't gone off quite as Tom had planned, and he blamed it on his poor
arithmetic. He should've given them hundreds, with at least two hundred for Chick. The fifties had made him seem a cheapskate: Ebenezer
Janeway, counting his pennies in the season of goodwill. But to make it
up to them now would look like plain bribery, which of course it was.

Pissed-off with himself, Tom went to buy a last-minute Christmas
tree—a dwarfish noble fir, one of the few left in the outdoor lot of

Chubby & Tubby's hardware store. He rode back with it tied to the roof of the VW and spent the rest of the afternoon scouring the house for the string of lights, the ornaments, and the stand. Beth must have pinched them. He called her at Belgrave Pointe, or Pointé, as he riled her by pronouncing it. When she picked up, he could hear Finn in the background, talking to someone else. The condo sounded Christmassy—peopled, convivial, with his son's voice the loudest and happiest in the room.

"I put them down in the basement," Beth shouted. "In a box marked 'Christmas Stuff.'"

Tom heard a male voice saying, "Who's the Tickle Monster, then?"

"I was wondering . . ."

"I can't talk now. We're kind of busy here," Beth said, and hung up.

We. The small word stung.

He got the flashlight from the tool-drawer in the kitchen and found the key to the basement padlock on his ring. Stepping outside, he saw the pert, striped, foxy face of a raccoon, standing on its hind legs with its paws on the lid of the garbage can. In the beam of the flashlight, the animal's eyes were bright scarlet. Ostentatiously unhurried, it eased itself on to four feet, and shuffled off into the bushes, back arched, head low; striking, Tom thought, a conscious attitude of resentful pique. Treading softly, listening for the movements of the raccoon, he went down the brick steps to the basement and undid the padlock on the door.

For a moment, he couldn't think why everything was in sharp silhouette—the lawnmower, the cot where Finn had slept when he was a baby, his changing-table, a leaning tower of cardboard boxes, the dangerous stepladder from which Beth had fallen in her second trimester. Past the junk, beyond the black rectangle of the furnace, rose another, mobile silhouette. Chick.

"Sorry," Tom said, half-blinded by the glare of the halogen lamp that hung from a nail on one of the joists. Feeling his way cautiously across the uneven floor, he reached the furnace and stood there blinking, fazed, slow to take in what he saw.

"Is good, right? Must be close to the work!"

With Christmas so much on his mind, Tom's first thought was of an illuminated nativity scene in a dark church—oxen, sheep, wise men, manger. A sleeping bag was spread on the earth beside two carpet remnants, one maroon, the other pale blue. A hanging spiderweb of wires connected a toaster-oven, a fan-heater, a telephone. A television—much bigger than the one upstairs—was on at low volume, and hooked up, apparently, to the cable system. Clothes were tidily piled on a familiar yard-sale couch. Finn's cast-off board books—*Goodnight Moon* and *Green Eggs and Ham*—lay on the sleeping bag beside a copy of *People* magazine.

"You don't have no beef with it? Is cool with you, huh?"

This was a new note: the contractor was pleading with him. In the cone of sterile light cast by the halogen lamp, Chick's face was as white, knobbly, and protuberant as a freshly-dug root vegetable. He was wearing a black T-shirt with a photograph of Madonna screen-printed on its front.

"No, you can camp out here."

"For the job," Chick said.

Tom was light-headed with relief at his discovery of the contractor's living arrangements. They meant that he was not about to be deserted, as he'd feared. He nodded amiably at the TV screen. "What are you watching?"

"'Ohio Five-O.'"

"*Hawaii.*"

"Hawaii," Chick said, in his new submissive voice.

At the edge of the cone of light stood a rusty bucket—the only clue as to how the contractor managed things in the plumbing department.

"You can use the bathroom upstairs," Tom said.

"T'anks."

"No problem."

Palm trees, in bright sunshine, flashed past on the screen. McGarrett was on a car chase.

"I was just looking for a box of ornaments for the Christmas tree . . ."

"I find for you." Chick walked confidently into the darkness and came back bearing the box labeled CHRISTMAS STUFF in thick red marker-pen letters. The *i* had a circle above it, not a dot—Beth's signature.

"I make ornaments. Long time ago. Work in ornament factory. Shit job. Real bad money."

"Really? Where was that, Chick?"

"Fuzhou." His soft pronunciation of the name made it sound like a confidence exchanged in the dark of night.

"Not Everett, then."

"No. Fuzhou."

All menace had left him. For a moment as brief as the opening and closing of a camera shutter, Tom saw a picture of Chick as a scrawny kid on an assembly line, putting little wire loops into the heads of spun-glass angels, and thought: *All I have to do is remember this.* When he took the box, it felt empty. They made things light in China.

"Goodnight, Chick."

"Goodnight . . . Mister Tom."

Goodnight Moon.

The deal was that Finn would spend Christmas Eve with Tom—Beth had a party to go to—and all three would lunch *en famille* at the Queen Anne house on Christmas Day, then Beth would take Finn back to the condo.

Tom was in the bathroom shaving on Christmas morning when he heard Finn pound across the floor downstairs to catch the shrilling phone. He patted his face dry, in no hurry to spoil Finn's proprietary satisfaction with his skill as a telephonist. God knows where he'd picked up the expression, but he had lately taken to saying "This is the Janeway residence" in as gruff a voice as he could muster.

The living room was awash in scraps of wrapping paper from Finn's stocking-stuffers. Santa's footsteps, planted by Tom the night before with a Wellington boot dipped in flour, had spread across the carpet like a patchy hoar-frost.

Finn held out the phone. "She wants to talk to you."

"Don't say 'she,'" Tom said, reaching for the receiver. "Hullo—Beth?"

"Tamás—"

"Ma! Happy Christmas!"

"Tamás, what is a 'karndow'?"

"I can't think," Tom said, struggling to think. "Why?"

"Finn say he and Beth have got a new karn—"

"Oh, I know. Of course. Yes, Beth bought a new car." He lowered his voice and shielded the phone from Finn, who was on his hands and knees playing with a Tonka Toy fire-truck. "It's a Honda," he said. "You must have misheard."

"But he say that he and Beth are living in it, Tamás."

"Pardonable exaggeration." He hoped that the grindingly artificial ring of his laughter would be lost in its satellite transmission to England. "You know how people are with new cars, Ma."

A note of doubt persisted in her voice as she went on to thank Tom for the case of wine he'd sent her via the Internet. She'd taken a bottle with her to Christmas lunch at the Nagys', and Andras Nagy had said that it was a very good wine. "Andras is a—oh, how you say it? *Inyenc* . . ."

"Wine buff . . . gourmet . . . connoisseur?"

"Tamás, I am sure Finn say 'karndow.'"

"*Honda,*" Tom said, making it sound as much like 'condo' as he could. "We haven't unwrapped your parcels yet, Ma. We're going to unwrap all the big presents at lunchtime. It's not yet ten in the morning here—can we call you back at about nine this evening, your time?"

"I just want to say 'Happy Christmas' to your Beth—"

"Well, she'll be back any moment now, she's just slipped out . . . How's the weather over there?"

"Windy," she said.

When Tom put the phone down, Finn looked up at him. "Daddy, why were you talking funny?"

"Funny how, Finbow?"

"'Vee unwrap all zee beeg prezentz . . .'" He sounded like a monocled Nazi in a 1950s war movie.

"Oh, I don't know. When I talk to my mom, I sort of pick up her accent."

"Granny Katalin don't talk that funny."

"I know. It's very bad of me. It just seems to happen."

Shortly after eleven, Beth arrived at the back door carrying a single large, beribboned parcel. She had rain in her hair, and her black pants were splashed with mud. Embracing Finn, she said to Tom: "It looks like the bomb went off out there."

The happy-family charade began. Finn was given the go-ahead to burgle the pile of "big presents" around the tree, and Tom caught the look in Beth's eye when he unwrapped his electronic dog: it was the look of someone at an auction sizing up a rival bidder on the far side of the room. When the outer casing of Beth's large parcel was ripped apart to reveal a cunningly-assembled cube of smaller parcels, Tom felt a spasm of reciprocal anxiety that he'd been outclassed by the stuffed moose, the creative construction kit, the Math Shark, and the Pokémon Battle Stadium. By the time the magic kit (top hat, wand, and cloak included) made its appearance, Tom saw the gifts as a cruel and unusual punishment that he and Beth were visiting on Finn, with whom the roofing-felt dog Anthony had been a bigger hit than anything he'd been given for Christmas. Unwrapping, exclaiming, and laying each present carefully aside, Finn bore the infliction with a dignity that it did not deserve.

"Look, pumpkin!" Beth said. "See the pretty necklace Grandma Katalin sent me?" She held a multicolored folk-arty beadwork choker to her throat. "Isn't that kind of Grandma?" With a sideways grimace at Tom, she returned it quickly to its box.

"You haven't opened mine," Tom said.

"I'm sorry—I didn't get you anything. I didn't think—"

"It doesn't matter."

Putting on a mime-show of eager anticipation for Finn's benefit, she undid the knotted silver cord. "It's *very* heavy . . . what *can* be inside?" she said, then "Oh, God." Finally, dully: "It's beautiful."

"There's a butterfly inside it," Finn said.

Beth held the Baccarat globe as if it were a hand-grenade from which the pin had been removed. "You shouldn't have. I can't—"

"I just liked it," Tom said, wondering if he'd secretly known all along that the paperweight would serve to chastise her. At the time, he'd attributed the purchase to simple uxorious absent-mindedness, not unconsciously calculated vengeance.

Beth, kneeling on the floor beside Finn, leaned across him to peck Tom on the cheek. "It's . . . exquisite," she said, and Tom thought, *The torture, is what she means.*

He was taking the chicken out of the oven, to baste it for the second time, when she came into the kitchen. "Anything I can do?"

"No, I've got everything under control here, thanks."

"Have you seen the new Woody Allen movie, *Sweet and Lowdown?*"

"Heavens, no. I hardly ever go to the movies now, and anyway I realize that I've developed a sort of loathing of Woody Allen over the years. He's so—transparent." Spooning fat from the pan over the pallid corpse of the bird, he thought how strange it was to hear himself talking to Beth like this, as if they'd just met.

"Funny: I'd have guessed he'd be right up your street."

Scenting danger, Tom said, "Is it any good, the new one?"

"Well, it's pretty to look at and the music's nice."

"Jazz?"

"Swing, his usual. It's got Sean Penn in it—he plays kind of an American Django Reinhardt, but there's this British actress—"

"Listen, Beth—" With the chicken safely back in the oven, he told her of his mother's phone call.

"You haven't said anything? Jesus, Tom!"

"It's Christmas Day, for godsake. I can't tell her on Christmas Day!"

"There've been whole weeks of fucking days. How long do you mean to keep from telling her—the rest of her natural life? Let me get this straight. You want me to get on the phone and lie through my teeth so you can . . . I don't believe it. I've never heard of anything so cowardly and dishonest. It's insane! I mean, it's *insane* insane! Oh—yes, pumpkin?"

Finn was suddenly with them, in his top hat. "Mom? Pick a card!"

"Oh, honey." She picked a card. It was the wrong one.

At Finn's insistence, they had to pull the Christmas crackers that Grandma Katalin had included in her care-package for Tom, which also included a Star of Bethlehem card, a boxed jar of thick-cut marmalade, a Shetland sweater, a fixtures calendar for West Ham United's 1999–2000 season, and a check for £50. Tom and Beth put on the flimsy paper crowns that fell out of the crackers, and Finn ate lunch wearing the top hat.

On every count, lunch was a severely qualified success. The brussels sprouts were burned, and required surgery to amputate the blackened bits. Finn spilled his glass of cola into his mashed potatoes and chicken. Beth tried to restore a little seasonal spirit into the occasion by recounting the story of a Dilbert cartoon.

"'Must control fist of death,'" she said, leaving Tom awaiting the punch-line. When none came, he said, "I think you had to have been there," which precipitated another five minutes of silence between the parents, who eventually reunited in an attempt to help Finn with a trick involving three paper cups and a disappearing yellow pom-pom ball.

"Abra—cadabra!" Finn said, flourishing his wand. He lifted the cup to disclose an obstinately undisappeared ball.

"Look, Finbow, you need—"

"To be a good magician, you have to—"

"I'm not a magician." He took off the top hat and planted it on the table. He looked glazed and weary, defeated by Christmas. When Beth put her arm around his shoulder, he shrugged it off. "I have to take Anthony for a walk."

Tom called his mother. When he'd thanked her for her presents, he mouthed "Please?" at Beth, then passed her the receiver and listened gratefully, She wasn't a good liar, but when he closed his eyes and tried to imagine her auditor in the Romford flat, it sounded good enough.

"Thank you," he said when she hung up.

"I hate myself." Out of old habit, she gathered up the plates and took them to the sink. Shortly afterwards, she and Finn left—Finn in the back seat with his spoils piled beside him and Anthony in his lap. Tom watched the tail-lights disappear through a blur of rain and (he was ashamed to admit) tears.

Shut up in the study, feeling too bereft to read or think, he spent a wastrel hour on the Internet. England, he learned from the BBC, was flooded and gale-torn. A man had been swept to his death from a promenade, six people airlifted from a ship in trouble off the Northumbrian coast, hundreds evacuated from low-lying areas of Kent and Sussex. Power-lines were down all over the country, roads blocked by fallen trees. A few flakes of snow had fallen at the London Weather Center, confounding the bookies, who'd offered odds of 50 to 1 against a white Christmas. The Queen had delivered her Christmas speech.

Tom clicked on the Queen, and up she came—powdered, permed, bespectacled, and wearing blue. On the tiny screen inside the RealPlayer window, she was a talking postage stamp. "More than ever," said the famous cameo head, "we are aware of being a tiny part of the infinite sweep of time when we move from one century and one millennium to another." She appeared cross, and grew crosser. "As I look to the future, I have no doubt at all that the one certainty is change, and the pace of that change will only seem to increase." The Queen's mouth, its musculature shaped by a long life of dutiful forced smiles, looked as if it were chewing on some tough and unfamiliar meat. "I for one am looking forward to this new millennium," she said, in a tone of candid insincerity.

He checked his e-mail—no messages—and drifted downstairs, where he made a half-hearted attempt to tidy up the rubble around the Christmas tree. He opened windows to clear the living room of its sad smell of bubble gum, fallen pine needles, the trace of Beth's cologne. She hadn't taken the paperweight, which lay on the floor partly covered by its overturned silver box. Holding it was like cupping a rainbow in one's hand: the purple-bodied butterfly seemed to suck every last candela of light out of the afternoon, darkening the room around it. The smudgy, marbled wings glowed orange, green, red, blue, yellow, and violet, the colors rippling and swelling in the glass. Its eyes were pinpricks of turquoise. It was ridiculously lovely.

He was swept by a sudden wave of pure desolation. As it passed, he felt himself floundering in panic, out of his depth. Someone else seemed to place the paperweight, in slow motion, on the mantelpiece; someone else, breathing in gasps, to go down on his knees and bury his face in the couch. He wondered, with oddly dispassionate curiosity, whether this someone was having a heart attack, and whether he should dial 911 on his behalf. Then he and the someone merged back into each other, and shuffled into the kitchen in search of a glass and something high-proof to pour into it.

Nursing the last dregs from the bottle of geneva, he sat at the table and did the three-cup trick with the yellow pom-pom balls. He was in need of magic: Houdini himself would find it hard to escape from this particular afternoon into the neutral territory of morning. There was *Some Like It Hot*—borrowed from Blockbuster in preparation for a solitary Christmas night—but Tom could not now bear the prospect of sitting alone in front of the TV. He saw all too well the long dark hours, crowded with thoughts of the family he had lost as casually as one might lose an umbrella on a bus.

He tried the Tatchells' number, but they were out, and he could think of no one else to call. He knew what men in his predicament were supposed to do. He ought to pack a bag and drive to the Pacific coast, or down I-5 to California, but then had to remind himself that he was afraid of driving at night in the rain. He could head downtown and find a perch on a barstool; but he disliked bars and had no wish to become a stock character in a *New Yorker* cartoon; besides, even bars would be closed on Christmas Day. Finally, he went down to the basement and invited Chick to supper.

The contractor was sitting cross-legged on his sleeping bag, watching "Rugrats," and tinkering with a partially disembowelled refrigerator. He acknowledged Tom with a distracted wave of a length of copper tubing, which he pointed at his mouth: his lips were pursed shut on half a dozen small screws. He picked them out one by one and laid them in careful order on a spread in *People.* "Goddamn Mexicans," he said. "They goof off on me. 'No work Navidad!'"

"Christmas."

"Christmas." Echoing Tom, he made it sound as joyless a word as any in the language.

Tom delivered his invitation. Chick considered it. "Hah. Chicken." He squinted up at him for a moment, then stared broodingly at the scattered components of his refrigerator. Tom feared the fridge was going to win. "Okay, sure."

Chick, a confident foot-in-the-door intruder, was an uneasy guest, declining to sit down, declining wine, beer, apple juice, and water. While Tom was putting the meal together, he stood close by, moving when Tom moved and speaking, when he spoke at all, in grunted monosyllables.

"Would you like to put the salad on the table?"

"Wah."

"There's plenty of broccoli. You eat broccoli?"

"Wah?"

Tom crossed from the sink to the stove; Chick shadowed him. Once, Tom turned and caught him making a rapid inventory of the Christmas remains with quick, stealthy eyes. He'd better put the paperweight away in a safe place, he thought, or Chick—a true magician—would make it disappear. Yet he had brought a companionable human heat to what would otherwise have been a frigid void. Needing his warmth, Tom chattered at him, keeping up a running commentary on everything from the time it would take to steam the broccoli to the disposition of the knives and forks, but couldn't tell if he was taking any of this in.

Chick refused to sit down until Tom was seated at the table.

"Salt? Pepper?"

But Chick had eyes only for his plate. Deferential Chinese good manners, Tom decided. The whirring hum of the fridge was joined by the considerable noise of Chick masticating his food: it sounded as if a large mammal were trampling through brushwood inside his mouth. Perhaps that was Chinese good manners, too.

Tom tried another tack. "I was thinking of watching a movie tonight . . ."

"Movie."

"Yes, an old favorite of mine. A comedy. Very funny. With Marilyn Monroe, you know?"

The name appeared to make no impression.

"She was sort of the Madonna of her time."

"Cool," Chick said, spraying the table with small fragments of food.

"We could take our plates through there and watch it now, if you like."

"Okay."

So they decamped into the dark living room, Chick squatting cross-legged beside the Christmas tree. Tom fed *Some Like It Hot* into the VCR and fast-forwarded through the trailers to the beginning of the film. The car chase got under way and the police opened fire on the hearse with machine-guns, bootleg whiskey spouting from bullet holes in the coffin. Tom, already snuffling with laughter, looked across at Chick.

"Very old movie," he said. "No color."

"Nineteen fifty-nine, I think. Billy Wilder."

Tom could see Chick's jaws working methodically in the busy, glimmering light cast by the screen. Otherwise, his face was perfectly expressionless. Tom's laughter grew thinner, fainter, more self-conscious by the minute. Of course the whole idea of asking him up to dinner had been a pathetic mistake, and the desperation that had inspired it was shaming. Clammy with embarrassment, hanging his head to hide the expression on his own face, he thought, *Get a fucking grip!*

"Freaky!" Chick honked, scooting up into a chair so as to get a better view of the screen.

On the Chicago station platform, Jack Lemmon and Tony Curtis were in full drag, hobbled by tight skirts, and late—like Marilyn Monroe—for the train that was to take them to Miami with the all-girl band. The dialogue was drowned by the noise of Chick's demented giggles.

For the rest of the movie, the armchair could hardly contain him as he rocked back and forth, muttering to himself, letting out guffaws that aproached the decibel-level of shrieks. Every time Jack Lemmon showed on the screen, Chick hugged his knees and grinned in horrible anticipation. It was always Lemmon, and not Curtis or Monroe, Tom noticed, who sent Chick into fits of unhinged rapture; and Lemmon, unlike Curtis, took his transformation seriously. For a tantalizing moment, Tom had the sensation of inhabiting Chick's skin and watching the movie through his eyes; but the moment was quickly punctured by another falsetto whoop from the armchair.

When Joe E. Brown delivered the film's final line, Chick picked it up and ran with it. "'Nobody perfec'!'" he caroled, as Tom reached for the remote. "'Nobody perfec'!'"

"I was afraid you weren't going to like it."

"I like."

"I'd never have guessed."

Chick was still looking, wistfully, at the dead screen. "He make joke on *America*," he said.

"Yes. That's it exactly, isn't it? Well, of course he was originally German—Austrian, actually, I think," Tom said, then realized that Chick meant the movie, not the director.

As he was returning to his quarters in the basement, Chick stuck his head around the kitchen door, cackled "Nobody perfec'!" and was gone.

6.

The house shook to the thunder of construction. A diagonal shaft of sunshine, radiant with dust, fell through the new glass of the window on the stairs and reached the Christmas tree, which stood in a litter of browning needles and fallen ornaments, some in jagged silver smithereens. The contractor had removed the front door from its hinges, and chilly gusts of wind from outside added wood-shavings and sycamore leaves to the swirls of drifting paper. The disembodied talking heads of Chick, Lázaro, and Jesús were visible at floor-level in the doorway like characters in a glove-puppet show, yammering at one another in an acrimonious Babel of English, Spanish, and Chinese over the unearthly ensemble of sledgehammers and saws.

"*Enano!*"

"*Besa mi culo!*"

"Yo' fuck!"

Tom hid the butterfly paperweight behind a great black-backed poetry anthology by Louis Untermeyer—surely no temptation there— and bicycled off to Ken's Market. He returned to the house in time to hear Chick utter a sentence that sounded like the battle cry of a wounded tomcat in a rooftop territorial dispute. Shrugging himself into his old winter overcoat, he set off in the Volkswagen in search of peace and quiet.

He was crossing the grating of the Fremont Bridge when the conversation with Beth began. She seemed to be riding beside him in the car, a sullen storm-cloud in the unseasonable brightness of the morning. She was so unjust. He shifted from second into third with an abrupt swipe that made the gearbox shriek.

"Sorry," he said. Then, "Look . . ."

He drove on, wrangling with her silently through the stop-and-go traffic. As he swung right on to the Lake City Way exit from I-5, he said aloud, "I never dreamed you would turn out to be so bloody shallow."

The city frayed out into the ugly suburbs, the flag-bedecked car dealerships, strip malls, lumber-yards, Taco Bells, and martial-arts studios rendered still uglier by the unforgiving sunshine. Meanwhile, Beth—that spoiled ingrate—goaded him from the passenger seat.

"You never once bothered . . ." he said. "You might have had the common decency to . . ."

When a woman in a red Jeep cut in ahead of him without signalling, he slammed the heel of his hand on the horn. "Thoughtless fucking bitch!" Then, stuck behind a slow-moving U-Haul van: "Will you get a fucking move-on?" To Beth he said, "You've betrayed me, you've betrayed our child, and you've betrayed yourself."

His tires screeched as he yanked the car into the parking lot of a 7-Eleven. He stood, bristling, at the counter, waiting for the clerk, a turbanned Sikh who was talking into a mobile phone, to acknowledge his presence.

"Box of Marlboros. No, not those—the red ones."

The price shown on the till was a surprise. He dug into his pocket for more change.

"Matches?"

Yes, of course—one would need matches.

That'll show her!

But he was able now to grin at the absurdity of the thought. When he returned to the car, he was back in control, and alone. Buying the cigarettes had exiled Beth to the margin of his attention, and as he settled into the traffic flow, counting the street numbers to his turn-off, he found his anger gone.

He'd last come out here about a year before Finn was born. Ian Tatchell had discovered the footpath along Sammamish Slough, which he described admiringly as "possibly the flattest twelve-mile walk in the entire American West." Tom and Ian, together with the Tatchells' black mutt, Engels, had spent a summer Sunday afternoon ambling along this undemanding trail, stopping at intervals to visit what Ian insisted on calling "pubs." With help from the street atlas, Tom found his way to the same brick-strewn clearing where he and Ian had parked six years before.

More canal than river, the slough ran between thickets of dead rushes. The water was beer-colored, its surface lightly scrolled with calligraphic doodles of current. Ian had claimed there were salmon in it, but the water looked like lifeless industrial effluent. If he were a fish, Tom thought, he'd hold his nose for the duration of the long swim upstream from Lake Washington to Lake Sammamish.

The paved trail led, in its early stages, through a nondescript civic park, surprisingly empty of people. A bald and skimble-shanked old man in running gear—apparently on the brink of death—panted past, and then two powerfully-built Valkyrie types whizzed by, hunched athletically over their Rollerblades, gloved hands swinging within an inch or two of the ground, blonde ponytails flying from behind identical black helmets. But mostly Tom had the path to himself. Limbering up gently for the walk to come, he strolled the easy mile to the first "pub," a windowless cinder-block bunker, painted purple, with a Budweiser sign over the door. Here he stopped for a vile microwaved cheeseburger and a glass of beer that he nursed but did not drink.

The dirty ashtray on the bar prompted Tom to burrow deep inside his overcoat for the Marlboros. There was nostalgic pleasure in disrobing the box of its cellophane wrapping and tweaking the foil covering aside to expose the triple-banked, cork-colored muzzles of the cigarettes. Feeling like a clumsy amateur, he shook one free from the box and lit up. The smoke tasted foul, like leaf-mould; trying to inhale, he felt immediately giddy and nauseous. After the third determined drag, he stubbed it out, snapping the cigarette in two, then paid the bartender and resumed his walk.

Past Woodinville, the trail entered a kind of no-man's-land, a scruffy border-country of allotments, or, as Beth called them, "pea-patches," collapsing sheds, hen-houses, horse-paddocks, overgrown truck-farms. The slough was fringed by bare poplars and dense tangles of blackberry and salal. The forested hills were scarred with outcrops of new tract-housing, and from the road that rimmed the eastern side of the valley came the growling surf of continuous traffic. This unlovely, accidental, unincorporated landscape featured regularly on the late-night local news, where Tom had seen the home videos of bears and cougars that regularly blundered out of the wilderness to take up residence here. He shared the animals' confusion: each time he looked beyond the brambles to the fields, he saw them differently—now rural, now suburban, now wild, now tame. A tawny mountain lion would find perfect cover in the tall sedge grasses that grew on the fields' edges; a black bear would make its den in the ruined outhouse of that abandoned farm. Bred to revere ambiguities of the academic, literary sort, Tom warmed to the double meanings in this wide, untidy stretch of countryside—as vividly un-English a place as any he'd ever seen—and amused himself by picturing Sussex with bears, or cougars in Wanstead.

He stopped at a King County public toilet and sat for a while on the wooden bench outside it, placed there in loving memory of Holly W. Klingman, 1938–1997. Wondering if a cigarette would taste differently in the open air, he discovered it did. This time, when he took the smoke deep into his lungs, trapping it inside his chest for a few seconds before exhaling, it was as if the last five years had never been, and he was back—in a feat of pure magic—to being himself again, at home after a long spell abroad. There was a fresh ripple to the landscape now, a sharpness of focus he recalled from the past, but which had eluded him through all the fog-bound years of his abstention. He smoked the cigarette down to the filter-tip, marveling at the sudden, intense lucidity that had come to him out of the blue, an unexpected gift.

He walked with purpose now, lengthening his stride, the skirts of his long coat brushing against his calves. He thought—for the first time in months—of his unwritten, unwriteable book, that brimming cardboard box of scattered riffs and takes on polymorphous, polyphonic, polycentric America. The trouble was that the box contained descriptions of a thousand trees but not one glimpse or glimmer of the forest.

"On your left!" The bicyclist sped by, a grotesque insect in his metallic sheath of Day-Glo spandex.

The people who dared to see America whole were greenhorns and tourists. Chick had said, "He make joke on America," and it was true. That was Billy Wilder's genius: he was at once utterly knowing, in an old-world way, and utterly fresh-off-the-boat. If the stuff in the box was ever to turn into a book, Tom would need to hijack the eyes and ears of someone considerably more innocent and more assured than he was. He'd have to sack his Public Radio persona, the mild Hungarian-born English prof, and find an altogether more interesting character to do the job.

Like a black paper cut-out against the sky, a raptor of some sort was hovering a hundred feet or so above the slough. Tom took it for a bald eagle, then, squinting more closely, decided it was a red-tailed hawk. When he'd first arrived in the Northwest, the only birds he could name were starlings, crows, and house-sparrows; the rest of the garden birds were nameless, strange, exotic as parakeets. He'd learned them, one by one, out of a book, as greenhorns must. Nowadays when he caught sight of a varied thrush or a western tanager, he didn't race for the binoculars hoping to earn a footnote in ornithological history. His eye had dulled with experience. The character he was looking for should be as scandalizeable as Tom had been when he first spotted a red-shafted flicker in the yard. When he described the flicker to Beth, she said that she'd once read about a bird like that, in the Book of Revelation.

There were several possible candidates for the post Tom had in mind. He thought of William Cobbett, growing rutabagas on Long Island; maybe he could dig up Cobbett for the book, just as Cobbett had dug up the bones of Thomas Paine. Fanny Trollope, perhaps? That "vulgar, pushing woman," as Robert Browning called her, with her failed "Bazaar" in Cincinnati, had a wonderfully imitable style—garrulous, snobbish, and funnier than she deserved to be. Or Dickens, in *American Notes*. Tom remembered him mounting a performance of dutiful romantic awe at Niagara Falls . . .

Pastiche was his medium; he could do those voices.

He could almost hear them in his head: Mrs. Trollope at the food court; Cobbett on stock options; Dickens, in frock coat and gaiters, on the ski-lift at Snoqualmie. These would be his characters. He'd try and summon the vigor and arrogance of England in the nineteenth century in order to catch something of the vigor and arrogance of America in the last days of the twentieth.

He lit another cigarette. The idea had no shape, no architecture, but it felt like the precious *donnée* that had escaped him for so long. He'd begun *Tunnels* and *The Few* on less. It would at least entitle him to bear away stacks of books from the library. He needed to look at some of the less famous English visitors to the U.S.—Captain Basil Hall, for instance. And Captain Marryat. There must be many that he'd never heard of. He would read them all. Before he could start to write, he would need to become a Victorian literary tourist himself.

It was as if a long inviting room had suddenly opened itself to him: flower-smelling, book-lined, tall-windowed, furnished with big deep leather chairs, a wood fire burning in the hearth. Here he would live for the next few months—and on a mentally expansive scale, in keeping with the room's generous proportions. After the miseries of the last weeks, it looked like deliverance. He could be happy here, he was sure of it.

Smiling at his luck, Tom stopped and flipped his cigarette into the slough. When the butt hit the surface, quite far out, it was met by a great finny swirl in the brown water and a splash like that of a dropped brick. For an instant, Tom saw the hole in the water where the fish—if fish it was—had been. The cigarette was gone.

Hardly believing what he'd seen, he broke off the filter from another cigarette and lobbed it hopefully out. This one sailed slowly and erratically downstream on the current until it was lost to sight, but he had glimpsed Leviathan.

It was sunset and abruptly, shiveringly cold when he turned off the trail to find another of Ian's peculiar pubs. He downed a Glenfiddich and water ("No ice!"), smoked two Marlboros, and asked the bartender to call a cab. Then he rode back to his car, staring out at the dark landscape and daydreaming about his book. The word *"green"* should be in the title somewhere: green for greenhorns, green for the color of American money, green for "the grass is always greener . . ." *The Green Stuff*? With, or without, the article?

*   *   *

On KIRO 7 Eyewitness News that night, the lead story was about Mayor Schell's cancellation of Seattle's millennial festivities. From the tone of the report, one might have thought that the millennium itself had been put on hold. Still looking a little shaky from the beating he'd taken over the WTO riots, the mayor blinked at the journalists and said the risk of a terrorist attack on Seattle Center and the Space Needle was too great for him to ignore. "These are unusual times," he said. "We don't want to take chances with public safety. We want a safe and family-friendly transition into the next century. It's safer to be prudent." The late-night network wits would eat this up, and the mayor seemed to know it. With his big conk of a nose and baggy bloodhound eyes, he had the air of a man gloomily resigned to becoming a national figure of fun.

Next up was an item about the search for yet another missing child. Children seemed to disappear as frequently as cats on the suburban fringes of the city—shots of neighbors combing woods and frogmen leaping into ponds were a regular feature on the local news—and Tom paid little attention to the story until the floodlit live reporter said "Sammamish River Trail." The screen filled with a picture of a little girl: Hayley Topolski, aged six, her big cheesy grin full of absent teeth. In voiceover, the reporter said that Hayley and her brother, Taylor, eight, had been playing hide-and-seek near the slough under the supervision of their fourteen-year-old sister, Maddie. Hayley had been hiding. When she was gone for over half an hour, Maddie raised the alarm. The King County Sheriff's Department had issued a composite sketch of a "person of interest" in the case.

Unlike the usual Wanted Man drawings, this sketch was of a monster. A cigarette protruded from fat banana lips. The creature's hair, perched atop a massive domed forehead, was a collapsing heron's nest. Recessed black-button eyes were overhung by copious, shaggy, cross-hatched brows. Tom's first, fleeting thought was that the artist must have copied the picture of the Giant from a nineteenth-century edition of "Jack and the Beanstalk," then touched it up with details from the Wolf Man, Godzilla, and King Kong. Then he saw that the sketch was a grotesque caricature of himself.

"The man is described as white, five-foot-nine to five-foot-ten, with gray Afro-style hair, weighing around two hundred twenty pounds . . ."

The news shifted to a different crime-scene, but the image that Tom continued to see on the screen was of his own face, ridiculously, repellently transfigured. He grabbed the remote and aimed it at the set, thumbing through the channels in search of another glimpse of the blubber-lipped savage. On KOMO, a hoarse-voiced bully was peddling used RVs; on KING, Paul Schell was cancelling the millennium again; on the cable news station, a commentator was grieving over the latest Seahawks loss. But there was no real doubt in Tom's mind. That hair, that egghead cranium, that cigarette: it had to be him. Someone had made a preposterous mistake, and he'd better put them right.

The phone in the living room had never quite recovered from an experiment in which Finn had plastered the keypad with peanut butter; the numbers stuck fast if you pressed them ever so slightly too hard, and it took three attempts to get 911 ringing. And ringing and ringing and ringing. Tom was indignant: what if he were trying to report a fatal accident, or an intruder in the house? At long last—by which time the intruder would surely have shot him dead—the emergency operator came on, sounding impatient even before he had a chance to state his business.

"Ah," Tom said. "Good evening. I wonder if I can have a word with somebody from the King County Sheriff's Department?" He pronounced *King* and *County* and *Sheriff* as if they were Sanskrit or Urdu words—conveying, or so he hoped, his status as a public-spirited citizen with no direct prior experience of policemen.

The sound came from a long way away—a thin chirruping, like the cry of a baby bird, that grew steadily closer until Beth was awake enough to snake out a hand from under the covers and yank up the phone from the floor beside the bed.

"Yes?"

"Beth!"

"Debra?"

"Beth!"

"What?"

"Oh my god, Beth—you mean you didn't see the news?"

*   *   *

The duty officer in the Sheriff's Department thanked Tom for his cooperation and his quick response. He was asked to spell his name twice, to recite the number he was calling from—"That checks out"—and told to expect a call in the morning.

"You got a work number where you can be reached?"

"I work from home."

"You'll probably be talking to Detective Paul Nagel."

Tom clung to the name. It gave a welcome touch of ordinariness to this strange night-excursion. "I didn't see those children," he said.

"Well, maybe you saw something else. Might not mean anything to you, but it could to the task force."

"There's a task force?"

"She's not the only kid who's gone missing in that neighborhood."

So a serial predator was on the loose—and the best the police could do was show that stupid, brutal cartoon on TV? No wonder most crimes went unsolved. Suppose the child had been Finn? Tom slammed the receiver back into its cradle.

He was up drinking coffee hours before the phone rang at eight-thirty, and Detective Nagel sounded too casual by half. "I got hell's own morning on my hands today. You should see the stack of reports I got to deal with. What was that—you having an earthquake up there?"

"Builders," Tom said.

"Amounts to the same thing. Like I was saying, my morning's shot. How would two-thirty this afternoon accommodate with your schedule?"

Time dragged. Tom tried to interest himself in the construction of the porch. The rising skeleton of bare fir reminded him of the balsa-wood framework of the model airplanes that he used to build up in his childhood bedroom—those dedicated hours with an X-Acto knife, his fingertips horny with balsa cement. Chick was squatting athwart a narrow beam and inspecting an aluminum carpenter's level.

"I think green paint for the deck—a dark forest-green," Tom said.

"You got it," the contractor said without looking up.

They were cross-bracing the interior of the porch. From deep inside the structure one of the Mexicans—Jesús or Luis—peered at him so intently that Tom felt himself blushing. For the rest of the morning, he blamed it on his paranoia, but the memory of that look kept returning to him—the insolent stare of someone recognising a newly famous face.

He drove through the wet—more mist than rain—to the King County Courthouse. At Third and James, lowlife types in hooded sweatshirts stood smoking on the sidewalk, and with more than twenty minutes to kill, Tom joined them, adding his solitary plume of smoke to the criminal air. When a woman passer-by raked him with a savage glance, he ground the cigarette under his heel and headed inside, seriously afraid that the next stranger might actually assault him.

At the security checkpoint, he caused a brief commotion when he set off the alarm—a vile high-pitched jangling that made it sound as if he had an Uzi stuffed down his trouser-leg. Fishing out his hoard of keys from the deep pocket of his overcoat, he realized that in this building they'd look like the tools of an unusually well-equipped burglar. A Hispanic guard sorted through them slowly and officiously, singling out the large, ancient, two-fanged key that unlocked the Ilford coal-shed. He showed the keys to a female colleague, who treated Tom to an exasperated shrug and waved him through.

He gave his name to the receptionist in the Sheriff's Office, who curtly told him to sit down and wait—Detective Nagel was busy on the phone and taking no calls. The narrow hallway was like a third-world doctor's waiting room, with harsh fluorescent lighting, plastic chairs in ill-assorted colors, and a battered side-table on which news magazines were stacked. The egg-shaped face of Jeff Bezos stared out from the cover of *Time,* which had anointed him Person of the Year. For the benefit of the receptionist, Tom made a show of stretching himself out comfortably, putting on his half-moon reading specs and burying himself in the magazine. *Jeffrey Preston Bezos,* he read, *had that same experience when he first peered into the maze of connected computers called the World Wide Web and realized that the future of retailing was glowing back at him.* Looking up, he noticed from the name board on her desk that the severe receptionist had the unusual patronym of Crymes.

When Paul Nagel eventually showed up, he stopped short of Tom and nodded. Experts on "Antiques Roadshow" wore the same expression when someone brought in an original Sèvres vase or a hitherto unknown painting by John Copley: it was the nod of an appraiser in the unexpected presence of the real thing.

"Thomas," he said. "Come on—I'll take you through."

As he led the way along the corridor, the detective said: "You're a professor at the U?"

"Yes."

"You might say I'm a student of yours. I take a course there in the evenings. An extension course in family law."

"Not my field. I'm a writer, really."

"Yeah, I'm a writer, too." He gestured toward the open door of his office, a bare space lit by a single flickering overhead tube, the desk copiously littered with scraps of paper. Following Tom inside, he glanced at his computer monitor and clicked a button on the phone, then said: "It's been one of those days. Here, you being a professor, I don't have to read this to you. Just read it through and put your autograph where it says, will you, Thomas?"

So Tom waived his constitutional rights while Nagel filled in another form that—again—required him to spell out his details.

Without looking up from his laborious ballpoint penmanship, the detective said, "You saw the little girl that's gone missing? On TV? Hayley?"

"Yes, I did."

"But you didn't see her on your hike?"

"No."

"Look." Like a card-sharp, Nagel dealt out half a dozen photographs across the front of the metal desk. There was a posed school photo of Hayley, dressed up as if for church, smiling obediently at the camera; birthday-party photos, with Hayley circled in red among her friends; Hayley, laughing, astride the bronze pig in the Pike Place Market. The pictures were heartbreakingly familiar; Tom had nearly identical ones at home.

"You got kids of your own, Thomas?"

"Yes, one. A boy. He's four and three-quarters."

"I got two. Boy and a girl. Eight and ten. So we're speaking here as concerned parents, right? What's the name of your boy?"

"Finn."

"That an Irish name?"

"My wife's family was originally from Ireland."

"Okay." Nagel leaned back in his chair and intertwined his fingers behind his dark-bristled skull. "Let's try it this way. Leave the pictures there—they just might remind you of something you've forgotten. I want to hear about your hike. From the beginning. And take your time. I want to hear the whole goddamn thing."

With many prompts and questions from the detective, Tom's walk took a long time to tell. As a narrative, it was hopelessly lacking in motive, plot, significant events, and dénouement. Its only supporting pillars were the eight cigarettes he'd smoked, which at least provided a flimsy chronological framework for his afternoon. Otherwise, it was a mess of trivial contingencies. Tom finished with the cab ride back to his parked car. "And then I drove home." As he said it, he thought, *This is the silliest story I have ever told.*

"Okay, that's good. We're getting somewhere. Now . . ." Nagel checked the pages of his yellow legal pad. "Eleven-forty. You're in the 7-Eleven on Bothell Way, like you said. Clerk there—an East Indian guy, remember?—says you were kind of antsy and bad-mannered."

"You've been talking to the clerk in the 7-Eleven?"

"'Angry man . . . had trouble making correct money . . .'" the detective read from his notes. "You tell me why that was, Thomas."

"I'd just been having an imaginary row with my wife."

"Well, we've all been there before. Move on about fifty minutes. It's around twelve-thirty, and you're in the Cloverleaf Bar and Grill. The bartender says you asked for a beer but didn't drink it, ordered a cheeseburger but didn't hardly eat it, then lit a cigarette but didn't smoke it. Still arguing with the wife, huh?"

"No, no, it was over by then. I was . . ." Tom struggled to regain his standing in this humiliating dialogue. "Anyway, that place serves about the worst cheeseburgers in western Washington."

"We've all been there, too. Now here's something, Thomas. I hate to sound over-personal, but we have to talk about it. We've already talked to a lot of folks who saw you on your hike, and just about all of them agree on one thing. They say you were talking to yourself. You know, mumbling. Is that something you do a lot of, Thomas? Or are we back to bawling out the wife?"

Appalled, Tom said, "I . . . don't know. I don't think so. You see, I was thinking about writing, and—"

"You mean, you think up a line and say it out loud to see how it sounds?"

"Well, yes, that sort of thing."

"Yeah. I do that too. But not in this building." Nagel laughed. "I wouldn't want to blow my pension. Anyhow, let's move along here. Bar in Redmond. Waldo's. This is coming up on a quarter to five. Like you said, you had a scotch and water—you made a big deal about not wanting any ice in the water. Customer there says you seemed like you were in a pretty good mood about something, and that you talked to him about the Sonics."

"He talked to me about the Sonics."

"He says you were quite a fan."

"I was just agreeing with him. I don't know anything about basketball. I don't understand the rules."

"The point is, Thomas, the guy in that bar in Redmond is a happy, outgoing sort of guy. Chats with strangers, shows an interest in sports. Very different, wouldn't you say, to the guy we heard about in Bothell and Woodinville?"

"It was just that—I'd had an idea."

"Want to tell me about it?"

"It was an idea for a book. It had nothing to do with . . . It was about British travelers to the United States in Victorian times."

Nagel blinked at Tom across the desk, his face gray in the fluorescent light. His skull would have interested a phrenologist; through the thinning, close-cropped fur, you could see strange swellings and contusions of the bone beneath the skin.

"You see, here's my problem. I want to eliminate you, Thomas. You just look a little weird. Plus you're a smoker, and that creates a bad association. I got better ways to spend my time, and so do you. But then I got to deal with this—"

He passed a clipboard across his desk. "You'll see quite a few anomalies there, but those little black crosses with circles around 'em are sightings of you."

The clipboard held a smudgy, photocopied map of the area, with the Sammamish Slough running top to bottom through the middle. The pecked line of the trail had been touched up in green marker. About two miles of its length was enclosed in a narrow red oblong. Small, circled black crosses with numbers beside them were sprinkled across the entire surface of the map.

Watching Tom, Nagel said: "You can ignore those. People saw you all over. We had calls from Wenatchee and Spokane. Just look at the ones along the trail."

The numbers were confusing. Following the route of his walk, Tom saw 1007, 1218, 1615, 1305, 1150, 1702, 1350, 1600, 1425 . . . Now that everyone wore digital watches, people remembered time in ridiculously specific terms, but half the reported times were wildly wrong and some were fantastic. Yet there was an underlying pattern in the muddle—a sequence of numbers that chimed reasonably well with his own memory of the afternoon.

"How many calls have you had?"

"Last I checked, they were right up around three hundred. But that's including people like your neighbors and faculty and students at the U."

Neighbors? Students? The idea presented itself as a door better left unopened. "What's this red sausage-shape?"

"That's the time period when the victim went missing. Three-ten to three-fifty. I plotted it according to the best times I could get on your hike. Those times look about right to you, Thomas?"

"Yes, I think they do . . . Yes, that would make it start just after I left the public toilet, which seems about right to me. Give or take ten minutes either way."

"You see anybody in that toilet?"

"I told you before—I didn't go in. I just sat outside on the bench and smoked a cigarette. The second cigarette."

"Now, you see the red cross?"

It was a few hundred yards north of where the slough was crossed by NE 124th. Tom remembered the bridge. "That's where Hayley went missing?"

"Yes. So you get my problem?"

The red cross was in the exact center of the sausage.

"What was it that you didn't see, Thomas?" The detective laid out two more photos on the desk. "Let's forget Hayley for now. These are the other two kids. Maddie—she's the teenager—was wearing pink fleece pants and an aqua bomber jacket. Taylor was in blue jeans and a puffy silver down jacket with a hood."

"I didn't see them."

"They saw you."

"Did they see me—before, or . . . after?"

"Around three-thirty. Maddie was starting to worry."

Tom stared at the map and the photographs. Nothing stirred in his memory except Mrs. Trollope and her great money-making schemes in Cincinnati in 1828. That he remembered clearly, but of Maddie and her brother there was no trace. "I'm sorry, I just didn't notice them. I was thinking of other—"

"Okay. Now, one more time. I want you to walk me through this section, from the toilet to south of the bridge."

Tom did his best, but there was no more to tell than there had been first time around. He described how he had stopped to watch the red-tailed hawk. He could still see its shivering wings as it hovered over-head, as attached to its position in the air as a kite to the end of a tight string.

"Yeah, you said. I like to see the birds, too."

"You don't think that perhaps—a bear? or a cougar?"

"Nope. We'd have found remains." Nagel stared at the blank Sheetrock wall of his office as if a window there offered him a long view over fields or the sea. "She's the third kid to disappear in this vicinity in two years. All girls. Last spring, they recovered the body of one of them near Sandpoint, Idaho. The other's still missing. You're *here*, Thomas," he said, and leaned forward to prod irritably at the map.

"Well, it was about, I suppose, ten minutes after that, say, oh, a quarter of a mile, when I stopped and lit another cigarette. That would be the fourth." The look in Nagel's eyes was not encouraging. Tom explained that he had stood and watched the current for several min-utes. "You see, that's when the idea of the book really seemed to gel—I mean, I'm only telling you this so that we can—"

"Could you see the bridge from where you were?"

"I don't know. I was looking at the water. I was *thinking*. When you live in your head, you sort of blot out the external world, you know?"

"So you couldn't really see anything—like you'd gone blind. Is that it?"

"No, not exactly, but it's a very partial kind of vision. For instance . . . But, no, sorry, that would be totally irrelevant."

"In this job, nothing's irrelevant. Tell me."

So Thomas told him, bringing to the story more verbal energy than he had been able to muster all afternoon.

Nagel heard him out, unsmiling, and met the tale's ending with silence punctuated by the irritable drumming of his fingertip on the desktop. "A fish ate your cigarette."

"Yes."

"You know what, Thomas? I think you're the most goddamn self-absorbed guy I ever met."

"You sound a bit like my wife." Tom's laugh was snickering, conciliatory, meant to take the heat out of the moment.

"Tell her I'm on her side." There was no humor in the detective's voice. Chin cupped in his hand, he spoke in a weary monotone. "I want you out of this investigation, Thomas. You're no good as a witness, and you didn't do it. Trouble is, I don't see a way of clearing you, not right now."

"Perhaps I could give a blood-sample. Or take a polygraph test?"

"What good would that do?"

"I don't know. I just thought it was what you did."

Nagel gazed out through his imaginary window. "You don't remember nothing. And the other folks—all they remember is you. It's kind of the same deal when you come down to it." He gathered up his photos and put them in a drawer. "The level of probability is that the task force will be requiring for you to be re-interviewed again."

"Well, of course—any time."

"You're not a citizen."

"I'm a British citizen."

"So you'd have a passport."

"Yes."

"You have any travel plans?"

"No."

Once they were out in the corridor, Nagel surprised Tom by putting his hand on his shoulder.

"Sorry if I was a little short with you in there. It's been a rough day."

"I'm sorry to be so useless to you. I wish to hell I'd been more observant."

In the lobby, the detective gave Tom his card. "You want to go out of town for any reason, call me. You think of something—any damn thing—call me. You never know, maybe you'll get your memory back. Start remembering what you saw on that hike of yours and you'll be doing yourself a big favor, Thomas. It could be a couple days, could be a week, but we'll be in touch." He held out his hand. His mouth was bent into a tired minimal smile.

"I meant to ask," Tom said. "What is it you write?"

"Screenplays," Nagel said, in a gnarly tone that prohibited further questioning.

Tom arrived back at the house with fifteen minutes to spare before he had to leave for Treetops. An e-mail from Beth was waiting in his Inbox.

> *Hi, Tom:*
>
> *That PICTURE! How awful for you, but I'm sure you're getting it all sorted out now and everything will be back to normal in a day or two. Hope so, anyhow! God, it must have given you a shock to see it! Were you really hiking on that trail when it happened? Did you see those kids? I feel for the parents. Horrible. With everybody talking about this, I'm sure it would be a huge embarrassment for you to deal with Treetops right now, so I'll pick up Finn at five and he can stay at my place tonite. That arrangement will be best all around—hope you agree (?)*
>
> *Take care.*
> *See ya,*
> *Beth*

See ya? The phrase made him shudder, and Tom found the whole tone of the message suspect. Beth would never normally spell *tonight* like that, nor did she usually go in for block capitals and exclamations. She was concealing something behind this mask of pert chattiness, and he doubted very much if saving him from embarrassment was her true motive for hijacking Finn.

Tom had been counting on Finn as his lifeline to sanity. He needed to be boiling pasta for him and to sprawl beside him watching "The Crocodile Hunter" on "Animal Planet," and hearing his knock-knock jokes; he needed to bathe him, and tell him a story at bedtime, and snuggle with him under the covers.

He dialled Beth's number at work and got her voice-mail. He thought of driving to Treetops to forestall her but didn't have the guts, imagining with horrid clarity the terse marital wrangle conducted in front of Finn's teachers, classmates, and their parents, all of whom would be rooting for Beth.

Without Finn, he couldn't bear to cook pasta, so he cobbled together a sorry Spanish omelette for his supper. The eggy bits were burned and the potatoes tasted raw, like cubes of radish. Forcing himself to eat, he was seized by a new thought. They'd want to search his house. They always did. It was the first thing you read about. *The police conducted a search of his apartment* . . . If they came to the house, they'd find Chick and the Mexicans. And if they found Chick and the Mexicans, they'd hold him responsible. As Beth said, "Remember Zoë Baird." He'd be—what was the legal term?—an accessory after the fact. They could probably deport him for harboring illegals—and not just could, but would.

He saw himself being hustled, under guard, on to a British Airways flight, with Finn sobbing in the background, held there by goons. He thought, *I am not being rational about this,* but the more he thought, the more likely it seemed that his fears were a form of merciful pre-science. There was still—just—time to act.

Two cigarettes later, he braved Chick in the basement.

"Wanna beer?" The contractor opened the door of his new fridge, revealing an illuminated nest of thinly stocked shelves.

"Thanks, but I won't just now. Look—this is desperately inconvenient, I know, but something's cropped up. You see, the police may be coming round."

"Police? You call police?" Something dark and nasty was brewing in Chick's face.

"No, no. I no call police—" Hearing himself stumble into pidgin, Tom wanted to claw the words back from the air. "It's just that . . . Well, they might show up here, you see. To talk to me. And if you and the Mexicans were here, I thought . . . Of course, it'd be different if you were a citizen, or if you have a . . . green card?"

"I got driver's license," Chick said, as one might say "I got a gun."

"Yes, but I think what you really need, probably, is a green card, isn't it? I just don't want to land you in trouble, that's all. It's only going to be a matter of a couple of days. After that—"

"Jesús say he see you on TV. I tell him no. He dumber than a box of rocks, that guy."

"There's been a stupid mix-up. They're trying to sort it out. But just for the next day or two, it might be best if you weren't here. I'm sorry."

"He say you in deep shit." Hunch-shouldered, scowling, Chick gazed morosely over the contents of his den.

"He's wrong. That's totally untrue. But he'd be in the shit if the police found him working here." Tom wanted suddenly to punish Jesús.

"Mexicans say no worry about police. INS only."

"That's not the way I read it. And if you guys are undocumented, that's going to be my responsibility, isn't it? Then I really will be in the shit."

"Porch ain't done still. Need wooding. Today get paint, forest-green, like you say."

"Great—look, I'm only suggesting that you lay off work, like, you know, tomorrow and the day after. Of course I want you to come back," Tom said, addressing the TV set, the pile of folded clothes on the couch, the toaster oven, the fridge, the carpet samples. The orderly rectangle of ground the contractor had cleared in the wilderness of basement-stuff was far cosier than the Belltown condo. Chick had been studying Dr. Seuss and drinking 7-Up. The carpenter's level lay on top of the TV, and a wooden shim had been carefully placed between one foot of the stand and the bare earth on which it stood. Tom had never imagined turfing someone out of his settled home, and he felt unexpectedly ashamed.

"I'm sorry."

The contractor shrugged.

"I hate to spring this on you . . ."

Chick stared back at him from under the fatty violet bags that overhung his eyes, his face a mask of pure woe.

"Look, the moment I get this business sorted out, I'll call you. On your pager . . ."

"Maybe," Chick said, and began to roll up his sleeping bag.

Beth read:

Fishing for winter steelhead is like sex. Some days you just want to roll over. Others, it's the only show in town.

Debra had appointed herself the fishing columnist at Oroonoko.com, and her studio was littered with new gear bought on expenses: the frog-green waders in which Finn had gallumphed around the room, waving the landing-net at imaginary butterflies; the rod and box of gaudy tin-seled flies he'd been forbidden to touch. Finn now sat huddled under a blanket, busy with his Game Boy, and from the plaid mound in the arm-chair came a stream of thin electronic chirps and peeps as he repelled the host of alien invaders.

"I don't know," Beth said. "I just don't know."

"About my column?" Debra said, alarm spreading through her face.

"No—sorry, I haven't finished reading yet. I think the opening's very strong."

"You think it's okay? The opening was hell."

"Really, it's quite funny. Let me finish . . . "

I was using a No. 10 shooting head (my casting sucks). I tied on a Peacock Woolly Bugger, and got a great tug on my second cast into the riffle under the alders.

Psyched, I cast again and lost my Woolly Bugger (my one and only, as you guessed) in a tree. So, back to the flybox! The Green Butt Skunk (its neck is green, but its butt is actually bright yellow) caught my eye . . .

It took Debra another thousand words of mishaps and near-misses before she finally got her fish.

"It reads great," Beth said. "A little heavy on the parentheses, per-haps. You could lose one or two of those, I think. The only other thing that struck me was, I'd like to see a tad more about the river—you know, the color of the water and that kind of thing?"

"Yeah, nature. I've never been any good at that. Human-interest's really more *me*. But did you like the part about the fish looking like a winking silver platter?"

"Sweet image."

" 'Winking' was the hard word to get."

"I can see. It would be."

At last Beth got to talk—in cautious code, with Finn in the room—about Tom.

"Of course I don't think so. Of course not. It's inconceivable. But—"

"You don't think he did, but you don't know he didn't. You don't, like, *totally* know, right?"

"Maybe. I guess."

"That's so like me and Joel. The not knowing."

"He couldn't have."

"The times I said that about Joel."

"He's just not programmed that way. It's not in him."

"Ted Bundy worked for the Samaritans answering phones. Everybody thought he was the kindest, most understanding guy. Until they found the bodies of those women up on Taylor Mountain."

"You'd never find Tom doing that. He's way too self-centered."

"Joel did."

"What?"

"He worked for the Samaritans," Debra said, making it sound like murder.

"My big worry is what to do about . . ." Here Beth nodded in the direction of the beeping plaid hump. "Of course *c'est trés important pour le garçon de voir son père—tu comprends?*"

"Sorry. Me no spikkee. Me from Rapid City, South Dakota, remember?"

So Beth said, *sotto voce:* "Important . . . for . . . Finn . . . to . . . see . . . his . . . dad."

"Got you," Debra said.

"I talked to the doctor today. *His shrink,*" she whispered. "I don't know if I should take it seriously, but she has some real concerns about this character that . . . my ex . . . tells him stories about—like bedtime stories? He's called . . ." She glanced over at Finn, then wrote *"Mister Wicked"* on the back of a page from Debra's fishing column and passed it across to her.

"Mister *Wicked?*" she said, then, snapping a hand up to her mouth, "Sorry."

" 'Mister Wicked!' " Finn's head emerged from under the blanket. "He's cool."

"Pumpkin, I was just telling—"

"You know what? Everything he wears is black. He wears a black hat, and a black jacket, and black pants, and he's got a 'lectric rainbow bow-tie. He works it from a switch in his pocket. When he switches it on, it whirrs round and round. He goes all over Seattle doing wicked things."

"Thank you, pumpkin."

"And there's Moira the witch. She's Mister Wicked's friend. She can fly around on her magic Hoover, and she helps him do his wicked stuff . . ."

"That sounds cool," Debra said.

"They are cool. They're the coolest people. They're *wicked*." He pulled the blanket over his head and returned to his war, but then popped out again. "Mom? Can I go to my dad's house tonight—please?"

"No, pumpkin. We've been through this. I told you, maybe to-morrow."

"Can you tell me a Mister Wicked story?"

"Finn, I don't know how."

"It's easy. You have to start 'As was his wont . . .'"

"Do go back to your Game Boy, honey."

"Sorry to have started this," Debra said.

"You couldn't know."

Beth and Finn left for the eleventh floor a few minutes later. As they were going out the door, Debra said, "For the next column, I thought I'd fly to New Orleans for a long weekend and fish for red drum in the bayous. Want to come?"

"I wish, but I'd get fired. We open in Chicago in March, and the whole site's gone totally insane."

Later, when Finn was safely asleep, Beth called upstairs on the phone. Debra thought Mister Wicked a very ominous sign indeed; it would be crazy to trust Finn to the sole overnight care of "that man." Tom could visit Finn at the condo, "but only when you're there." Beth's instinct was to believe that both Karen Eusebio and Debra were vastly exaggerating the dangers, yet she was was depressed to find herself in a minority of one.

She was tempted to dial Tom's number, but delayed doing so until she'd brewed a mug of camomile tea, and then she was too sleepy to face the inevitable chess-moves and fencing-maneuvers that any con-versation with Tom required. But she dreamed of him that night, and in her sleep he was neither evil nor unkind.

For the first time in ages, it seemed, Tom could hear the peevish chur-ring and keening of the crows. Without Chick and his crew, the house was forlornly silent. Listening to a faint noise that he could not immediately place, Tom realized it was the *thump-thump-thump* of his own heart.

He went down to the basement. Chick had removed all his possessions, along with the old couch, and a flattening of the earth beyond the furnace was the only sign that anyone had ever lived here. He was so thoroughly and completely gone that it might have been tempting to doubt his existence, were it not for the junk-staging that clung to the west side of the house, and the half-built porch, now criss-crossed with red plastic tape to warn off unwary callers at the front door. Yesterday's racket of saws, shouts, and hammering now came back to Tom as a companionable memory, and he would have given a great deal to hear it return.

He was summoned upstairs by the pealing of the phone.

"Hello?"

There was a man's voice at the other end—elderly, reedy, emphysematic. "There's a few things I'd like to discuss with you, if I may," it began, amiably enough. "You murdering pervert Jew—" What followed was only partially comprehensible, but the gist of it appeared to be that Tom was living proof of the truth of *The Protocols of the Elders of Zion.* He banged the receiver back into its cradle.

It must be because of my hair, he thought. Who was this unhinged old toad? A neighbor? Some loony professor-emeritus at the U, or a fellow-shopper at Ken's? He recalled a shuffling, shrunken, papery-skinned geezer who often stood ahead of him in the checkout line with his cans of catfood and frozen turkey dinners. Was it him? Certainly, the voice would fit. And if the man knew his name and phone number, he must know his address, too. In a country where eccentrics routinely drove their opinions home with bullets from semi-automatic handguns, there was much to fear from even the most bent and arthritic basket-cases. He might have to bring his oxygen supply with him when he called, but he could still kill.

When the phone rang again ten minutes later, Tom waited for the answering machine to pick it up. From the loudspeaker came a slow, drawling, Oxbridge English voice saying, with unsettling aptness, "Oh. Tom. Just wanted to find out if you were still in the land of the living."

"David—it's me. I'm here. Let me turn off the machine . . ."

"Ah, an actual human voice, how nice. How are you? And the book? Not interrupting in the middle of a sentence, am I? How's Betsy? How's the kid?" Having disposed of the pleasantries, Scott-Rice got down to business. He was "rather hoping" that UW could see its way to paying him $15,000 up front on his fee, plus the airfare, as he'd prefer to buy his own ticket in London.

Listening to these demands, Tom realized he hadn't heard from Shiva Ray in over a month, which was unusual. To Scott-Rice, he said that he thought there were still a few odds and sods of paperwork to tie up, and that he'd drop a note to the department chairman to find out where things stood.

"I'd be v. grateful if you would," Scott-Rice said. "To tell you the truth, I'm in a bit of a hole. The Inland Revenue boys . . . they're being ridiculously unreasonable. My accountant tells me it's time to throw a bone to the wolf, or whatever the phrase is. But I'm having a spot of bother finding the bone. It's rather a big bone, actually: twenty-five grand. But if your chaps could stump up fifteen thousand American by January twentieth, I think I might just be able to put it together . . ."

"I can't speak for the department, of course, but I'd be amazed if we could get anything for you by then."

"The b-word has been mentioned . . ."

"The what?"

"Bankruptcy." Scott-Rice made the one word sound like three.

"Oh, dear, is it really that bad?"

"Bad? You can't have a bank account. Or a credit card. You have to pay for everything in cash. I can't imagine anything worse."

For a moment, Detective Nagel and the missing child slipped Tom's mind, and he felt the faint warming glow of *schadenfreude*.

"And everybody knowing . . . the public disgrace of it. I tell you, this is about as serious as it can get."

Clearly, there was no point in speaking to Scott-Rice about his own predicament: compared with having to pay cash for everything, it would hardly qualify as a predicament at all.

"So you can see why I'm counting on you."

"Of course I'll do whatever I can, but—"

"Well, just remember, will you, that I am facing total ruin? I mean, it's like that bloody Dickens novel, you know the one. The Marshalsea."

"Little Dorrit."

"Yes. And where the hell is *she* when I need her? That's what I'm obviously lacking—a devoted daughter with twenty-five thousand quid in readies."

The more Scott-Rice blew his financial troubles into comic opera, the more Tom wished he could unload a few of his miseries on the scapegrace novelist. But he knew Scott-Rice. He'd never catch his ear. He thought—briefly—of his comfortable bank balance, and of Beth's ever-multiplying stock options. She was now, he very much suspected, a technical millionaire. But they'd never get it back. Nobody who gave Scott-Rice money ever did.

"Heigh-ho. I must say I cannot imagine life without my flexible friend."

"Can't you ask your publisher to help out?"

"Don't talk to me about fucking publishers. They're all run by bloody accountants now. It's as bad as dealing with the Inland Revenue. Worse. You heard that poor old Terry got booted out by the Nazis?"

"No, I didn't—"

"Well, he did, a couple of weeks before Christmas. On his ear. Now I have to deal with a dreadful spotty teenager. Looks like the office boy. Named Kevin. Kevin! Can you beat it?"

"I ought to call him . . ." Tom said.

"Oh, you won't get any joy out of that, I can tell you. What do you imagine he reads? Comics, I would think. Comics and girlie mags and balance-sheets."

"I mean Terry, not Kevin."

"Oh, Terry. Yes, I suppose one should. But with my problems . . ." He sighed extravagantly. "It's dog-eat-dog in London now. It's brutal. Hobbesian. People getting murdered on the street for their cellphones. Carjackings everywhere. In broad daylight. I can't tell you how much I'm looking forward to escaping to Washington State for a breather. Mountains. Water. Pine trees. Those little baby oysters . . . How I envy you the peace and quiet of it!" He made the sound of sniffing the Seattle air down the telephone line like a wine buff inhaling a rare bouquet. "Heaven!"

When Scott-Rice finally hung up, his last words rang in Tom's ear. "Remember: total ruin!"

*　　　*　　　*

Life's toughest trials, Tom read, *should not be faced alone*—a sentiment that exactly mirrored his own feelings as he leafed through the Yellow Pages. The listings for "Attorneys" ran to nearly one hundred pages, the lawyers pitching their wares like barrow-boys in a street-market.

> THE NAME'S BENNETT. I'M A LAWYER.
> I KEEP PEOPLE OUT OF JAIL.
> IS YOUR FUTURE AT STAKE? PROTECTING THE
> RIGHTS OF THE ACCUSED IS ALL I DO.
> IF YOU'RE IN TROUBLE, YOU NEED EFFECTIVE,
> AGGRESSIVE DEFENSE.
> DON'T GET LOST IN A LEGAL MAZE!
> WE'LL FIGHT FOR YOU!
> PROFESSIONAL, DIGNIFIED, AGGRESSIVE.
> IF IN CUSTODY, CALL COLLECT.
> JAIL VISITS.

The advertisers mentioned a spectacular variety of crimes in which they specialized, from traffic violations to capital murder, but the plight of being a person of interest wasn't included. Nobody, apparently, had cornered the market in mistaken identities. In the end, Tom called Hamish McTurk of DeWitt, Olmsted, Grabowski, Lu & McTurk, hoping he would turn out to be an expatriate Scot with whom he could talk in his own language.

The voice that came on the line was not Scottish. This branch of the McTurks must've left the Highlands during the Clearances. But the lawyer had heard of—and, better still, had heard—Tom Janeway.

"Well, I'll be darned," he said. "Hey, Phil? Know who I'm talking to? Tom Janeway. Guy who does those commentaries on NPR." Speaking back into the phone, he said: "Phil's another fan of yours. We're big listeners in this office. Last pledge drive, we gave a thousand dollars to KUOW."

"I'm glad to hear it."

"Bet that's where you heard our name, huh? We're sponsors. We like to think we're pillars of the public-radio community, supporting quality talk of the kind that you do so well, Tom. Hey, do me a favor, will you? Say something with an *r* in it."

"Barracuda," Tom said. "Brambles. Bankruptcy. Arrested."

"I'd know that voice anywhere. Phil—stick around for a minute. I'm going to put him on speaker. Listen for the *r*'s. That's your radio signature, right, Tom—those *r*'s? They really knock me out."

"The thing is, I've run into a bit of a problem."

"Hear that? 'Prrroblem!' You're a sport, Tom. I wouldn't do this to you, but I know you got a great sense of humor. You make me laugh. Like, what you said about the dot-coms a little while back? Getting sunlight out of cabbages? I've quoted you on that. That was a great line, Tom."

"Cucumbers. Extracting sunbeams out of cucumbers. It was from—"

"You can't say it plainer than that. I don't know that anybody's stuck it to the bubble economy better than you did, Tom. I'd really like to have a tape of that broadcast. Okay, Phil—see you. Phil sends his regards, Tom. Now, what were you saying?"

Two minutes later, he pronounced this to be Tom's lucky day, for he was still free for lunch. Less than an hour later, lawyer and client met in the lobby of the Rainier Club on Fourth. McTurk, close to Tom's age, was small, bald, and snub-nosed, like a retired welterweight boxer: his pinch-waisted suit, cut from a fierce black-and-white houndstooth check, was hard on the eye, though when they shook hands, Tom keenly felt the shabbiness of his tweed jacket and his conspicuous want of a necktie. The attorney's tie was decorated with a crowded regatta of little sailboats flying rainbow-striped spinnakers.

"I'm afraid I'm rather underdressed," Tom said.

"Hey—that's your prvilege. You're a Bohemian."

As they climbed the stairs, Hamish McTurk nodded at a vast mud-colored canvas representing a logged forest, clearly inspired by photographs of the wrecked landscapes of Ypres and Paaschendaele. "Guy who painted that picture—Ken Callahan—used to hump Mary McCarthy when she was in high school. She was a famous author from here in Seattle." McTurk appeared to offer this as an example of acceptable Bohemian behavior in his broad-minded city.

When they were seated, in overstuffed high-backed chairs, at a large window-table in the third-floor dining room, Tom broached the subject of his questioning by the police, but McTurk waved his hand sweepingly across the linen tablecloth.

"My motto? Never let legal business interfere with a good lunch. We'll talk about that back in the office, and I'll put you on the clock. But from what you said over the phone, you got nothing to worry about. So—enjoy." The attorney's eyes went on walkabout around the dining room, and to everyone he recognized he delivered a high stiff-armed salute. Then he said, "Yeah—'sunshine from cauliflowers.' Like I said, I tell that line to a lot of people. Kind of encapsulates the whole dot-com culture."

"Cucumbers. Of course, that's Swift's phrase. When Gulliver visits the Grand Academy of Lagado, he meets this guy . . ."

"Swift?" There was a fierce courtroom snap in McTurk's question.

"Yes, Jonathan Swift. It's a famous passage from *Gulliver's Travels*."

"And you can do that?"

"Well of course you—"

"Okay, let's call it fair use. I thought you made that one up, Tom."

"I attributed it to Swift in the broadcast."

"Maybe I just wasn't listening too closely. Anyway," McTurk said in a concessionary tone, "it's a great expression, whoever wrote it—you or Jonathan. Sums up the business plans of ninety-nine percent of these start-ups."

"You know, I met a man on Bainbridge Island once, who's planning to get fabulously rich making 'digital smells.'"

"I remember—you said that on the radio. Some kind of crazy-ass box you plug into your PC . . . Which actually sounds smarter than half the rinky-dink ideas getting funded in this town. Most of these so-called entrepreneurs? I'm just waiting for the day when I can go into McDonald's and watch them flipping burgers."

"Have you heard of a man called Steve Litvinof?" Tom said, warming to the prospect of doing a satiric hatchet job on GetaShack.com.

"My oldest friend," McTurk said, alarmingly. "Steve and I were at Syracuse together. Both Dekes. Now Steve, he's a different kettle of fish altogether. He's got a business plan that looks like a business plan. You ever diddle around on his site?"

"Actually, my wife works there."

"So you know. When everybody else was dreaming up schemes to attract advertisers with content, Steve thought his way out of the box. At GetaShack, the advertisers are the content. The customers think they're getting into a virtual community, right? What they're really getting is commercials. It's like TV without the programming, like a newspaper with no news. Know how Steve described it, a couple years back? He said it was like interactive Yellow Pages where everybody pays: the realtors pay, your restaurants and coffee houses pay, movie theaters pay . . . the supermarkets . . . the dry cleaners . . . That's a revenue stream most sites would kill for."

"My wife does the . . . I suppose you'd call it content."

"The little black T-Bird? The tour-thing? Yeah, that's cute. And better than cute, it's real cheap. I tell you, Tom, I got lucky when Steve asked me to put a few bucks into the float back in '96. Oh man, now that's a serious chunk of change!"

Tom tinkered with the venison pot-pie as Hamish McTurk laid into a filet mignon so rare that a pool of blood formed around it on his plate.

"You sail, Tom?"

"No, I never have."

Not missing a beat, McTurk described his sailboat in lavish technical detail, all of which was lost on Tom. He was talking about "lazy-jacks" when a departing clubman stopped by their table.

McTurk seized his hand. "Bill! Of course you know who *this* is! Tom Janeway—does those great commentaries on 'All Things Considered'? You've heard him, right? On the radio?"

Bill slowly shook his head and gave Tom a befuddled smile. Within five minutes, the same exchange was repeated with a man named Larry and another called Scott. Then McTurk called "Norm!" at a receding gray suit, which turned around and came to the table for the standard routine. Norm hadn't heard of Tom either, but when he was gone, McTurk said, "So now you've met the King County Prosecutor."

"For the first and last time," Tom said. "Fingers crossed."

"You slay me with those *r*'s, Tom, you really do. Hey—"

Tom feared yet another introduction, but it was only the waiter.

"Bring us the menu again, will you?" To Tom, he said, "I have to warn you: I'm a big dessert man."

Tom ordered coffee. McTurk had profiteroles in cream-and-chocolate sauce.

"So who do you deal with at NPR? Bob Edwards? Jacki Lyden? Robert Siegel? Corey Flintoff? You know those guys?"

"No, I work with a producer in D.C., just down the line. I've never actually met her face-to-face."

McTurk wagged his cream-laden spoon. "But you'd know where to go, right? If you had a concept?"

"Well, I'd probably start by talking to Miriam—my producer. Or perhaps to someone at KUOW."

"I don't talk to franchises, Tom. See, this is confidential, but Phil and me, we've been talking for a while about this. We've identified a market gap in public radio, and I want to pick your brain here a little."

"Yes?" Tom and McTurk were the only people now seated in the room. The waiters huddled by the desk, waiting to set the tables for dinner. Tom shared their impatience.

"It's a big niche, Tom. It's the law."

"Really?"

"Think about it. Everyone runs into a legal problem sometime in their lives. Like you calling me up today. Divorce . . . child custody . . . landlord-and-tenant . . . DUI . . . or maybe you accidentally took something out of a store without paying, or you got some inappropriate behavior going on at the office. Everybody's been there. Even you. Even me. And what do you want to do? You want to talk to an attorney, Tom."

"Yes." Tom could hear the longing in his own voice.

"So you talk to us, Phil and me. We're the Law Guys. We bat your problem around on air for seven, ten minutes. Maybe we solve it for you, maybe we send you to a specialist. We're smart. We're funny. We're experts. Between us, we do basic criminal, family, driving, injury claims, consumer rights, immigration—and that's a real hot topic with a lot of listeners—plus employment and financial. You with me, Tom?"

"Yes," Tom said, thinking how little he would relish hearing his own problem batted around on air for the entertainment of a nationwide audience.

"You could call it 'Bar Talk.'"

Tom laughed cautiously, uncertain if this was meant as a serious title or a facetious joke. "Well, it certainly isn't something for Miriam Glazebrook. It'd have to go to someone *much* more senior. I'll happily ask her who you ought to send it to, if you'd like." Surely Miriam knew the chief rejection-slip writer at NPR—and would enjoy Tom's telling of this trying lunch.

"I'd appreciate that, Tom. But you get the concept—like a legal Click and Clack?"

"Oh, yes. I think it's . . . major."

They collected their coats, and as they walked down to McTurk's office on First, Tom told him that at least he'd got rid of his crew of illegals.

"Why'd you do that? You planning on reporting them to the INS?"

Tom explained the danger of having his house searched, with a Chinese squatter in his basement.

"See? That's why people need the Law Guys. You never had a problem there, Tom. Even if the cops did come around, they wouldn't be interested in your builders. Patrol car stops a wetback on a highway for speeding: the cop'll ask for his driver's license, but can't go for the green card, because that'll land him in a violation-of-rights situation. The police don't see illegals; it's none of their business." He laid his arm, clad in thick camel-colored alpaca, across Tom's shoulder. "It's like I said. Everybody needs to talk to an attorney."

In the Skylight Room, Sally said, "Go on, Finn, you take the last brownie."

Finn didn't get it. The teachers were being nice to him. He'd had the first turn at the sensory table, and the last of the brownies. The moment he finished his picture of two dogs in a park, with a grinning yellow-crayon sun overhead, Sally pinned it up on the wall and said, "Isn't that a great picture? You *have* used your imagination, Finn!" But he'd done much better pictures than that, and nobody ever put them on the wall.

He excused himself to go to the bathroom. When he was halfway down the hall, the principal, Midge, stepped out of her office to smile at him.

"Well—Finn!" she said. "Good morning. How are you?"

"Fine." He hurried past. She had a really spooky smile, like a monster's. Her lips were pulled right back, and you could see her gray old teeth sticking out of her gums. Spencer's mom had given him the same creepy smile, when usually she just said, "Oh, hi, Finn," in a vague, flat voice, like he wasn't really there. Caro's dad had squatted down beside him with that big smile and asked, "How's it going, Finn?" Weird, huh?

It was good to sit alone on the toilet. He carefully pulled a stringy booger from his nose and ate it. A fly buzzed against the pane. Did flies have dreams? What would you dream about if you were a fly? The toilet was a good place for thinking. When he flushed, he closed his eyes tight shut, because he hated to see the poop and the paper get all swirled up together in the bowl. He didn't know why that was, but it was really gross. When he was three, he thought it was scary. Now it was just gross.

Washing his hands, he growled at his reflection in the mirror over the sink. He had death-ray orange eyes and vampire teeth. He was the Night Creature. He could fly over rooftops and stare into people's windows without them seeing him. They called him Mister Fearless. Out in the corridor, he spread his black cloak and glided noiselessly over the linoleum floor. As he passed the principal's office, she didn't even turn her head from the screen of her computer. He was perfectly invisible, just a ripple in the air, like a draft.

"Hello, Finn. Were you in the bathroom all that time?" That smile again. He really liked his teacher, but the smile made her look like a stranger. She was handing out empty milk cartons, construction paper, and drinking straws. "We're going to make pirate ships," she said.

Finn enjoyed making things, especially the glueing. For several minutes, nothing existed for him except the satisfying scrunch of the serrated blades of his plastic scissors on the construction paper. Ships were cool. He loved to ride on ferries, and building his ship made him think of the long, long ferry ride they'd taken in the summer, him and his mom and dad, to Victoria, in Canada, where the money was called "loonies."

"Did you hear what I said, Finn?" Sally had pulled up a chair and was sitting right beside him. He could smell her sweat. "I said . . . oh, never mind. Tell me what you're doing."

"I'm making a ship."

"Yes, but what are you doing with the paper now?"

"Cutting out the sails."

"We're all starting with the hull, Finn. The milk cartons—"

"I'm not. I'm starting with the sails."

"Well, it's your ship."

She put her arm around his shoulders and hugged him, squashing Finn against her big pillowy body. It was like being hugged by a hippopotamus. The lumpy weave of her cardigan hurt his cheek. He wriggled free, knocking a milk carton to the floor.

"Finn? Are you okay, honey?"

"I need privacy," he said.

Teacher Sally picked up the fallen carton, and her joints creaked as she got out of the small chair. "Okay, then." She looked tired, and her smile was brief and skimpy—an everyday smile at last.

When she was gone, he went angrily to work. He sliced his cut-out sail in two, took the straws that were supposed to be masts, and snipped them up, sorting through the bits to find arms, legs, and a body for his stick-person. He'd make the head from PlayDoh. He tried a lot of different limbs before they looked right, then he raised his hand. "Hey? Please? I want glue!"

"It gets worse," Paul Nagel said.

The detective appeared older than Tom remembered from their first interview. His face looked as if it had been moulded in potter's clay, and his blue eyes were bloodshot. It was Saturday morning, nine and a half hours into the new millennium. Had Nagel been up all night and on the bottle, he could hardly have been in worse shape; but it seemed unlikely that his wrecked face owed anything to Y2K festivities.

"We've had calls that put you on the trail back in February. The twenty-eighth. The day Tracey Groh went missing. She's the one they found dead in Idaho. You were seen walking there again on November seventeenth of '98, when Nicole Waxman—"

"That's ridiculous. I told you, Monday was the first time I've been there in six years."

"That's what you told me, Thomas, but other people are telling different."

"I—" McTurk had said that in any future interview he should be accompanied by his attorney, but Tom had come alone. It seemed to him that to enter the courthouse building in the company of a criminal lawyer could only deepen his troubles. He disliked McTurk, whose last action had been to slide the bill for lunch into the new folder labeled "Janeway," but he badly wanted him by his side now. It was as if solid ground had abruptly given way to a bog of floating moss, and that no matter where he planted his foot, he'd find himself up to his neck in black slime. "They're wrong. I wasn't anywhere—"

"In a case like this, a lot of people start remembering things that didn't happen."

"Thank you."

The detective opened a tin of Sucrets and began sucking on a lozenge. Tom smelled the mint on his breath.

"Something you didn't tell me, Thomas. Your wife . . . Elizabeth. Few weeks ago, she moved out of the marital home. She's living in a condo in Belltown."

"Why should I tell you that? It's nothing—"

"Things sometimes have to do with things in ways you wouldn't believe. Your boy, Finn: you got a parenting agreement for him?"

Humiliated, Tom explained the weekly schedule that he and Beth had worked out, but didn't mention that he hadn't seen Finn since Sunday.

"That sounds pretty close to joint custody. You find it difficult to swing that quality of access, Thomas?"

"No. She and I just divided up the week, and because the house is so close to his preschool—"

"You're lucky. My kids? They get to stay with me two Saturday nights a month . . ."

"You have them tonight?"

"No."

"That must be hard. I find it hard enough with—"

"My wife's dad hired her a big-time lawyer. From San Francsico. An older broad, a real feminist. In court, she tied my guy up in a bag and took him out with the garbage. I should have had a woman, too. Should've seen it coming. That's why I'm studying family law at the U. You'd think, me being involved with legal work and everything, I'd have all that shit figured out. But I wasn't too bright. Came out of that courtroom without a pot to piss in nor a window to throw it out of." Nagel glowered, as if the lawyer from San Francisco was sitting in Tom's chair. "I'll tell you something, Thomas. When it gets to the divorce, you better find yourself a smart female attorney."

Feeling greatly encouraged by this shift in the detective's tone, Tom said, "You know, I'm not sure, but I think I did remember something."

"Yes?"

"The bridge—the one near where . . . There's a parking lot there, not big, just a square of gravel by the side of the road?"

"I'm with you."

"It may not have been the only vehicle there, but there was one that

I seem to remember—a scruffy sort of camper van. Not a minivan or an RV, but the prefab add-on kind . . ."

"Truck conversion?"

"Yes, that would be it. It was dirty-white, with a bit of yellow on it, I think. But old and scratched-up. All the shine was gone from the body-work. I believe I saw floral curtains in the windows."

"You notice the license plate?"

"Oh, I couldn't possibly remember the num—"

"I'm not asking you for the numbers. Was it an in-state plate, or out-of-state?"

"Alaska!" Tom said, astonishing himself. "I'm almost sure it said 'Alaska.'"

"That's pretty good, Thomas. In fact, that camper has Washington plates, but the shell says ALASKAN, the company that made it. It's an '84 Dodge truck with an Alaskan shell. The owner—he lives in that wreck—was walking his dogs and says he was way up in Bothell when . . . Well, it checks out. But I think we're finally getting somewhere. You remembering this camper—it shows you live in the same world as the rest of us, some of the time anyhow. Which I was beginning to doubt."

Chick was nowhere to be found. Tom left three messages on his pager, and drove slowly around the reticular grid of streets looking for the black pick-up truck. Everywhere he saw contractors of the grander sort, but Excellent Construction had vanished into the city's wintry labyrinth. On Queen Anne's eastern brow, Tom stopped the car and looked down over Seattle, incontinently sprawled over its lakes and timber-spotted hills. From here, the gray slurry of development appeared not to stop until it reached the snowfields of the Cascades, some forty miles away. The contractor and his band of Mexicans might be anywhere. Chick had no habits that Tom knew of, no contacts or connections: he'd popped into existence like the plants that suddenly appear on new volcanic islands, their seed carried there in seagull shit. He was a creature of pure accident, it seemed to Tom, and there was no predicting the next rock on which he might take temporary root.

Back at the house, a long strand of plastic tape had broken loose from the porch deck and was flying in the wind, a wild red question mark. Gingerly straddling two raw joists, Tom let himself in by the front door. As he was turning to close it, he could have sworn he saw a lightning-bolt, though he heard no thunder and the sky above was empty except for a few streaks of high cirrus. He looked up and down the street. There was no-one about. He must've been imagining things.

Up in his third-floor eyrie, he retrieved the still unfinished ALIENS.doc, but was too jumpy and distracted to write. He found his copy of *American Notes,* but reading Dickens on the Atlantic Ocean in a hurricane roused only a sharp, unwelcome memory of the turbid water of Sammamish Slough. Finally, Tom did what he'd shied away from doing for the past several days: he went on the Internet in search of Hayley Topolski.

He clicked back and forth between the online editions of the *Seattle Times* and the *Post-Intelligencer,* following the story as it grew from the kernel of a bare police report into a ripe journalistic tragedy. Tom's own role in it was smaller than he'd feared: the "person of interest" sought by the police at the outset had come forward and been interviewed by detectives. A spokesman for the King County Sheriff's Office declined to release his name and said he was not regarded as a suspect.

More than a hundred volunteers had combed the neighboring fields, and the slough had been dragged. A volunteer was quoted as saying, "At least we didn't find what many people were afraid of finding." Neighbors had spent Saturday tying ribbons to the branches of the poplars along the trail to remind people of Hayley. An impromptu shrine had arisen outside her house, where well-wishers left cards, prayers, cut flowers, balloons, teddy bears, and Beanie Babies. A candlelight vigil had been held at the Community Baptist Church on the outskirts of Woodinville.

Hayley had entered the limbo of the missing, where she was spoken of, insistently, in the present tense, but in terms that took her death for granted. "She is a little piece of sunshine," said her pastor. "She's a wonderful little girl," her kindergarten teacher said. "She's a well-behaved sweet girl." "She's a quiet girl who laughs a lot." To these people, Hayley had become the incarnation of childhood itself, and they talked as if what had in fact gone missing on Sammamish Slough was innocence itself. As a neighbor said, "She is an angel." It was left to Maddie, her older sister, to strike the lone realistic note: "She loved karaoke." And for a moment, Tom was able to see her as a real child, jigging, out of sync, mike in hand, to Britney Spears.

Hayley's parents—in their "routine of anguish and agony"—had given no interviews, but Tom could picture them from the reports. He was a loader operator, she worked part-time at Denny's; their ranch-style bungalow on Route 202 was described by the *Times* as "modest" and by the *P-I* as a rental. Both Ed and Sharon were on their second time around. Maddie was the child of his previous marriage, Taylor of hers.

How often, then, must the Topolskis have been gripped by the instinctual, reflexive paranoia that keeps parents watching out for their children's safety? Tom thought of Finn, at two and three, tottering at speed down supermarket aisles: in the time it took to grind half a pound of coffee beans, or choose the greenest bananas, he would be lost to view around a corner, with Tom ricocheting from trolley to trolley and shopper to shopper in a torment of anxiety. The day Finn was born, the world suddenly filled with baby-snatchers, child-molesters armed with bags of candy, drivers yakking into cellphones who carelessly squashed small bodies beneath their wheels, along with the unguarded machinery, deep water, precipitous stairwells, electrical outlets, sharp knives, and prescription drugs that made any child's survival to adolescence seem an against-all-odds miracle.

A couple of years ago, Finn had disappeared on the crowded beach at Golden Gardens. It was hot, in the eighties, the air stinking of suntan lotion and barbecue smoke. Tom and Beth, talking fondly and intently, had relaxed their guard for a few instants, and when they looked up he was gone. In raging panic, Tom waded into the sea, fully expecting to see a pale shape like a drifting jellyfish in the suck and swash of the tide, while Beth sprinted across the low dunes to the parking lot, having spotted a man hurrying a child towards a car in the far distance. Finn, as it turned out, had attached himself to another family and was helping two girls to build a sand-castle; but in the nearly ten-minute interval, Tom experienced fear of such pure intensity that he hadn't known it lay within his being to be so possessed by a single emotion. It was a feeling beyond, or beneath, language, a howling emptiness in the heart. He'd seen Finn dead. Later, he plowed groggily through the sand to the rest-room by the swings and vomited himself dry in the toilet.

The Topolskis would have lived through all the usual false alarms and learned, as Tom had done, to try to control such mad blazes of apprehension. Your child always turned up safely in the end. Always. Then came the day when yellow ribbons were in the trees and flyers on telephone poles, and all those fears—banal, irrational—became true prophecies.

Poor Maddie. Tom imagined her father shouting, and the blaming, appalled gaze of her stepmother. She'd let thirty minutes go by before looking for help. Only thirteen, and lacking the in-built fright-machine of a parent, she'd probably thought Hayley a tiresome brat when she failed to answer, and kept on walking. Tom could see her in her bomber jacket and pink pants; an anemic pinched face, with damp fair hair hanging in rat-tails around her ears; and earrings—big braided hoops of many colors.

She hadn't worn earrings in the snapshot on Paul Nagel's desk, Tom was certain of it. Only memory, unbidden, unexpected, could have supplied that detail. She was stopped on the trail, with the boy dawdling ten or fifteen yards behind. Hands deep in the pockets of his overcoat, head down, he passed them both. Dickens was on his mind, or at least Dickens's America, an enormous and unlovely landscape of swamps, jails, and lunatic asylums. Concentrating hard now, he stared into the inky foliage of the holly tree, seeing the arch of the bridge that carried the road over the slough, and beyond the arch, on the trail, something, or someone: not so much a figure as a shifting disposition of space and shadow.

A cloud of bushtits took wing from the holly, and the image, such as it was, crazed over like a windshield hit by a rock. Lighting a cigarette, Tom set to reasssembling it piece by piece. He got the bridge in view again, and the muddy puddle underneath it that had made him step out into the rough grass on the bank of the slough. *Stop there.* Leafless brown brambles. A poplar. A stand of tall, parchment-colored sedge. It was like Find Waldo, except that Tom didn't know if he was scanning the picture to find Hayley, her presumed abducter, or a casual passer-by. But he was convinced that the picture was somehow incomplete, that memory was withholding the crucial bits of information that would make it spring into full focus.

Then he got it. He knew where he'd seen Maddie's cheerful hoop earrings—just yesterday, on a checkout girl at Ken's. He wasn't recovering memories but building a fiction, planting a bogeyman under the bridge to please Paul Nagel and get himself off the hook.

Thirty feet up, harnessed by a rope to the trunk of a big old fir, Chick got his rental chain-saw going by holding the toggle of the starter-cord and letting the saw itself fall free. The sucker screamed, like someone was killing a pig. He'd learned this trick from Lázaro, who called it "gravity start." Hauling up the live, throbbing saw, Chick narrowly avoided cutting off his right leg at the knee. He grinned down at Lázaro and Ernesto, leveling the saw at them like a gun.

Trees were a major liability in this rain-soaked city. Their spreading roots made sidewalks heave and crack. They leaned at tipsy angles. When the wind blew, they tipped over, flattened cars, took down telephone lines, and crashed into the roofs of neighboring houses. You got a tree in your yard, you better have good insurance.

Chick had ambushed the old lady while she was taking shopping bags out of the trunk of her Coupe de Ville. It was as if she'd been expecting him, so quickly did she agree that the fir needed to come down. His first thought was to ask $250, but when he said $500, she jumped at the price like it was real cheap. Lázaro had gone up first, taking off the branches. Chick watched him carefully, then claimed the bare trunk for himself. He was excited by the chain-saw's manic ferocity and noise, and liked the idea of himself, high aloft, armed with this great howling two-handed weapon.

Lázaro showed him how to make the deep notch in the trunk on the side where you wanted the tree to fall. Legs braced, throwing his whole weight out hard against the harness, he drove the chain into timber soft as meat, spraying himself with resin-scented dust. Down in the yard, the Mexicans held the line that Lázaro had tied to the trunk ten feet above Chick's head. He gave them a thumbs-up sign. At the end of his second cut, a chunk of wood the shape of a fat watermelon slice fell neatly out of the tree, and he maneuvered himself around the trunk to make the back-cut. This was the difficult bit. You had to stop just before the chain reached the angle of the notch, so the treetop was still joined to the trunk by a thin hinge of uncut wood. Biting his lip, he went in as far as he dared, then looked up to see the tree above him shudder indecisively for a second or two before it slowly teetered over, like a wilting flower, and then slammed with a bounce onto the lawn, exactly along the line he and Lázaro had planned for it. The din of the saw made the fall appear soundless, but he felt the thump as the tree hit the ground. It was beautiful to see. His first time, too.

From his perch atop the amputated fir, Chick surveyed roofs encrusted with moss, plants sprouting from gutters, splayed siding, swarming ivy, sagging porches, houses choked in greenery. Wherever his eye rested, he saw work: between the rotting stuff that needed to be rebuilt and the growing stuff that had to be cut down, a man could keep himself busy for a lifetime and never even make a difference. Things rotted so fast and grew so fast that the size of the job would always stay the same.

He stopped the chain-saw and lowered it to Lázaro, who set to work slicing the fallen section of trunk into logs. A black guy had a firewood lot down on Rainier and paid $40 a cord. Or they could sell the wood direct off the trucks. It was a fine call, time against money, and he hadn't yet made up his mind. Feeling for toeholds in the rutted bark, he clambered down to where Ernesto stood with a shit-eating smile on his face.

Chick followed the direction of the smile and was shaken to see that it led to Mr. Don, sitting at the wheel of his high-riding 300-horse Ford truck. He was mouthing words, but the noise of Lázaro's sawing drowned them out and Chick had to step down on to the sidewalk to hear.

"That's a pretty line of business you're into—being an arborist."

"Is a job," Chick said, fighting his habit of deference. He didn't like the Mexicans seeing him standing while Mr. Don was seated; him looking up and Mr. Don looking down.

"There's a handy profit in trees. I'm happy for you. Here." From his top pocket, he brought out two small cigars and passed one out of the cab window.

Although he hated smoking, Chick thought that to share a cigar, boss to boss, would impress the Mexicans, so when Mr. Don produced his lighter, he leaned into the flame, sucking warily. The lighter reeked of kerosene; the smoke tasted unpleasantly of cherries.

Breathing feathery contrails from his nostrils, Mr. Don said, "I've missed you."

"I be busy."

"I got to worrying. You know, about where you're at and what you're up to."

Chick stifled a cough. "Been doing okay."

"Yeah, so I see." He nodded at the black pick-up. "You did a fine job there. You're a hard worker, pardner. I admire that."

Standing at his full height, Chick could see Mr. Don's dog curled up snoozing in the passenger seat, like a pile of tarred rope. "Scottie," he said, trying to deflect attention from himself.

"You been working on your English. Listening to you now, I could take you for an American. Hey, you even look like an American."

Chick grinned and scuffed his heels. "Nights I study. Read a whole bunch of books." He did, too: he could recite *The Cat in the Hat Comes Back!* now, every word.

This was no time for play.
This was no time for fun.
This was no time for games.
There was work to be done . . .

"That's a wonderful thing—reading. Maybe you should go to school, get yourself a college degree, become a professional. You got the brains for it. You ever thought about signing up with a community college?"

"No, Mr. Don."

"You ought to. Fellow like you, hell, you could be anything you wanted. You go back to school, I bet you could get yourself an M.B.A."

"Maybe I do that."

"You'd be doing yourself a good turn. See, it's like this. There's only one thing bothers me about you, Chick."

"What's that, Mr. Don?"

"You stole my Mexicans."

Chick emptied his face of all expression and dropped the cigar into the grass. "Job be finish. He over. I find new job for Mexican boys."

"Well, let's just say you had 'em out on loan when I had no particular use for them. But now I want 'em back. Hey, Ernesto! Go get Lázaro for me, will you?"

"They like work with me." Chick knew Mr. Don's terms: $8.50 an hour, and for cow-work. Chick paid $9.50, and the work was good—no fucking with asbestos and stuff. Even if he paid eleven bucks, he'd still be fat.

Lázaro came shambling down to the sidewalk in a yellow hard-hat and ear-muffs, smiling his usual vacant, apologetic smile. He shrugged at Chick, then at Mr. Don, who began talking fast in Spanish. Chick studied Lázaro to guess at what was being said. "*Sí*," Lázaro said, pushing his muffs up behind his ears, "Okay . . . *sí* . . . *sí* . . . *sí* . . ." Each time he spoke, he glanced sideways at Chick. Mr. Don appeared to be telling a long rambling story, with Lázaro listening to him like an obedient child. Chick was angry at his exclusion from the scene, and angrier still at Lázaro for his nodding, droop-shouldered, submission.

Chick thought, *Twelve dollar an hour.*

Mr. Don turned to him, and switched back into English. "Nice visiting with you. I'll see you when I see you." As the truck pulled out, he called, "And don't forget about college."

"What he say?"

Lázaro wouldn't look at him, directly. "He say we go to his yard at eight in the morning, or he talk to friend he know in INS."

"He shitting you, man. Guy do bad stuff. Guy do asbestos. He no talk to INS, no way."

"He know where we live, on Greenwood."

"He tell you crock-of-shit story to scare your bones."

"Is not we." Lázaro gazed at the ground as if a secret was buried there. "Is you and he."

"Tell you what. Here's the deal. Thirteen dollar. I pay thirteen dollar an hour." Chick held out his hand and put on his grinning, management face, like the boss in the Men's Wearhouse commercials. "I guarantee it."

Lázaro's hands stayed locked in his jeans pockets. He shook his head. "That guy—what he say, he do."

They brought down the remainder of the tree, Lázaro handling the chain-saw. By the time they'd piled the two trucks high with logs, the afternoon was darkening into chilly night, and lights were coming on in all the houses. They left the boughs on the lawn, in sawdust deep as a dirty fall of snow. When the old woman came out, Chick forestalled her complaints by waving his hand dismissively at the mess. "Yard waste," he said, taking hold of one of the smaller boughs as if he were about to haul it off. But once he had the $500 in his hand, he dropped the bough where it stood and walked to his truck.

They drove in convoy to the wood lot on Rainier, Lázaro riding with Chick. Gridlocked in the rush-hour traffic around Mercer, Chick said, "Okay, you and Ernesto, you go with him. Jesús, and Dany, and Victor, and Sandro, they go with me."

"He say everybody go with him."

"You crazy, man. Work make you sick. He pay shit."

Lázaro sat low and crumpled in the seat. His big hands, criss-crossed with bloody scratches, were spread wide on his knees. "Sorry, Chick."

"Why you sorry?"

Lázaro sighed. "No only me I look out for. I got wife. I got kid."

"Hey," Chick snickered, leaning across to lightly slap Lázaro's knee. "Nobody perfect!"

"When's my dad going to be here?"

"Soon."

Face pressed to the glass, Finn looked out into the dark and watched the snow. The tiny flakes, far apart, were darting every which way like fish in a tank. Many of the flakes appeared to be falling upwards, as if the sky was sucking them back from the ground. As soon as they touched the railing of the balcony, they turned into boring raindrops. Squinching his eyes tight, concentrating as hard as he knew how, Finn willed the world otherwise. The snowflakes grew plump and feathery, whitening the darkness outside, settling on the city in drifts and hillocks, turning cars on the streets into bulgy, ghostlike shapes. They'd have to close the schools. You could build a snowman right in the middle of the road, and make snow angels. There'd be just kids out there, snowball fights and sleds, and the soft crunch of snow under your shoes. And it was all so very nearly happening.

"I think it's sticking."

"I don't think so, pumpkin. It's not cold enough for it to stick."

"But it will be. It'll stick in the night. When we get up tomorrow, we'll have tons and tons of snow."

"It's not in the forecast."

"You don't know everything."

"No, but I don't want you to get your hopes up and then be disappointed in the morning." His mom came over to the window. "It's hardly even what you'd call sleet."

"It's snow." Finn felt her hand in his hair. If he could make her believe in it too, it would happen. "Look over there. You can see it's snow." But he heard the whine of doubt in his own voice, and seemed now to be looking out the window through his mom's eyes, seeing what she saw: smuts of gray ice, melting into rain. It wasn't fair. She was spoiling everything. Without his mom there, Finn was certain there'd be proper snow.

The ding-dong doorphone chimed, and Finn charged across the room to answer it. "Daddy?" Everybody who came to the building sounded like a twangy space alien, and his dad's deep, crackly "Finbow!" came in from like Mars, or Jupiter. He pressed the button and let himself out of the apartment to wait by the elevator doors.

He flattened himself against the wall, so his dad wouldn't see him, and listened to the sighs and groans that rose from deep inside the shaft. He heard laughter from a lower floor, but it wasn't his dad's. With an elevator, you never knew quite who was coming, and had to be prepared for surprises.

When his father stepped out of the cage, he seemed unsure about which way to go. "Here I am!" Finn shouted, launching himself like a flying dog. Hugging Finn tight, his dad gave him a rough bristly kiss. Finn quickly squirmed away, wiping his mouth with the back of his hand. His dad smelled all wrong, like he was somebody else. His breath came out of him in moldy gusts that made Finn think of burned bacon and cat pee and dead flowers.

"Oh, Finn—I've missed you."

"I missed you too," Finn said, in a small, hurried voice. He was staring at his dad's lips, which always looked bigger than other grown-ups', but never so big as now. They were patterned with hundreds and hundreds of tiny criss-cross lines, like the wrinkly skins of the banana slugs who lived in a mason jar in the Skylight Room. Finn didn't want to kiss those lips. Beginning to panic, he buried his face in the long damp coat, feeling his dad's hands on his shoulders, holding him close. But the sense of strangeness wouldn't go. The sour, old-man smell was in his clothes, too. Something was happening to his dad, Finn didn't know what, but he suddenly wanted to be back in the apartment with his mom.

Inside, Finn watched and listened intently while pretending to gaze out the window at the snow.

"You look better than I expected, " his mom said. "You've got your color back, at least. How is it?"

"How do you think it is?" His dad sounded cross. He sat down in the couch, still wearing his black overcoat. "Of course it's not uninteresting. I don't quite know how I'd rate it as an experience, though. Somewhere between major dental surgery and winning a free weekend in Grozny or Kosovo."

"You're cleared now?"

"It's rather hard to tell. I think so. Well, I think so most of the time, when I'm not going through bouts of howling paranoia."

"Vooze avay voo le jon-darm on core?"

Finn really hated it when his mom spoke French.

"Yes. A couple of days ago. I like him, actually. He's a good egg. Except that he says he writes screenplays, and I have a horrible feeling he's going to ask me to read one."

"Eh lonfon? Laperteet fee yet?"

"Zilch. Disparoo sawn trass."

"Can you imagine what they must be going through?"

He saw his dad's eyes swerve over to him, then move quickly away. "Yes, I can."

They were talking bad stuff, in special voices, not wanting him to be there. Finn didn't know exactly how people had a divorce, but he thought his mom and dad might be having one right now. There was something dangerous and secret going on, like they were getting ready for a big shouting fight and he'd have to hide.

Then things seemed to get more normal. After phoning for pizza, his mom said that the only wine she had was weeks old, but she got it out of the fridge. His dad tasted it, said it had gone to vinegar, and drank it anyway. When Finn looked out the window, he couldn't see a single speck of white in the rain.

"It won't snow tonight, Finbow. The temperature's getting warmer. This is the beginning of the Pineapple Express."

"What's the Pineapple Express?"

"It's hot wet air blowing up here all the way from Hawaii, where they grow pineapples. It brings high temperatures and heavy rain."

"I want the Snow Express."

"Well, you'll need a cold wind from the northwest, blowing across the ocean from Russia and Alaska. The north wind doth blow, and we shall have snow . . ."

"And what will poor Robin do then, poor thing? With his head up his ass and his mouth full of glass, he'll have to shit out of his wing, poor thing."

"Finn! Where did you learn that?"

"In pre-school. With his head up his ass—"

"All right. Once was quite enough, thank you."

When they sat down at the table to eat pizza, his dad asked him boring questions about Treetops and what he'd been doing. That stuff wasn't interesting to talk about, and he'd forgotten most of it; besides, it was *over*. But his dad went on at him like he had to remember every stupid thing, which he wouldn't want to even if he could. "I don't know," he said, or "It was okay." He was actually relieved when his mom began to talk, in French, about "la fair Sammamish".

"I don't think so," his dad said. "It was a very momentary brush with celebrity. That sketch must have been on screen for all of ten seconds."

"What are you talking about?"

"Oh, nothing, Finbow. Just a silly picture of someone I saw on TV."

Later, when his dad was in the bathroom, Finn whispered, "My dad smells funny."

"I know. He's been smoking those stinky cigarettes again."

"Is he going to die? Spencer's grandma died. She died of cigarettes. She smoked fifty cigarettes in one single day."

"Don't worry, pumpkin—he'll stop. We'll tell him to."

When his dad came back, Finn said: "You got to stop smoking cigarettes, or you'll die."

His dad looked not at him but at his mother. "What's this—the maternal propaganda machine?"

"He brought it up, not me."

They stared at each other across the table. Finn could hear them both breathing. If anybody said anything, he thought, it was going to be something really mean. He waited, looking from face to face. At last his dad stretched out his arm to Finn and said, "You're right. It's stupid. I won't do it anymore."

But Finn wasn't sure he could trust him. It sounded like he was just saying it.

"My friend Spencer, his grandma, she died. Her lungs went black and got all shriveled, and then she went to the hospital and died. They had to burn her up. Then they had a big party and made Spencer wear a tie."

"That's so sad," his mom said.

"I don't think they were sad." He tried to remember what Spencer had said. "I think they had fun."

"Well, I expect Spencer's grandma is in heaven now."

"No she isn't. She's in a jar. They put her in a jar and buried it in the ground. That was after they burned her and there wasn't nothing of her left, except white ashy stuff. She didn't hardly fill a little jar."

"That's pretty interesting, Finbow."

"She was rather old, anyway. Can I have ice-cream?"

At bedtime, his dad took charge and started a new Mister Wicked story when he was still in the bath. As was his wont, Mister Wicked was reading the classifieds in the *Seattle Post-Intelligencer,* where he spotted an ad for an old Washington State ferry, really cheap at $99.99. Neither Mister Wicked nor Moira knew how to drive a ship, so they had a few accidents.

The story continued in bed, but Finn was only half-listening, distracted by the cigarette-smell and by the strangeness of being with his dad in the condo.

". . .'You loony old fool!' Moira shouted. 'Look what you've done now, you nincompoop! You dunderhead! You great galumphing lummox!'"

"Are you going to live here now?"

"What? No, Finbow, I'm just visiting this evening."

"You could sleep in my mom's bed."

"That's not an option."

"You can sleep in my bed, if you want. I don't care."

"Thank you." His dad kissed him on the forehead. "But not tonight. After you're asleep, I'm going back to our house on the hill."

"Okay." Finn felt sort of relieved: he didn't really want that smell in his bed all night. When his dad went on with the story, he soon lost track, imagining himself somewhere else—not in the condo, not in the house on the hill, but in some place snowy, like up in the mountains, where the snow was so deep that whole houses got buried underneath, and every tree was pure white. When he closed his eyes, he saw the dazzle of it, like glittering sugar, stretching all around him as far as he could see. Beside the deep purple shadows of his own footprints marched the smaller, shallower pawprints of his dog—whose name changed from dream to dream, and who sometimes had no name at all. With his tail like a tall black flag against the glaring white, the dog plunged ahead, throwing up exploding puffs of snow, but stopping every few moments to check on him. The dog was super-smart: he knew tons of stuff, and he was really, really kind. When Finn got tired, he and the dog would build an igloo. They'd snuggle together inside their snow-house, and the dog would keep him warm.

"Debra, I can't come up. Finn's already asleep. And no, I don't think Tom has a clue about what's happening to him. He was talking about his 'ten seconds of fame.' I mean, it's all over the fucking city. You know what he said about the detective on his case? 'He's a good egg.' Can you imagine? It's what Brits do for character analysis, you know? He's a good egg. Or a bad egg. They're subtle that way. That's why none of them believe in therapy—they do the egg thing instead. Why they went to war with Hitler? He was a bad egg. Like this detective's a good one. Jesus! No wonder he can't process. That's always been Tom's problem, he just can't process . . ."

Then she remembered to ask: "How's the column coming?"

The only message on the answering machine said: "Okay, I got that number. I'll call him right back. Yes? Oh. Paul Nagel, King County Sheriff's Office. Message for Thomas Janeway. Sorry about that article in the *Stranger*. Yeah—I'm talking to his voice-mail right now. Thomas? Uh, about that article. I wanted you to know that if it came out of this department, it didn't come from me. But my guess is that those god-damn kids figured it out for themselves, and futzed it up, like the media always does. Anyway, like I said, I'm sorry, and our media-relations officer will make a clarifying statement. Feel free to call if you've got any questions." The terminal click was followed by a mechanical soprano voice saying, "Wed-nez-day. Ten. Forty. Seven. A. M. End of. Final Message."

When Tom tried to type into the address bar on the computer monitor, his fingers seemed to have drifted out of contact with his brain. He got *wsw, wwe,* and *wqw* before he managed to get even the *w*'s in line. The site took a maddeningly long while to assemble itself on the screen, in shivering bricks of text and picture that eventually resolved into the police artist's sketch, alongside the old Jerry Bauer photo from the dustjacket of *The Few,* and a caption in thick black letters designed to resemble prison bars: BURDEN OF PROF. The table of contents added a subtitle: *In Search for Missing Child, Finger of Suspicion Points to Famed UW Writing Teacher.*

"Oh my Christ."

He clicked on the link. Behind the arrow and hourglass, the pixels reconfigured into yet another photograph, in rather poor focus, showing Tom apparently caught in the act of burgling his own house. A tubby figure in a long coat, bent forward in a posture of clownish stealth, was in the middle of taking a giant step across the deck to the front door—an image utterly incomprehensible to him. Had they faked it in a photo-lab? Then he realized they'd snapped him unawares while he negotiated the joists of the unplanked deck, stepping high to clear the cat's-cradle of Chick's red tape. But in this context he might as well have held a pistol in one hand and toted a sack of swag over the shoulder of his villain's overcoat.

He scrolled through the text that ran beside the picture, vile phrases jumping out at him from the cascade of moving type. *UW's Euro-weirdo po-mo writing prof with a regular spot on NPR's "All Things Considered."* Christ! *Pretentious*—that was an unnamed student speaking, and here was *pompous* from another. *Labored Victorian parodies . . . Known to favor female students with uninvited extracurricular attention.* That was outrageous; they couldn't say that, he'd bloody sue them. Somehow they'd got hold of his never-used second name, Bódog, which they translated as Lucky, and used in the next bold subhead: **Lucky Tom.** Impudent bastards.

Suspect.

Two-year manhunt for Sammamish slayer.

Suspect again.

. . . . behind his affected manner . . .

Nothing in his experience came near to preparing Tom for this, and the sheer appalling novelty of it made him giddy. Only in fantasy could he find even a remote precedent. On transatlantic flights, after the tepid dinner and second miniature of brandy, all blinds pulled down for the movie and the light from the overhead reading lamp splashed meagerly on his open book, Tom regularly imagined that the washing-machine churn of the engines would suddenly be interrupted by the captain's voice over the intercom, saying, in the laid-back midwestern drawl of his trade, "Ladies and gentlemen, I regret to inform you that the aircraft has developed a serious mechanical problem. Please immediately adopt the braced position, as shown in the card in the seat-pocket in front of you, and say your prayers. God bless all of us. Thank you." This was somewhat like that, except that this couldn't be banished by returning to one's book. This was—as it were—*it.*

. . . behavior students characterize as "inscrutable."

Frantically scrabbling through the contents of his wallet, spilling over the floor, he found Nagel's business card and dialled the number. The detective answered on the first ring.

"This is insane," Tom said. "It's insane beyond belief."

"These things happen with the media," Nagel said, sounding much like the airline pilot. "It's an unfortunate development for you, of course, but we've issued a statement, which is all we can do."

"Who did you issue it to? What does it say?"

"Hang on, I'll bring it up on my screen . . ."

On his own screen, Tom read: *One clue may lie in the Victorian Lit course that Prof. Janeway taught two years ago. The reading list for that course includes* The Strange Case of Dr. Jekyll and Mr. Hyde *by noted Brit author of the 1800s, Robert Lewis Stephenson . . .*

"Okay. I got it here. It's short. I'll read it to you. 'King County Sheriff's Department wishes to make it clear that, contrary to allegations in local media, Thomas Bódog Janeway is not considered a suspect in the disappearance of Hayley Jane Topolski (6), although he remains a person of interest in the continuing investigation.' I can e-mail it to you if you want."

"*Although?* What do you mean—*although?*"

"I'm not following you, Thomas."

"It's an adversative conjunction! It means that whatever you said before, you're taking it away, or taking part of it away, or modifying it. That bloody *although* means, 'He's not a suspect, *but,*' and it's the *but* that everybody hears, not the *not*. Don't you see? Anyone who reads this libellous shit in the *Stranger* is going to think, 'Well, of course he's a suspect really—they just haven't got enough evidence on him yet.' You have to change that statement. Right now, before it gets around. Instead of the *although,* you need a full stop, I mean a period, and—"

"You have an issue with the grammar."

"It's not just grammar—it's the whole implication of the thing."

"What it says, Professor, is that you are not considered a suspect."

"*Although.* Not just *but,* but *although,* which is even worse."

"It could've said 'is not yet considered a suspect,' or 'is not considered a suspect at this point in time,' That's commonly used terminology in statements like this, but in your case we made the decision not to use it. Because of that *Stranger* article. Because this department is being proactive in counteracting a false impression created in the media."

"*Person of interest!*"

"Yeah. That wasn't my call. That was like a departmental decision. If it was down to me, I'd most likely said *witness.* It's a fine line. We're dealing with bureaucracy here, and the question went all the way up to the sheriff."

"It's just another way of saying *suspect!*"

Tom heard slow breathing coming down the line. Not friendly.

"A person of interest is a person of interest. Means we may need to talk to them further. Means there could be still things we got to find out about them. Means—"

"What words mean is what people think they mean, and what people think *person of interest* means is *suspect!*"

"I'm a reasonably patient guy, Professor. I got a low metabolism. I don't blow easy. But talking with you now, I'm beginning to see what those creeps at the *Stranger* are getting at."

"You don't understand. I'm sorry, but I'm just trying to explain that language is what we—"

"This department has gone out of its way—way out of its way—to accommodate you in your concerns, Thomas. Soon as that article appeared, before it's on the street, even, we issued a statement. A factual statement. A statement that says you're not regarded as a suspect. Now you tell me we got a comma where we ought to have a period, and *person of interest* doesn't mean 'person of interest,' it means 'suspect.' We're not in your composition class. Professor. We're not asking you to *critique* our goddamn statement. Are you hearing me?"

"But how am I supposed to *live* with this?" Tom's voice was cracking. "I mean, my whole *reputation*."

"A little girl has gone missing. We're in the middle of a criminal investigation. Probably—though I hate to say this, and don't quote me on it—a homicide investigation. And you seriously think, pardon my French, that this department gives a rat's ass about your personal self-esteem?"

7.

A visored biker in damson-colored leathers delivered the cellophane-sheathed envelope from—Tom read as he signed for it—the Department of English, University of Washington. Only urgent Shiva Ray business could possibly account for the extravagance of a messenger service, and while the letter inside did indeed mention Shiva, he was not its main subject.

Dear Tom,

It falls to me—regretfully—to let you know that an emergency departmental meeting was held this morning, at which it was resolved that under present circumstances your presence in the classroom would prove a "distraction," and that you should therefore be placed on temporary paid leave of absence.

Allow me to tell you (in confidence) that this motion was passed by just one vote, and that I was not myself in the majority. In fact, I argued as strongly as was within my power that any such action would be in violation of your basic civil rights, and that it would bring discredit on the department and on the university. However, my voice was not, alas, heeded.

My thoughts, as well as those of many of your colleagues in the department, are with you at this difficult time. I hope very much indeed that you will be able to return to the classroom in a matter of weeks, if not days. Your courses here are highly regarded by students (pace the obnoxious screed in the Stranger*), and your teaching will be widely missed for the duration of your absence.*

If I may put some positive "spin" on this unfortunate affair, it may be that you can use this period of leisure to tie up the loose ends of the Ray Foundation Fellowship arrangements (have you spoken to him lately?), as well as to make progress on your (long-awaited!) next book.

Cordially yours,

The signature looked like a small explosive device trailing a long fuse. Below it was a translation: *Bernard S. Goldblatt, Chair, Department of English.*

And chair, Tom thought bitterly, was a good word for plump, bland, velveteen-upholstered Bernard, though banquette would have been better, since he could comfortably accommodate so many people at one sitting. *Argued as strongly as was within my power* would mean that he'd let out a mild whinny of surprise, as when the Milton course was dropped from the core undergraduate syllabus. The evident distress in his letter surely arose from the embarrassment of having to write it, not from any principled unhappiness with the motion. *Violation of civil rights* wasn't at all Bernard's line of country; that question would have been raised by political types like Russ Van Strand and Greg Weems, both of whom would have pitched in energetically on Tom's behalf. Typical of Bernard to slyly claim for himself any available kudos, after presiding over the vote with the expression of mild, studied quizzicality intended to make you see his shallows as ironic depths. As a graduate student, Bernard had spent a year at Oxford, where his chief academic acquisition, Tom suspected, had been that Gioconda smile.

Bernard wouldn't have lifted a finger. He was certain of it.

Tom thought vengefully of his fogeyish edition of the poems of Gray and Collins, which a *PMLA* reviewer had praised as the "indispensable" successor to the Austin Lane Poole edition of 1917. "Editions" were Bernard's specialty: he was a besotted collector of books with a mild, touristic interest in their contents. Tom thought of his curly silver hairpiece, and his addiction to the tag *mutatis mutandis*—which he no doubt trotted out after counting the hands raised around the table. Feeble, ingratiating, fraudulent Bernard!

Was he in fact the architect of this whole thing? Tom wouldn't put it past him. He would've seen the *Stranger*, panicked, called a meeting . . . No, that would have been out of character, for Goldblatt had never instigated anything: he'd waited to see which way the wind was blowing, then gone with the wind. Behind his cowardly letter, Tom detected the shadows of those perennial callers of emergency meetings, Lorraine Cole and Yolanda Bunche, who'd had it in for him ever since he first arrived. Having backed Camilla Taruk Sanchez for the Weyerhaeuser job, they'd always treated Tom as an illegitimate pretender. The *Stranger* article gave them the chance they'd been waiting for, and gutless Bernard would've played along, as was his bloody wont.

He looked out longingly across the water to the great glass eyesore that hid the Klondike building from view, and had the phone in hand before he heard, in vivid premonition, the weary flatness of Beth's tone when she recognized his voice. He hung up without dialing.

If only he had Finn—but he could imagine all too well the stares at Treetops, and the principal calling Beth, "just to make sure it was all right" for Finn to go off with his father. Tom knew he wasn't man enough to brave such gross humiliation.

It occurred to him that it was nearly three in the afternoon, and he'd eaten nothing all day. On his way down to the kitchen, passing the new window on the stairs, he saw a car drawn up behind his VW, and two pale moonlike faces gazing out, clearly hoping to catch a glimpse of the man who was not regarded as a suspect. He shrank into the shadows, a fugitive in his own house.

The fridge was bare. He found two elderly eggs, a single stick of butter, the hollowed remnant of a pint tub of mint chocolate-chip ice-cream, a cracked nub of parmesan, three cartons of yogurt, all past their sell-by dates, one Jell-O chocolate pudding, a doubtful package of Bunny-Luv baby carrots, along with a hefty mass of decaying organic matter, much of it rotted beyond recognition. Tom ate an eccentric lunch, then went on to the Internet. After visiting the BBC and downloading the *Guardian* crossword, he found himself prowling the aisles of HomeGrocer.com, where he aroused no curiosity as he loaded up his trolley with enough supplies to see him through a lengthy blockade. With no neighbors to dodge in the produce section, no check-out girl who'd once babysat for Finn, the online store was a haven of solitude and leisure. He enjoyed the luxury of indecision, picking up items and putting them back again. Camembert or Brie? Or both? He settled for both. In a surge of bright optimism, he laid in Froot Loops and Apple Jacks, Gold Fish and Triscuits (and to hell with blue-green algae and Beth's crackpot diet). He lingered in the wine department among the Oregon Pinot Noirs, finally choosing three bottles of Ken Wright and three of Cristom. All in all, Tom spent an hour at HomeGrocer, his most nearly happy hour in recent memory.

He had become—as he put it in a tart e-mail to Beth—a virtual Alexander Selkirk. Downstairs, all the curtains were drawn against snoopers. Encouraged by his grocery shopping, he'd moved on to MyLackey.com. His uniformed lackey had arrived in a primrose-yellow van, bearing copies of Fanny Trollope's *Domestic Manners of the Americans* and Franz Kafka's *The Trial* from the Elliott Bay Book Company, a bottle of Teacher's from the liquor store, nicotine chewing gum from Bartell's, and, from Blockbuster, videotapes of *Double Indemnity, Sunset Boulevard, The Apartment, The Fortune Cookie,* and *The Lost Weekend.*

The lackey—who looked barely old enough to have bought the whisky on Tom's behalf—had to go around to the back door to make his delivery, where he seemed determined to keep his distance. Tom signed his form, thanked him, tipped him ten bucks and, trying to break the ice, asked him how things were going.

"Going okay."

"And you're quite comfortable with your job-title?"

"What?"

"You know, 'lackey.'"

"It's fine. We get stock options," he said, then fled.

Selkirk, marooned on Juan Fernandez Island in the South Pacific, was said to have occupied his first weeks of isolation by carving his name on trees. Tom wrote e-mails—to the president of the University of Washington, to the editor of the *Stranger,* to the King County sheriff. Though the emphases in each message were different, the theme was the same: Tom had taken an innocent walk along a much-frequented public footpath—no, "trail"—and by "mere contingency" had passed the scene of a child's tragic disappearance. No one had seriously suggested that he had spoken to, much less abducted, that child. So far as he understood, the only thing that distinguished him from other hikers was the fact that he had been seen to smoke cigarettes ("an unwise habit, but not as yet a criminal one") and, naturally, that he resembled himself and no one else. For this, he had been vilified in the press, had lost—even if temporarily, and with pay—the job which had brought him here from England, and been rendered an object of public contumely and derision. His house was under siege, his family life thrown into chaos. He had, so he wrote, come to this country as an immigrant, inspired by the Jeffersonian ideal of life, liberty, and the pursuit of happiness, and was now seeing these inalienable rights alienated beyond likely hope of recall. As the father of a young child, he, too, grieved over the fate of Hayley Topolski, and had willingly assisted the police as much as he could. Yet as an immigrant, and as a student of America, he was shocked to learn how very fragile was the essential framework of fairness and decency on which he had always believed this country was founded.

There were rather too many grandiloquent flourishes, he feared; and as he finished each letter—sharpening the phrasing with every successive message—he filed it in Drafts, for later revision. While writing, he had to hang up on three anonymous callers; and once, from the bathroom, he saw another carload of looky-loos drawn up outside the house.

Surprised by the spring in his step as he went back up to the study, Tom realized how strangely energized he'd become by the drama of this situation. Far from the blank depression and despairing languor he was expecting, there was a liberating fizz of adrenalin in his blood, and he felt a couple of stiff drinks above-par. The keyboard was calling: there was work to be done.

Writing about war in *The Few,* Tom had often teased himself with the question: how did soldiers *do* it? Did they brush their teeth out of automatic habit on the eve of battle? How did they manage to get a wink of sleep? If Tom himself ever had to face the rockets' red glare and bombs bursting in air, he was pretty sure that his bowels would give way and that he'd cower in a whimpering heap, waiting for the bullet with his name on it. Yet the most ordinarily timid people were called up to fight and some came back covered with decorations, like his history master at Ilford, a gentle, snuffly man, like a tame hedgehog, who'd won a Military Cross for outstanding bravery at Anzio. How had old Willy Wadsworth done it? Come to that, how had Tom's parents made their flight—with his infant self in tow—from Budapest in '56? That was another mystery, for his parents clammed up whenever he raised the subject.

Tom knew nothing first-hand about life under duress, or how you survived it. There was the delivery room at Swedish Hospital when Finn was born, but he'd only been a squeamish and alarmed spectator there. Doing finals at Sussex? Hardly. That afternoon at Golden Gardens was the nearest he'd come—but only for ten minutes, which in truth probably lasted no more than four or five. Now, though, he was undergoing an experience that gave him at least an inkling of what it might be like to be at war, and he felt quite unexpectedly buoyant. It was a bit like being in the school play: disguised from yourself, as from everyone else, by a protective layer of pancake make-up, you could unashamedly kiss the girl before an audience full of teachers and parents—or shoot the enemy, bang-bang, with a real gun.

He tidied up his drafts and launched them into cyberspace. Still in an avid writing mood, he retrieved ALIENS.doc, finished the piece in a fluent twenty-minute burst, and sent it to Miriam in D.C. with a covering message that asked her to call when she had a spare moment. He uncorked a bottle of Cristom's Mt. Jefferson Cuvée, put together an asparagus omelette, sat down to lunch with *The Trial*—a book he hadn't looked at in more than twenty years—and prepared himself for a long and dullish slog. That someone must have been telling lies about Joseph K. had become a line so famous that it had taken on the irritating power of a billboard slogan seen many times too often on a freeway. Yet six pages in, to his great surprise, Tom found himself laughing aloud.

*　　　*　　　*

When the churring doorbell broke into the scene in the cathedral, he didn't answer it. It rang again, but he kept his eyes firmly on the printed page. Then whoever was perched outside on the joists began knocking. Tom crept on tiptoe in his socks to the front door, where he crouched down on his haunches and prised open the letter-slot. All he could see was the front of some wrinkled trousers, then there was a blur of gray flannel, and the trousers gave way to a pair of staring eyes.

"Sorry—am I calling at a bad time? I was taking the dog for a walk, and just happened to be passing . . ."

It took him a moment to connect the voice with Ian Tatchell. "Well, if you've got Engels with you, you'd better go around the back."

When Tom opened the kitchen door, Engels—grizzled now, and noticeably lame—lolloped gamely inside to explore his old haunts, if his memory went back that far. Since Beth had pronounced Engels "not good with Finn," even less had been seen of the Tatchells.

"New deck, I see," Ian said. He was wearing a green, vaguely Tyrolean hat, and carried the stick that had appeared during his first attack of gout.

"Well, bits of a new deck, at least. What can I offer you—wine? Scotch?"

Tatchell made a show of consulting his watch. "Oh, I think it's a shade on the early side for me. Actually, I lied. I'm here under strict orders. Sarah says that unless I can collar you for supper at our place tonight, I'm going to find myself eating take-out macaroni cheese from Ken's. So please don't think for a moment that I give a shit about your welfare. This is pure self-interest."

So poorly did a dinner invitation fit with Tom's current conception of himself as an outcast that he felt obliged to turn it down. "Do thank Sarah, of course, but—"

"Oh, don't be such a stick. Bloody come."

"Well, put like that . . ."

"Have you ever tasted Ken's fucking macaroni cheese?"

"Your dad did something bad." Spencer was washing his hands in the sink of the boys' bathroom.

"He did not."

"Did too."

"Did not!"

"He did. It said in the paper. Your dad—he had his picture in the paper, 'cause he done bad stuff. My mom said not to tell."

Catching sight of Spencer's face in the mirror, Finn was shocked by its seriousness. "Not true!" he bellowed. "You're telling lies again, Spencer! I'm warning you!"

"Am not. I saw your dad's picture. In the paper. He did something bad with a kid—"

Finn flung himself forward, knocking him down. He didn't exactly know how to fight, but he'd watched dogs do it, and he went for Spencer like a dog, growling, clawing, biting. He couldn't really see what he was doing because he was fighting and crying at the same time, but he got a mouthful of T-shirt and plump flesh between his teeth, and bit hard down. That made Spencer scream real good.

Later, in the principal's office, after Beth had come to take Finn home, Midge said, "I never really thought that boy was a Treetops child."

The Tatchell house on Garfield was a dislodged chunk of England marooned in the Far West. In 1988, Ian and Sarah arranged to meet Ian's parents in New York for Christmas: on December 21 the senior Tatchells flew out from Heathrow on Pan Am 103, and died over Lockerbie. So Ian, a lifelong spartan leftist, found himself in possession of the family pile in Dorset. He sold the house, but shipped its contents to Seattle. The gilt-framed Tatchell forebears—a solid, bourgeois crowd of serious women at writing desks, bewigged judges, vestmented bishops, and military men in antique uniforms that made them look like drag-queens—now shared their quarters with the likes of Gramsci, Adorno, Raymond Williams, and Ian's complete forty-year run of pastel-spined *New Left Review*s. Wherever you looked, there was an elephant's-foot wastepaper basket, or a Victorian games table, or a dress-sword hung in a scabbard on a wall. Ian had originally hoped to dispose of most of this stuff on the antiques market, but Sarah, who was from Poughkeepsie, refused to let a single object go. She, unlike Ian, knew who everybody was, and could recite the lieutenant-general's campaigns and the European travels of the lady at the writing desk.

Tom had always found these exotic fragments of England disconcerting. Between the Tatchell house in rural Dorset and his own in suburban Ilford lay a social gulf as wide, at least, as the Atlantic Ocean; and a smaller, subtler version of that gulf seemed to divide the house on Garfield from his on Tenth West. But in one respect they had an intense natural affinity: both houses brought to clean-living Queen Anne Hill an atmosphere redolent with homely English clutter and homely English dust.

Sprawled in the torn leather armchair that was missing a caster and had once belonged to the corseted Victorian general, holding a glass of rot-gut red wine (funny how the rich—and Ian was now rich beyond the dreams of most professors—clung to cheap wine as if to an ardent moral principle), Tom felt at liberty, in another country.

Sarah said, "It sounds like something out of Kafka."

"I've been reading Kafka," Tom said. "And you know something? He's just like P. G. Wodehouse. He's funny. I never got it before. Everybody knows how Kafka used to read chapters from *The Trial* aloud to his chums in Prague and crack up laughing, but I always put that down to something very weird indeed in his sense of humor. It never made me laugh. But it did this afternoon, when I saw that Joseph K. is really a first cousin to Bertie Wooster. First off, he's a whole lot richer than I bet you remembered. I thought he was meant to be an impoverished sort of clerk, but he's much grander than that. He gets invitations to swank Sunday lunches on yachts, keeps a stock of vintage brandy and a closet full of suits, and lounges about on sofas smoking cigars. The cook brings him breakfast in bed every morning. Once a week he has it off with a prostitute, and the rest of the time he's fending off respectable girls like Eleni and Fräulein Grüber. It's easy to see him as a fuddled Wodehouse bachelor, heavy on the bottle and short on the gray matter.

"In the Wodehouse version, you'd have Bertie waking up one fine morning with a king-size hangover. He rings the bell for Jeeves, who mysteriously fails to shimmer in with one of his patent tissue restorers. Instead, Bertie hears strange voices coming from the next room and gets up to investigate. The room's full of—not secret policemen, but aunts. With Aunt Agatha as the Inspector."

"And Sir Roderick Glossop," Ian said. "The ghastly Honoria Glossop would make a natural Kafka fan, by the way. When she was engaged to Bertie for two weeks, *The Trial* was probably one of the books she made him read. After she dosed him with Ruskin. 'I read solid literature till my eyes bubbled . . .' Sounds like Kafka to me."

"They were only a couple of years apart. Wodehouse, oddly enough, was the older. Perhaps they read each other? The lightest and the darkest writers in modern lit. And if there's a Wodehouse comedy in *The Trial*, Bertie's world is all set to become a Kafka nightmare."

"If it wasn't for Jeeves."

"Well, if you could smuggle Jeeves into *The Trial* for a day or two, Joseph K.'d be strumming away at 'I Lift Up My Finger and I Say Tweet-Tweet' on his banjolele."

"I wouldn't do it if I were you. You'd be put on trial for desecration."

"Of Kafka or Wodehouse?"

"Both."

"Can I have one of those?"

"I thought you'd given up."

"I did. But then I took it up again, as an experiment. Funnily enough, cigarettes seem to be the proximate cause of my getting into hot water. The reason everyone remembered me on the walk I wish I'd never taken? Because I was a smoker."

In the large kitchen, the table was laid with crested family silver. Ian passed over Tom's Ken Wright Pinot Noir in favor of a second magnum of Italian diesel fuel. Liberating the rack of lamb from the oven in a pungent gust of burned rosemary, he said, "Well, you've provided the best entertainment I can remember in ages. There's nothing that historians like better than to see their colleagues in English make utter fools of themselves. We've been quite agog."

"So you know about the emergency department meeting?"

"My dear, I've heard so much about it that I feel I was there."

"I suppose it was the women," Tom said.

"Who called the thing? No, I gather they were pretty much on your side. The whole parcel of nonsense was cooked up by the 'new men,' the my-turn-to-change-the-diapers brigade. I think they were demonstrating their solidarity with the world's children, or something. Who's that frightful little prick with the tonsure and the granny glasses?"

"Russ Van Strand?"

"Yes, that's the one. He was at the bottom of it, going around with a long Anabaptist face, and batting on about how the university's in loco parentis to its students. Sententious creep."

Russ and Emily had a son a few months younger than Finn. They'd come to supper a couple of times, and just before Christmas, Russ had talked to Tom about setting up a sleepover at their house in Wallingford.

Tom said, "I thought it would've been Lorraine Cole and Yolanda Bunche."

"An underdog's an underdog, even when it's a male underdog," Sarah said. "And if this Russ wanted to shoot himself in the foot, he couldn't have made a better job of it. In loco parentis? Why not just run up a flag in defense of patriarchy?"

"Russ Van Strand would make a rather weedy patriarch," Ian said.

"I'm astonished. I thought they hated me."

"They probably do," Sarah said. "So they'll feel doubly virtuous for taking your side."

"In this whole ridiculous business, the most interesting character seems to be your department chairman."

"Bernard?" Tom said. "He's never seen a fence he didn't want to sit on."

"Well, so I hear. But not this time. He's blown all his fuses. Impossible to get a sensible word out of him, apparently. Pop-eyed with fury, he blathers on about McCarthyism and the Dreyfus affair—and Thomas à Becket, Joan of Arc, Galileo, and Guy Fawkes, I wouldn't wonder, poor old bugger."

"Bernard?"

"Yes, so a lot of people are saying. He's turned himself into a sort of tourist attraction, like the statue that weeps real tears on Lady Day." Ian slopped more wine into his glass. "It seems that you vividly remind Bernard of his younger self. In the Sixties, at Yale, when he was coming up for tenure. Someone outed him in an anonymous letter, and there was a whispering campaign about boys—not students, just boys in New Haven. I think Bernard liked to cruise the waterfront in those days. Anyway, he didn't get tenure."

"I never heard that."

"Nobody had. That's the amazing thing. I mean, he was a fixture here when I arrived a hundred years ago, and sexless as a potted plant. He was quite roly-poly even then. Now we're landed with the revisionist Bernard, queen of the New Haven docks. It's rather hard to imagine."

"He wrote me a letter. I took it as empty guff. But he meant it?"

"Oh, yes. All this time nursing the injustice done to him by Yale, waiting for a catalyst to unburden himself of his misery—and here you are. You're providential."

"Russ went to Yale."

"There you go. The Yalie calls his stupid meeting, and something in Bernard goes pop."

"Where does Bernard live?" Sarah asked.

"In Ravenna," Tom said. "In a tiny, fussy house. A sort of settler's shack, painted blue, and furnished with eighteenth-century first editions. He's got a chihuahua." This last word was unexpectedly difficult to pronounce. After a mangled first attempt, Tom managed to lasso it, more or less, on his second.

"A maltese, in fact," Ian said. "We ran into them once on campus, and Engels mistook it for his breakfast. We haven't spoken much since."

At the sound of his name, Engels laid his long gray-mottled snout on the table and crooned dolefully at the remains of the lamb.

Tom excused himself and headed for the downstairs lavatory, but walls, door-jambs, and pieces of furniture conspired to barge into him. Once safely locked inside, he rinsed his face with cold water and blinked ferociously to bring the world back into focus. He nodded—as at old acquaintances passed in the street—at the framed Fritz the Cat cartoon by R. Crumb, the Diego Rivera print of a woman bowed into servitude by her basket of lilies, and the black-and-white photo of boys in striped caps, blazers, and white flannels, at the bottom of which "Tatchell, I.K.L., Castle House" was identified as Captain of Cricket for 1957.

Leaning forward on the toilet seat, elbows on his knees, face in his hands, Tom gave vent to a muted groan of exasperated self-mortification. If only by the law of probabilities, one had to be right sometimes. But the law also states that if a coin has come down tails for a hundred times in a row, the odds on it coming down heads on the next spin remain at fifty-fifty. For the hundred-and-first time, or so it felt, Tom had made the wrong call. Tails again. He bitterly regretted his waspish, two-sentence e-mail to Bernard Goldblatt. Wiping himself, he simultaneously performed a bloody act of assassination, exploding Russ Van Fucking Strand's silver Dodge Caravan by remote-control. As he washed his hands, his face in the mirror looked alarmingly unfamiliar: seedy, rubicund, fish-eyed.

Back in the kitchen, the air was gray with smoke, cheese and grapes had appeared on the table, accompanied by an ancestral cheese knife and an ancestral pair of grape scissors, and the Tatchells were wrangling happily about Senator John McCain, who, Sarah said, was all set to trounce George W. Bush in the New Hampshire primary.

Mindful of the law of probabilities, Tom said, "I think Bush is going to win."

At 7 A.M., Steve Litvinof's army in the Klondike building, genderless in its uniform of cargo pants and sweat shirts, was in an advanced state of combat fatigue. Many cubicles appeared empty, until one saw their occupants sprawled on the floor in sleeping bags, to which they'd retired shortly before dawn. Rumpled, slack-jawed figures in Aeron chairs nursed triple- and quadruple-shot espressos. Some peered at their screens with the baffled intentness of the snow-blind. Others chattered urgently, but hardly cogently, into their telephone headsets, for it was already nine o'clock Central Time and everyone had to keep pace with Chicago.

The site was due to open there in seven weeks and two days' time, and everything—but *everything!*—hinged on making a success of Chicago. It was the biggest city GetaShack had tackled thus far, and the first city east of the Mississippi. For the last fifteen months—which was as far back as almost anyone could remember—Steve had been saying the name Chicago as if it were the Holy Grail. The Windy City was the great test of Steve's vision of electronic metropolitan communities, founded on the universal weekend passion for snooping around other people's houses. If it played in Chicago, it would work around the globe, this marriage, surely made in heaven, between the virtual and the local.

Steve had taken San Francisco by stealth over the course of a year, moving quietly from neighborhood to neighborhood, sneaking first across the Bay Bridge into Oakland, then, weeks later, across the Golden Gate into Marin County. But buoyed by the recent surge of investment in the company, he'd promised to take Chicago by storm. On March 4, more than a hundred neighborhoods were to go online at once.

In what people now called "physical Chicago," every commuter route was punctuated with billboards that changed each week in a teasing ad campaign—this week's message was GET A . . . LIFE?—and parallel campaigns were running on local radio and TV stations. By the launch weekend, it would be hard for anyone living in the region to be unaware of the site. If San Francisco had fallen to word-of-mouth, Chicagoland would capitulate to the trumpet blasts of prime-time commercials—whose cost was going to at least double the company's burn-rate in the next quarter.

With less than two months to go, Steve was afraid they'd run smack into a wall of arrogant old-economy midwestern cynicism—"the stock-yard mentality," as he called it. Realtors were reluctant to come on board until more merchants had signed up, and merchants were holding back because of doubtful realtors. There were still several neighborhoods whose streets were entirely empty of links to click on, and many more in which you'd find only a couple of houses and a Bank of America. Worse yet, some forty neighborhoods didn't even exist—no maps, no texts, no links, no nothing.

Half the marketing department had been relocated to the Chicago Hilton. Steve himself was spending two and sometimes three days a week on Michigan Avenue, taking the midnight flight out of Sea-Tac on United, landing at O'Hare at five-thirty, drumming up business in wall-to-wall meetings through the day, then reappearing in the Seattle office at around nine o'clock the same evening, looking shattered and dangerous. He was said to fly coach.

Meanwhile, in anticipation of a triumph in Chicago, the stock rose by $21.00 in the first two weeks of January. Eleven of eighteen portfolio analysts tracked by Zacks were rating GSHK as Strong Buy, with a High Risk caveat attached. But inside the Klondike, there was none of the usual euphoria at a new hike in the stock-price; rather, the Nasdaq numbers were seen as a measure of the burden that was increasing, daily, on everybody in the building. To dampen the inflated expectations of the market now would imperil the Chicago operation, and put GetaShack.com itself in jeopardy. Pills and powders were trading freely from work-station to work-station: No-Doz, Xanax, coke, diazepam, methamphetamines, Ativan, Halcyon; uppers, downers, rollers, soothers, wakers, sleepers. The smokers' ghetto on the First Avenue sidewalk drew a dozen new regulars, as did the Mexican restaurant a couple of blocks south on Second, where the techies drank Tequila Screwdrivers at strange and antisocial hours.

The elevators began to smell of people who'd skipped their last several showers. The company masseuse now spent most of her time reading Harry Potter books in her unpatronized spa. The laziest of Steve's employees felt compelled to at least feign distracted frenzy, and were surreptitious about their visits to Priceline.com for bargain getaways to Acapulco and Honolulu.

Even Robert, Beth's assistant, seemed to have grown up fast. "It's getting to be like the Donner Party," he said. "Soon we'll have to eat our dead."

In this overcharged atmosphere, one person was entirely at ease. Suspended from Treetops, Finn roamed through Editorial like a Parisian *flâneur*, helping himself from the bowls of power bars and M&Ms, drinking from a can of chilled soda. Seven dogs lived on the floor, and he knew all their names, visiting each in turn with Milk-Bones. He hung out in the kitchen-area, where you could explode free packs of popcorn in the microwave, and played on the Ms. Pac-Man game machine. Then he drew pictures of the seven dogs on the whiteboard, with markers from the supply closet.

He really liked GetaShack. Everything was free. Nobody messed with him. Nobody yelled or got mad. He never saw anyone bossing someone around. Everybody did their own thing, like playing on their computer or talking to their friends on the phone, whatever. When they got tired, they took naps on the floor. They didn't have to ask when they went to the bathroom. They just went—and often grabbed a fistful of candy on the way back.

Looking over this labyrinth of brilliant cubicles, Finn saw a world he could admire and comprehend. He liked it best when he crouched on his haunches and could see, below the partitions, the enormous interesting disorder of disembodied legs and feet, shopping bags, shoes, slithering black cables, wastebaskets, handbags, backpacks, printers, laptops in shiny leather cases, toy robots (he mapped these carefully), sleeping dogs, and sleeping people. He watched one bare foot attached to a hairy ankle—much hairier than his dad's—that was tapping up and down on the floor. The cool thing was, he couldn't begin to guess who the foot belonged to. It had big yellow curling toenails. As he watched, the words of a song attached themselves to the movements of the foot:

Row, row, row the boat,
Gently down the stream.
Throw the teacher overboard
And listen to her scream.

Beth was everywhere and nowhere in her corner cubicle. Hyde Park was on the screen, which also framed a half-written letter to Treetops in a window. Dr. Karen Eusebio's answerphone was on her headset, Robert was signaling to her over the top of the partition, and on her lap was the hard-copy text of a piece on Wrigleyville by a *Chicago Reader* writer. Though the machine was not immediately in view, she heard the hoarse chuckle of the paper-cutter on the fax announce yet another document requiring her urgent attention. Even as she pulled an *I'm not here!* face at Robert, while asking Dr. Eusebio, in her politest Smith College voice, to call her back, Beth's mind was otherwise engaged.

Since waking at four-thirty that morning, she'd been conducting a one-sided quarrel with Debra, who the previous night had casually, even gaily, convicted Tom of offences that would send him, strapped to a gurney in the state penitentiary at Walla Walla, to a lethal injection. "Everybody says . . ." she kept on saying. Beth had hung up on her in mid-sentence, then collapsed, shuddering with sobs, on to the couch, terrified of waking Finn. For a period of seconds, she had actually imagined the gurney—first the saline drip, then the anesthetizing barbiturate, then—before anger and a proper sense of the ridiculous drove the hideous picture from her head.

How dare she?

Of course Tom was hopeless. As far out of touch with other people as he was with himself, he was like fog in human form. But for Debra to call him a psychotic predator, and to suggest that his swift incarceration was "frankly in his own best interest," was unforgiveable. It was sick.

Everybody says? That would be Debra herself, yakking to her Oroonoko friends around the water-cooler and making it sound like she'd had dinner with Ted Bundy.

A loud ping from the computer drew her attention back to the screen, where both Hyde Park and her Treetops letter had been eclipsed by a message from Steve Litvinof. Over Christmas, the techies had rigged the system so Steve could bypass the mailbox with Hot Wires that plonked themselves directly on to the screen of his victims. Outlined in large blood-red asterisks, they were headed "From Steve." When Robert saw his first Hot Wire, he nasally intoned: "For I your God am a jealous god, and thou shalt have no other gods but me."

This one read:

forest glen

i just went there and i take exception with your guy he targets wrong demographic and cool in the online environment is smart not smartass plus when i go to a neighborhood i want to visit a place not a software application i want more tactile I WANT TO SMELL IT like lakeview is strong but forest glen sucks mostly cos guy has bad case of the snoots and thats not what were about

remember we have a customer obsessed culture in this company and always ask self question do i want to buy in here? in lakeview i want to be part of that community in forest glen what i want to do is sneer

recommission and dont use guy again?

aloha steve

Beth knew Forest Glen was no good. She'd put it up only as a temporary filler for one of the many blank spaces on the map, but she ought to have known that Steve, a notorious micromanager, would instinctively sniff it out and hold it up to scorn. Maddeningly, as usual, he was right.

Like a small spider scuttling by on the extreme periphery of her vision, the thought crossed Beth's mind that when she next encountered her ex-friend in the Belgrave Pointe elevator, she'd tell her what she really thought of her dipshit fishing column.

"Hi." Finn had appeared at the entrance to her cubicle, holding in his hand a flashing, chattering, moving toy.

"Hey, pumpkin. How are you doing?"

"Good. Jason gave me this robot. To keep."

Beth couldn't quite think of who Jason was. "Cute," she said.

His mom, Finn noticed, looked like she had bruises around her eyes. She looked like a stranger.

"I'm sorry, pumpkin. I'm sorry I'm so busy."

"That's okay." He wanted to get another power bar and go see Sasha the pug.

"I'm trying as hard as I can to get you back into Treetops—maybe even tomorrow."

"I don't want to go back to Treetops. Everybody hates me."

The looky-loos, or the police, were breaking in.

A thrashing noise down by the front door was followed by a series of peremptory bangs. When Tom incautiously shifted his head on the pillow, it was as though a steel knitting needle had been driven through his skull, an inch or two above and in front of his ears. Maneuvering himself into an old bathrobe of Beth's, he was strangely weightless, his whole being distilled into the throbbing pain between his temples and a pure, thin, high-octane fury at his visitors, who by the sound of things were now ramming the door with a telephone pole. He grabbed his glasses from the bedside table.

"For Christ's sake, stop! I'm coming!"

He descended the stairs in a single movement that felt like a bungee-jump from a high bridge. In the curtained darkness, he couldn't tell if it was night or day. Flinging the front door open, he found a single blue-coated figure kneeling on the porch and hammering a nail into a plank.

"Oh. It's you."

It was neither night nor day. The streetlamp showed as a fuzzy corona in the saturated air. Under the hood of his gleaming anorak, Chick's upturned face was pale and owlish, the features indistinct in the half-light.

"Hi—how ya doin'?" There was a warning absence of inflection in the contractor's voice.

"I left messages for you, on your pager. I drove around looking for you."

"Yeah." Chick banged home another nail, and it could hardly have hurt more than if he'd pounded it directly into Tom's frontal lobe. "Been flying around like a fart in a whirlwind."

Again the voice was flat, whispery and, to Tom's ear, laden with rancour. "I'm glad to see you."

"It's not a problem." His hammer was raised.

Tom squinched his eyes shut in preparation for the blow, and said, "Lázaro and the others? Not here today?"

The contractor stared at him. Tom had seen as much human warmth in the eyes of the Komodo dragons in Woodland Park Zoo.

"Not here today." The phrase came back with a mocking echo of Tom's question still attached to it.

"Look, I'm sorry about the other night. I was in a panic. It was quite unnecess—"

"A *panic*," Chick said, with a distinct note of interest.

"Yes. Panic. It's when . . ." With his Wooster-sized hangover, Tom was not of much use as a dictionary. "When you get irrationally frightened about something." Now he'd have to explain *irrationally*. He was on the verge of doing so when a weird smile, not friendly, spread across Chick's face, and Tom saw himself in the smile: his limbs sticking out like a giant's from the tiny bathrobe, the stink of stale alcohol and night-sweat on him, his ash-gray wilderness of hair.

In self-defense he said, "I need to make some coffee. Do you want some?"

"No coffee." Chick picked up the *New York Times* from the edge of the deck, rose to his feet, and handed the paper to Tom. "Please—I go toilet. Gotta make a dump."

In the kitchen, spooning coffee with an unsteady hand into the filter-basket, Tom heard the sound of rushing water overhead. Was Chick taking a bath up there? He shook the newspaper from its blue plastic sheath and tried to read, the print wobbling in and out of focus. Even familiar words looked strange and misspelled. It was voting-day in the New Hampshire primary. By the end of the second paragraph, he had to start over again to make any sense of the story. Then the name Seattle jumped out at him from a neighboring column. There'd been an air crash—that much, at least, he managed to glean from the swarming text, before the contractor appeared, walrus-like, the silky hairs of his moustache plastered to his upper lip. For a crapulous instant, it seemed that Chick had just escaped from the air crash.

"Sorry?" Tom said, looking up over the top of his glasses.

"Nine hundred dollar."

"What?"

"Nine hundred dollar. To finish porch."

Tom realized that Chick must have been talking to him for quite a while beforehand. Strange how time passed in a bad hangover: everything seemed to happen either in slo-mo or fast-forward, with all the normal bits left out, as in some experimental film.

"Oh—yes, of course." Conscious of having behaved badly, Tom felt that $900, which he still thought of as £450 in real money, was the least he could pay in reparation.

In excruciating slo-mo, the contractor set off on an indignant tirade about the cost of paint, as if, having come prepared for an argument, he was unwilling to be cheated out of presenting his case. There was no stopping his English now: it flowed out of him in a babbling stream of vernacular. "Totally," he kept on saying—and "gazillion" and "el ropo" and "scumbag." Tom nodded obediently. "Fuckwits!" Chick concluded, then went back to the deck to resume his mind-splitting percussions, in which he was immediately joined by a radio, turned up to full blast on a rock station. As Tom tried to disentangle the facts of the crash from the paper, he heard Eddie Vedder singing "Nothingman."

An afternoon flight from Puerto Vallarta to Seattle via San Francisco had gone down in the Pacific near Malibu. "Skies were clear," the *Times* said. The pilots had reported "mechanical difficulties," and asked permission to land at LAX, shortly before the aircraft plummeted into the sea from 17,000 feet. Tom imagined that fall. It must've taken minutes, not seconds—ample time to take stock of what was happening, and to reflect on how one had so very nearly not been on this flight at all . . . how one should really have been at home, or at work, or still lazing on the beach back in Mexico. When a plane went into free fall, how long would it take to lose consciousness? An eternity too long.

Beth had talked of taking Finn to Puerto Vallarta, "if there's a lull in the Chicago jihad."

There'd been five crew on board and eighty-three passengers. Coast Guard boats and rescue helicopters had found floating bodies but no survivors. Clergy and "grief counselors," those gruesome death professionals, had marshalled at San Francisco and Sea-Tac airports. Tom pictured going to meet Beth and Finn, only to encounter some hand-wringing, sickly-smiling, Uriah Heepish reverend. What would one say? "Not today, thank you"?

*The public address system at the airport made periodic announce-
ments that anyone waiting to meet a passenger on Flight 261
should report to a ticket agent.*

You'd probably think that you'd misheard the number. The ticket
agent wouldn't tell you anything, of course. She'd instruct you to go to a
special room, a long walk away from the counter, which would turn out
to be full of people with crumpled faces, weeping, shaking, blankly staring. But you'd have guessed by then; you'd be steeled for it. There'd
even be a kind of relief at having one's fears so extravagantly confirmed, like the patients who said "Thank you" to the doctor for telling
them they had six weeks to live. The hardest thing would be to manage
one's getaway from the grief counselor and find a private place to cry.

Either his hangover was gone or the outside world now conformed
so exactly to the symptoms that his sense of radical disconnection had
evaporated and he was back in tune with things. There was no passenger list in the *Times*. Eerily certain that he would know someone who
had died, he went upstairs, coffee in hand, to search the Internet for
more recent news, pausing on the landing to hear Chick, timing his
hammer-blows to a band of yelling banshees on the radio.

An e-mail from Miriam Glazebrook had appeared in his Inbox.

Tom,

*Thank you for "Aliens." It's timely, eloquent, and funny—and I
see no problem with length. Unfortunately, the consensus here
is that in the light of your present situation in Seattle we can't
broadcast it immediately. As you will know, KUOW is running
a pledge drive later in the month, and the station is understandably anxious not to rouse irrelevant controversy among
listeners. It would of course be impractical to broadcast the
piece on ATC with our Seattle and Tacoma member-stations
opting out. However, as soon as the situation changes, I'll
arrange a recording date with you. It's a fine piece!*

I'm very sorry about this, but I'm sure you'll understand.

Best,
Miriam

Tom surprised himself by feeling resigned—almost indifferent—to this offhand slap in the face. So he was now *persona non grata* in Washington, D.C. Where next—the *New York Post?* Fearing that he might return to brood over the wording of her message, he clicked Delete, and vanished Miriam Glazebrook from the screen.

The *Post-Intelligencer* site was full of the crash. Alaskan Airlines had named the five crew-members, but no passengers as of yet. There were articles on the safety record of the MD-80 jetliner and the probable cause of Flight 261's shocking fall from the sky. Tom read them all avidly, hungry for each new detail.

Flying scared him. He always insisted on a window seat—partly for the view, but partly so that he could keep a close eye on the rivets in the wings, lest they show signs of metal fatigue. He never slept because he couldn't rid himself of the belief that his own consciousness was a vital factor in keeping the aircraft aloft. If he nodded off, he'd wake to find the plane disintegrating in mid-air, or never wake again. So he'd sit up hollow-eyed through the night, listening for give-away rattles in the engine noise and watching the drink in his glass to ensure that it stayed absolutely on the level. At the end of a transatlantic flight, he'd leave the plane exhausted by the effort of sustaining it at its correct altitude and bringing it safely down onto the tarmac. Through the snarl of the reverse-thrust, when they arrived at Heathrow in a December fog, Beth had asked how much BA paid him for his strenuous work on their behalf. She might mock, but the death of Ian's parents in the Lockerbie crash confirmed all his fears.

He was an expert on air disasters: on long vigils between Seattle and London, Tom had dealt with terrorist bombs, engine failure, flocks of starlings in the jet-intake, fractured fuel lines, incompetent pilots, absent-minded air-traffic controllers, ice on the wings, lightning-strikes, shorts in the wiring, collisions, fires in the cargo hold, running-on-empty scenarios, instrument failure, turbulence, malfunctioning landing-gear, and forklift trucks obstructing the runway, among others. But the apparent cause of this crash—to judge by the reports of a desperate conversation between the pilots in the air and mechanics on the ground—was something to which he'd never given a thought: trim tabs. It seemed that the horizontal stabilizer attached to the tail of the aircraft had probably gotten stuck.

If a plane lost control of its horizontal stabilizer, it would have
no way to keep the nose pointed at the right angle up or down.
Gravity would force the plane into an uncontrollable dive.

Well, that made sense. In Tom's mind, the entire catastrophe boiled down to the likely fact that one fine morning somebody forgot to oil a widget.

The *Seattle Times*, the afternoon paper, had posted the latest information on its Web site, where Tom found his expected news. He *did* know someone on that flight—the *Times's* own wine correspondent, Tom Stockley, who had given a talk on Washington State wines to the faculty wine club shortly after Tom's arrival in Seattle. It was Bernard Goldblatt who'd introduced them afterwards. Tom's namesake was affable, unpretentious, and appeared to be on intimate terms with every winemaker in the Northwest. Before Finn's birth, Tom and Beth sometimes bumped into Stockley and his wife—also killed in the crash—at a small Greek restaurant on the south side of Queen Anne Hill. They were slight acquaintances, not friends, but Tom felt a short, fierce pang of sorrow for his unwitting alter ego among the dead.

Yet an unseasonable cheerfulness stole through him even as he scanned the list of victims. Beside the tumbling plane and those eighty-eight abruptly terminated lives, his own difficulties shrank to the size of a nuisance like a bout of flu or a lost credit card. It was as if the crash had set him free—free, at least, to fish out Miriam's message from the Deleted file and reread it in a state of composure. *And fuck you, too!* he thought, but with a jauntiness he never could have summoned half an hour before.

Waiting in line at the bank with a check for $1,000, he saw himself in black and white on the TV monitor: a queer-looking piece of work filmed in bird's-eye profile. Watching the screen, he rotated his head from side to side, trying to get a full-face shot so that he might look upwards and locate the hidden camera. It was only when the teller impatiently called "Next, please?" that Tom became aware of the figure he was cutting in the public eye: a person of obviously criminal aspect behaving like a loony. The reassuring thing was that no one apart from the teller appeared to be paying him any attention to him at all.

Over the din of the radio, he paid Chick off in virgin hundred-dollar bills.

"You heard about the air crash?" Tom had to shout.

"Wah? No, all that shit go to the Dumpster."

The phone was ringing. Tom took the call in the kitchen, holding his left hand over his ear to blot out Chick's horrible music.

"Thomas! I am over Washington! London to San Francisco—the polar route. You are under a cloud—"

So even Shiva Ray knew.

"One can't see a blind thing. Such a pity. Hudson's Bay was so beautiful—you know, the thrilling region of thick-ribbèd ice?"

"Measure for Measure?"

"Oh, Thomas, you're too clever for me. Always fun to talk to you. I just thought I ought to give you a bang on the pipes to ask what news?"

"There's been a plane—"

"Oh, that, yes, I heard it on the BBC. Ghastly. I can tell you that stepping aboard at LHR this morning, I did have a very slight twinge of the cobbly-wobblies, but what I meant was my fellowship."

"Well, DeLillo can't do this year, but he may be able to come in 2001. We've still got feelers out with Saul Bellow and Margaret Atwood—oh, and Roddy Doyle, too. Of course David—Dave Rice is coming over in April, which is getting awfully close—"

"Dave *Rice?*"

"Yes, you told me to invite him. In November. You'd been reading *Crystal Palace,* and—"

"Ah, yes. Dave Rice. Of course. But Thomas, do you really think he's quite big enough for us? Is he *major?*"

"Well, I only wrote to him because you were so keen to have him. He's your pigeon. We can hardly uninvite him now. Besides—"

"Yes, yes, yes, so we shall have Rice for breakfast, but not, I hope, for lunch and dinner, too. Now, what about that African chappie . . . who do I mean?"

"Wole Soyinka?"

"There you go—Woley. What about him?"

"I think of him more as a playwright than a novelist, but yes, we could certainly sound him out, if you're keen."

"I am keen. Ask him, Thomas. Ask Woley. He is major."

"Shiva—it's none of my business, of course, but I know the development office is getting a bit anxious about finalizing the arrangements, especially now that Dave Rice is very nearly with—"

An exasperated snort came down the line from seven miles up. "I tell you, *somebody* in that bloody office needs a firecracker putting up his bottom. Every time I talk to my chief financial attorney, he's still waiting for the paperwork to come back from your development wallahs. Weeks go by! Everything's there on the silly bugger's desk. We need two signatures. The trials of bureaucracy! It makes me *seethe*."

"God, Shiva, I'm so sorry. As soon as I get off the line, I'll call the department chair and get him onto it. That's terrible."

"Tell him to personally insert the firecracker. I only wish I could be there in person."

"I'll talk to them myself, if necessary."

"I wish you would, Thomas. Now, on a more pleasant topic, I have to tell you I am starting a new venture. It's all terribly hush-hush at present, but I can tell you this. It's big. It's global. And it's free. London—I was only there for twenty-four hours—simply loves it. Wall Street's positively frothing at the bit. And if you can light that firecracker and get the bumf back to me pronto, I think I shall make my gift to the UW in stock. We're talking about going public in June. I like June. It's a good month for an IPO, in my experience, and if we open at, say, 12, you can bet your bottom dollar that we'll close the day at 24. Double your money! We'll have Saul Bellow in our pocket then."

"Wonderful," Tom said, thinking that what was really needed now, and urgently, was $35,000 cash for Scott-Rice's residency—suddenly an intimidatingly larger sum than it had seemed when he allowed David to twist his arm. However, the university had obviously behaved atrociously toward Shiva, and it was up to the university to fork out now, whether or not his gift translated into instant money in the bank.

"Well, after London, I'm feeling in such a good mood that not even the sillies in your development office can put me off my stroke. I tell you, Thomas: London swooned. Ah! a gap in the clouds—"

As nearly always with Shiva Ray, the connection was lost in mid-sentence—but not before Tom picked up a distant but explicit howling at the other end of the line, accompanied by a frantic *blart-blart-blart* on a horn. Fire trucks, he thought dully, do not usually fly over Washington State at 39,000 feet.

For the next several minutes, a complicated game of pinball seemed to be going on inside Tom's head, with flippers, pop bumpers, and flashing lights. When the ball finally rolled home, he was surprised by how little surprise he felt. Shiva had never been quite real to him, and this unmasking of his unreality came as welcome confirmation that Tom's skepticism was—*pace* Beth—not always totally misplaced. He only wished he'd had the nerve to broadcast his early doubts about Shiva's merry grandiloquence. But in this city where money truly did grow on trees, Shiva Ray was no more inherently disbelievable than Jeff Bezos or Steve Litvinof or Paul Allen or Howard Schultz.

He went upstairs to write to Bernard Goldblatt, then to David Scott-Rice.

> . . . *It seems that we've all been taken for a ride by a fantasist with a cellphone. Not exactly a con man, I think, though perhaps he has a grudge against UW. I see him as an out-of-work programmer, hanging out somewhere in Silicon Valley and dreaming up "business models" for imaginary dot-coms. He probably believes in them—and may well believe that his gift to us will actually be forthcoming, if only he can hook up with the right venture capitalist and make the multi-millions that are his natural entitlement. His enthusiasm for literature, though naïve, seems genuine. He's obviously quite inventive, and I can't see any very good reason why he's not a bona-fide billionaire. It just happens that he isn't.*
>
> *I really don't believe that there are any straws to cling to here. When I heard the fire truck, I knew for certain what I've always half-suspected, though I'm afraid I've been gutless in not voicing my doubts. Our great benefactor hasn't got a bean.*

While he was writing, an e-mail from Beth arrived, headed *Fw: Finn.*

Chicago crisis means I have to pull an all-nighter here. Can you pick up Finn from the office this afternoon? See below.

"Below" was a message from Midge at Treetops.

Beth:

I spoke with Dr. Eusebio. After reviewing the special circum-
stances of the incident in the boys' bathroom yesterday, and in
light of Finn's current parental situation, we have decided to
readmit him to the Treetops community, under certain condi-
tions.

Until he starts kindergarten in September, he will remain
here on probation. In the event of another disruptive incident, I
shall have to ask you to remove him permanently, in which case
no rebate will be payable from the monthly tuition.

Thanking you for your cooperation (we do have to worry
about the other kids!!),

Midge :-)

Bafflement was Tom's first response, anger his second. He didn't know
if he was more angry with his wife or with this supposed educator,
whose bloody smiley-face richly deserved to have a fist put through it.
On balance, he decided that he was marginally more angry with Beth,
for not telling him about whatever the hell it was that had provoked this
abominable letter. He dug into the top pocket of his jacket and extracted
the bent cigarette that he'd put there at the Tatchells'.

No matches.

With the precious cigarette between his lips, he went downstairs to
light it from the gas cooker.

As he passed the front door, Chick came through it.

"Problems!" he announced with maddening complacency.

"Nothing," Finn said.

"It must have been about something, Finbow."

"Spencer's really stupid" was all he would say.

They were stalled in heavy traffic on First, just across from the
entrance to Belgrave Pointe. The interiors of stores and restaurants had
begun to glow like stage sets in the quickening dusk, and Finn's face was
turned away, toward the window of a gallery that sold expensive, inau-
thentic Indian kitsch. Beyond the floodlit display of thunderbirds,

monster-masks, painted chests, and dream-catchers stood three women, one of them profusely gesturing with her hands.

Following Finn's gaze, Tom said, "She must be the interpreter. She's using sign-language. Now you have to figure who's the deaf one, who's the customer, and who's the shopkeeper."

"That's the customer—the one in the coat. And she's the deaf one, too. She looks as deaf as a pole."

The car gained thirty yards, then stopped alongside a Korean convenience store.

"Your mom did tell me a bit about what happened at Treetops." Tom reached his arm around Finn's skinny shoulders and gave him a quick squeeze. "Thank you, Finbow."

"You're welcome."

"I love you, Finbow."

"Love you, too." But his voice was small, and his attention fixed in a pretence of interest in the Korean storekeeper, glowering over a newspaper at his empty counter.

Tom had no idea of what to say. He could not bear to think of Finn protecting him from what was being said at school. A clever father, he thought, would know how to lift this impossibly grown-up burden from his child, but in the presence of this small, tense figure gazing determinedly out of the window, Tom felt childishly helpless. "Finbow?"

"What?"

"Just . . . Finbow."

"Can you go on with the Mister Wicked story?"

So they shunted forwards, in the wake of a MyLackey van, father and son both feigning absorption in the adventures of Moira and Mister Wicked and their ferryload of kids on the high seas. Tom had a sudden, unhappy pang of *déjà vu,* thinking of himself and his own father on their Saturday-afternoon trips to Upton Park to watch West Ham. At Bell Street, they passed the cause of the jam, blazing flares illuminating a violent fusion between a jumbo pick-up and a red convertible, attended by half a dozen police vehicles and two ambulances. As a patrolman flagged them past, Finn kept up a running commentary: "It's an injury accident . . . They're pulling out the dead people . . ."

"Please, don't look."

"I can't see any blood. There'd be lots of blood, you'd think. Look, Dad! One of the dead people's talking!"

For the rest of the way home, both of them were relieved to have accidents, instead of Mister Wicked, to talk about. Finn had heard about the plane crash.

"It's really sad," he said. "But if I was on that plane, you wouldn't need to worry. I can swim."

Chick had nearly finished planking the deck. Seeing Finn, he said, "Hey, kid, where your dog?"

"He's at my mom's. We saw an accident. It was humungous. There was blood all over everybody."

"Finn—there was not!"

"There was too. I saw it."

Chick apparently misunderstood. "Maybe I make you new dog, huh?" He slapped one of the gray, vaguely-Ionic columns that supported the porch roof and said to Tom, "I see what I can do."

"Sure," Tom said, though his rotting columns were the last thing he now wanted to be reminded of. Chick claimed to have found spongy wood in three of the five, and his parting shot had been "You looking at a fat chunk of change," said with a cackle that had rung in Tom's ears all the way to the Klondike building.

That evening, Finn pulled off a string of narrow victories at Animal Snap and went to bed at eight, a tired and happy conqueror. When he was asleep, Tom slid out from under the covers and went upstairs to find an e-mail from David Scott-Rice waiting for him. It began, without salutation, "Do you honestly expect to hold me fically reponsible for your own iditic credulity?"

"Fically"? Tom checked the time of the message: 4:45 P.M. here, drunk o'clock there. Somebody ought to tell Scott-Rice to hold his pissed night thoughts in Drafts. His latest was all over the place—now belligerent, now whining, sometimes addressing Tom as a public institution, sometimes as a treacherous friend. He threatened legal action, wallowed in the miseries inflicted on him by the Inland Revenue, appealed to "our years of fighing a side by side in the tenches of Gub Street," then he threatened legal action all over again. "I shall be consuting my lawyers in the morning." Lawyers, in the plural?

Although he was referred to in one sentence as a "rat," Tom felt, on the whole, more sympathetic than not to Scott-Rice's drift. Certainly, he was owed something—if not the promised month's residency, then at least a decent fical compensation.

Dear David,
Can you let me have a shorter, more formal (and more temper-
ate) version of this? I need something that I can show to the
authorities, and I doubt if you'd want this to circulate around
the U. So far as my rodentlike character will permit, I'll do the
best I can on your behalf.
     —Tom

Chick's current berth was an eight-by-eight storage container on Nick-erson, rented ostensibly as a place to keep his tools. He thought the $75 a month extortionate, but the container had climate-control and a light socket from which he was able to run his growing collection of appliances. For a further $9.50, the storage company supplied him with a P.O. Box number and his own private mailbox.

He was doing all right. As Charles Ong Lee, he had very nearly $9,000 on deposit at the United Savings & Loan Bank on Jackson Street, where most of the tellers spoke Chinese. American was his language now, but it felt safer to confront the mystery and seriousness of money in Chinese. After a careful discussion with the banker, he'd chosen to invest his money in money—in the currencies of all the nations, as hour by hour they rose and fell in relation to one another, forever changing in value. His money-market account made his dollars seem like living things, like horses jostling for position in a race. As the banker had explained it, his money would be continuously busy, working, always growing, making profits out of losses. The dollar drops—so you make more dollars with your yen. The yen drops, there's the Deutschmark. Wolfing down a Big Mac, he took much comfort from the thought of his unwearying, industrious, ingenious money earning enough to pay for the burger in less time than he took to eat it.

He kept his bank book safely buttoned into the homemade inside pocket of his jeans. At work, he'd feel its reassuring pressure, exactly where a girl might place her hand in a caress—another thought that made him smile. But for now, money was more exciting than any girl. He'd take care of that in time, when his money had made enough money for him to buy a good one.

What Chick most needed now was Mexicans. He wasn't asking for many. Even two would be enough. Whenever he saw Mexicans aboard a truck, he followed them, and twice had made a confident, grinning approach, only to meet with incomprehension and unfriendly stares. Lázaro was too scared of Mr. Don to help him look, but told him of a place downtown where Mexicans in search of work usually hung out. There was nobody there. Every construction site and house-remodel was using Mexicans, and the river had run dry. Chick felt cheated. He wasn't greedy: two Mexicans only, and he'd be in the timber business, clearing maybe four hundred bucks a day. With no Mexicans, he'd be lucky to make $120, which over the last few weeks had come to seem dangerously close to chickenshit Mexican wages. Too small margin!

Scarcity of labor was on Chick's mind when he became aware of another overnight resident in the storage compound. An hour before dawn, his neighbor materialized into the lamplight: an older man, white, wearing a suit and necktie. His wrists were spindly, his stomach sagged, he walked like a duck. Chick thought, *$7.00 an hour,* as he sized him up from the shadows. Even this unhealthy-looking *gweilo* would be better than no help at all. Keeping out of sight, he tracked him around the block to a blue Dodge Neon—late-model, too. As soon as he was behind the wheel, the man thrust his jaw forward, blinked his eyes, and became a twenty-dollar man. Pulling away from the curb, he was like some bigshot sales-executive leaving his own gravel driveway after saying goodbye to a wife.

Next morning, Chick showed himself. The man looked through him like he wasn't there. Putting on the controlling smile he'd copied from Mr. Don, Chick took two steps forward. The man flinched, making an agitated, fluttering protest with his hands, then turned and hurried to the gate, exposing shoe-heels that had worn to bare half-moons on their off sides. Beyond the fence, he glanced quickly back through the chain-linking, and from his face you'd guess that evil spirits were after him.

Watching the shamed man scuttle away in his beggar's shoes, Chick felt pleasantly richer, like he'd just found a silver dollar in the street.

Although Treetops had never been quite high enough to justify its name, it did start life on the third floor of a commercial building on Queen

Anne that also housed a pizza restaurant, a gym, a travel agency, and a New Age book-and-crystal store. Two tenancies later, it had sunk into the basement of a Unitarian church, where the classrooms—Cypress, Sycamore, Space Needle, Olympic, and Skylight—no longer bore any relation to what could be seen from their windows, which let in so little natural light that the preschool had to be lit, all day and year-round, with power-thirsty 150-watt bulbs.

Holding Finn's hand as he walked down the steps into this subterranean world, Tom was a character in the books he'd pillaged to write *The Few;* he was Kenneth, on the run from Colditz, braving a stronghold of the Waffen S.S. with forged ID and phrase-book German. At the entrance to Skylight, he kissed Finn goodbye, aware of Spencer staring at him from behind a tower of building blocks, and of Sally acknowledging his presence with a simper and a nervous little flap of her hand.

"Have a great day, Finbow."

"Can you pick me up early? Please?" Finn's face was wan; he, too, was in enemy territory.

Tom hugged him tight. "Yes, after you've had lunch. If it's a nice day, we'll go to the zoo."

"Promise?"

"Stick a needle in my eye." He rumpled Finn's hair and abandoned him to the Nazis.

He still had to deal with the *Oberführer* in the office. Steeling himself against the interview—Beth had said it was essential to thank Midge for permitting Finn's return—Tom pretended to interest himself in the notices on the cork-board: the fund-raising auction, the breast-cancer marathon, a bassinet for sale. To these messages, he found it uncomfortably easy to append another: the ghastly composite drawing, under a headline screaming WANTED in boldface 72-point type.

When he appeared in the doorway, the principal speedily recycled a look of frank astonishment into something very like the colon-hyphen-and-parenthesis of her e-mail signature.

"I just wanted to say thanks for—"

"Well, we're glad to do what we can. And you know we're very fond of Finn. It's just that . . ."

"He did have some provocation. As I understand it, he was only trying to defend my good name."

"Spencer's mom was most upset. Quite understandably."

The words *And how do you think I fucking felt?* sprang instantly to mind, though Tom managed not to voice them. Instead, he said, "I hope she recovers."

"We'll all be keeping our fingers crossed for him," she said, in a tone that didn't even pretend to hold out much hope. "He's a very . . . creative child."

He escaped the principal's office, thinking that Beth would have handled this altogether differently. He reached the double fire-exit doors leading to the street at the same time as another departing father—one of several identically trim, close-cropped, boyish men whom Tom could never tell apart. He was already pushing on the panic-bar to swing the door outwards when the man—Scott, or Brad, or Todd—placed his hand immediately behind Tom's and said, "You first."

Thinking this a clumsy acknowledgement of his fifteen-year seniority, Tom ignored it and held the door open, waiting for the man to pass.

"No, please." The man then made a shoving, *giddy-up!* gesture with his hands.

Tom shrugged and walked up the steps. Not until he was crossing the street did he realize the insolent little bastard meant to see him safely off the premises. At the door of the VW, he turned in time to catch the guy brazenly staring from the top of the steps, a one-man neighborhood-crime-watch vigilante. Driving back to the house, riven between mortification and blind fury, Tom missed a YIELD sign and was indicted by a moss-green Range Rover with a needlessly loud horn.

Chick was waiting for him. So were five pillars he must've yanked from the jaws of a tear-down—a timber baron's mansion, circa 1900, by the look of them. Oxidized paint clung to the timber in tarry, brownish dribbles.

"How you like these guys? They good, huh?"

Beside the slender gray columns that Chick had condemned as unsound, they seemed monstrous. Cut down to fit the porch, they'd be as comically obese as five sumo wrestlers squatting in line.

Chick stroked a swollen wooden belly. "No rot! I fix him up, he be like new. I tell you, you not know your house when I done finish!"

Tom was sure that he had first found the pillars, then made up the story of the rot, but knowing was one thing, and arguing quite another.

"Cheap," Chick said. "I get for you at bargain rate."

"How much?"

"For all together, I pay"—he eyed Tom closely—"One hundred fifteen dollars."

Tom had expected a thousand or more. The figure was meaningless, really, for Chick would make his killing in labor costs, and the pillars were obviously stolen. Tom had never wanted them in the first place, yet here he was nodding his approval, smiling weakly with relief, agreeing that the damned things were spectacular value for the money.

"Your lucky day, right?" Chick laughed.

The front door had to be left open, to allow him to run the extension cords for his tools inside. The house filled with the sounds of the radio, the chain-saw, the sander, and with the resinous stench of fir. Sawdust drifted through the door and got tracked upstairs to the bathroom. The contractor could be seen in blurred outline, working in the eye of a small, sulfur-yellow tornado. Soon after eleven in the morning, it began to rain, and the dust that had settled thickly over the front yard turned to the color and texture of dirty clotted cream.

When Tom left the house, he barely recognized Chick behind his flaxen eyebrows and moustache. His rimed cheekbones made his eyes appear to be sunken even deeper than usual into his skull.

He turned off the sander. "Hey, I show you something."

Two of the gray columns had been removed from the porch. He propped one of them against the edge of the deck, then took a hammer, raised it above his head, and brought it down hard. The column snapped in two like an Italian breadstick, releasing a puff of white dust from the fracture.

"Rot. You think I shitting you."

Tom then braved the Skylight Room for the second time. Hurriedly bundling Finn into his coat, he tried to pass himself off as an average standard-issue dad whose composite picture had never been shown on TV or published in the newspapers. As they were leaving, Sally came over to murmur confidentially that Finn had had "a good day," which Tom took to mean that for once he'd failed to inflict grievous bodily harm on another child.

It was too wet for the zoo, so they settled instead for life-size papier-mâché dinosaurs at the Pacific Science Center, which was blessedly empty on this weekday afternoon. The few people who were there paid Tom no special attention, so far as he could observe: outside his immediate neighborhood, it seemed, he was becoming safely anonymous again.

Hayley's disappearance had ceased to be a news item. The blunt truth, Tom supposed, was that the Topolskis weren't sufficiently rich or photogenic to hold the wandering eye of the media for long. Had Hayley come from a lakeside mansion—had she been a JonBenet Ramsey—things would have been different, but a kid going missing from a rental bungalow in trailer-park country was a story without legs, and it had been quickly submerged under the pile of newer stories: the Greenlake rapist, the Laurelhurst axeman, the Tacoma gang killings, the cop who shot and killed a black motorist for no apparently good reason, the Sonics streaker, and the crash of Flight 261. And as Hayley Topolski slipped from public view, so did Tom Janeway. It had been ten days since he'd heard from Nagel, and he wondered if the detective, too, had wearied of the girl and moved on to a new case.

Finn was at the controls of a robotic T-rex. Blank-faced, lower lip thrust forward, he made the creature swing its huge head up toward the rafters and give vent to a dolorous, sobbing roar. Tom, sitting on the bench in the center of the gallery, put on a show of clownish terror, but Finn ignored him. The dinosaur sank back, then turned its head inquiringly at him, and roared again. This time Tom stared into the small dim-witted eyes without a smile, trying not to blink. For the longest time—a minute at least—the tyrannosaurus remained stock-still, until Finn jiggled a button and released his father from its wounded, prosecutorial gaze.

Bangers and mash—Finn's favorite supper—were on the kitchen table when Chick appeared at the back door with an expression of such sly self-satisfaction that Tom prepared himself for catastrophic news. Rivulets of dusty rain trickled from the creases of his disreputable blue coat, and his eyes went on a methodical reconnaissance of the food on the plates and the stove.

"Have you eaten yet?"

"Won't say no. Hey, kid—you wanna see something?" He reached into one of the many compartments of his coat and brought out a squirming bundle wrapped in a filthy towel.

"It's a puppy! Dad, it's a puppy! Can I pet him?"

"Sure," Chick said, and let the animal loose on the floor.

Finn was down on his hands and knees. "Doggie? Doggie, doggie, doggie? Oh, he's so cute! Dad, look!"

The thing was buff-colored, stoutly built, with vestigial legs and protruberant thyroidal eyes. A dachsund and a pug must have figured somewhere in its troubled ancestry, but other forebears came to Tom's mind, including the tree frog, the brown rat, and the pot-bellied pig. "What exactly *is* it?" he said.

"Is a dog," Chick said authoritatively. He picked it up, lifted its tail, and pointed its rear end at Tom. "Girl dog." He returned it to the floor, where Finn resumed his doggie-doggie-doggie talk in high-pitched singsong.

"Got a name. Sugar." He turned to Tom. "Like in the movie."

"Sorry?"

"Like the movie." Chick wiggled his hips about and mimed strumming a ukulele. "Sugar."

"Oh—*Some Like It Hot*."

"Yeah, the movie."

"Shooo-gar?" Finn said in his doggie voice. "Shooo-gar!"

At the stove, with his back turned, Tom shoveled sausages and potatoes on to a third plate, furious at being blindsided. "Finn, put Chick's dog down, wash your hands, and come and eat your supper." The sausages bounced from the impact when he set the contractor's plate in front of him.

"Is Sugar your doggie?"

"Your doggie now, kid."

"*Mine?* She's mine?" Finn's face fell apart from the inside outwards, eyes welling, mouth shifting shape, asymmetrically, like a red moon jellyfish. First he flung himself at the contractor, then at the puppy. "Sugar! Oh, Sugar! You're *my* dog! Daddy!"

"Well, isn't that kind of him. Chick—how much do I owe you?" He saw Chick's face assume the insulted look that he feared most, and immediately backed down. "Thanks. He's always wanted a dog . . ."

"I've always, *always* wanted a dog! Sugar! How big will Sugar grow?"

Chick extended his hand to terrier-height and slowly raised it until it would have sat comfortably on the head of a mature Irish wolfhound. "So big," he said.

"I don't suppose it came with anything like a . . . collar, or a leash?"

"Buy at store," Chick said shortly, pronging his second sausage.

"Do wash your hands, Finn, your food's getting cold. You can play with it later."

"She's called Sugar."

"You can play with *her* later."

The puppy went sniffing, in small, purposeful circles, around the perimeter of the kitchen floor, then stopped abruptly, faced its audience, and went into a crouch, head craning upward, ass thrust out. Its brow wrinkled into furrows, and its pop-eyes looked as if they were about to take leave of their sockets. Its hindquarters began to shudder. No one spoke. It was a tragic performance: Isolde, played by an overstrung amateur, Tom thought, singing her death-aria, the *Liebestod*. Finally, the puppy reached the *Ertrinken versinken unbewusst, höchste Lust!* bit, and stepped aside, leaving behind a surprisingly large, perfectly formed coil of excrement, like a gleaming fossil ammonite, on the white linoleum.

"Good *doggie!*" Finn said, and held out one of his sausages.

"Oh, Finn—don't feed it from the table. Please."

But the animal was already messily disposing of the sausage, exposing needle-like white fangs. Tom had forgotten to order paper towels from HomeGrocer.com, so he cleaned the muck off the floor with toilet tissue, soiling his fingers in the process. The stink was formidable. He uncorked a bottle of red wine and poured himself a large glassful, which he took down in medicinal gulps. Then he remembered his guest. "Chick? Would you care for some?"

"Sure," he said, though the wine stayed untouched by his plate.

"Can Sugar bark?" Finn asked.

"Yeah, big-time. Wanna see?" Chick turned himself around in his chair, pulled a threatening face, and raised a clenched fist above his head. The dog cowered, whimpered, and shuffled backwards on its stomach, then went into a fit of frenzied yelping, as if it were being disembowelled. It managed to hit notes that Tom had not previously realized were audible to the human ear.

"See? Bark good!" Chick, grinning, turned to Tom. "Guard dog."

"Sugar! It's okay. Poor Sugar. It's okay, Sugar. He didn't mean it. He was playing. I love you, Sugar."

"Where did you find it?" Tom said, wondering what miserable history had taught the animal to respond like that to a raised hand.

"Like I tell the kid, I make him new dog."

The puppy did indeed look very much like a piece of Chick's handiwork, with the same singular, ingenious, makeshift character that distinguished his scaffolding and the new pillars on the porch.

"American dog!" The contractor laughed extravagantly at his own joke.

"Daddy? You can hold Sugar if you want."

Tom was tolerant of cats—he'd grown almost fond of Hodge—but had never cared for dogs and their unwinning combination of savagery and pathos. He gingerly took hold of the puppy, which gazed at him with prematurely wizened cynicism, then tried to sink its teeth into his fingers—not very hard, but hard enough.

"Ouch!" He handed it back to Finn, who phoned his mother with the astounding news, but got her voice-mail on both numbers. "She needs obedience classes," he said. As "Animal Planet's" most loyal viewer, he'd always been a fountain of canine lore. "We have to get a clicker. And a training leash. A rawhide bone. And dog food. We really need dog food, Daddy. Can we go to Ken's?"

"What does she eat?" Tom asked.

Chick mulled the question over. "Sausage," he said.

"Sit, Sugar, sit! Sit! Good *doggie!* Look, Daddy! No, doggie, *no!* We'll get you some real chew-treats."

Elbows on his knees, chin cupped in his hands, Chick was smiling at the dog and boy with proprietorial, Pickwickian benevolence. He glanced at Tom and winked. "Happy like a pig in the shit, huh?"

The cap was off the jar of mustard. The half-eaten remains of supper littered the table. Looking from his own empty glass to Chick's full one, Tom saw a tableau of family life. He surprised himself with the thought *We're a family!* Masked faces and crossed purposes were part of that. So was the temporariness of the arrangement. Families didn't last long nowadays, and this one was going to break apart at any minute, but its ephemeral character made it no less authentic; quite the contrary. Every family, he thought, gets the dog it deserves, and the weird-looking Sugar seemed suddenly to fit right in, as if she'd always been lurking in the household in shadow form, but had waited until this moment to take substance.

Unpeeling a tablet of nicotine gum from its foil, Tom said, "Where are you living now?"

"I got a place. Rental."

"It's just that, you know, if you still needed somewhere . . ."

The puppy had Finn's pant-leg between its teeth and was shaking it from side to side. Between shakes, it produced a falsetto snarl, like a midget two-stroke engine on a model airplane.

"No, doggie! Sugar, *don't!*"

"*Wang! Wang! Wang!*" Chick bared his own snaggled teeth at Sugar, who instantly let go of Finn and wang-wanged back at the contractor in fluent, shrill Chinese.

"Ice-cream, anyone?" Tom said, hoping to hold his ad hoc family together a little while longer. "Anyone for ice-cream?"

"Chess!" Beth said.

In a lull in the Battle of Chicago, Beth and Robert were eating late at Flying Fish. The din was so tremendous that they had to lean close, across the narrow table, to hear each other speak. Beth was having the rockfish in pineapple and anchovy sauce, Robert the Thai crab cakes with lemon-grass mayonnaise. Beth was paying.

"Chess?"

"Yes. I'm no good now, but I was pretty good when I was little." Robert wrinkled his nose as he always did when he was being self-deprecating. "Hey, when I was in fourth grade, I was Michigan state champion. I made it to the nationals, but got creamed in the semi-finals by this East Indian kid, from Oxford, Mississippi. Rajiv. I mean, I was nerdy then, but Rajiv was a mega-nerd. He had glasses *this* thick, all done up with Band-Aids and stuff, and he talked to himself out loud through the games. I think it was having to look at Rajiv over a board for, like, four hours, that made me decide that chess wasn't really me."

Robert framed the word "me" by raising his hands and making bunny-ears with his index and middle fingers. That was another Robert habit—absenting himself from his own words by putting apostrophes around them, though not so often that it was predictable or irritating. Beth rather liked it.

"Now I'm just a recreational player."

"And you play with this guy in Sarajevo every day?"

"Branko. Most days. Only one game. We meet up on this chess site at eleven in the morning for me, nine at night for him."

"How long do these games last?"

"Not long. Half an hour, forty-five minutes."

"I've never caught you at it."

"That's my firewall working. My real-time boss scan."

"And all this while you've been two-timing me!"

"Everybody needs a little something to take their mind off the Ayatollah. Think of where you'd be without Finn."

"The Ayatollah?"

"The way he buttons his shirts right up to the top. Those suits."

"Oh, he's not so bad. At least he's not the Geek Messiah."

Robert produced an exact, but tactfully muted, imitation of Jeff Bezos's screeching laugh, which made Beth giggle. Then he held up his hands—mock-arrested—and said, "My fault. I never should've mentioned him. But don't let's talk about Steve, it'll wreck our dinner."

"Okay. So what's with your Serbian friend—Branko?"

"He's pretty witty."

"So you call each other up?"

"No. I meant his chess. He's always making moves that make me laugh."

"You can be funny in chess?"

"Oh, yes," he sounded mildly puzzled. "I've never actually talked to him. We just log on."

"It sounds like the perfect relationship. Where you just log on." It occurred to Beth that this was what she and Robert had been doing for the last hour or so. They'd just sort of logged on.

"Yeah, I was thinking that too. Like Bishop, D3 to C4. King, G8 to H8. Queen, E4 to F4 . . ."

"Checkmate?"

"Spassky resigned. That's Reykjavik in 1972. It's classic. But you wouldn't want to have any kind of relationship with Bobby Fischer. Or Spassky." He laughed. "To be a real chess player, you need to be a serious psycho."

For dessert, they split a banana split. As Beth was rearranging the position of her legs in the cramped space below the table, their knees touched. Neither of them nudged or pressed, but neither withdrew. They were not calf to calf, exactly; more, Beth thought, like jean to jean. She wasn't even totally sure that Robert had noticed.

When the bill came, he said, "I'd better get going or I'll miss the bus to Capitol Hill."

There was just enough uncertainty in this announcement for Beth to say, "You could always crash at my place. It's right across the street. Finn's with my ex, so his room's free—I mean . . . if you wanted . . ."

Which—shyly, becomingly—he did.

The police were in the house. Uniformed officers were putting things into transparent plastic bags. They had already taken away Tom's computer, a Gap Kids catalogue, an envelope of photographs of Finn in the bath. A woman officer was showing a male colleague a book whose title Tom couldn't see: as she riffled through its pages, graphic disgust registered on the man's face.

Tom tried to speak, but terror seemed to have paralysed his vocal cords. All he could manage was a strangulated *urrrgh!* to which his visitors paid no attention whatsoever as they went on stowing his possessions in evidence-bags.

Working downwards through the house, they were nearing the end of their search of the second floor, and it was only a matter of time before they found what was hidden in the basement. Tom had lived with the knowledge of its presence, but had told no-one. He hadn't done it, or, rather, had no memory of doing it, but he'd known about it, and that knowledge would ensure that he would soon be cuffed and driven off in the police van. It had caught up with him, as he supposed he'd always secretly known that it would, and now he was going to be horribly punished.

An officer pushed past him with a bag full of Finn's clothes.

"We've got your number, mate," he said, surprising Tom with his south-of-the-Thames accent. He was wearing a black helmet with a large eight-pointed silver star on the front. As he went on down the stairs, Tom wondered, dully, what a Metropolitan Police constable could be doing here in Seattle.

That couldn't be right. A wash of relief flooded through him as he realized he was dreaming. He knew how to escape from bad dreams.

You had to take a deep breath and somehow force it past the silencing constriction of your larynx. All it took was an effort of will.

Policemen were still coming out of his room and Finn's, bags in hand, but he knew them to be chimeras. Putting his whole being into the attempt, he filled his lungs with air and yelled himself free of the dream.

He woke to the empty house, the police gone. Yet he was not in bed, as he'd expected, but in the basement. The air smelled sickly-sweet, like putrid fish, and although it was the middle of the night, he was fully dressed. A black, rubber-barrelled flashlight was in his hand. He shone it on the spiderwebs slung between the rafters, the stacked boxes of junk, the murmuring furnace. Bracing himself for what was to come, he stepped past the furnace to the flattened rectangle of earth where Chick had set up his encampment.

It was there, as he'd known it would be: an untidy parcel, the size of a fat child, wrapped in a dirty blue plastic tarp and tied with coarse garden string. The crinkled tarp, a patchwork of shadows, appeared to have leaked. An irregular dark stain had spread over the dirt on its western side, like a coastline of fjords and promontories. That was new, surely. He squatted on his haunches, shining the flashlight on the ground all around it. The black specks were rat-droppings. Beth had called in a pest-control company a couple of years ago, but the rats must have returned. This close, the stench was unbearable. Tasting vomit, choking it back, he tried to undo the string. The raffia had frayed, and he couldn't keep the light on the knot. A black rat, wet fur plastered to its body, wriggled out from inside the tarp and scurried into the darkness beyond the furnace.

Tom screamed. As he woke this time, his hands and knees were scrabbling for purchase on a hard floor that canted violently upwards into the vertical. Groping, he found that he was lying crosswise on the pillows at the head of the bed, face pressed against the wall. The dark bedroom remained connected to the basement by the fading echo of his scream, which must have been loud enough to wake the neighbors and terrify Finn.

He listened, but no sound came from down the hall. Half in, half out of his dream, he clumsily pulled Beth's bathrobe around his shoulders and, suffused with dread, stumbled towards Finn's half-open door.

In the ghostly blue of the Mr. Moon nightlight, Finn's body was sprawled across the bed, his cheek snuggled against Squashy Bear, the covers down around his thighs. Holding his own breath, Tom listened for his son's. He had to hold his good ear close in order to catch it, but there it was—regular, unhindered, like a light wind over water. He pulled up the covers and settled them around Finn's shoulders. A whiffling noise came from the cardboard wine box beside the bed, so the puppy, too, was still alive.

He made his way groggily downstairs, where he sat at the kitchen table with his head in his hands. The abundance of life in Finn's room should have cheered him, but he was not cheered. The stain on the earth, the blue tarp, the knotted string, were hardly further from him now than they'd been in the dream—if indeed he wasn't dreaming still. The smell was in his nostrils, a rich, cloying odor that you might momentarily mistake for some misbegotten hybrid damask rose. It seemed possible— or at least not impossible—that this was the dream's third instalment, and he might soon scream himself awake into a further episode, every bit as deceptively solid as the present.

He had to untie that knot and find out who or what was wrapped in the tarp. The shapeless bundle could as easily hold a fetid slumgullion of butchered parts as a whole body—the torso of one victim, the severed leg of another. If a bit of Hayley Topolski were in there, that was the least of its contents. For all his inattention on that afternoon, he couldn't feel so utterly, abjectly guilty for whatever it was that had happened to the child, not even in a dream. Finn, then? The family that had died on him—died of his casual neglect, like an unwatered plant? Yes, and yes, but it was more, and worse, than that.

Innocent people don't have murderers' dreams.

"Daddy?"

Tom had no idea how long Finn had been standing there. He was holding Squashy Bear. He looked afraid—not the usual night-fright that could be quickly banished by outstretched arms—but afraid of his father. His face, creased with sleep, was feverishly white, his eyes wide. He looked as if he knew.

"What is it?" Tom's voice came out as a thirsty croak.

Before Finn could answer, Squashy Bear began to wriggle and squeal.

*   *   *

Beth was the first to wake. Not moving a muscle, she watched Robert, or as much of Robert as she could see in the predawn light through her one open eye. His boyish mop of thick albino hair fell in a ragged fringe across his forehead. There was a slight ironic smile on his face, as if his lips knew no other way to settle. Listening to the surf-like sound of early traffic on the Alaskan Way Viaduct, she found the sight of him, without his glasses, entirely beautiful, and felt herself undeserving of the sight: it was like waking to a treat delivered by accident to the wrong person in the wrong room, but no less nice for that. Stealthily, she fished her hand out from under the bedclothes so she could check her watch. It was later than she'd hoped.

She whispered: "Robert?"

No response. His eyelashes were albino, too.

She tried again. "Robert, honey?"

One eye opened. Then the other. His natural smile enlarged. He appeared wholly, and delightfully, unsurprised to see her.

She smiled back for a moment, and said, "Remember Chicago?"

8.

"Thomas?"

The voice at the far end of the line was worn to a throaty whisper.

"Yes?"

"Paul Nagel. I got a virus. And some news." He sounded as if he were calling from his deathbed. "Hayley's been found."

Tom thought, *I knew that*. He said: "Alive?"

"No."

"Oh."

"Scumbag reptiles. They buried her in a creek near Moses Lake. Over the mountains. The remains are coming back today."

"They?"

"Man and a woman, if you can call them that, which I wouldn't want to. Twenties. Caucasian. We got a license number and descriptions. Folks thought they were her parents. Maybe they were related—that's being checked out now. There's an uncle in Idaho. She'd been . . . abused."

"I'm sorry."

"What's to be sorry about?" A note of impatient ferocity had entered the whisper. "You're free and clear. Oh, yeah, you even have a fucking alibi, not that you need it—and I wish to God I didn't have it neither."

"I'm not following."

"January one? Oh-nine-hundred? Hayley was in Ellensburg. We have very positive ID on that. She was *alive*, for fuck's sake! And where were you, Thomas?"

"I've no—"

"Of course you wouldn't. Sorry, I forgot. You were here in this office, talking to me."

"So if—"

"Yeah, right. Everybody was in the wrong fucking place, wasting everybody's fucking time. It happens. The dad never even said he had a brother, and nobody thought to ask about that. No, we had to get fixated on weirdo-looking smokers with amnesia. I'm not trying to be a comedian, Thomas. The kid was alive for five days, minimum, after she went missing, and that makes me sick to the bottom of my fucking guts."

Tom wanted to say that he understood, that he knew he wasn't blameless in the matter of Hayley's death. But in this dialogue he was cast as the Fool, and Nagel would allow him to say only foolish things. "I think I know how you must feel."

"You don't know squat, Thomas." Nagel's voice crackled like dry leaves in a late-summer breeze. "You don't have the least goddamn clue about how I fucking feel." He hung up with what sounded to Tom like a racking sob.

There was no lift of spirits, no sense of release, as Tom replaced the phone in its cradle. He, too, felt sick to the bottom of his fucking guts. He sat staring numbly through the study window, into the black tangle of the holly tree with its clustered berries. He seemed to have divided into two people. He observed his second self reaching for pen and paper and writing out a list of supplies for Finn's ugly little puppy, which was asleep in the box at his feet. This other person wrote *Cage*. Then *collar + lead*. Then *clicker?* And *rubber bones*.

Tom watched him doing it, glumly envying his heartless, mechanical composure.

". . . in this world except death and taxes," Mr. Don said. He was sitting at his roll-top desk, from which a white drift of papers was spilling to the floor. "Know who said that? Before I did? Benjamin Franklin. He was quite the humorist. You ought to read him sometime."

"Maybe I do that, Mr. Don."

"You probably seen his picture on the hundred-dollar bill."

He'd come here to negotiate for the Mexicans. He had no great hopes of success, but he was prepared to pay $1,000 for the whole crew, and it seemed a good-luck sign that he'd arrived to find Mr. Don groaning over his tax forms.

He was still groaning over them, showing his back to Chick—scribble, scribble, scribble—and keeping him waiting. Finally, he swivelled around in his chair. "Okay, what can I do you for, pardner?"

Chick laid out his terms. Mr. Don's meaty, sunburned, turtle-like face showed no expression as he stared at a spot on the ceiling above Chick's head.

"Be all I can pay, Mr. Don."

At last Mr. Don looked directly at him. "I wouldn't want to take your money. I got a better idea." He tossed a cheroot in his general direction, and Chick had to go down on his knees to pick it off the floor. "Know my steam barge?"

"Sure I do." It was the gray ship at the end of the dock that looked like a floating factory, its superstructure as big as the American's house and encrusted with a labyrinth of pipes and catwalks. Chick had long admired it for its air of serious business, though he could never figure out what anybody could do with such a thing. He'd asked Lázaro, whose answer—"make steam"—only added to the ship's attractive mystery.

"It's a sad story. I paid thirty-four grand for that sucker at auction. Got it off the Navy. I had big plans for it. Thought I could sell it foreign. Steam barge that size new, you'd be looking at a million-five, a million-six. I called all over the marine business, spent a thousand bucks in advertising. Guess what? No takers. Now I got buyer's remorse." Mr. Don tapped his cigar on the old brass spittoon he used as an ashtray.

"See, what I'm thinking here is, if you and me go into partnership, I can cut my losses. The scrap market's tanked on me, but I can still unload the non-ferrous metals. There's ten grand in brass, and more than that in copper, plus the lead ballast. Say thirty-five thousand total. We strip all that good stuff out and then we sell the son-of-a-bitch. That's another twelve, maybe. You following the math on this?"

Chick was following, but wasn't impressed.

"You got one problem. To even get at the good stuff, and make it legal, you got to get all the wiring out, for the PCBs. And the asbestos. There's more asbestos in there than you can shake a stick at. You should see the lagging on the boiler alone. There's three truckloads of that shit, maybe more—and I'm not talking pick-ups, I mean the biggest god-damn moving vans you can rent from U-Haul. You'll have to find a wilderness-area somewhere, like up in the North Cascades, in the national park, or out by Ross Lake. And if you're not careful, you'll end up doing jail-time. Which I'd hate to see."

Chick felt insulted. This wasn't partnership; it was $12 an hour, or less, by another name, however Mr. Don tried to talk his numbers. Rolling his unlit cheroot between his fingers, he studied a spot on the ceiling above Mr. Don's head and said, "I don't think so."

"Wait. You haven't heard the kicker yet."

"The kicker?"

"Yeah. You get to be the owner. That's your guarantee. No way I can sell what isn't mine—that's breaking the law."

"I don't get it."

"It's like this. The way things stand, we go partners and each one of us lands up with around twenty-three grand at the end of the day, right? Which is okay for you, but bad for me. That sort of business makes me feel sorry for myself every time I see my ugly chops in the mirror. I already paid the thirty-four for that sinker, remember. Plus it's been rotting out there for a year, costing me a hundred fifty feet of dock space. I need the loss. If I sell it to you today, I get to write off the difference between what you pay and what I paid, *and* the charges for all that dock space I been renting out to myself."

"I don't want no steam barge, Mr. Don."

"You haven't heard my price yet."

"What price?"

"A hundred bucks. One Ben Franklin bill."

"Why you want this?"

"Simple self-interest, pardner. If you got title to that ship, I make sixty-eight thousand, or twice what I paid. If I retain title, I only make twenty-three. So if you buy it, you're doing me a forty-five-thousand-dollar favor."

"Like win-win."

"Right. You win, I win. The brass, the copper, the lead, the barge, I buy all that back from you at half of market. You don't even have to find a buyer, I'm sitting right here. You get to hire the Mexicans for as long as it takes—three weeks, a month—starting next Monday. I need 'em to finish up a job for me first. Then *you* can look after their health insurance and Social Security taxes."

Chick sniggered.

"Course the real price you'll be paying is in sweat-equity, which is a kind of equity the IRS won't ever know about."

A little while ago, Chick thought, he would've been baffled by the logic of this proposal, but now he saw it clearly. It was like the money market, as Mr. Qiu had explained it to him at the bank: Japanese yen go down, people in Japan crying, but you're laughing because you gobble up their money cheap with high-rising German marks. Loss makes for profit. Lose money, you make money. All the big American companies knew this: their value was reckoned by the size of their losses, so the bigger the loss, the richer they got. Even the fifteen-dollar dog fit this pattern. Mr. Don wanted to give him the ship so he could make more money, which was the exact-same reason why Chick had bought the mutt for the boy. It was like Mr. Don said: win-win!

"How I buy from you?"

"Well, first you give me a hundred-dollar bill. Even better, I'll give it to you on credit. Then we make out a bill of sale. We go to the bank at Fishermen's Terminal and get it notarized. Then—bingo!—you got title."

Mid-afternoon, Tom drove Finn and Sugar to PETCO, where Finn basked in the celebrity conferred on him by the squirming puppy in his arms, whose vicious and eccentric appearance seemed to unreasonably enhance its popularity. A woman Beth's age stopped Finn to ask him if it was "a little boy dog or a little girl dog," and two girls at the checkout, cooing extravagantly, fed it miniature colored bones, which it seized from their fingers much as the Tasmanian devil Tom had seen on "Animal Planet" went for the tethered carcass of a dead sheep.

They came away with $160 worth of dog-essentials piled into the trunk, along with a book titled *The Dog in Your Life,* which Finn made a heroic attempt to read aloud on the way home.

"Getting—a—puppy—is—parrot—of—the . . . I don't get it."

"Spell it."

"A-m-e-r-i-c-a-n . . ."

"American."

"Is parrot of the American drum."

"Dream?"

"Yeah, getting a puppy is part of the American dream!"

"Brilliant, Finbow."

Leaving boy and dog to frolic in the kitchen, Tom went upstairs to his computer. Just in from Beth:

I read the Times story. Horrible about the child, but so glad to see the bit about you. They even apologised, and everybody says that's unusual.

It's crazy here. Instead of me picking up Finn from you this evening, can he stay with you tonite? I may be able to have him tomorrow, but I'm not sure yet. Depends on the craziness at work. (Chicago!)

—B.

Tom, who'd been dreading an evening of remorseful solitude, replied that he was happy to take Finn for the next few days, and that Beth was not to worry. He was heading for the *Times* site when he heard Finn shouting downstairs.

"Oh, *no!* Oh, Sugar! Bad doggie! *Bad* doggie! *Dad?*"

In the living room, the puppy was crouched, snarling, in a nest of shredded paper.

"What happened?"

"I only went to the bathroom." Finn scooped up the puppy and held her to his chest, eyeing his father fearfully. "Is it very, very bad?"

"No, Finbow, it's not." Tom saw from Finn's face that he'd half-expected his pet to get euthanized for its work on Mrs. Trollope's *Domestic Manners of the Americans.* He picked up a chewed fragment:

> *a noble boat,*
> *as they are called were*
> *ple balcony, sheltered by an awning; chairs and*
> *son, nearly all the female passengers passed the whole*
> *d vessel was the Lady Franklin. By the way, I*

That book-idea, Tom thought, was no bloody good anyway. Stuff Fanny Trollope. He laughed. "It's a literary-critical dog. It's a patriot dog, Finbow. So where did you put its real food?"

"Oh, man!" Lázaro's shoulders, usually hunched and sullen, were shivering with laughter. "Know what he call you? Harry Onassis." His dark, cratered face had never looked so full of life.

"Funny guy." Chick hoicked a gob of phlegmy spittle onto the asphalt.

"He make you buy the shit-bucket."

Both men looked across the shipyard to the steam barge, whose immense evening silhouette blocked the view beyond.

"He not 'make.' Me and him do deal. Win-win."

"He win, man. He always win."

"You don't know fuck. I got title."

"He win taxes, you win trouble." Lázaro was on the brink of another laughing fit.

"What you mean?"

"He in deep shit with εPA, with Coast Guard, with city, even. Lady write letter, say it fuck her view. He say last week he going to tow that thing out to sea, way deep, and pull plug—only he scared the Coast Guard see."

"Then he say bye-bye to all that good non-ferrous," Chick said contemptuously. "Is brass. Is copper. Is lead. Plus barge. Follow the math!"

"Is all trouble, man."

"Is business."

"εPA come looking, man. Coast Guard, and city too. Guy set you up."

Chick scowled, disbelieving; then believing, and again disbelieving.

Maddened by the sight of Lázaro's idiot grin, he lowered the shutters on his eyes and forced his mouth into a smile. "That what he think. Maybe."

"I tell you, man, end of month, he charge *moorage*—thousand dollar, minimum. You not pay, he say get that fucker off my property. You the owner! Gotta move it! How you do that? You screwed!"

"He say that?"

Tom made a cabbage-patch run to the university—a low-flying raid under enemy radar. Mount Rainier was "out," the campus unseasonably pretty in February sunshine. He kept his head down and walked fast, a moving target.

He encountered flak at Padelford Hall, when he stepped into the elevator. Russ Van Strand was standing there, and, like him, going up. The assistant professor found an extremely interesting knot in the grain of the wood paneling, and gave it the full semiotics treatment. His miniature purple nylon backpack, stuffed to its limits with books or provisions, looked brand-new. As the door slid shut, he mumbled, "Good to see you back."

Seeing no adequate reply to this, Tom said, "Going hiking?"

"No, why?"

"You look—equipped."

At the third floor, Van Strand shot out like a greyhound bounding after an electric hare. He turned right, Tom left. The unwelcoming bare office, swept clean in his absence, reminded him unpleasantly of Paul Nagel's grim quarters in the King County Sheriff's Department. He wrote out a schedule of visiting hours and posted it on the pin-board beside his door, along with a notice saying CLASSES RESUME AS NORMAL FROM 3/9/00, then sent a round-robin e-mail to the eleven M.F.A. students in the Fiction class. He pulled down *Sister Carrie* from the shelf and pretended to read Dreiser before he braved the hallway and called on Bernard Goldblatt.

If Tom's troubles had awakened ghouls from Bernard's past, it was obvious the department chair had wasted no time in laying them to rest. Alarm spread over his face the second he saw Tom standing in the doorway, and his eyes were pleading. Before they had finished exchanging mild pleasantries, Bernard was off and away on the "prickly" subject of the Ray Fellowship. Tom had suggested in an e-mail that the university might, in charity, still honor its commitment to Scott-Rice, who clearly had a following among the students.

"Totally impossible. Totally." Bernard treated Tom to his ironic Oxford smile, the silver hairpiece twinkling in the sunlight that fell aslant into Bernard's south-facing office. "That's a year's salary for a perfectly competent Renaissance man. I mean, just look who's teaching Shakespeare now!"

Tom didn't know who was teaching Shakespeare, and wasn't about to ask. "Given the circumstances, I'm sure David would settle for less—or perhaps we could get him to teach a whole semester for the same price."

"We're practically drowning in novelists as it is."

Tom could see his point all around him. Bernard's office was furnished ceiling-to-floor with uniform editions: Austen, Benn, Burney, Defoe, Edgeworth, Fielding, Radcliffe, Richardson, Smollett, Sterne . . . He was practically drowning in poets, too, though they took up less space. This collection made it rather hard to argue the importance of David Scott-Rice. *Tristram Shandy* and *Crystal Palace:* Compare and contrast.

"I mean, you can teach the Victorians—well, at least to undergraduates. No, I've had it out with Development, and the absolute best we can do is offer him our sincere apologies with a check for a thousand dollars."

"I dread his response."

"Well, they're very concerned about the form of the apology, and would much prefer no apology at all. At any rate, we'll have to clear it with the lawyers before we send off anything in writing. There's also the question of exactly how we describe the check—if, indeed, we have to produce one."

Trying to reach Bernard the human being, his moral champion during the emergency, Tom reckoned his best hope was to address himself to Bernard the dog-lover. In the deferential tone of a beginner seeking advice from an acknowledged master, he told the story of Finn's puppy. It didn't go down as well as he expected.

"Clarissa passed away. A year ago next week. Cancer of the bladder."

"I'm sorry. I didn't know."

"Most people did. I had quite a number of condolence cards."

So that was that. On his way out, Tom said, "I just wanted to thank you for—"

"Absurd business," Bernard said, dismissing it, and Tom, from further consideration.

Returning to the house, Tom was shocked. Chick had spent the morning painting the new deck and pillars with gray primer, and the house now bared to the world a mouthful of immense tombstone teeth, set in an expression of irrational—no, maniacal—exuberance. No amount of forest-green paint could disguise that ghastly grin. It was as if the contractor had given the house his own face.

Inside, the puppy was howling in her crate—a sopranino tirade accusing Tom of unpardonable selfishness and neglect. When he let her out, she cowered and promptly puddled on the carpet. He mopped up after her, while she gazed at him with a look of wrinkled doubt and sor- [...] en much [...] se it in a dog. When he showed [...] e sniffed at it disdainfully and backed away. He got out her leash. From some remote cranny in his memory, a strange word surfaced.

"Walkies?"

He thought he saw a flicker of response in her mud-colored eyes. She submitted to having the leash clipped to her collar, and waddled, almost amiably, to the front door.

On the street, Tom felt ridiculous. He might as well have been towing a toy duck on wheels—except that Sugar's wheels seized up at regular intervals, and he'd hear the rasp of paws on concrete as he dragged the puppy's dead weight behind him. "Sugar!" he kept muttering, *sotto voce*. "Sugar, *no!*" Though "Sugar" didn't appear to register with her, there were a couple of occasions when she looked up enquiringly at the word *no* as if that were her true name.

He scuffed his heels and stared at the sky while she buried her nose in cracks in the sidewalk. He yanked her away from piles of unscooped dogshit. The walk to the market took on the epic dimensions of an Oregon Trail as Tom grew hungry and the puppy flagged. Though Ken's was in sight, it appeared to be receding over the far horizon. For the last four blocks, Sugar had to be portaged. He tied her to the ice-machine outside the store, where she sank into a comatose brown heap.

He came out with his shopping a few minutes later, and found a dog transformed. She was straining at the end of her lead, tongue lolling, tail throbbing, her stunted forelegs bicycling in air.

The woman who was crouched in front of her looked up. "You don't mind if I pet her? What's her name?"

"Shoo-gar," Tom said in unthinking mimicry of Finn.

"Oh, cool. Chinese. Siu Ga! Siu Ga!"

The dog pranced from foot to foot, panting so frantically that Tom thought she might drop dead of a spontaneous explosion of the heart.

"It's not mine," he was quick to say. "It's my four-year-old's."

"She's such a cutey. You have a boy or a girl?"

"Boy." The woman reminded him alarmingly of Beth—not Beth now, but as she'd been in the days before she went off to work for Steve Litvinof. They had in common a black leather bomber-jacket, slim hips, fair hair, and a nice asymmetrical smile, higher on the left than on the right. Not much, but enough to disconcert.

"Hey, I know who you are . . ."

She was scrutinizing him. How many milliseconds would it take, he wondered, for her to make the connection?

"You're Tom Janeway."

"Yes."

But she was still smiling.

"I've heard you on NPR. And I read your book . . . *Corridors?*"

"*Tunnels.*"

"That's right, *Tunnels.*"

Amazing.

"My husband gave it to me for Christmas one year. I'm a big Dickens fan. You want to know the part I really loved? When you had Quilp putting the moves on Becky Sharp and getting hauled off by General William Booth. That was hysterical."

"Ah, you must be in the trade," Tom said. "Teacher? Or just finishing up your Ph.D.?"

"Me? No, I'm in marketing."

That was the line he liked best.

Walking back along Sixth Avenue, Tom appraised the dog with different eyes. He had to admit she had a certain skewed and low-slung charm. Obviously a social asset, she might yet prove the means of his reintroduction to the world. If her desire was to stop by a cherry tree, sniff shit, and eat grass, that was fine by him.

They were just passing Garfield when a car slowed beside them, its electric passenger window rolling down. "Hi, Tom! Hi, Siu Ga!" Then she accelerated away.

It was an encounter blessedly without consequence. The woman was married; and even if she hadn't been, her unsettling likeness to Beth would have put her safely out of bounds. But the uncomplicated airiness of their exchange gave him an inkling, a glimmer, of a life still hidden from his view, and it was pleasant to think of how the woman would never know the meaning of the gift she'd so casually bestowed on him.

On a flying visit to the house, Beth looked wrecked, her eyes sunk in sleepless violet bruises. "I can't stay long," she said as she came through the door.

Finn introduced her to Siu Ga.

"Oh, look at her. She's *so* cute!" To Tom she said: "Has it had its shots?"

"I doubt it."

"You ought to take it to the vet's. Like, tomorrow. I mean, where did your Chinese guy get it from? It probably has—well, god knows what. Distemper? Worms? Ear-lice? It could have rabies."

"Well, she's bitten me a couple of times, and so far I'm not foaming at the mouth."

"You'll have to keep it here. There's a no-pets rule in my building."

"You could always take her to work . . ."

Beth scowled. "I thought you hated dogs."

"Well, I seem to be coming round to this one."

Turning away from Finn, Beth whispered, "It's incredibly ugly."

"She grows on you. By degrees."

"Better you than me. Oh, pumpkin—she's having an accident. On the kitchen floor."

Finn had grown adept with the sandwich bags, and cleaned it up with proprietorial pride.

"It was on the paper, almost," he announced. "She's *nearly* paper-trained." *The Dog in Your Life* had supplanted Mister Wicked stories at bedtime, and the puppy was already sitting on Finn's command. Or so he claimed.

"How's Chicago?"

"What? Oh, it's a nightmare. The opening got pushed back three weeks, and Steve's losing it. Have you seen what's been happening to the stock?"

"No."

"It's all over the place. Yesterday it looked like it was going into free fall. Then it recovered. The CFO keeps on sending out don't-panic messages, which of course just adds to the general hysteria. Lots of crazy rumors are going around . . ."

Yet Beth's tone was detached, even amused. Tom was tempted to mention 1720, and the South Sea Bubble, but remembered the last time he'd raised that subject, and said, "Rumors of what?"

"Oh, you know—lay-offs, downsizing, mergers. Steve flew to San Francisco last week, and everybody got paranoid. There's a Silicon Valley company called RealWorld . . . I heard we'd definitely been sold. But it turned out to be a family funeral. If Steve goes to the bathroom now, that starts another rumor."

"Are you getting any sleep at all?"

Beth squinted at him, as if he'd said something odd. "Not much. It's like they say—twenty-four/seven."

"Can you stay for supper?"

"Uh-uh. I promised I'd be back in the office by eight, and I sort of ate already. Thanks, though."

"Are you sure it's worth it?"

"What?" She gave him that funny, sharp look again.

"This . . . life you're leading. You look flat-out exhausted."

"It's just temporary," she said. "Just till Chicago."

She played with Finn and the puppy for twenty minutes, then left.

Finn looked up and said: "My mom really, really loved Sugar."

Chick was on a stepladder painting the pillars, the radio going at his feet. He'd wanted to use white, but the American insisted on this ugly green, an offense for which he'd make him pay. But he liked painting— the good smell of it, the feel of the loaded brush in his hand, the lavish unrolling of color on the gray. He was lost in his work, cocooned in music, when he heard a voice shout "Mr. Lee?"

Chick plotted a route of escape before looking away from his pillar. A short bald man in a yellow coat, with highly polished brown shoes, stood on the porch steps. He looked too rich to be an official, but he carried a leather document case. The car parked under the tree was a black BMW—no logo on it, and with private plates. "What you want?"

"Home improvements!" the man shouted, then pointed at the radio. "Can we talk?"

Chick put the brush down, lowered the volume of the music, and waved the man imperiously back. "Wet paint!"

"Excuse me." The man retreated to the edge of the sidewalk, from where he had to speak with face upturned and raised voice raised. "I called Donald Dahlberg, who said I'd probably find you here."

How did Mr. Don know this? "You friend of him?"

"No, I just talked to him on the phone."

"Where you work?"

"I'm an attorney." The man reached into an inside pocket and produced a business card, which he held out as bait. "My name's Hamish McTurk." He began to step forward, but Chick held up his hand, palm outward, like a traffic cop.

"What you want?" Though small, the man looked strong, and had a fighter's lumpy potato-face. Chick decided to change his route: through the front door and out the back.

"Oh, I just dropped by on the off-chance . . . Hey, I'm only the gofer here, but I've got a client down in Galveston. Texas, you know? More a friend than a client, really. He's in the energy business."

"What you want?"

"Mr. Lee? You think maybe we could find some place to talk? Go get a coffee together, or just sit in the car? Five minutes is all it would take."

Chick was encouraged by the uncertain, experimental look of the attorney's smile. "Talk for why?"

"Your steam barge?"

"Not for sale," Chick said, watching the man closely.

"No, of course not." The attorney laughed, a thin, cracked whoop. "No, he was thinking charter. Short term. Per diem. A temporary arrangement. Any chance there's an open slot on your schedule?"

Chick moved to the side of the deck and nodded at the open front door.

As the attorney set foot on the steps, he said, "Don Dahlberg said it had just changed hands." Then, once he had his head inside the door: "Nice house!"

Taking care to stay behind him, Chick pointed through the living room toward the kitchen.

"Always wanted to go to China. Never made it, though. Now the Great Wall—that's something I'd love to see. Have you visited the Forbidden City? The Silk Road? Friend of mine at the office, he and his wife took a cruise down the Yangtze, and said it was *fabulous.* I was looking at the photos just the other day. Great country."

Chick had forgotten about the dog. It was squealing inside its crate on the kitchen floor. The crate shook, claws scrabbled, bits of brown fur showed against the ventilation slats, followed by a single wild eye. The attorney looked at the crate, grinned, opened his mouth to speak, but was forestalled by a shrilling howl. Chick kicked the shuddering crate several inches across the linoleum. The dog whimpered once and went quiet.

"You got to admire a people like that. I mean, think of the things you guys invented. Gunpowder. The umbrella. The magnetic compass. I'm a sailor, of course, so I like to dabble in maritime law. I do criminal, family, immigration . . . That's the bread-and-butter side. But what I really like to do is maritime. What part of China are you from, Mr. Lee?"

Chick pointed at a chair.

The attorney unbuttoned his coat and seated himself at the table. "I love to travel. I got to get over to China some day. That's one promise I really mean to keep."

Leaning against the stove, arms folded, feet planted wide, Chick watched the attorney spring the locks of his document case, and saw his eyes glance nervously at the crate.

"And that's another thing—the cooking. You got one of the top cuisines in the world. If not *the* top. Couple I was telling you about? They say they ate like kings around the clock."

"What you want with steam barge?"

The man riffled through his folders and pulled out a single printed sheet. "You know the Orinoco Delta, Mr. Lee? You been to Venezuela? My Galveston friend's out there now. All shallow water and mangroves. What he liked about the sound of your vessel is the draft. Six feet, right? He had a notion it might just work, but it's no big deal to him. Hell, he's probably got a dozen people looking at steam barges for him right this minute."

"Why he want?"

"Sorry?"

"Why he want!" At the sound of Chick's raised voice, the dog began to wail again.

"Well, I hardly need to explain to you—"

"Why he want steam in Venezuela?"

"Oh, I see what you're getting at. I don't believe they've got the same viscosity problem on other fields. Just on this one. Funny, isn't it? You'd think in that kind of equatorial climate—"

"You tell *why!*" His hands were bunched into fists.

"You mean—well, as I understand it, which probably is a whole lot less than you do, the oil down there's like Jell-O. Just won't pump. I don't know why I'm having to say this, Mr. Lee, but you got to fill that whole reservoir down there with steam—right?—so the oil heats up and thins, and 'Thar she blows!'" The attorney looked emptied by this explanation, emptied and sick.

Chick imagined the swampy brown water, the mangroves, the mosquitoes, the congealed oil, the tall skinny frame of the rig, the see-sawing pumps. Without a steam barge . . . At last the great gray boiler-house with its chimneys, pipes, and walkways had a real purpose. Mr. Don's big-money dreams made sense now.

"You want day-rental for Venezuela?" Chick laughed, enjoying the attorney's humiliation.

"Well, if the price was right, I guess he might conceivably . . . But you say it's not for sale, so—"

"You show me." Chick pointed to the piece of paper. The attorney passed it to him: a muddy photocopy of a page torn from a ship-magazine. October 1998. The ad for the steam barge took up the bottom half of the page: a picture, mostly black, of the barge being towed by a tug-boat, a paragraph of technical details, and Mr. Don's name, address, and phone number. Chick had hoped to see a price, but that was something people in the marine business would know without being told.

"Have any of the specs changed?"

"No change. All same."

"I could try calling my friend from the car, if you'd like, just to see if he's still looking . . ."

"You watch out. Wet paint!"

Twice the attorney went outside to his car, returning each time with questions, and an expression that was hard to figure. Chick made a call of his own, to Mr. Qiu. Over the next half hour a price for the steam barge was negotiated—$379,000, subject to survey, and payable within four days by banker's draft. The number was too low, Chick knew, and he was at first affronted, but then agreed, sullenly, with a nod and a grunt. At least this poor deal would further anger Mr. Don if he were ever to learn the terms of the sale. If Mr. Don had sold the steam barge, he would've got $500,000, minimum, which made the whole thing even funnier.

The attorney drove away just as the American pulled up, his old Volkswagen rattling into the space vacated by the new BMW. Chick turned up the volume of the radio before the American got out, and when he stood under the tree, a pile of books in his arms, looking up at the porch, Chick pretended not to see him, and laid another swath of paint onto the primer.

Later in the afternoon, when he stopped by the shipyard, Mr. Don's pick-up was gone.

"He go to Vancouver," Lázaro said. "Buy a ship. Not back till Monday. Hey, this morning he say EPA come looking for you."

"Yeah. The fuck tell him where I do work." He looked down the dock to the steam barge and laughed. "Wah!" He spat into the asphalt. "Fuck set me up."

On Sunday morning, Tom was in his eyrie at the top of the house, trying to draft a letter to David Scott-Rice. He'd got as far as *Dear David, I,* but the last ten minutes had been spent wondering how to proceed from there. From the second-floor landing came the sounds of obedience-training—Finn shouting "No!" and "Bad dog!" in his deep Santa Claus voice, the puppy answering with a volley of yips and barks.

Tom back-spaced on the *I* and typed: *Your first impulse will be to shoot the messenger, but*

A ferry was crossing to Bainbridge Island, trailing a long skirt of ripples behind it in the windless gray.

I've talked to the department chairman, and

"Sugar, no! No, no, no!"

"Finbow," Tom called. "Cool your jets, please. Or take her downstairs."

I'm afraid the university is going to take the line that

There was a disturbance, like a sudden snow squall, outside the window, and Tom looked up to see a flock of birds settling on the holly tree—or, rather, not settling but fluttering about it, as quick and random in their movements as a cloud of gnats, skipping daintily from branch to branch, trading places, covering the tree so thickly that they appeared to be a kind of mobile foliage, a mass of shimmering olive, with, here and there, winks of gorse-yellow, winks of scarlet. Even through the double-glazing of the window, he could hear them at it—a continuous metallic zinging like the tuneless fiddle-bowing of cicadas in tall grass.

"Finbow! Come up here—quick as you can!"

Though he knew waxwings from the bird book, he'd never seen them in life. He got the binoculars off the windowsill and brought the holly tree into swimming close-up. The birds were better than their pictures—trim dandies, the sheen of their plumage bright beyond reason in the gloomy overcast.

"What?"

The puppy was nipping at Finn's heels.

"Look!"

"Birds," Finn said, sounding cheated.

"Waxwings. Here—" He passed him the binoculars, and Finn sighed theatrically before holding the glasses to his eyes.

"You see their crests?"

"Yeah. They look like they got bike-helmets on."

"Try counting them. How many do you think there are?"

"Millions."

"What are they doing?"

"I dunno. Nothing. Playing?"

"I think perhaps they're eating berries."

Yet, as Finn said, they appeared to be up to nothing in particular. Not feeding, not fighting, not mating, they seemed impelled by simple restlessness and exhibitionism, like college athletes showing off their muscles.

"Can I go get a cookie now?"

"Oh, if you have to." Tom took down the Peterson guide from the shelf and looked up the cedar waxwing: *sleek . . . gregarious . . . nomadic . . . fly and feed in compact flocks.*